PRAISE FOR RICHARD COX'S NOVEL OF HIGH-FLYING SUSPENSE
GROUND ZERO

"A TOP-NOTCH THRILLER . . . The continent-hopping pace is swift, the plot intricacies delightfully eye-popping, and the technical detail solidly convincing."

—Publishers Weekly

"A REAL GEM . . . Authentic and hair-raising . . . All too scary in light of today's headlines."

—Ocala Star-Banner (Fl.)

"GREAT ENTERTAINMENT . . . A novel that crackles with international excitement!"

—Press-Register (Mobile, Al.)

"A ROARING CLIMAX!"

—Ft. Wayne Journal-Gazette (In.)

Don't Miss These Richard Cox Thrillers—
Also from Berkley Books . . .

GROUND ZERO
THE ICE RAID

ABOUT THE AUTHOR: Both a pilot and Reserve Paratroop Major, Richard Cox was for seven years Defense Correspondent for *The Daily Telegraph,* and has reported wars, revolutions and other disasters first hand. He has been flying since he was 21 and his first job on leaving Oxford was with one of Britain's largest aircraft manufacturers. His international bestselling novels combine his unique experiences with world-wide intrigue.

Berkley Books by Richard Cox

RICHARD COX

THE KGB DIRECTIVE

This Berkley book contains the complete
text of the original hardcover edition.

THE KGB DIRECTIVE

A Berkley Book / published by arrangement with
the author

PRINTING HISTORY
Hutchinson edition published 1981
Berkley edition / March 1988

For information address: The Berkley Publishing Group,
200 Madison Avenue, New York, New York 10016.

ISBN: 0-425-10414-1

A BERKLEY BOOK ® TM 757,375
Berkley Books are published by The Berkley Publishing Group,
200 Madison Avenue, New York, New York 10016.

PRINTED IN THE UNITED STATES OF AMERICA

10 9 8 7 6 5 4 3 2 1

Acknowledgements

I owe a debt of gratitude to organizations who helped me with this book, notably the Accident Investigation Branch, the Royal Aircraft Establishment, the Police and the Transport and General Workers Union.

More especially I would like to thank Elizabeth Batchelor, John Bruce-Lockhart, Bob Ford, Ned Kelly, Ron Nethercott, Geoffrey Wilkinson, a KGB captain who frequently gave me lunch before his deportation from Britain, and Sheila Pincus who typed the manuscript.

Because the threat of sabotage in industry is so real, the technical processes described in this book include one deliberate mistake. I shall be delighted if any reader suggests where it lies.

Richard Cox

1

A chill November wind chased the dead leaves along Kensington Palace Gardens, whirling them in eddies down the avenue. The road sweeper, manipulating a long broom, made a desultory show of clearing the gutters, the collar of his donkey jacket up around his ears, a woollen cap pulled tight down on his skull. He trudged slowly past the Russian Embassy, a gaunt Edwardian edifice behind a wall, and glanced through the gates, noting the registration of a car parked there. When he next bent down to shovel up a pile of leaves, he murmured the number into a miniaturized tape recorder concealed in his coat, then pushed his cart on again. Of the many ways in which the British Security Service kept watch on the Russians this was the most basic.

High within the Embassy itself a middle-aged man glanced down through his net-curtained window, saw the sweeper, chuckled gently to himself and returned to reading the document he had just received. As he perused it further the expression on his broad, jowled face hardened and the humour died. Colonel Maxim Petrovich Grigoriev was fifty-six years old and feeling it. He had been in London too long already. During four years he had lost patience with Britain and his tasks there. Now, to add to his burdens, came this infuriating provocation. He looked again at the headline in the newspaper.

There followed several paragraphs of overexcited journalistic prose, spiked with such adjectives as 'chilling' and 'extraordinary', claiming that details of a highly secret document had come into the hands of the author: a document moreover which he had 'checked with Western intelligence sources, who are satisfied that it is what it seems.'

Beneath was a passable picture of the KGB's Chairman Andropov, standing among a group of Soviet leaders, with a translation of what purported to be a letter from the less senior General Kutuzov to Grigoriev himself. This bore the subsidiary headline

The KGB's Directive to their London Resident

Dear Comrade Colonel,
I attach herewith the new Directive to the London Residency. This Directive number 61 has been approved by Comrade Chairman Andropov and lies within the strategic framework laid down by the Central Committee.

There are few basic changes in the Directive. The strategic aims of the Central Committee and the role of the KGB in achieving these aims have been consistent since Directive number 26. . . .

At this point the reproduction ceased, ending dramatically in a carefully torn edge of the translation. Then, below, came the concluding phrases:

Affairs are going well for us in Britain: but no rashness is justified. The action taken by Douglas Home showed that the British knew much more than we calculated. It could be repeated. Move slowly, time is on our side.

Again the translation, reproduced as a facsimile letter, ended in a torn edge. Beneath came a single photographed line of Cyrillic script and the signature, 'Ivor Kutuzov', written firmly and clearly, the strokes of the 'K' bold and hard, the loop of the 'z' characteristically flamboyant.

'Not bad,' Grigoriev muttered to himself. 'Not bad at all.' He recognized the picture too. It had been taken during a

May Day parade in Red Square several years ago. As Chairman of the Komissariat Gosudarstvennoi Bezopasnosti, the Committee for State Security, known universally by its initials KGB, Andropov was seldom photographed.

It was even less usual for one of the subsidiary directors to be as much as named. In fact Kutuzov headed the First Chief Directorate of the KGB, the one which dealt with foreign operations. Under his control were departments handling Administration and Support, Specialized Operations, and Geographical Areas. The Third Department was one of the latter and dealt with the United Kingdom, Australia, New Zealand and Scandinavia. This appeared an illogical grouping, and indeed Scandinavia was included more for historical than current reasons. Of the old British Commonwealth countries the other major Dominions were now more relevantly linked to adjacent areas rather than Britain: Canada to the United States; South Africa, due to its extreme revolutionary potential, to the emergent nations of black Africa.

Grigoriev reached into his desk drawer for a magnifying glass and studied the reproduction of the single Russian line and the signature. The translation 'Move slowly, time is on our side' was accurate. As for the signature, if it was a fake then it had been done by someone who had seen the original.

Patiently Grigoriev re-read the whole of the translated letter, shaking his head and tapping the desk with his fingernails. The wording was all slightly wrong, even for a translation. Take the reference to Sir Alec Douglas Home's expulsion of 105 diplomats in 1971, following the defection of the traitor Oleg Adolfovich Lyalin. This setback to the KGB's activity was so graven on everyone's memory that it never needed to be referred to. The phrase in the letter about 'the British knew much more than we calculated' rang false. It implied an acceptance of blame which Kutuzov would unrelentingly have pinned on his predecessor. The First Chief Director of the Moscow Centre did not indulge in self-criticism. Otherwise this story had certainly caught the spirit of his true instructions. Consistency. The slow grind. The knowledge that in the end the bourgeois capitalist democracies would collapse. This was how the Kremlin thought, confident that any reverses were as insignificant as the brief retreats of an incoming tide. He knew it because it had been his life for a quarter of a century. And he was becoming bored by it.

The Colonel lifted his eyes, leaned forward and squinted down through the net curtains which made long-range photography of papers on his desk impractical. Below in the wide street the sweeper was shovelling more leaves into his dirty galvanized-iron box, shoulders hunched. Across the shoulders of his donkey jacket were the letters 'RBK&C'. Grigoriev read them mechanically, as if they were a useful distraction. The Royal Borough. What did the man down there care for his masters, either real or pretended? He kept up the façade, edging the length of Millionaires' Row in the wet, a policeman of the cold war on his beat.

'Hell!' exclaimed Grigoriev, bracing himself. 'If that slave hasn't caught the British disease, why should I?' Once again he began to labour through the key phrases of 'Directive 61' as it had been summarized in the newspaper.

> To exploit Britain as a base for creating a revolutionary situation in Western Europe ... destroy parliamentary democracy ... undermine the total economy; and in particular to destroy the prosperity of British industry through the strike weapon ... violence and intimidation should be encouraged ... other revolutionary groups are never allies ... Marxism the only serious political and social alternative....

In essence the theme was correct. The Kremlin's policy had not changed. The aims were the same, the means the same. Penetrate the Labour Party, the unions, the media, education. Grigoriev shook his head slowly and grunted. He was a big man, a typical Slav, running to fat a trifle maybe, though still fit. He needed physical action. But the one place where there was immediate, violent action – Northern Ireland – was denied him. Relationships with the IRA were never dealt with through London. In the old days there had been real excitement. He remembered landing once from a submarine off the coast of Norway, slipping ashore far down the Ballsfjord near Tromsö in the darkness of a winter night. The captain of a ferry boat had spotted the submarine as it slipped out towards the sea at dawn and for two days the Norwegian navy had hunted it without success. His own mission had never been discovered. Now that was an operation he had enjoyed.

But Britain. Grigoriev found the lassitude which pervaded every level of society affecting him. The huge majority of British people simply did not believe that revolutionary change was possible, desirable or imminent. So far as he could see they lived only for football and pay rises. Even the militant left was hopelessly divided. When he first arrived he had ached to introduce some order into their rivalries. However, his activities were depressingly circumscribed by his own seniority. As head of the KGB's London Residency Grigoriev was not permitted to run agents himself; subordinates like Rusopov did that. His own cover as a Counsellor (Commercial) in the Russian Embassy was a pretence without any serious spice of danger. He presumed the British knew who he was. They would not demand his recall except in the most extreme circumstances because it would result in the expulsion of their own Head of Station in Moscow. Tit for tat. The 1971 expulsions had been a once-in-a-generation affair. Why then, he pondered, had the newspaper article not named him? Maybe the British officials who had so clearly inspired it were reluctant to stir the pot too much. But the explanation was not satisfactory. Nor could he be sure, the more he considered it, that this apparent plant was a forgery. The gist of it was accurate. Could it be that the phraseology was blurred by fading memory rather than deceit: the memory of someone who had seen past correspondence between Moscow and the London Residency? Someone who had enjoyed access to the KGB files a few years ago. Someone able to hand over a genuine letter from Kutuzov. A traitor, in other words. It was not a pleasant thought.

He sat for a good half hour, turning over in his mind the various ways in which to counter the scandal which must follow the publication of 'Directive 61'. He had been sent this advance copy of the *Sunday Echo* by a contact in the National Graphical Association, the union whose members were principally responsible for the newspaper's printing. They had achieved a production hold-up. But only a minor one. Most of the intended edition would be printed. Today was Thursday. This material must be in Kutuzov's hands by tomorrow and the Director himself must decide on a course of action, apart from the obvious flat denials. The Director had to be involved, given the potentially compromising circumstances.

Suddenly Grigoriev remembered the reception downstairs. The Defence Attaché, a Major General, was throwing a party. The normal proportion of officers and civil servants from the British Ministry of Defence had been invited. One of them had been selected at his special request. He would have to be there. Methodically he put away his papers, secured the steel cabinets, twirled the combination locks, re-checked the entire room, then deposited the keys in their special box and went for a wash before descending. In his dark blue suit, the trousers a little tight over the stomach now, and the cloth stretched over his broad back, he looked like any one of a thousand Soviet diplomats. He would have worn the same suit whether he was checking harbour facilities in Malta or touring a ball-bearing factory in Sweden. It was his unofficial uniform.

The ground-floor reception rooms in the Embassy were reached through wide double doors in the main hall. As Grigoriev came downstairs the first guests were coming up the steps from the outside, where the chauffeur-driven cars would be lining up to disgorge their occupants. Soon the hall would be full of couples waiting to be announced to the host by a British flunkey, dressed in a red tailcoat, who asked their names in a stage whisper, then bellowed them out like a sergeant major on the parade ground.

Grigoriev nodded to the flunkey and walked through the double doors. The Major General stood just inside, flanked by his wife and the Military Attaché. He was in full uniform, medals sprouting from the lapel of his khaki tunic in a row of shining discs which slanted halfway down his chest. He greeted Grigoriev familiarly. 'Welcome, Maxim Petrovich.' After all, in everything except outward appearances the KGB Colonel was his senior. Grigoriev shook hands courteously with the wife, nodded to the effusively smiling Military Attaché and moved on into the room, neatly gathering up a glass of vodka en route. The drinks were held by a waiter on a silver salver. Grigoriev knew the vodka would run out early, as would the diminutive portions of caviar on squares of toast. Allocations of Russia's national delicacies were strict. The General's party came too soon after the 7 November celebration of the anniversary of the Revolution for the quantities to be anything but small. Grigoriev liked his vodka. He gulped the first glassful down and rapidly secured a replacement.

The room filled up quickly. People gathered in knots of three or four, officers from the Soviet bloc and her allies all in uniform, everyone else in civilian clothes. A woman photographer took flashlight pictures for a diplomatic magazine. Despite the high ceiling the noise grew. For perhaps half an hour Grigoriev did his duty, exchanging stilted small talk with strangers, noticing the occasional pretty wife of a guest. Their best friends could not claim that many of the Embassy wives were attractive. They were dumpy, plainly dressed women who tended to congregate in corners, ignoring everyone else. The Colonel's own spouse was at home in Moscow: she had a job in a Ministry which she had refused to abandon. He missed her. But their children were grown up now and there was no reason to deny her a career.

Rusopov, his assistant, materialized, nudging him discreetly. 'The Air Commodore is over there, Comrade Colonel.' Only fellow Party members called each other 'Comrade', like members of a special club. Of Russia's

257,000,000 population only 1,000,000 were Party members. Within this controlling elite existed a closed system of patronage, a secret roster known as *nomenklatura* of those selected by the Party bosses to hold the most sensitive positions. These men and women, at whatever level, from villages to the Politburo, wielded great power and enjoyed enormous privileges. Grigoriev was one of them.

He followed Rusopov's glance and studied the Briton for a moment. The Air Commodore was of medium height, with a craggy face and unfashionably short hair. He wore a noticeably well-cut grey pinstripe suit, a pale blue shirt and a striped club tie. Not the usual airforce officer, thought Grigoriev; pilots often looked uncomfortable out of uniform. This one, for all his intent expression, appeared completely at ease as he chatted to a younger man. Possibly that was why the British had transferred him to the Procurement Executive in the Ministry of Defence from the Defence Sales team. In either job he was of keen interest. Grigoriev eased his way past another group and introduced himself.

'Grigoriev. Counsellor of the Embassy.' No point in wasting words on additional platitudes. He affected a slight stiffness of manner to emphasize the point that he was one of the hosts.

The younger man responded first. 'This is Air Commodore Stringer. I'm Defence Correspondent of the *Sunday Echo*.'

Grigoriev shook hands, looking the journalist over sharply. A few defence correspondents were usually invited to these receptions: not only did they serve as a catalyst to conversation, if they knew their jobs they were very well informed. The Americans reckoned any top-class defence writer knew 98 per cent of NATO's secrets, but refrained from revealing them in print.

'We were just discussing the new airliner,' remarked the journalist provocatively. 'Quite a project.'

'Ah.' Grigoriev was non-committal.

'The government has given Western Aircraft the go-ahead on the 207,' the journalist explained. 'In answer to a question from Norman Huntley, Western's local MP, the Industry Secretary announced a government contribution of three hundred million pounds towards the estimated six hundred million it's going to cost. Half, in other words.' He let slip a calculated indiscretion. 'A half share in Britain's final bid to stay in the big league of civil aircraft construction.'

'Bit of an overstatement, don't you think?' muttered the Air Commodore suavely. Although he realized that the journalist was deliberately stirring things up, he still disliked hearing his country denigrated. 'As I'm sure our friend here knows.' He smiled crookedly at the Russian, a smile that never reached his eyes. 'We have a wide variety of international collaborative projects on hand. Military and civil.'

'With respect, Air Commodore, the military can afford the high additional costs of collaboration. Civil projects can't.'

Stringer bridled. That phrase 'with respect' caught him on the raw. 'With equal respect,' he remarked cuttingly, 'our aircraft industry is in damn good shape and the 207 is an outstanding design.' He would have liked to say more. He was well briefed because the 207 had military applications which were being kept under wraps. However, it was safer in present company to shift the subject. 'In any case, if you want an example of a civil collaborative success, how about the Airbus?'

Grigoriev listened politely, but his brain was racing. He had the keenest possible interest in the 207 project. That was why the Air Commodore had been invited tonight. But for the other distraction he would have known today's news.

'This announcement was in the Parliament?' he asked.

'Three hours ago,' said the journalist. 'Nicely timed so we could get our copy away for the early editions.'

They were interrupted by a Belgian diplomat joining the conversation. Grigoriev slipped away. A few minutes later, negotiating his way through the press of guests, he found Rusopov again. Of all his staff Vladimir Sergeyevich Rusopov possessed the most agile, technically oriented brain. A graduate of the Academy of Sciences, he could have pursued a distinguished career in industry had not his strong Party affiliations led him through the Komsomol to the KGB. He still looked like an intellectual, rather thin with untidy hair, a diffident smile and spectacles. His post as a Second Secretary (Scientific) in the Embassy was ideal. As well as the undercover work which principally concerned him, he was genuinely sought after as an adviser to visiting trade delegations. His whole appearance and manner were worlds removed from the KGB 'heavy' of Western imaginings and he was one of the most successful operators in the London Residency. He admired his senior because, in their opposite ways, they were both professionals, and Grigoriev in turn felt an almost fatherly affection for his protégé.

'Ah, Volodya.' As he spoke Grigoriev quietly stretched out his glass to a waiter for a refill of vodka. 'Can you spare a moment?' He was glad to have his assistant at hand and called him by the familiar diminutive of Vladimir.

'Of course, Comrade Colonel.'

'Let's go through.' Grigoriev led the way to the last of the three reception rooms, a curious Gothic appendage to the main building, with high, coloured glass windows, potted plants and the aura, if not the temperature, of a hothouse. 'You are aware,' he asked as soon as they were in a corner and alone, 'that the British are going ahead with the 207?'

'I heard a few minutes ago.' Rusopov looked impassively at his superior, knowing what he was after. 'All we need is confirmation that manufacture will be at Frampton.'

The information was released while the reception was in progress. The 207 would be constructed by Western Aircraft Ltd at their Frampton factory. Three prototypes would be built initially.

The following morning Grigoriev waited impatiently for his assistant's summary. Today was a Friday. If he could complete his proposals fast enough, they would catch the afternoon's diplomatic bag and be on General Kutuzov's desk first thing Monday. And be an excellent antidote to the aggravation of the fraudulent 'Directive 61'.

'Good morning, Comrade Colonel.' Rusopov paused on the threshold of his superior's room, as he always did, not merely out of respect for rank, but because the first request was so often to fetch some document or other. Today proved no exception.

'Tell the clerk to bring the contact files.'

An hour later the two men had reminded themselves of the basic management and trade-union structure at Frampton.

'We are certain that our original political assessment was correct?' demanded Grigoriev.

'In more ways than one. The last government made a commitment to the workforce at Frampton factory that the level of employment there would be maintained whatever happened. It's a highly charged political issue. If the 207 is not built at least seven thousand men would be unemployed. There are three marginal parliamentary seats in the area and neither party dare risk closing Frampton. Quite apart from the promise made to the unions.'

'So there is as much at stake as our first reports to Moscow suggested?'

'The journalist you met last night expressed the situation accurately several weeks ago.' Rusopov thrust forward a newspaper clipping stuck to a thin piece of backing paper and dated '*Sunday Echo*, 19 October'.

After four years of indecision the future of Britain's only major independent civil project hands in the balance. If Parliament does not soon agree the funding of the 207 airliner then the few prospective foreign customers lined up will finally lose interest. Hugh Johnson, President of the key American purchaser, Atlantic Airlines, was outspoken yesterday. 'The 207 is tailor-made for our domestic routes,' he told me. 'But if your boys don't get off their asses and build it, we shall be forced to look elsewhere. We can't hold off re-equipment decisions any longer.'

The question facing MPs as they debate the aerospace industry is a simple one. Are we who were once a leading world manufacturer to drop out of the civil market for ever? Do we become a mere sub-contractor? Or is the line of brilliant designs like the Viscount, the BAC 1-11, the HS 125 business jet and the Anglo-French Concorde to be followed through into the 1980s and beyond? It is not merely the jobs of seven thousand skilled men at Frampton which are at stake. It is the future of a whole industry.

'He exaggerates, of course,' commented Rusopov. 'What reporter does not? But in essence he is right. It took the Germans a quarter of a century to recover from the enforced closure of their industry after the war. If the British cease to make large civil aircraft the design teams will be broken up, their ability to manage major projects will decay, they'll be out of the market for ever.'

Grigoriev grunted. Rusopov understood his ideas perfectly. 'How long does it take to build a prototype airliner?' he demanded.

'If the designs are already complete and they start cutting metal almost immediately, they might have the first 207 flying in a year to a year and a half.'

'Then we have no time to lose.'

'I agree, Comrade Colonel. Once the Director approves we shall have our hands full.'

For the first time in many months Grigoriev felt the same sudden contraction in the pit of his stomach as he had felt when he had slid into the rubber dinghy in the Ballsfjord, the same tense excitement as when he had cornered a spy in a deserted tenement in East Berlin. He knew he was on the brink of action.

2

Driving cloud hung over the Frampton skyline, grey and ominous. The wind moaned around the tower block. 'Roll on Christmas,' muttered Ken Norris, as he parted the thin bedroom curtains and glanced out. Patches of grass below were white with frost and ice fretted the windscreens of parked cars. He wondered if his own would start. He wasn't taking the bloody bus to work in this weather.

'Christ, what time is it?' Marion shifted in the wide bed, blinking at the dull light.

'Go back to sleep, love. It's not six thirty.' As a community worker she started a full hour later than he had to clock in at the aircraft factory. Usually he only woke her just before leaving.

She turned herself over, away from the window, her naked arms embracing the pillows, snuggling into the soft warmth where he had lain. The bed was one of their few extravagances, virtually the only concession Ken had made when she moved in with him six months ago. She had categorically refused to sleep in the bed his estranged wife had used. They had made the most of the new one. Marion Robbins was a woman of deep sexuality, masked in public even before she met Ken by the offbeat way she dressed and by her one serious inhibition. She was ashamed of her own middle-class family. In effect she apologized for her origins through her job as a social worker in a deprived part of the city. This self-consciousness was at the core of Ken's attractiveness to her as well. He wasn't merely aggressively on the way up. He had an uncompromising working-class directness which her own relations completely lacked, with their social snobberies and petty dramas. He even insisted on simplifying her name to Mary.

Ken closed the curtains so that the light should not disturb her, then pulled on his trousers and went down the short passage to the bathroom, closing the bedroom door quietly. Though he had once called her a bourgeois bitch during a quarrel, he would never have brought her to live with him if he hadn't respected her. She wasn't only attractive, she had a touch of class. He liked that. Although he swore habitually both at work and in his thoughts, he kept his language clean in front of her.

The bathroom was a mess, underclothes draped along a nylon wire, towels in a heap, a rim of soapy grime on the basin. 'I wish she'd bloody clean the place more often,' he thought. He wiped away the dirt and shaved. Then he went to the kitchen and made them both a cup of tea. When he got back to the bedroom she was fully awake, sitting up and huddling the blankets round her shoulders.

'Oh, thanks.' She took the cup. 'Just what I needed.' She looked at him. 'Are you going to ask for the time off?'

'It's union business,' he said defensively, reaching for his shirt. 'A meeting's a meeting.' He had to be alone on this trip to London, no question about it.

'Christmas shopping, more like. You want to see the lights, that's all. I've half a mind to come with you.'

'I'll be on the first train back when it's over. Shops'll be shut before I even get there.'

'Not on Thursdays. They stay open late in the West End.' She bit her lip, regretting she had spoken.

'I'm not that ignorant! Listen, Mary, I'm going for the Youth Committee, not the shops. Right?' Feeling he was being too harsh, he crossed to the bed and gave her a teasing hug. 'You're after a present, is that it? Should have guessed, shouldn't I?'

He pulled on a thick polo-neck sweater, then took his leather jacket off the peg behind the door.

'Very fancy,' she said mockingly, but the admiration in her eyes gave her away. Ken Norris was a good-looking man in his early thirties, powerfully built yet slim and not afraid of spending the £140 a week he earned on things he liked. Plenty of women would give a lot to be where she was.

He walked across to the bed, chucked her under the chin and kissed her on the mouth. 'I should be back by midnight. Don't wait up if you're tired.'

To his relief the three-year-old Ford started despite the cold. He joined the slow traffic through the city, listening to the seven o'clock news on the radio, mentally noting the latest negotiating position taken by his union in a dispute with British Leyland. The Transport and General Workers Union was the largest in Britain, an organizational colossus of two million workers in trades from aircraft manufacture to road haulage. Its leader, the General Secretary, was one of the most powerful men in the country. Ken Norris's main aim in life was simple. In twenty years time, sooner maybe, he was going to be in that office and a national figure. He was well on the way. The driving urge in Ken Norris's life, the longing for power, derived from childhood and the sufferings of his mother. Widowed by an industrial accident, reluctantly given a pitiful pension by his father's employers, she had struggled to pay for his upbringing by serving in a draper's shop. The late 1950s and early 1960s might have seemed rosy to the Tories, but the Norris family, living in two rented rooms in north London, never had it good. Never at all. Not even before the disastrous day when his mother was accused of stealing a length of braid in the shop. It would have been a senseless thing for her to take. She and Ken needed bread, not braid, and she had not stolen it. None the less, it was missing from her counter and she was sacked. The ill-repute stayed with her. Thereafter she could only find work locally as a cleaner. Young Ken grew up imbued with a hatred of the bosses and a determination to make good himself and secure her old age.

He went to work at sixteen for a small engineering firm, joining the T&G rather than the Amalgamated Engineering Workers because he was unskilled. He'd been bringing home a regular pay packet with immense pride for under eighteen months when his mother died. He was left only with the hatred. He'd already become a Communist Party member and, now alone in the world, he responded readily to their suggestion that he move to Derby and seek work at Rolls-Royce. Within a few years he became a shop steward there. If he was still only a semi-skilled worker he was a highly skilled activist.

He was twenty-six when he married Carol, a girl from Islington whom he'd met one weekend when she was on holiday in the Peak District. He always thought it funny that he had to go all that way up there to meet a girl whose home was two miles from where he used to live. She was vivacious and intelligent and took readily to the suggestion of moving south again when the idea of going to Frampton came up. Western Aircraft was expanding. He found a job there easily. Within a year he'd achieved shop-steward status again. But the next twelve months brought the end of the road for Carol. They had not been blessed with children, his politics began to worry her, and, more intrusively, she realized how little room there was for her to come first with a man so corrosively dedicated to avenging the past.

Norris never fully understood why Carol walked out. He had thought she approved of his ambitions: he was anticipating getting himself elected as Convenor of the Joint Shop Stewards Committee at Western Aircraft next time round. Anyway she left and before long he met Marion and she moved in.

As he approached the factory, his mind was on the Convenorship. So few union members wanted responsibility that anyone prepared to shoulder it could hardly fail. He chuckled to himself. They were an unambitious lot of bastards at Frampton too, not like Derby. No political motivation. That was why he'd come to the West Country. It was wide open.

A few moments before 7.20 he was checked through one of the factory gates, cracked a joke with the blue-uniformed works policeman, parked the Ford, and began walking briskly towards what Western Aircraft called Production Centre Three. Broadly speaking all the small assemblies were manufactured and treated in the 'Top End Shops'. Then the parts – everything from the smallest detail to huge wing spars, machined out of solid aluminium – were taken down to the assembly hangars: literally taken down, because the factory's extensive buildings sprawled over a low hill.

Western Aircraft had a distinguished history. It had been founded before the Great War, in the days of wood-and-string aeroplanes, when the electric trams clattering through Frampton's centre were symbols of progress and modernization. In those far-off days the grass field from which the first aeroplanes flew was several miles clear of the city. The wooden sheds sprang up in farmland at the foot of the hill. The original directors of the company, men fired with visions about the possibilities of flight, prudently acquired rather more fields than they needed immediately. They wanted to keep the area free of obstructions. But even their dreams never foresaw a tarmac swathe of runway one and a half miles long cutting through the countryside, though they did buy the hill up which the factory's offices and buildings expanded. As this private industrial enterprise grew, so did Frampton. Housing estates edged out around the airfield. Now the population density had increased to the point where some local politicians wanted to ban the flying as a hazard to the homes of the very workers who built the aircraft.

This campaign began when Western Aircraft was already past its prime. From 30,000 employees in the Second World War its payroll had shrunk to 7000. Many of the sheds past which Ken Norris hurried, his coat collar turned up against the wind, were now as forlorn and disused as the concrete air-raid shelters which burrowed into the ground beside them. As he walked, he glanced down the hill through a gap in the buildings. A grey painted Land-Rover was slowly pulling a small, sleek private jet from the maintenance hangar to the runway. 'It's all right for some,' thought Norris angrily. 'The bosses don't bloody go by train.'

Centre Three was a complex of buildings, joined by covered walk-ways. One was the process facility where Norris worked. Although it had four entrances of its own, the biting wind was persuading men to reach it by the most sheltered route. This was through the press shop. A painted sign by the door announced 'Production Centre Three'. Workmen were jostling to enter, stamping their feet against the cold, greeting each other and joking.

'How's yer luck, Ken?' asked one convivially.

'Great.' Norris grinned and stuck a thumb up. That was his standard reply. He was always OK, by definition. His mates brought him their problems. Never the reverse. Looking after union members was the clue to his success as an organizer. 'How's the old woman, then?' He knew Perce's wife had been ill.

'Still poorly.'

Norris nodded sympathetically as they passed through the door. 'Don't forget we have rest homes,' he said. 'She'd be eligible.'

'I'll remember that, Ken.'

The two men separated. Norris glanced at his watch. Seven twenty-six. He hurried on past groups of men standing around by their machines chatting, reading newspapers, killing time until 7.30. Overhead hung a painted sign:

Think Ahead
Think Cost
Think Quality

The time clock in the process shop was near the door. Reaching it, he pulled his card out of the rack, punched it into the slot and replaced it. Another day had begun. He paused, caught by the thought, wondering what they wanted from him in London, then walked more relaxedly to the area where he worked.

Ken Norris was a grade A operative, a skilled man responsible for the final corrosion proofing of aircraft parts after their heat treatment, a process technically known as anodizing. Aircraft construction had come a long way since Western Aircraft's beginnings and the days of fabric, wood and wire, though a tiny proportion of piano wire was still used in the factory, duly handled by a solitary member of the Musicians Union. No trade union ever let slip the tiniest toehold here. The inter-union rivalries at Frampton, with twenty-three involved, were pretty nearly as sophisticated as the techniques of construction: as more and more T&G members had become skilled, so its competition with the craft union, the Amalgamated Engineering Workers, had intensified. In his way, Ken Norris exemplified the growing status of the T&G, whose members were now predominant in the treatments complex. The unions not only fought the management, they fought each other.

The anodizing process involved dipping metal parts in a series of liquids, including a mixture of chromic acid and sulphuric acid – a pickle, they called it. Acrid odours drifted up from the long tanks. Norris peered down into one, the surface of the acid covered by what looked like hundreds of ping-pong balls gently jostling each other. To a large extent these chroffles cut down the evaporation of the solution, heated to 60° C, and were easily pushed aside when a part was lowered into the tank. Such fumes as did escape were sucked away by extractors. He sniffed. The system wasn't working too well. If he needed a complaint, this was ready made. Anyone working with chrome had to have a medical check monthly, by law.

The foreman appeared, conspicuous in a white coat with red cloth flashes on collar and cuffs.

'Been a hold-up back there,' he said. 'Snag on one of the ovens during the night. The lads from pyrometry are checking it. Is your last batch through yet?'

'We finished all but a couple yesterday.' Norris jerked his head at two curved pieces of aluminium sheet, hanging in a special rack.

'Finish them off. Then you might as well grab a cuppa.'

'Matter of fact, I want to see Mr Burnett.'

'What's it this time, Ken?' The foreman was only mildly curious. On union business the shop stewards invariably dealt direct with the shop manager, bypassing him.

'Youth Committee. Have to go to London.'

The foreman nodded. 'Yes,' he agreed, as though he might somehow have had a say in the matter himself. 'You'll have to see Mr Burnett about that.' He moved away, the ever-patrolling lowest representative of the management.

Bloody old fool, what the hell does he think he knows, muttered Norris to himself, watching the foreman go. He looked round for his companion. No one could accuse him of being work-shy.

'Come on, Les. Let's get these two out of the way, then.'

Together the men lifted the first aluminium pressing, fitting it to a bar hoist with which it would be lowered into each tank in turn. Norris picked up the route card for the part, checking the processes ordered, even though he knew what they would be. Then he swung the pressing over and down into the first tank.

When the anodizing was complete and the parts were in the drying oven, where they would remain for twenty minutes, Norris told his mate, 'Right, I have to see Burnett, OK?' and set off briskly towards the Shop Manager's office. As he walked, he saw Burnett in the distance, dark-suited, moving down a line of machinery, and altered course to intercept him.

Bob Burnett was the key man in Norris's day-to-day work; equally strong willed, physically resilient, technically highly competent. An ex-apprentice, he could have taken over almost any of the jobs in the area he controlled at a moment's notice. The men respected his ability even though if he ever had laid a finger on one of their jobs they would have all downed tools in seconds. Less grudgingly, they admired his playing with a local soccer team on Saturdays. For all the occasional snide remarks about Bob being ambitious and on the make, it was hard to see him as a class enemy when he came from the same background and the same schools as themselves, spoke with the same burring Frampton accent. Norris, by origin a Londoner not a local, recognized him as a tough opponent and devoted much thought to ways of undermining his authority. Both men knew they could be on a collision course at any time, but maintained a superficial politeness in their dealings.The continual, abrasive confrontation of many Midlands factories had not yet been imposed on Western Aircraft.

'Could I have a word, Mr Burnett?' He gave the request an inflexion implying he had to.

'Give me ten minutes.' Burnett glanced at him. 'In the office.' He resumed what he was doing. He had a considered style for dealing with Norris. Don't let him bug me, but be available quickly. Play it cool, yet friendly.

The Manager's office was small, basically a part of the shop floor partitioned off, but with a carpet, desk, table and enough upright chairs for a small meeting.

'Have a seat, Ken,' said Burnett when Norris entered. 'What can I do for you?'

'Couple of things.' He pulled out a folded piece of paper and handed it across. 'Only came this morning. I'd have to catch the three thirty train.'

Burnett scanned the paper, which was a roneoed sheet calling a special meeting of the Youth Committee of the International Aircraft Workers Federation. 'Pretty short notice, isn't it?' he remarked casually, masking his suspicions. The International Aircraft Workers Federation was a Communist front organization about which the management had recently received some frank advice from the Confederation of British Industry. 'Who else is going?'

'Just me.' Norris was too intelligent to lie about something so easily checked. 'The Joint Committee agreed a couple of months back – that I do this one, I mean.'

Burnett noticed the man's defensiveness. But if he had the blessing of the factory's Joint Shop Stewards Committee there could be no objection. He made a mental calculation. Shop stewards did union business 'on the clock'. For this evening Norris could reasonably book around four hours' overtime.

'Will you be in for work tomorrow?' he asked.

'As usual.' The confidence returned to Norris's slightly clipped style of speech. He reckoned he was over the hurdle.

'So what's the other problem?'

'Fumes. The extractors on the pickle tanks aren't effective. Could be injurious to health. You know the Hazardous Chemicals Act as well as I do, Mr Burnett.'

'Have you seen the foreman?'

'I told him I was seeing you.' Norris had deliberately skipped a stage in the procedure in order to make his trade-off clear to the Manager: prevent my London trip and you'll have a stoppage. This was the way the system operated. Both union and management held ammunition in reserve.

'I'm a bit busy, Ken.' Burnett appreciated the bargain and guessed that the fumes, which caused recurrent trouble, would now be held over as a counterbalance for some future dispute. Not that he could ignore the request. 'If the foreman can't get the extractors sorted out, I'll come and have a look myself.' As he would. With the 207 project under way, his own instructions were to avoid unnecessary confrontations.

'All right, Mr Burnett.' Norris yielded.

'So, what time do you want to go?'

'About three.' The shop steward's relief was evident in spite of his self-control. As he left the room Burnett wondered what was so important about a Youth Committee.

The weather had cleared. Pale winter sunlight slanted onto the flaking bark of the plane trees. Inside the Embassy Rusopov re-read the file, repeating details softly to himself in

REGISTRATION CARD*

No. 27816

(Photo of Norris)

1. SURNAME, GIVEN NAME AND PATRONYM Norris, Kenneth Arthur

2. PSEUDONYM Yuri

3. SINCE WHEN IN THE NET

4. ADDRESS a) OFFICE

b) HOME 44a Harold Wilson House, Minehead Rd, Frampton

5. PLACE OF WORK AND POSITION Western Aircraft Ltd, Grade A worker in Production Centre Three. TGWU shop steward.

6. FINANCIAL CONDITIONS Adequately paid but accepts gifts and expenses

BIOGRAPHICAL DATA:

Born in London 1948. Separated from wife Carol. Since 1979 has so-called common-law wife, Marion Robbins of bourgeois origins. Worked in Rolls-Royce plant, Derby. Moved to Western Aircraft 1978. Elected shop steward 1979. Member of Shop Stewards Committee.

Came to notice during trade union visit to Tupolev works 1969. Resigned CPGB 1972 on our advice. Black Sea holiday 1974 with wife Carol. Second holiday alone 1977. Advised leave Rolls-Royce. Joined Frampton North Labour Party 1978. Member of Constituency Executive Committee 1980. Intelligent. Ambitious. Hates capitalist classes.

*Certain Russian words are open to different English translations.

order to memorize them. The contact procedure had been laid down by Moscow Centre with the usual exactitude.

. . . Carrying a copy of *Flight* magazine and standing near the barrier to platform five. As Yuri approaches, case officer is to say, 'Hallo, what a surprise. How is Aunt Edith?'

Yuri is to reply, 'Fancy seeing you. She is out of hospital now.'

Case Officer is to ask, 'Have you time for a cup of coffee?' and introduce himself as Peter.

After this Yuri is to be taken to an approved place, dependent on weather and time of year.

Fantastic, thought Rusopov, so at least I am allowed initiative if it rains! It was too cold for the park, impossible in a café. There was only one alternative agreed by Moscow, one which demanded the certainty of having shaken off surveillance, of shaking it off well before the contact. Even assuming Yuri remembered the simple instructions given him a year ago, responded to them, and was therefore willing, Rusopov could not risk frightening him at such a crucial moment by having to evade a tail. Wanting to remind himself of the man's appearance, he took out the registration card. He had not met Yuri himself yet.

Rusopov studied the small photograph cut from a seaside holiday group. It was relatively old. He doubted if Yuri's hard features had altered, but his hair could be longer. If Rusopov succeeded in this evening's aim of being able to add the date to item 3 on the card, then he would have a replacement picture taken.

At 1 p.m. Rusopov left the brown stone Embassy building, went through the gates, past the solitary policeman sitting inside a sentry-box-sized hut with glass windows that made it more like a lottery ticket booth than a guard post, and strode out to the Bayswater Road. He would spend the next four hours losing any tail in the shops and side streets of the West End, then take the underground to Paddington, just another traveller with his coat collar turned up against the wind, though an anxious one in spite of himself. For more than a decade the KGB had cultivated Yuri against such an eventuality as this. Today he had to be consciously brought into the net. The moment of truth was always critical.

With a slight jolt the train rumbled forward again. A tinny voice came over the loudspeaker: 'Ladies and gentlemen, this is Paddington Station. Paddington Station.' The platform slid alongside, porters gazing up at the train windows. The Frampton Inter City express was a money-spinner. With another quiver, the carriages stopped. Doors swung open, passengers began hurrying down the platform. Norris took his time, staying with the crowd but not blindly. At the barrier he showed his day-return ticket, walked a few steps and pretended to look at the big station clock.

'Why, Ken, what a surprise.'

He spun round, caught off balance. A thin-faced man in a brown overcoat stood there smiling, a magazine prominent in his left hand.

'How's Aunt Edith?'

'Better, thanks.' Norris recovered himself.

'Have you time for a coffee?'

'I could use a drink.' He was unnerved by the way the stranger had appeared.

'The bars are closed at this time, I think.' Rusopov could depart from the script now, but colloquial English vanished with it and his individual mispronunciations became more evident. 'I suggest to go somewhere private. My own flat is not so far. We can walk.' Without waiting for an answer he led the way to a side exit, a road only taxis took, where he could tell if he was followed, his trained eye noting the few people both behind and in front of them. By the time they reached the corner of Sussex Gardens he was satisfied that they were not under surveillance.

The house was divided into five flats. Rusopov rang the bell quickly before sliding his key into the lock.

'I stay here temporarily,' he explained, 'while my own apartment is decorated. I like to warn my friend in case he is in.' The explanation was plausibly close to the truth. The flat was loaned to him occasionally by a left-wing London University friend who willingly accepted the fiction that he wanted solitude to write a spare-time scientific paper. It was part of Rusopov's cover, approved by the Centre, to build up a reputation for being less than satisfied with the restrictions of diplomatic life.

The living room of the flat was lined with bookshelves. Pottery ornaments, folkweave and a couple of abstract pictures gave a little life to an otherwise rundown decor. Norris sat down, the sofa creaking uneasily beneath his weight.

'What drink do you like?' The Russian hovered near a side table.

'Whisky and water, if you don't mind.' Why not indulge himself? He had come a long way. More to the point, he could use some Dutch courage.

'I am so glad you remember our friend's arrangement.' Rusopov smiled encouragingly as he poured from a bottle. 'I have been looking forward to making acquaintance with you. This is a pleasure. My name is Peter, by the way.'

'Glad to meet you.' Norris half rose again, then abandoned the attempt and accepted the drink. 'What about this meeting, then?' he asked after taking a good, solid gulp. 'We haven't much time.' Even though he knew the notice had been a summons from the Russians, he half believed the Youth Committee might be in session. Certainly he was going to pretend he did.

'Postponed at the last moment. I am so sorry.' Rusopov did not hesitate. If this was how Yuri elected to play it, he would tag along. 'We were able to contact the others by telephone. Oh, but don't worry. We will of course refund the expense.' He gave himself a drink, turned the radio to a music programme and then sat down, facing Norris across the low glass-topped table. He had prepared what he was going to say meticulously and he wasn't going to rush things. 'For me, this is a real bonus. I had wanted to ask your advice. Now, instead of some hurried words before the meeting, we can relax.'

'Well, I'm in no hurry, I suppose.' Norris swigged some more whisky. 'What's the problem?' He was gaining confidence and with it his normal directness.

'We Russians are a peace-loving people, as you know yourself. We are constantly worried by the threat to peace made by Western militarism.' Rusopov made the despairing gesture of a father unable to control a child. 'In spite of our troop withdrawals from Germany, the so called Western Allies continue to re-arm!'

Norris nodded. He knew the theme from reading *Socialist Worker.*

'I thought you might advise on what an individual could do in Britain to stop this. You agree all freedom-loving people should act for peace?'

'I go along with that,' said Norris cautiously. 'But how do I come into it?'

'Did you realize, my friend, that the 207 project at your factory is a military one?'

'You must be joking.'

Rusopov leaned forward intently, exploiting Norris's surprise. 'I am serious.'

'We've been told it's a civil airliner.'

'It will be ordered as a troop transport by your airforce.' He reached into his coat pocket, extracted an envelope and produced a magazine cutting. 'Already the American magazine *Aviation Week* has the story.'

Norris read the clipping. He doubted if anyone on the shop floor at Westerns would give a damn. They'd built military aircraft since the factory was founded. There was subcontract work on American strike planes going through now. What counted to his mates was cash in their pockets. The only possible issue he could imagine making out of it would centre on failure by management to keep the workforce informed, and that would be bloody slender. However, since he wanted to know where this conversation was leading, and the Russian clearly hoped he would be outraged, he was prepared to be.

'They never told us!' he said, with a show of anger.

'Your government have tried to keep it secret. Inevitably, they have failed. The lies of the imperialists are always exposed.' Rusopov spoke without venom, his quiet self-confidence oddly at variance with the histrionic phrases long ground into his vocabulary. Watching the shop steward's face, he believed that the message was getting across. 'How much do they ever tell the workers?' he asked. 'What do you expect from your present government but betrayal of the workers' interests? In my country the union would be consulted from the start.'

'So are *we* supposed to be!' Norris clenched his fist angrily. 'Wait till I get back!' He lapsed into silence for a moment, thinking this one out further. But he couldn't seriously visualize it as an issue and there was a limit to his theatrical ability. He tried to shift on to an aspect of life at Westerns which genuinely did raise emotions.

'You know about Frampton?' he asked. 'Well, I'll tell you. Western was going to be nationalized, made part of British Aerospace. It wasn't because the management conned the workers. They talked the shop stewards into believing they'd lose out. Said Western had its own identity and traditions. If they got nationalized all the decisions would be made hundreds of miles away, in Weybridge or Hatfield or wherever British Aerospace thought the living was soft. They said it would be the end of Western building complete aircraft; they'd be on subcontract work within a year. The moderates supported them. Bloody lunatics like Charlie Brook. Jesus wept!'

'Brook?'

'He's one of the heat treatment inspectors. And the ACTSS steward. Bloody pain in the arse.'

'You mean?' Rusopov risked making a quick note on a scratch pad. Everything else he already knew. Indeed it was precisely because of this unwelcome situation at Western Aircraft that the KGB had steered Norris there. But this was a new name. 'Tell me about Brook.'

'He has a lot of graft in the Joint Consultative Committee at the factory. Labour Councillor, Chairman of the Constituency. Solid as they come. And they all respect him. Get rid of Charlie and we'd be in business!' Norris grinned suddenly. 'Don't worry, Comrade, I'm working on it.'

'What is ACTSS?' Rusopov pronounced the initials laboriously, as he scribbled them.

'Staff union. Association of Clerical, Technical and Supervisory Staffs. Part of the T&G in fact. Which makes things easier.'

Rusopov concluded his brief note-taking. He only wrote down complicated details, otherwise relying on his memory when recording contact with an agent.

'You spoke of consultation,' he prompted. Norris had veered off the subject in his tirade against Brook.

'The rest of the stewards weren't as bone-headed as Charlie. In exchange for no nationalization they got a new agreement on consultation over policy, production targets, manning levels, all the usual. So,' Norris stuck his fist forward, thumb up, a favourite gesture, 'we should have been consulted. If the 207's going to be military they should've asked us.'

'It is truly monstrous.' Rusopov could see his opening coming.

'Believe me, Comrade, if I can hit the bosses where it hurts them, I will! They did for my mother. I'll bloody do for them one day.'

Rusopov already knew Norris's family history, because the shop steward had poured it out one evening to a friendly Russian girl on his second Black Sea holiday, a girl the KGB had thoughtfully placed at the same table in his hotel.

'You have good reason, I know,' Rusopov said. 'What do you consider the best way to attack the management at Frampton?'

'Bring the lads out! Not that the shop floor gives a crap about whether they're making bombers or airliners, so long as the pay goes up. No, brother, what we'll stir 'em up on is infringement of rights. Breaking agreements. They have a right to be consulted, haven't they? Well, they weren't. Next thing we know the management'll be bringing in work study again. That's the line I'll take. I'll have them all out.'

'Are you sure that a strike is the correct weapon for fighting this gross betrayal of the workers?'

'It's the only one we have.' Even as he said it Norris realized the falsity of the assumption.

'Within the legalistic framework of a capitalist society,' Rusopov conceded, 'that may be true. But the framework is designed for the enslavement of the workers.'

'Too bloody right.'

'Something much stronger should be done.' The Russian smiled hesitantly and brushed a lock of hair away from his eyes. He was close to the proposition now and he wanted this moment fluid, indefinite. If Norris reacted adversely he would draw back immediately. 'Of course, I am a scientist more than a man of action. I tend to think in theories.' He lowered his voice a fraction, thinking how delicately all things were balanced. If the room were bugged, then the music ought to obscure his voice without making the shop steward wonder why he had the radio on in the first place. 'Frankly, my friend, I believe that the best theoretical solution is destruction of the 207 project. World events are at a crucial turn. Détente between East and West is endangered. Almost any action is justifiable to halt the imperialist arms race.'

Norris nodded slowly, his stock reaction to any tricky argument, but his thoughts were whirling. What did the man mean? Blow up the factory? Jesus Christ, no way. Wouldn't stop production anyhow. Not in a place the size of the Western works.

'The principle's OK,' he said at last. 'I reckon the 207 should be stopped. Question is how.'

The moment had come. Clearly the shop steward was prepared to envisage action. Rusopov took the plunge, making a play of nervousness by twirling his steel-rimmed glasses in his fingers. 'In theory the prototype 207 might crash through a design fault. If so, then potential buyers would be frightened away. There would be very bad reports in newspapers. Time would be lost. Enormous sums of money wasted. Many adverse reactions in your Parliament.' Rusopov smiled to himself. The KGB could guarantee that. 'I believe the project would be abandoned. What is your view?'

'You could be right.' Norris kept his comments short, he had only a hazy idea of how the top strata of the aircraft industry operated. 'Has the 207 got a design fault, then?'

'It would be possible to introduce one.' Rusopov allowed more confidence to creep into his approach. 'Speaking as a scientist, I can see several technical possibilites. For example, the milling machines.'

'The Marvins, you mean?' Norris thought of the squat, grey-painted, computer-controlled Marvins, quietly throbbing as their rotating bits scoured into solid metal under a continuous stream of milky coolant. They had some of the most advanced equipment in western Europe at Frampton.

'Highly sophisticated machinery,' said Rusopov. 'But if the computer program gives a wrong dimension and a piece of metal is made too thin, it might never be queried, because people think computers are gods. The computer cannot be wrong.'

'So the metal cracks one day under stress and . . . bang!'

'Exactly.' Rusopov smiled openly. His pupil was learning fast. 'Now, purely theoretically, there must be other departments where some fault could be introduced.'

'I've heard of fuel lines being blocked with wirewool. That's the sort of thing used to happen at Derby.'

'But when the engine fails the cause is discovered, yes?' Such sabotage was the kind a well-intentioned idiot would try. Rusopov dismissed it politely. 'I would prefer a technique which cannot be traced so easily.' The interview was going well, but he had a gut feeling that Norris could still be frightened off. Better to keep the discussion theoretical. 'As a scientist, I find the whole question intriguing. For instance, in your own department there is a possibility for causing stress corrosion, is there not? What happens if a part is improperly heat treated?'

'Cracks under stress.'

'Precisely. The sheet of aluminium alloy is softened before being pressed into its final form. After pressing treatment by heat is essential to precipitate the aluminium copper molecules out of solution and into conformity with the new shape. If this is not done the aluminium is liable to stress corrosion.'

'You're the scientist, brother.' Norris was becoming tense.

'Do you think I am right that if a part were given only a little heat treatment it would appear normal, yet would fail under stress?' It was a loophole question. If Norris chose to disagree he could back out with no loss of face.

'Yes.' The response took a long time coming. 'I reckon that's right. If it got past the inspector no one would know.'

'My friend.' Rusopov half smiled, shaking his head in a self-deprecatory way. 'I am too much the academic. As I told you when you arrived, I would like advice. Do you think my idea could be carried out in the heat treatment, if need arose? I know it is theoretic. Is it also practical? Only a man in your position can tell us.' He hesitated deliberately. 'We must of course hope there are other ways to stop this dangerous project. Meanwhile could you advise on my theory?'

There was silence. Phrases echoed in Norris's mind, images like newspaper headlines. Spy in factory. Russian agent exposed. 'If you don't mind,' he said at last, 'I'd like to think about it. I'll be in touch, OK?'

'All we ask is your comments,' said Rusopov, his expression remaining friendly and reassuring. 'Nothing more. Your assistance would be greatly appreciated.' He risked throwing in additional bait. 'On another matter, quite separate, we are expecting to help you.'

'What's that?'

'You will be elected Convenor next year. We have friends

who can make sure support is withheld from your rivals.' The promise was not only meant to tempt; it was reinsurance for Rusopov himself. Apparently reliable trade unionists had been known to tell the police about attempts to recruit them.

'I'd rather you fixed Charlie Brook for me!' Norris's grin was savage, without trace of humour. 'Listen, brother, I'd like to sleep on this, OK. No offence meant.' He moved awkwardly towards the door. 'Thanks for the drink.'

Rusopov followed him. 'No need to worry. If you can advise us, that is good. If not, we understand.' He opened the door. 'You can find the way down? I have things to do here, if you excuse me.' He shook hands and Norris left.

From the window Rusopov watched discreetly to see if there was any surveillance. A car started up as Norris emerged into the street, but it swung into a U-turn, away from Paddington. All was well. He sat down again and made rough notes of everything that had been said, wondering whether he had failed or not. Later, back at the Embassy, he would compose a proper 'Course of Meeting' report. He would have to admit that ideology had proved an insufficient motive. Could Afghanistan have had the same effect as Czechoslovakia? On an intellectual perhaps. Hardly on someone as ruthlessly self-interested as Norris. Ambition might be the key. He had definitely responded to that lure. And he hated this man Brook. Maybe with the addition of money he could be brought into the net. If he returned, that was. Otherwise they would have to recruit someone else. Rusopov sighed. As the Centre never ceased to remind its cadre workers, as KGB staff operating under diplomatic cover were called, they were in a difficult and complex business. But it was a challenge, an unrelenting challenge, and Vladimir Sergeyevich Rusopov, like many of his fellow countrymen, was a talented chess player.

3

The winter seemed interminably depressing to Jim Donaldson. He loathed offices, yet his recent promotion to Deputy Head of the Accident Investigation Branch kept him more desk bound than ever. The AIB was a small and little-known part of the Department of Trade. Its twenty-three inspectors were responsible for enquiring into all accidents to aircraft in Britain, or to British-registered aircraft overseas. Donaldson himself was a man of average height, with a pleasant, unassuming manner and determination which showed mainly in his deep-set blue eyes. He was a former pilot, having flown first with the RAF and latterly with British Airways. Now in his late forties, he was a most experienced investigator. But he had never fully accustomed himself to 'flying a desk', let along to living in the city.

The Accident Investigation Branch's offices used to enjoy one of the most expensive views of London: an uninterrupted prospect of the Thames. Recently the AIB had moved to the drab confines of Victoria Street and he longed for an escape more than ever.

However, as deputy head of his department, he could scarcely pray for his job to take him away from London because only a major airline disaster would do that. It might be the Dan Air Boeing crashing into a mountain on Tenerife, or a two-seat light aircraft coming down with engine failure into a Kent hopfield. The casualties could run from hundreds to none, the damage from millions of pounds to a few thousand. It would take a catastrophic disaster to release Donaldson from the administrative chores of his seniority. He was caught.

One February morning, when the wind whistled through the trees in St James's Park and the forecast was of snow, the Chief Inspector called him in and announced a change of routine.

'Jim,' he began without preamble, 'we're going to follow through the production and flying of Western's 207. Same as we did with Concorde. The Minister's decided that as this is our make or break attempt to stay in the world market we can't take enough precautions.'

'I don't blame him.' Donaldson grinned. 'With three hundred million quid of government money backing it he's got a big personal commitment there.'

'You need to be more tactful about our political masters.' The Chief Inspector did not smile back. He was a small, rather thin-faced man who worried constantly about government spending cuts affecting his department's efficiency. 'If you're not careful you'll queer your pitch one day, Jim. Remember the old saw. We propose and our masters dispose. It was never more true than now. Thank God they are disposed to let us get acquainted with the 207 ahead of any possible trouble.'

'When would you like me to go down?' The growing enthusiasm in Donaldson's voice reflected his sudden realization of all that this meant. He'd flown Meteors at Frampton, long ago. So had Bill Broughton, now Western Aircraft's chief test pilot. The whole area was home territory.

'It's occurred to you that this will have its pleasant side?' The Chief Inspector could guess what was going on in his deputy's mind. 'Go as soon as you like. I want you and McPherson to treat the 207 as your special baby. Familiarize yourself thoroughly with its design, its construction and – eventually – its flying characteristics. God forbid it should have problems. But if it does, then you two ought to be ready-made experts on them.' He paused. 'Not to the detriment of your other work, you understand. The Minister won't permit any increase in staffing or expenditure.' The Chief Inspector allowed himself a slight smile. 'Don't think of it as an extra duty, Jim. Think of it as a perk.'

'No comment,' said Donaldson, thinking how typical this was of politicians. He mistrusted the whole bunch of them. Indeed, his resolute refusal to allow political considerations to influence his investigations had led him into an outright confrontation with the previous Minister. But he had stood firm on his duty to be impartial and the Minister had been forced to back down.

'You must admit it's a step in the right direction.'

'True.' Donaldson relaxed. 'Thanks for sending me. I know Frampton of old.'

'A fact of which I was not unaware,' said the Chief Inspector wryly. 'Not,' he went on, indulging in a rare display of double negatives, 'that the 207 doesn't deserve one of our best men. As you remarked, there's a lot at stake on the project, a hell of a lot. If there's anything down there you don't like the look of, say so. The factory may not be pleased, but the Minister will.'

'They're giving us the treatment, Jim, and no mistake.' McPherson spoke softly, looking at the huge black Daimler waiting in the Frampton station forecourt.

'Don't you believe it, Mac. That's for some VIP, not us.' Donaldson was an instinctively unostentatious man and found it difficult to appreciate that since his recent promotion he was some sort of VIP himself.

A grey-uniformed chauffeur with a peaked cap approached them and enquired their names. 'Then we've only to wait for the Air Commodore, if you gentlemen don't mind.' He moved away, scanning the area for likely senior officers.

'What did I tell you?' said Donaldson softly. 'We're just being given a lift.'

A moment later a man in a dark suit walked briskly up to them and introduced himself, while the chauffeur scurried round to open the car doors.

'I don't think we've met,' he remarked amiably, keen eyes sizing up the two strangers. 'I'm Air Commodore Stringer from Defence Procurement. I believe we're all being shown round together.'

Half an hour later, sitting at one end of the long board-room table, the portrait of the founder of Western Aircraft frowning down on them, Donaldson was forced to admit that Mac was right. They were all three getting the treatment. The Chief Executive, whose name was Wormley, welcomed them personally, explaining the programme for their visit while an assistant served coffee in porcelain cups. It was clear that Western were anxious to impress their visitors. But Donaldson suspected that the glossiness of their reception might preclude asking any really basic questions. His own aim as an operations man was to assess the flying qualities of the 207; Mac's as an engineer was to look critically at how it was built. An hour alone with the Chief Designer would be infinitely more valuable than the protracted lunch in the directors' dining room scheduled for them today.

After coffee there was a presentation on the 207's potential as a short- to medium-range airliner, with some special slides depicting it in RAF colours embarking troops.

'Essentially,' explained Wormley, as a coloured graph showed estimated seat demand on a variety of European and American domestic airline routes, 'this project will fill the gap between the old BAC 1-11 or the Boeing 727 and the much larger capacity designs like the Boeing 757.' Another graph flashed up, depicting costs of operation on various routes in terms of passenger seat miles. 'We believe, we have long believed, that the most economical size of airliner will carry between a hundred and twenty and two hundred passengers. Everyone knows the market's there. That's why Douglas stretched their DC 9 into the dash eight version. Fokker are trying to capture it with their F 29.' He smiled.

'We think they're building a trifle small. Our 207 will take around a hundred and ninety seats.'

'And what's it going to cost?' Donaldson asked.

'Say eight million pounds a copy and you won't be far wrong. But there'll be a tremendous saving in fuel costs. New engines coupled with the sophistication of this design will give forty per cent less consumption on a five-hundred-mile sector than current aircraft.'

'How long before you have one in the air?' Stringer demanded.

'We started cutting metal three months ago,' answered the Chief Executive confidently. 'The first sub-assemblies will come through soon. We should have two aircraft test flying in spring next year. From then to airline service would be about two and a half years, which is when the market will be ready.'

'May I ask if you intend to freeze the design?' asked Donaldson. This was a crucial question. If Western did not, in American phraseology, 'freeze the design', but tried to go on incorporating new technological advances during production, then the 207 would be greatly delayed.

'We shall *try* to freeze it.' Wormley glanced meaningly at Stringer. 'If our customers will let us.' The RAF was notorious for demanding design changes during production. So was British Airways. 'Atlantic Airlines have indicated they will accept 207s as of this year's standard.' He went on tightly, 'We hope to keep the schedule. We are determined to start test flying next March.'

Air Commodore Stringer sat silent. He knew that if the 207 was compatible with the new Air Staff requirement for a transport, the Procurement Executive would be demanding innumerable modifications.

'Well, then.' Wormley was pleased that tackling this question head on appeared to have made the Air Commodore yield. 'Shall we start our tour of the works?'

The Daimler was waiting outside and as Wormley ushered them into it Donaldson asked casually if they could call at the

Flight Test Centre.

'That's not on the itinerary, but no doubt we can fit it in.' Wormley was now happy to accommodate his guests. 'We'll stop on the way to the assembly hangar. Anyone particular you'd like to see?'

'Bill Broughton's an old friend.'

Wormley spoke to the driver and settled himself back into the deep leather upholstery of the limousine, then pointed out various buildings as they progressed down the hill towards the airfield. A momentary surge of memories overtook Donaldson as he looked out at the huge arched roof of the assembly hangar, the broad runway and the cluster of RAF buildings beyond. Hidden in the trees was the mess where he and Broughton had lived when they were young pilot officers. He had known every yard of that runway, there was a farmhouse close to the airfield perimeter, just where he used to turn off on to the perimeter track after landing. He wondered if it was still there. And what had happened to the squadron shields and trophies in the mess bar? It was all as distinct as yesterday – and a quarter century ago.

Wormley's precise, patrician accent cut into the reverie.

'We can afford ten minutes here, I think.'

The chauffeur was holding the car door open. Donaldson jerked himself back to the present. They were beside the single storey Flight Test Centre and a burly man in pilot's white overalls was coming out to greet them, a crinkling smile on his broad face.

'Good morning, sir.' Broughton greeted the Chief Executive with respect, went through the formality of being introduced to the Air Commodore and then clasped Donaldson's hands in his. 'Well, speak of the devil. We'd heard you were here. Good to see you again, Jim. What are you up to?'

'Mac and I are getting ourselves acquainted with the 207.' Donaldson introduced McPherson.

A gust of wind caught them, ruffling Broughton's hair, and he hastened them into the building to his office.

'So you'd like some flying, would you?' Broughton didn't

need to be told.

'If the management is agreeable.' Donaldson turned to the Chief Executive. 'Ideally I'd get a type rating on the aircraft. The more I know about her handling characteristics the better.'

'I hadn't appreciated that you were an airline pilot, Mr Donaldson.' There was antagonism in Wormley's voice. 'Happily I have never been involved with your branch before. Western has had very few accidents.'

'It's no reflection on your record that I want to fly the 207 in due course.' Donaldson kept his tone equable despite his growing annoyance. 'Because they think of us as sorting through wreckage, surprisingly few people realize our inspectors must have ten thousand hours and have held an Airline Transport Pilot's Licence. Mine is in date.' He gave Wormley a deprecating half-smile. 'It's worth our understanding an airliner's handling characteristics.'

'Hmm.' Wormley checked himself. He had been about to suggest that the AIB should pay for Donaldson's flying. 'You do understand that we won't be able to afford any interruption in the schedule?'

'I can promise that any interruption would be minimal.'

'I'll let him wind the wheels down occasionally,' Broughton interjected cheerfully. 'Don't worry, sir. Once the test programme is under way there's plenty of routine flying. Someone has to handle the take-offs and landings.' He turned to Stringer. 'Now, Air Commodore, I imagine your time's limited. Our main facility down here is for briefing, of course. . . .'

When they left the Flight Test Centre Donaldson knew he had an ally where he needed one. The visit then swung smoothly into its preordained path. They were taken up by a steel cage lift into the roof of the assembly hangar to look down and see how the production line for the 207 would be laid out; this was where sections of the fuselage would be joined to each other, the wings incorporated, the tailplane fixed and the many internal systems fitted. But the point that struck Donaldson most keenly was the paucity of activity now. All the vast hangar contained was a few old planes being refurbished. As they went on to tour the other production centres this impression was reinforced. Western Aircraft's workforce was mainly occupied with subcontract engineering and small-scale stuff at that. It was obvious that the 207 project was crucial, and Wormley could scarcely play down the fact.

'We're into a two million pound research and development budget just to get the first 207s off the ground,' he admitted. 'And as you'll see in Production Centre Three, we're not wasting any time.'

Again, as they entered the building, there were the formal handshakes and introductions, though this time it was McPherson who took the lead in asking questions.

'Tell me, Mr Burnett,' he demanded, as the Manager began to show them round, 'just what is the procedure for handling materials here?'

Burnett hesitated.

'Go ahead, Bob,' said Wormley cordially. 'You do the explaining.'

'An order is raised on this department giving the specification of the material and the size required . . . then each part is allotted a route card.' As he talked Burnett reached for a rectangular white card from a rack by a machine and showed them it. 'The start date is when the card comes into the shop. . . .'

'Every stage is recorded, I take it?'

'Correct.' Burnett was completely self-assured. 'We're not taking any chances. For instance, press shop details like formers and spars would be followed right through heat treatment, flaw detection, corrosion proofing, painting; marshalled with the route card all the way. We know exactly what's been done.'

As the explanations continued Burnett guided the small party through the various areas of his department, stopping briefly at each, nodding acknowledgement to the foreman concerned. VIP visits were familiar events.

Ken Norris watched them pass and overheard Stringer called 'Air Commodore'. The reference reminded him. Following Peter's suggestion, he was going to attempt a little harassment of Charlie Brook at the next constituency meeting. Using the 207's military applications as a lead-in. Should have a bit of fun with Charlie, he thought viciously, and if it didn't work, well, there were other lines of attack to try.

'Friends, our Member's championship of the 207 project in Parliament has been unfailing.' Charlie Brook was nearing the end of his speech, sweating slightly now as he always did when trying to add a turn of eloquence to his slow, ponderous phrases. He reckoned he had the meeting with him, though there was a hardness about Norris's expression which he mistrusted. 'I tell you, friends, if Parliament hadn't voted the three hundred million we needed, there'd be little hope for several thousand jobs at Western. As our Member of Parliament, Norman's done us proud. Let's show our feelings by passing a motion of appreciation.'

As Brook sat down there was a general nodding of heads among the thirty men and women present. One or two clapped their hands weakly. The General Management Committee of Frampton North Constituency Labour Party was seldom prone to outbursts of enthusiasm and especially not on a winter's night in an underheated room. If Charlie Brook was sweating, the rest were shivering and fervently hoping it would be over before the pubs closed.

The Constituency Secretary, Bruce Gardner, a man of Norris's age but more intellectual in appearance and with a sly, sardonic expression around his mouth, looked around the gathering, caught Norris's eye fleetingly, and rose to his feet in turn.

'The motion's on the order paper, Comrades. Let's have a show of hands.'

'Does everyone here know it's a military plane we're building?' Norris's interruption was half shouted from where he sat. 'Why don't we add our congrats to the North Atlantic Treaty Organization while we're at it?'

'Is that a fact?' Another left-winger picked up his cue.

The meeting came alive in a crackle of questions and murmuring.

'Order, order.' Gardner held up his hand and then, instead of persisting with the vote, deftly thrust his own blade into the chairman. 'Let Comrade Brook speak.'

Charlie Brook accepted this unconstitutional suggestion with more confidence than either Gardner or Norris expected. Though he was long respected as a man of honour and principle, a devout Methodist churchgoer and the kind of man who formed the bedrock of the Labour Party, on many questions his knowledge was less of fact than of hope. On the 207, however, he was accurately informed.

'As I understand it, friends,' he said, firmly avoiding the term Comrades, 'the Royal Air Force may order a few 207s. Nothing definite. Just expressing interest.' He looked straight at Norris. 'And to my mind there's nothing wrong with that, either. If the RAF wants transports, I'd rather they bought them here than from the Americans.' He paused, and was rewarded with a mutter of approval. The majority on the GMC were moderates and much more alive to Anglo-American rivalry in the aircraft business than to any larger East–West confrontations. Frampton was very provincial, which Brook capitalized on instinctively because so was he. 'To my way of thinking,' he continued, 'what's good for Frampton is good for Britain. And orders for Western are good for Frampton. Now, if you've all done argufying, I'll once more propose the motion of confidence in our Member, Mr Norman Huntley.'

Gardner knew that he was beaten this time. Work for the aircraft factory was too potent a political talisman to be challenged, wherever it came from.

'Hands up those in favour.'

Prudently three of the five activists raised their right arms along with the rest. Only Norris and the other questioner stayed immobile.

When the meeting ended, instead of trooping round to the King's Head to cram a couple of pints into the few minutes of drinking time left, Norris walked briskly through the near-deserted streets to the river. He wanted to be alone. He had realized something during the meeting, something so fundamental that the thoughts connected with it refused to be sorted out and catalogued in his mind. But their central theme was clear. Charlie Brook was the obstacle to all his own ambitions. How could you change society with men like him in the chair?

When he reached the river he leaned on a bollard of the former dockside and gazed down into the dark water mirroring the few streetlamps along the quay and the faint outlines of ancient brick warehouses. In its day Frampton had been an important river port. The warehouses were empty now, people even talked of preserving them as memorials to the city's mercantile tradition. That's the bloody trouble, he reflected, they're all living in the past. Suddenly the realization that came to him during the meeting fermented, swelled into a mind-blowing concept. Charlie Brook was the heat treatment inspector. Suppose the heat treatment of part of the 207 was interfered with and the prototype crashed, then when the cause was traced where would the blame go? On brother bloody Brook. Talk your way out of that one, mate! You passed the f... ing part. You said it was OK. Not just a bloody reprimand. Not with three hundred millon quid up the spout and only a pile of wreckage to show for it. You can collect your cards, Mr Brook. Say goodbye to the lads on the committee, Charlie boy. On all the committees. You're the bloke who f.... d it up at Frampton.

A chill gust of wind caught Norris's legs and he huddled into his leather coat, turned away from the river and hurried back to the tower block where Marion would be waiting. His mind was made up.

The flat was warm. Marion was sitting on the floor in front of the electric fire in the living room, cradling a mug of coffee in her hands. She looked up as he came in.

'Go to the pub?' she asked.

'I'm not going to drink with that lot.' He shrugged off his jacket. 'Not unless I have to. Here, make us a cuppa, will you, love? I'm freezing.'

Obediently she pulled herself up, went to the kitchen and put the kettle on. 'So who's getting on your wick this time?' she called out.

'Can't you guess? Charlie Brook.' He was longing to talk to someone, though aware that to confide even in Marion might be dangerous. But he could tell her the rough aim.

'I thought everyone liked him?'

'That scab!' He threw his cheap plastic briefcase hard into the corner of the room, wishing he could hit someone. 'If we're going to take over either the factory or the constituency, he's the man we need to be shot of. He's nothing but a bloody reactionary.'

'So he got his motion through, did he?' She knew a bit about the meeting because Ken had been preparing for it all week.

'What's good for Western Aircraft is good for Frampton. The idiots always fall for that.'

Marion put the teapot and a cup on a small tin tray and took it to the living room, poured for him and then nestled down again by the fire. Outside the wind moaned around the high building.

'No kind of a night to be out,' she commented.

'We have to get rid of Brook,' he said, disregarding her change of subject. 'Once and for all.'

'You don't want to be on the Council, do you?' She was puzzled sometimes by his activities.

'Not unless it's necessary. If it was I would.'

'You could do a lot of good. Plenty of people in Frampton need help. I see more of that than you do, probably. Local politics ought to be about helping people.'

'You and your do-gooding.' He couldn't but laugh. Then, seeing the pain in her face, he relented. Maybe she really didn't understand. 'Listen, love,' he said, putting down his cup, leaning forward and gesturing with clenched fists. 'Politics is about power. We want power for the workers, right? How are we going to get it? Not by trusting a bunch of layabouts in Parliament who talk their heads off! We've got to control industry, Parliament, the lot. Reform the whole bloody shooting match. We've broken the power of the bosses in most factories. Though not at Western yet. That's why I want to be Convenor, right? Now the other thing we have to do is start making Parliament democratic. Which means making Members of Parliament directly answerable to the workers. How do we do that? We throw out the Norman Huntleys of this world and put in proper socialists. Men who represent the workers because they take their orders from the union that sponsors them and none of this voting according to their bloody consciences. We want to do down here what Scargill and the miners have done in Yorkshire. We want Western Aircraft nationalized and a Member of Parliament who knows what's coming to him if he doesn't toe the line.'

'So you really are getting rid of Huntley?'

'He won't be re-selected. Not when we have a majority on the GMC, which we will have. Bruce Gardner's a bright lad. He's already making it difficult for anyone we don't like to join the Party at all. The subscription's £5 now, which is enough to put most ordinary folk off, and the office is taking six months to process applications. We're only accepting activists in the Frampton North Constituency Labour Party.'

'Then why the fuss about Brook?'

'Because he has a big following, that's why. Trust honest Charlie. We need him out of the way. And I think I know how to do it.' Realizing he was close to saying too much, Norris fell silent.

Marion looked across at him. She did not completely follow the manoeuvres he was describing, but she was in no doubt about his ruthlessness in pursuing them. She admired it. He had exactly the determination her own family so lacked. But she was still mystified over one thing.

'Ken, darling,' she said, shifting towards him and resting her arm on his knee. 'I'm sure you'll succeed, but if you're not interested in politics yourself, what's in it for you?'

'Hadn't you noticed?' he asked acidly. 'We're taking the country over. We're going to run it our way. Isn't that enough?' He spoke as though explaining to a child, but his voice suddenly hardened. 'No one ought to be allowed to do what the bosses did to my mother. Our party constitution includes a certain thing called Clause Four. We're going to implement that if it's the last thing we do.'

She felt dreadful at her ignorance. 'What is Clause Four?'

'Jesus wept!' He had to restrain himself. She really was a stupid bourgeois cow sometimes. 'Clause Four, my love, is the Labour Party's commitment to nationalizing the means of production and distribution. Everyone knows that. The trouble is, some don't want to do it. Like bloody brother Brook. Now do you understand?'

It was worse than being sworn at. Her eyes moistened and she began to cry.

'Sorry, Mary,' he said, momentarily ashamed. 'I didn't mean to hurt you. Let's go to bed, then.'

She obeyed, mutely, and said nothing more that night, lying as far away from him as she could. The gulf between them seemed to grow all the time.

The next evening he warned her he'd be late for supper and took an evening excursion to Bristol on the train. He stayed exactly long enough to walk into the city centre, telephone Rusopov from a call box and ask for a meeting. Then he had a beer and caught the first train back from Temple Meads station. He was tensely aware that it mattered to adhere to instructions, but he forgot that Rusopov had suggested also having an overt reason for visiting any town he telephoned from.

'So we have him on the small hook?' Colonel Grigoriev looked up from reading Rusopov's second report on a

Course of Meeting with Norris. 'Is this production schedule a confidential document?'

'Industrially, yes. Within the meaning of the British Official Secrets Acts, I doubt it. The construction of the 207 does not appear to be treated as a military matter.' Rusopov picked it up from the table. 'However, Comrade Colonel, Yuri having passed a copy to us does compromise him. As you say, since last night he is on the small hook. The schedule also gives us most valuable information on the timescale to which we must work.' He paused. 'We are short of time.'

Grigoriev scanned the sheets of paper again, tapping them with a stubby forefinger, occasionally consulting a calendar.

'You say, Vladimir Sergeyevich, that according to Yuri the cutting of metal has begun. But he believes there is a shortage of certain supplies. It is February 20th. Assembly of the fuselage subsections starts in April. When will the parts pass through Yuri's department?'

'He thinks in late March.' Rusopov noticed the frown edging across the Colonel's face and interpreted it accurately. 'We must ask the Centre for urgent consideration of our proposals. If only we were permitted a more immediate method of contact. . . .'

'Let me see the last letter again.' Grigoriev cut his assistant short. 'Have we answered their questions?'

Rusopov shook his head. 'Not completely.'

He flipped open the file beside him and found the Moscow Centre's most recent instruction. The letter was in fact a photographic enlargement, made from a 35-mm negative. All letters sent from the Moscow Centre to Residents abroad were typed at the Centre, photographed, and the rolls of undeveloped film sent out by diplomatic bag. The packet containing the films was specially marked, so that the Embassy cipher clerk sent it upstairs untouched to the KGB Resident's office. Even had the cipher clerk opened it and developed the film, such a perilous act would have availed him little. The KGB maintained its own top-secret ciphers. One of Rusopov's duties in London was to supervise the decoding of letters. After making one enlargement of each, and one only, he destroyed the negatives. At regular intervals, normally annually, the enlargements themselves were destroyed. This meant that after a time the only copy of a given instruction would be held safely in Moscow. It also demanded an exceptionally good memory on the part of cadre workers abroad.

The photographic enlargement was annotated in Rusopov's precise, scholastic handwriting. Even within the cloak of its special cipher, the KGB used further protective codewords which in turn had to be translated before the letter made sense. Some, in KGB terms, were common usage. Others were individual to the particular agent or operation. Rusopov had not troubled with the normal ones, but had enclosed the less familiar translations in neat brackets.

Letter No. 4/0 of 13 January

Concerning No. 31 (Yuri)

We regard the study and cultivation of No. 31 (Yuri) as continuing to be full of promise. Therefore we request you to carry into effect the plan of work detailed in Letter No. 58/0 of 12 December and to report progress in this work as soon as possible.

'In my opinion, Comrade Colonel,' remarked Rusopov, moving round to look over his senior's shoulder, 'we have fulfilled the instructions in paragraph one.'

'Not so fast, Vladimir Sergeyevich.' Grigoriev raised a cautionary finger. 'The method of sabotage you have devised between you is far from satisfactory.' He sighed. 'We will come back to that. Let us consider the lesser problems first. How about paragraph two?' Again he ran his thick finger across the paper.

We agree with your proposal to pay No. 31 (Yuri) a certain sum of money. We authorize you, at the opportune moment, to hand to him up to £150, using the justification that he had told you about expenses incurred in dealing with No. 32's (Yuri's wife) lawyers. Give him to understand that, so long as he continues to collaborate with us actively, he can always count on our help.

'The moment is *not* opportune,' said Rusopov curtly. 'He even said to me, "For once it's not cash I'm after." In my view to offer him money at this stage might frighten him. He is motivated by ideology and ambition. Isn't that enough?'

'The Centre have ordered us to obtain his signature on a receipt.'

'If we need to put pressure on him, Comrade Colonel, we have the production schedule.'

Grigoriev shook his head stolidly. 'The joint consultation agreements at Western Aircraft entitled him to see that document. We are agreed it is not secret. We could embarrass him, but not blackmail him. He is still only on the small hook.' The Colonel shifted his bulk, leaned one elbow on his desk and looked up at his protégé. 'Volodya, my friend, as you will learn in time, there is never anything academic about running an agent. Ideology is the best motivation at the time of recruitment.' He laughed. 'The British know just how well it served to keep Philby, Maclean and Blake in the net. But with the small men: not enough. If you turn a useful idiot such as Yuri into a conscious agent then you need more basic leverage. Blackmail, money, sex. You must be able to put everything they live for at stake.' He gave Rusopov a gentle butt in the ribs with his fist. 'Come out of your ivory tower, Volodya. Be a realist. What do you think kept that naval petty officer on the hook: money and an extravagant wife of course. What's your estimate of Yuri's character?'

Rusopov considered this for a moment. 'Ambitious, self-interested, ruthless within the confines of his little world, but not sophisticated. He sees us as a big and powerful ally towards his own ends and deceives himself as to the dangers.'

'Then he is an animal on whom we may have to use the whip, my friend. You have said as much. And already there are problems with women, as the Centre appreciates. Look at paragraph three.'

We request you to report to us by the next luggage all the information known to you concerning No. 32 (Yuri's wife) with figures in the departmental files in connection with her visit to Sparta.

'Those facts should be known to the Centre already.' Rusopov disliked having his time wasted. Like many young Russians, he found the inability of different Kremlin departments to consult each other infuriating. Basically most of what this paragraph demanded to know, by the next diplomatic bag, were details held in the consular department of the London Embassy regarding Norris's wife's visit to Russia in 1974. It must have long been on the file in Moscow.

'You are too impatient, Vladimir Sergeyevich,' commented Grigoriev equably. 'The Centre's concern for every aspect of security is correct. Women are considered dangerous for good reasons. If his wife hated him enough to leave him, she could also betray him. We have to discover her present whereabouts.'

'I will put investigations in hand, Comrade Colonel. At least I have obtained full details of his mistress, Marion Robbins.'

'You say she sounds a stupid woman?'

'That may be more a reflection of Yuri's general attitude to women than the truth,' said Rusopov cautiously. 'At heart I think he is very small-minded.'

Grigoriev leant back in his chair. 'You know,' he said, half yawning as though more bored by the affair than worried. 'If it were not for the Centre's insistence, I should not have chosen Yuri for this operation.' It was as near as he would venture to the heresy of suggesting that the Director a thousand miles away in Moscow did not necessarily know best. He stretched his limbs, then straightened up. 'But, my dear Volodya, we must do as we are told.' His voice tautened. 'Technically, I presume the sabotage plan is faultless.'

'As near as it can be.' On scientific matters Rusopov was completely self-assured. 'The rear pressure bulkhead of the 207 fuselage will consist of a cone, made up of seven shaped pieces cf aluminium alloy sheet. Imagine it as the end of a cigar tube. The wings will be fixed halfway along the tube, the tail secured to the end we are interested in. If one of those seven pieces fractures when the plane is at high altitude, then the pressurized air inside will force its way out with such violence that the whole rear end will split, the tail will be destroyed, the plane will crash.'

'And it will fracture if it has not been heat treated?'

'Precisely, Comrade Colonel. The heat treatment takes twelve hours and is done overnight. The day workers switch the oven on before leaving. They recover the treated parts next morning. The man whom Yuri has found is an electrician on the night shift. He can switch off the oven in the evening and turn it on again in the morning an hour or so before the day shift starts. I have devised a method for making the temperature recording machine continue to operate, even though the oven is off. The parts will appear to have been treated. In fact they will be too weak to withstand the pressure of sustained high-altitude flight.'

'The theory is excellent. But . . .' Grigoriev frowned, 'I am not happy about the motivation of the electrician. How can Yuri guarantee that he will adopt sabotage as a means of revenge against the management?'

'This man Brunner is a dedicated revolutionary movement member. He has been openly advocating violent action against the capitalist bosses.' Rusopov smiled thinly. 'He is an excellent example of a useful idiot.'

'What you mean, Vladimir Sergeyevich, is that he is a dangerous Trotskyite. Untrustworthy, undisciplined, unstable.'

'And so will act in the heat of the moment,' argued Rusopov defensively. 'Psychologically it is a more sophisticated plan than I would have expected from Yuri.'

'It relieves him of the dirty work. What's so sophisticated about that?' Grigoriev shook his head. 'I doubt if the Centre will accept the employment of a Trotskyite, even as an unconscious agent.'

'We can at least put the plan forward, though. We have been ordered to report.'

Grigoriev pondered this briefly. It was true. Better this than nothing. 'Hell,' he exclaimed. 'All right. Now, we have also to answer the Centre's questions about the allegations in the British press against us.' He swung round and faced his assistant. 'Could the defection of Bogdan in the Philippines be responsible?' The Colonel was more concerned than Rusopov had ever known him before. 'Could there be any other leak?'

Chief Inspector Colin Sturgess of London's Metropolitan Police had to visit the headquarters of the British Security Service regularly for what were described as working-level meetings. The building, an imposing if elderly office block in the city's West End, was in an area known more for social high jinks, gambling and prostitution than the plodding routines of catching spies. The contrast always amused Sturgess. Department Five of Defence Intelligence, ineradicably known to the British public by the long-abandoned name of MI5, always seemed completely monochrome to him. There was more life and feeling around any police station in the suburbs than in this place dedicated to what everyone imagined was a dramatic and fascinating business. But then Sturgess had learned, since he transferred to the Special Branch, that very few things in DI5's line were what they seemed. He had risen fast in the police and, at thirty-four, was still young enough to be curious about the functioning of organizations he dealt with.

This March morning Colin Sturgess came to the headquarters by special request and although the procedures of showing his warrant card at reception, completing a form and being given a visitor's badge were as stolid as ever, he sensed a very faint tension when he was shown into the office of one of the Assistant Directors.

'Glad you could come.' The Assistant Director, grey-suited, was affable as usual in a brisk military way. 'Have you met Kit Fairfax?'

Sturgess shook hands, amused at the contrast between the two. Fairfax looked thirtyish, was informally dressed and, given a quick rumpling of the blond hair, could have passed as an art student. Then he remembered that the juniors here no more spent all their time in the office than his own detectives did. There was little point in the kind of plain clothes which were themselves a uniform.

They sat down around a table at one end of the office, on which three new white scratch pads with three meticulously sharpened pencils were laid out.

'Now,' said the Assistant Director, without preamble, 'we are dealing with the activities of certain Russian diplomats. We are under very considerable pressure to identify their contacts.' He picked up a plain manilla folder and slid out a sheet of paper and a batch of photographs, handing the paper and one picture across to Sturgess. 'This chap's easy. As you can see, we know who he is: a lecturer at London University with a third-floor flat in Sussex Gardens, Paddington. We'd appreciate anything you've got on him.'

Sturgess glanced through the description and nodded. 'No problem,' he said confidently. Although other police forces in Britain maintained their own Special Branch sections, it was the Metropolitan Police which kept the national records. The Special Branch in London had originally been formed to deal with Irish terrorists at the turn of the century and had been collecting data on suspicious persons ever since.

'The lecturer's flat is used by a Russian for meetings,' explained Fairfax. 'An identified KGB captain named Vladimir Sergeyevich Rusopov. He has cover as a Second Secretary Scientific at the Embassy.'

'Does the lecturer know?' asked Sturgess. 'I mean, know what Rusopov is up to?'

'Possibly not,' interjected the Assistant Director. 'On balance we want to avoid questioning him directly. We want Rusopov's use of the flat to continue.'

'I've rented a room opposite,' said Fairfax. 'That's where the photos were taken from.'

'This is a straight diplomatic picture of the Russian.' The Assistant Director pushed a well-defined glossy print of Rusopov's head and shoulders across the table. 'These are some of his visitors.' He pushed across a further five prints.

'Two are of the same person,' commented Fairfax. 'One taken in December, the other last week.'

Sturgess surveyed the pictures. The man who appeared in two was of medium build, wearing a leather jacket. In the second his lean face was well defined, though with an odd softness as if he had somehow been photographed in bright moonlight.

'Northern Ireland's given us a few techniques worth having.' Fairfax smiled. 'He wasn't even under a street lamp when I took that. The second time we got a tail on him too. He went to Paddington and caught a train.'

'To?'

'Reading, Swindon, Chippenham, Bath, Bristol, Newport and Cardiff. Except that it went west, that doesn't tell us much. He could have changed trains at any of those places.'

'Couldn't he have been followed onto the train?' Too late Sturgess realized that this was possibly an impertinent question. It sounded openly critical.

'Next time he will be. Until recently we haven't had the manpower.' The Assistant Director's expression was set. 'Strictly speaking we still haven't. It means taking surveillance off others. No,' he went on grimly, 'next time our man will have a ticket through to Cardiff and go wherever Mr Leather Jacket goes. Meanwhile any line we can get on an identification would be invaluable. Any line at all.'

The tension was unconcealed now. Whatever was up, Sturgess sensed it was something the Assistant Director did not like.

'I'll do what I can on all of them, sir. It's not a lot to go on, though.'

'Do your best.' The Assistant Director hesitated fractionally. 'I think it's fair to warn you, Chief Inspector, we're going to be needing more assistance than usual. I suppose you've seen the reports in the newspapers about a KGB plan to disrupt Britain?'

Sturgess stopped gathering up the photographs. 'I've read

it with great interest. Has it any foundation? Frankly, sir, some of it seemed a bit overwritten to me.'

'You remember the defector Lyalin? A bit before your time, I suppose.' The Assistant Director scowled. 'The government of the day leaked some of the take from him to the press. This is roughly similar. A defector in, hmm, another country has been debriefed by the Americans. He had knowledge of KGB operations in Britain which we, how shall I put it, which we believe his masters did not know he had. The Americans very kindly passed the relevant parts of the material to us. The government has now decided that, although no original documents are included, the substance should be leaked as it was with Lyalin. In order to alert the public to the dangers.'

'I see,' said Sturgess, though the name Lyalin meant nothing to him. 'Hence the pressure on you to identify all Russian contacts.'

'It's an error, in my view.' The Assistant Director's anger was coming to the surface. 'In the first place I don't think the public will necessarily believe a bloody word of the story. Not with the left as active as it is today. But far worse, it's forcing us to act more precipitately than we would wish.' Suddenly he cut himself short. 'This is not the official view, you understand, Chief Inspector. We exist to serve the government and a political decision is a political decision. But our resources are going to be very stretched.'

'We'll certainly do what we can,' reiterated Sturgess and made his retreat. He was afraid the old man would blow a fuse at any moment.

After he had gone the Assistant Director took a deep breath. 'Let's hope he comes up with something. Do you think I was right to fill him in?'

'I think so,' said Fairfax, who thought this fuss rather overdone and enjoyed the watching post in Sussex Gardens. 'There's no need to spell everything out, though perhaps we should have reminded him that Lyalin was the KGB officer concerned with sabotage in our aircraft industry.'

4

Colonel Grigoriev perused the letter from the Centre. It was personal to him and whereas intelligence instructions were numbered in the 'O' sequence, this was headed with an 'SK' denoting a counterintelligence subject. He frowned and grunted as he read. The first paragraph only was enough to worry the most experienced KGB Resident.

Letter No. 14/SK of 23 March
CONCERNING THE PLAN OF WORK

The aggravation of the international situation and the pressing necessity for the timely exposure and prevention of cunning designs of the enemy call imperatively for a radical reorganization of all our intelligence work.

He had expected some such order. The British newspaper campaign against KGB activity had been mounting and it must be deliberately coinciding with the overall deterioration in East–West relations. What he had not anticipated came further on.

We have considered the possible sources of the allegations being published against the legal apparatus of the London Residency and whether they could originate from either the traitor Bogdan or the traitor Myagkov. The latter is known to have revealed details of operations of the Third Directorate to the enemy. However neither defector, in our view, could have furnished the information now being leaked to the newspapers about our own Directorate.

Accordingly we instruct you to conduct the most rigorous investigation into the possible existence of a further traitor with past or present access to correspondence in the Residency.

When Grigoriev put the letter down he was sweating. Could he be nourishing a traitor on his staff? There were enough people involved. So-called 'legals' with diplomatic cover like himself and Rusopov, others posted as Embassy chauffeurs or clerks. These were the 'illegals', a phrase in no way relating to the legality of their work, but solely to their cover. Several of the Tass news agency team were KGB men sent officially to operate in Britain as journalists, and officially accepted as such, but lacking diplomatic immunity from arrest if they were caught spying. The 'illegals' ranged through many occupations from trade representatives to language teachers.

Then again, every Russian industrial purchasing contract involved inspectors, every cultural project had its co-ordinators. Of these some were full time KGB cadre workers, others were genuine technicians who had been co-opted for espionage work whether they liked it or not. Such non-permanent employees were known as 'collaborators'. There were literally hundreds in Britain.

Every person in this widespread structure of 'legals', 'illegals' and 'collaborators' was a Russian. Everyone was trusted to some extent, if not to recruit and run agents, certainly to obtain information. The minute you briefed a man on what you wanted to know you gave clues as to your overall objectives. Even people who had never seen a single page of the Plan of Work had some degree of knowledge about it. Worse still, one never quite knew what people told their wives. The strict regulations on secrecy had often before been broken in pillow talk.

The Kommissariat Gosudarstvennoi Bezopasnosti was only the newest in a long chain of State Security organizations in Russia, originating in the Cheka set up in 1918 to protect the infant Soviet state against counter-revolution and, in practice, little different from the Secret Police of the Tsars. Whether they were called Cheka, or GPU, or OGPU, or NKVD, or MGB or KGB, or several other titles, they had all been plagued by the fear of treachery. Since the 1939–45 war the list of defectors had been long, starting with the Military Intelligence clerk Gouzenko in Canada in 1946, and each traitor caused upheavals of a most unpleasant kind in the service he left.

There was only one person with whom Grigoriev felt he could discuss this acutely sensitive matter: Vladimir Sergeyevich. He pressed the buzzer and ordered Rusopov to come in.

Rusopov too had something urgent on his mind, but tactfully did not mention it immediately. He had seldom seen the Colonel so concerned.

'So the guts of it is that we're all under suspicion,' Grigoriev concluded. 'Obviously Moscow believes the British are up to the old trick of using a known defector to release embarrassing information from another source.'

'Myagkov must have had knowledge of our own First Directorate's work?' argued Rusopov.

'But of the Third Department? Of Directives to this Residency? Neither he nor Bogdan could have seen them.' Grigoriev shuffled through the growing file of newspaper clippings. 'Such material can only come from someone who has actually seen the mail.'

'Permit me, Comrade Colonel.' Rusopov reached out a thin hand for the file and scrutinized the most recent newspaper report. He went through it carefully, biting reflectively on his forefinger. 'This is the language of a person who has been told what a document contains,' he declared at last. 'Listen to this quotation: "It has long been clear that our main hope of achieving power in Britain is through our penetration of the Labour Party and the trade unions. The degree of influence we have in both is most satisfactory." That is not the language we use, Comrade Colonel. Those are not our phrases. Our sentiments, yes. Our words, no.' He bit on his finger again, then spoke with sudden decision. 'I do not believe the British are in possession of a document. At most all this derives from a generalized description. I cannot remember decoding a letter with those sentences in it. Not in the whole fourteen months I have supervised cipher duties.' He paused. 'Of course, only the Centre knows what was sent before then.'

'Hmm,' Grigoriev grunted. The assumption was not entirely true. It was impossible to remember everything accurately and during his own four years in London he had occasionally flouted the rules. The Plan of Work was not so much one document, as the British seemed to imagine, more a continuing series of instructions, often updated. He had kept copies of some crucial letters after the due destruction date in order to be certain of acting correctly.

'The devil of it is,' he admitted, 'the phrase "time is on our side" is such a favourite of Comrade General Kutuzov's that I can't recall when he last used it in a letter. The fragment reproduced in the newspaper could have come from orders to another Residency.'

'Anyway,' suggested Rusopov loyally, 'wasn't the defector Bogdan's wife employed in the First Directorate for a time? She could have told her husband. The leak could be . . .' he cut himself short before uttering the heresy.

'My dear Volodya,' remarked Grigoriev drily, 'if you propose telling the Centre that it is insecure, you are a braver man than I. No, for the moment we have our orders. The rigorous investigation must start. Equally our own security must be tightened in every way possible.'

The cue was tailor-made for the problem worrying Rusopov. 'Comrade Colonel,' he said, 'Yuri has been in contact again despite my instructions.'

'He has? Damn the man. When?'

'He telephoned last night wanting a meeting. He sounded agitated and says he cannot wait longer. This can only mean the production of the 207 is reaching the stage where our operation must be either carried out or abandoned.'

Anger suffused Grigoriev's face. He crashed his fist on the

table. 'This operation must be kept secure. Can't the idiot understand?'

'He is still only on the small hook. He could be frightened off.'

'Fetch the file, will you?'

While Rusopov was out of the room, Grigoriev regained his temper, recognizing that he had no reason to shout at his junior. The people at fault were back in the long low building hidden behind trees on the circumferential highway outside Moscow. The Centre seemed so busy looking for traitors that it couldn't make up its mind about operations.

'Well,' he asked when Rusopov returned, 'what did the last letter say?'

'They mistrust use of the Trotskyite Brunner, they criticize our failure to make Yuri accept money and they demand more information about Yuri's wife.' Rusopov looked up from the file. 'They make no further comment on the technical feasibility of the sabotage so presumably they accept it. They have allocated the electrician Brunner a codename, "Tourist". Why is not clear, but it must be a good sign.'

'Send a telegram. "We beg to receive your decision urgently on the matters raised in our letter, etcetera."' Grigoriev stood up. 'Say we are confident Yuri will accept money at the next meeting.' He paused, considering the Centre's likely reactions. 'Yes, and request instructions for future contact with him.' At least Moscow could take the onus for some of the risks.

Marion Robbins made her way cautiously down the narrow street, feeling herself watched from behind the lace curtains of the terraced houses. There was an indefinable tension in St Joseph's and she was seldom at ease there, especially as the evening came on. In recent memory these rows of two-storey brick dwellings, built back to back to house Victorian workmen, had been home to a close-knit, friendly working-class community, at one with the nearby shops and markets of Frampton's city centre. Now they were run down, with paint shredding from the door frames, the tiny front gardens strewn with litter. Many had their windows boarded up, mute testimony to a council road-building scheme which had forced the occupants out and then itself been abandoned. Today most of the locals were coloured immigrants, attracted originally because housing was available and cheap, now economic prisoners of high unemployment. St Joseph's was becoming a ghetto. Marion had wanted to work there, but was ruled out by her middle-class speech. 'They'd never trust you, my dear,' the director of the community centre had said, not unkindly, and allocated her the adjoining area, which was less aggressive. She was in St Joseph's tonight on Ken's behalf.

The street ended in a factory yard. The house she was looking for was not so far along. Number 47. She stopped outside. The walls were painted yellow and to her surprise there were thick net curtains even on the upstairs windows. Then she noticed the two bells by the front door. Ken hadn't told her the house was divided. She shifted the gate aside and rang the bottom bell. Nothing stirred. She tried the upper one and thought she heard a voice. She rang again. Footsteps slapped on the stairs inside. The door opened a few inches. She could dimly see tousled fair hair and a young man's face.

'What d'you want?'

The hostility rocked her, even though she was used to a rough reception in St Joseph's.

'You must be Jack Brunner,' she said, forcing a smile. 'Aren't you up at Western?'

'What if I am?' He was holding the door almost closed. 'Who are you?'

'I'm from the community centre. We'd heard there was a girl here wasn't too well.' In fact it was Ken who had known she was ill, but it was a white lie.

'Oh, Lee you mean.' Doubt softened his voice.

'I don't want to intrude. Is she bad?'

'You'd better come up.'

The door swung back. Marion saw the man was thin,

dressed in jeans and a grubby tee shirt. She reckoned he was twenty-two or twenty-three years old. He led the way up the linoleum-covered stairs, lit by a naked bulb, and pushed open the door to a small landing.

'If you go in the front I'll tell her. She's in bed.'

To Marion's surprise he knocked on the other door before entering the back part of the flat.

The front room was sparsely furnished: a divan with rumpled bedclothes on it, two old wooden chairs, a white-painted table, a pile of newspapers on the floor. She guessed Brunner had been in bed when she rang. Ken had told her he was on the night shift. A wall poster caught her eye. The picture was of a smiling soldier holding a rifle, a red flower protruding incongruously from its muzzle. She gazed at it for a moment, then picked up one of the papers. A banner headline glared up at her in red. 'VICTORY TO THE STEELWORKERS'. A lesser story began 'Witch hunt against the Left will be defeated'. Suddenly she realized these must be what Brunner sold outside the works. She remembered Ken's instructions. 'I don't want him to think anyone's snooping. It's for his own good. He's wearing himself out working nights and then selling papers in the day. The blokes are complaining he's half asleep all the time. He'll get the sack if he's not careful.'

Brunner's return startled her and she covered up by asking if she could buy a copy, fumbling in her straw basket for her purse. She never had been good at dissimulating. But far from noticing her confusion, Brunner seemed pleased. The antagonism faded from his face and he half smiled.

'People would understand a lot more if they read our paper.' He took the money and slipping it into a collecting box said, 'Did you know the CIA was infiltrating the Labour Party? We uncovered that.' He changed the subject abruptly. 'Lee says she's feeling better, and she'd like to meet you. Come on through.' As he moved away the light shone on his face and she saw that Ken was right: his eyes were dark-ringed and his cheeks drawn, he looked as if he hadn't had a proper sleep for weeks.

If the front room of 47 Carlton Terrace had been no real surprise to Marion, the back was. She had expected a bedroom. What she found was an office. Propped up by cushions on a narrow bed in the corner, dwarfed by a grey steel desk and a high filing cabinet, was a diminutive Chinese girl, her shoulders huddled into a dark blue donkey jacket which was far too big for her. Though she was in shadow, her pale face had a luminous intensity which struck Marion more than the fact that she was also exceptionally pretty.

'I am Lee,' she said in a firm but quiet voice. 'Tell me your name.'

'Marion. Usually people call me Mary. I work at the community centre.'

'So you know I am on social security.' It was not put like a question and before Marion could answer, the Chinese girl went on. 'Do you think it right that the government should be cutting unemployment benefit?'

'Definitely not.'

'Then we are on the same side,' said the girl decisively. 'Please sit down.' She articulated her words with precision, yet had no foreign accent. Marion guessed she was halfcaste, then caught her breath, as though this racialist thought could have been overheard. She sat down hurriedly on a typist's chair.

'The capitalist system is breaking up,' said Brunner abruptly. 'We must struggle to carry the working class to power.'

'Jack is right,' said the girl, neatly silencing him. 'All around us the world revolution and the movement of the masses is taking place.' Whereas Brunner's phrases sounded like a replay of someone else's speech, Lee spoke with calm and compelling strength. She was clearly the driving force behind everything he did.

When there was a break in the conversation Marion asked if Brunner sold the paper every day.

'It is the duty of all members to sell the paper,' he replied woodenly.

'In the evenings,' said the girl, 'we plan our campaigns and read the works of Lenin and Trotsky.'

'I'm terribly ignorant.' Marion blushed. 'What is the difference between a Trotskyist and a Marxist?'

'None,' said Brunner suddenly. 'We are all followers of Karl Marx. Trotsky sacrificed his life for the working class when the Stalinists murdered him.'

'They have taken power from the working class in Russia and created a Communist Party bureaucracy which is as bad as capitalism,' the girl explained, seeing that Marion was mystified. 'It's simple once you know the history. Marx created Socialism. But after him only Trotsky fought for the workers, while Stalin betrayed them when he became leader. That is why Russia has never achieved the true dictatorship of the proletariat which Marx preached, only a Bonapartist bureaucracy.' Lee gave her a searching glance. 'You should come to our meetings.'

'I can't tonight. I will another time.' Marion got up awkwardly. 'I never asked if you had a doctor, that sort of thing.'

'The movement looks after me.' Lee smiled defiantly. 'I'll get better soon. It was nice to meet you. Come again.'

'Let me show you out,' offered Brunner with unexpected politeness.

At the street door Marion thanked him. 'You look done in,' she said sympathetically.

'I'm all right.' The original antagonism flickered back into his face. 'There's a lot to do now she's ill.'

As Marion walked away it occurred to her that he had said a great deal in that last remark. He thought of the girl as 'she' and of her illness as long lasting. She wondered if he had any social life at all.

Night had fallen. When she got back to the tower block, only a few streets away, all the lights in the hall except one had gone and she appreciated the irony of its shining down on the notice 'If you don't stop vandalism in Frampton, no one will.'

There were cigarette ends everywhere and a smell of urine

incompletely overpowered by disinfectant. She pressed the lift button and went up. On the sixth-floor landing someone had stuck a beer bottle into the protective metal grille over the window. It hung by the neck from the rusting mesh. She felt a sudden hatred for the whole place. How could people in this sixteen-storey concrete monstrosity ever achieve a sense of community? The flats hadn't even got balconies. Nor a kids' playground.

Ken was in the living room, watching the colour TV, a plate of ham and baked beans balanced on his knee.

'Hallo, Mary love. How d'you get on?' He looked up but didn't move. 'Turn the telly down if you want.'

'You might have waited.' She eyed his food with annoyance, then shrugged off her coat and went to hang it in the hall, talking through the open door.

'They're an odd couple: if you can call them a couple.'

Unable to hear against the noise of the football commentary, he put the plate aside resignedly and turned the TV off.

'What was that?'

'I said they're an odd pair. She called marriage "an idealistic capitalist extra". God, I'm starving.'

She walked through to the tiny kitchen and began taking things out of the refrigerator. Frowning, he followed her.

'Well, let's have it then. What did you make of him?'

'He's dog tired all right.' She filled the kettle and plugged it in again, then lifted the remains of the sliced ham from its greasepaper and laid it on a plate. 'He's also very strange. Very strained too.'

'The blokes at work think he's a nutter. Like most of his lot. They don't count. The movement that matters is the Tendency.'

'He kept saying things as though he'd learned them by heart.'

'Probably had.'

The naked cynicism of this remark made her round on him. 'Why on earth are you so concerned about him then?'

'Because he maintains the electrics in our shop, that's why.

If he's half asleep when he's fixing wires someone else could get hurt when they switch on in the morning.' He spoke with a gravity which he hoped would impress her. 'We use a lot of power. I'd like him put right before there's an accident. Not after!'

'Then why don't you talk to Lee? He's completely under her thumb.'

'You mean the Chinese?'

'She's a really interesting person, Ken. I'd like to meet her again. Anyway, there ought to be a social worker visiting her. She's on supp. ben. and she's ill.'

Norris had wanted Mary to suss out the situation for him. He emphatically didn't want her hanging around Carlton Terrace. Not with the plans he had for Brunner. He took the plate of ham from her hand and put it down in a way that was distinctly menacing. 'I don't approve of that crowd. OK, I wanted a bit of background on Brunner, because he could be a threat to all of us. But I don't want you getting caught up with a bunch of bloody Trots! Tell the community centre to send somebody else, right!'

To his amazement, she turned on him.

'Just listen to me, Ken. A few weeks ago you were all uptight because I didn't know about Clause Four. But you're so busy, you never really explain anything. I never knew before that Trotskyites *are* Marxists, I thought they were opposed to each other. If you don't want me to learn from other people, you can find time to tell me yourself.' She picked up the plate and took it to the living room.

Taken aback, he followed her again. In fact his knowledge of Communist dialetic was minimal. He remembered trying to understand about the Russian invasion of Afghanistan by reading a three-page article in *Militant*. Five paragraphs had left him reeling. His kind of dogma was the simple, gut-feeling repetition of a few useful ideas, and most of these were Stalinist rather than Trotskyite.

'OK,' he began, making a brave attempt. 'We all know the decisions this government makes are based on defending the interests of the capitalist classes. Right? And capitalism's in decline. So we're not just going to sit and watch, are we? We're going to help it on with a few hefty kicks. Like nationalizing the two hundred biggest companies, taking over the assets of the banks and using them for the benefit of the working class. I'll tell you one thing about Marxism, love. It's always been part of Labour policy.'

'You'd hardly think so, sometimes.' Mary had her mouth half full but she wasn't going to let that past. She had begun to realize lately that Ken might send shivers of delight all through her in bed, but he was no great shakes as an intellectual. Clever in a cunning way, yes. Brainy, definitely no.

'You're right there, love. Look at Frampton North Labour Party for a start. Flaming hell. Huntley and Brook, like a bloody pantomime duo. But Charlie'll have his work cut out after the council elections next month!'

'You always get back to the same thing, don't you?' she remarked. 'Beating hell out of the moderates. Planning take-overs. That doesn't help the sort of people I'm looking after, you know. People on benefit need caring for, not fighting over.'

He didn't want this argument. 'Let's turn on the telly,' he said. 'Be the news soon.'

'You don't like having your ideas challenged, do you, Ken?' she said.

'Oh, shut up!' The moment he spoke, he regretted it. Her face became strained and her mouth set. He hastily went and sat beside her on the sofa. 'Sorry, love. I didn't mean anything. It's just those Trots get on my wick.' He put an arm round her. 'Love you, Mary. I don't want to hurt you.'

She held him close, half relieved, half still unhappy. Soon he took her to bed where, as though to make up for his temper, he kissed her gently, smoothing her hair, gradually arousing her into a crescendo of love-making, so that she fell asleep exhausted and totally happy.

In the morning, when he brought her a cup of tea as usual, he mentioned that he would have to go for another evening meeting in Bristol tonight.

'Well,' she said, 'I'll wait up, but please don't take it out on me if things go wrong.'

Donaldson's second visit to Frampton came at the end of March. On this occasion he was promised time with the Chief Designer. He especially wanted to understand more of the design concept of the 207 airliner. He was by himself, since Mac was busy investigating a crash. The Chief Designer, Frank Golding, was a tall, stooping man with thick bushy eyebrows, which made him the delight of the company magazine's cartoonist. In consequence he was better known to the workforce than most of the Directors, even though his own position was one level below the Board.

Western Aircraft's design team had been built up over years and Golding showed Donaldson round the large open-plan offices with pride.

'I have to be honest with you,' Golding said. 'If we had not received the government funding, we couldn't have kept this team in being. As it is, thank God, they're as keen as mustard. Now, I imagine you'd like to know the whys and wherefores of the 207. Let me show you.'

Using models and large-scale drawings, Golding began to expound the design philosophy.

'A low wing. Unnecessarily complicated to have anything else, in our opinion. You save a lot of complication on the undercarriage and you can give it a wider track.' He surveyed the six-foot-long model, sleek in the white and gold of the company colours. 'True, the British Aerospace 146 has a high wing. But that's only a seventy to ninety seater designed for short routes and if you're going to operate off unpaved runways in remote places, you have to consider possible ground obstructions.'

'So you're not so worried about short take-off capability?' Donaldson asked. His prime interest was in how this plane was going to handle from the pilot's viewpoint.

Golding smiled, momentarily twirling one eyebrow with

his finger tips, a habit which overcame him when asked a tricky question. 'Of course Wormley will be telling the customers that it doesn't need a lot of space. But the people we're selling to will only be operating out of proper airfields anyhow.' He pointed to the shape of the wing. 'You pay for short take-off. Remember the old VC 10?'

Donaldson laughed. 'Should do. I was a VC 10 captain. I suppose you're going to tell me it was designed for runways in Commonwealth countries which were promptly all lengthened for the Boeing 707.'

'Well, weren't they?'

'Too right! And we found ourselves using three per cent more fuel in the cruise because of a capability we didn't need any more.'

'We were determined not to listen to a lot of possibly transient local requirements, when one of the main markets for this aircraft is in North America. We're after economical operation, good clean flying characteristics and an aircraft which is easy to load and unload.'

Donaldson agreed again. There was little point rushing passengers and freight from here to there in fifty minutes if they then had to queue for fifteen minutes merely to get off. The more he saw of the 207 project, the more he liked Western's commonsense approach to its construction.

'Incidentally,' Golding remarked, 'there are two executives across from Atlantic Airlines.'

'Really?' Donaldson had old friends in this New York based carrier. 'Not Colonel Daly, by any chance?'

'Correct. He's booked in to see me after lunch. I'm sure Wormley would let you join them for a drink beforehand.' Golding picked up the phone, spoke briefly to the Chief Executive's PA and said, 'Well, that's all fixed. Now how about a look at the first assemblies?'

They left the design offices and walked perhaps a hundred yards to Production Centre Three, where once again Donaldson was introduced to Bob Burnett and shown round. More and more parts were being completed, emerging painted, and being made up into small assemblies.

'We're bang on schedule,' Burnett told them. 'In fact ahead of it in some respects, I'm glad to say. We'll be having the fuselage bulkheads through in a week or two now.'

He said this while they were standing near the twenty-five-foot-long anodizing tanks where Ken Norris and his workmate Les had just completed the two-and-a-half-hour treatment cycle of a batch of panels. Norris's attention had already been attracted by the presence of the visitors. He edged towards them.

Burnett nodded to him. 'How's it going, Ken?' Then, as a gesture, he introduced the shop steward.

'You've got a first-class aircraft building here,' said Donaldson encouragingly.

'Hope so,' Norris replied. 'Frampton needs the work, what with cutbacks everywhere else.'

It was a curiously unenthusiastic answer. As they passed out of earshot, Donaldson asked if Norris was in local politics.

'I'll say he is,' Burnett snorted. 'One of the militants trying to take over the local Labour Party. Not, mind you, that I let politics enter my job here. Never at all.'

Watching their retreating backs, Norris cogitated on Burnett's remarks about schedules. If the Russians didn't make their minds up soon it would be too late. There'd only be one chance with the bulkheads, one single night when the bulkhead panels came through. If Peter failed to come up with a decision this evening, they might as well call the whole scheme off.

The gruffness of the shop steward was soon chased from Donaldson's thoughts. Golding escorted him to the Chief Executive's offices and he had a pleasurable reunion with an American he hadn't seen for several years.

Colonel Harrison Daly was a former US Air Force officer who had for a time been the FAA representative in London and was now with Atlantic Airlines. His hair was greying, Donaldson noticed, but he had the same quiet dynamism as of old: and if things hadn't changed, he would be still capable of creating hell. Daly believed in getting what he wanted, which was presumably why Atlantic had hired him.

'Don't be deceived, Jim,' he quipped. 'I'm just along to carry the Vice-President's bags on this trip.'

'Don't you go believing that.' Daly's boss, John Conrad, had resumed talking to Wormley, but heard and glanced over his shoulder. 'If we place options for the 207, and I think we well might, then Harrison's going to be plenty busy. He'll be in charge of coordinating all aspects of the purchase.'

'Better buy yourself a house here before the prices go up again,' Donaldson joked.

'Well,' Daly grinned, 'if we do a deal, I'll be over here a lot. Maybe not quite that much, though.'

'How many planes have you in mind?' Donaldson could safely enquire. He had no axe to grind.

Again Conrad swung round and interrupted. 'Something of a leading question, that. But it's no secret that we're in the run-up to a considerable re-equipment programme. We'd hardly be in the market for less than twenty planes.'

Wormley appeared not to appreciate this convivial approach to a serious question and diverted the conversation by ordering drinks. Half an hour later Donaldson excused himself, though not before obtaining Daly's address and explaining briefly why he was here himself.

'See you around,' he said, 'I hope.'

'I'll keep my fingers crossed.'

Donaldson left. He was lunching with Bill and Margaret Broughton and didn't want to be late.

At 8 p.m. the same day, a thick-set man carrying an umbrella waited on the Paddington station concourse for the arrival of the Frampton train. He hovered near the barrier as the passengers crowded through, let Ken Norris pass him, then slipped away and followed some fifteen paces behind. The shop steward was nervous, especially leaving the station building and crossing Praed Street, when he looked intently behind him. The thick-set man unhesitatingly went on walking, overtook, and stopped to stare in a shop window until Norris disappeared round the corner, then continued after him at a leisurely pace, crossing the next road, London Street, before Norris did and staying a good fifty yards behind. However, at the corner of Sussex Gardens the man hesitated, glancing round as though uncertain where he was. Then he occupied himself consulting his diary under a street lamp until Norris had reached the front door of the house. Finally he put away the diary, hooked the umbrella over his arm, pulled out a packet of cigarettes and lit one, partially cupping the match in his hands.

In the flat Rusopov heard the door bell ring and walked quickly across the darkened room to the window. As he looked down the street the bell rang again. He watched the man on the corner shift his umbrella, saw the brief flare of the match and immediately hurried back in time to press the entry-phone buzzer as the bell shrilled long and insistently. Yuri was certainly nervous, he thought, but at least he wasn't under surveillance by anyone else. The match signal came as a relief. That morning, too late to alter this rendezvous, a further letter had come from the Centre. Its last paragraph had been disturbing.

> In connection with the measures which you know to have been taken by the counterintelligence against the London Residency and on account of the heightened subversive activities of the British against the plan of work, we instruct you to maintain maximum caution in further work with Yuri. You should immediately place your contact arrangements with him on a totally clandestine basis.

The order had been as impossible to carry out in time as it was longwinded. All Rusopov could do was wait with the lights off and rely on the emergency procedure. As a precaution he had told Yuri that if there was no one at the flat, then three-quarters of an hour later they should meet at a public house near Marble Arch. This would both prevent Yuri telephoning and, if he remained under surveillance, enable Rusopov to telephone him at the pub and rearrange matters.

It would be bad for Yuri's morale, but hugely preferable to a security breakdown. Now all was well he switched on a table lamp and the radio and opened the door.

'Come in, Ken. How are you?' He made the greeting as normal as possible. But Yuri was visibly agitated.

'Why didn't you answer? I thought you weren't here.'

'I am so sorry. I had a busy day. I fell asleep.' He ushered Yuri in. 'Allow me to take your coat. You must be cold. Whisky as usual?' Rusopov was quick to make an informant feel nothing was wrong. 'I do apologize,' he went on, bringing the drink, 'that we had to delay meeting. You know how it is. Some things are beyond one's control. Now tell me, how are things progressing?'

'Too bloody fast, Comrade. The bulkhead pressings will be through our shop next week.'

'Do you know which day?' Rusopov began to see why Yuri had made his agitated telephone call.

'Could be Wednesday, could be Thursday.'

'And will all the sets of pressings be together?' This was crucial. He could not visualize Tourist sabotaging the project two nights running.

'They're making five sets of detail for the 207. I found that out from a bloke in production control. Two for the test planes, one for the ground test airframe and two spare. There'll be eight pressings in each set. Forty altogether. But they're not large. I reckon they'll go through in the one night.'

'Excellent. Congratulations. This is precisely what we needed to know.' Rusopov smiled encouragingly. 'Now, what you call the sixty-four dollar question. Are we certain your Trotskyite friend will be on duty then?' Even in a safe house, even with the music masking their conversation, he wasn't going to mention Tourist's real name.

'We're not on overtime yet. Unless he's ill he'll be there.' Seeing the puzzlement in the Russian's face, he explained. 'We work a five-day week and he does four night shifts. There's only a fifth night shift Fridays if we're on overtime. Like Saturday mornings. He might not be chosen for overtime anyhow. It's an outside chance.'

'So he will be there?' Rusopov wanted to be certain. He found the British manipulation of overtime confusing. In the Soviet Union each worker fulfilled his set norm. At least, in theory he did.

'Should be.' Norris grinned. 'And he's properly steamed up at the moment, too. When they threaten him he'll go spare. Mary reckons he's half off his head anyway.'

'Mary? How is she involved?' Rusopov's anxiety returned.

'She made a social work visit,' Norris told him, unable to hide his self-satisfaction at his own ingenious scheme.

'It will not be wise for her to continue this contact.' Rusopov made the comment as much of a slap in the face as he dared. If Yuri were a cadre worker he would have castigated him for such a breach of discipline. Rusopov estimated conceit as one of his most dangerous traits.

'Don't worry, Comrade. She won't. It was a one-off.' He caught the anxiety in Rusopov's voice but he wasn't too worried. He'd made it up with Mary and so long as he treated her right she'd do as she was told.

There was no more Rusopov could say, except perhaps to discuss technicalities and he approached this circumspectly. 'Then you are convinced our plan is viable?'

'As good as can be. Short of doing it myself.'

'We don't want you at risk.' Rusopov hesitated. 'You do understand the technical principle? A battery can activate the recording machine as if the oven was on. But I do not think you need to tell an electrician this.'

'I might prompt him.'

'Be careful, my friend. As the months pass he must come to believe the conception was his own.'

'He will. Well then, Peter, we're on, are we?'

The way this was said clearly implied a quid pro quo. After fetching him a refill of whisky, Rusopov assured him that when the factory election came in November he would emerge as Convenor.

'By the way,' he probed, still needing to elucidate the

Centre's outstanding queries. 'Have you heard anything from Carol?'

'Funny you should ask.' Norris swigged his drink. 'The bloody bitch wants a settlement. I had a letter from her yesterday. She's back with her parents in Islington.' He fumbled for the envelope, crumpled from being in his jacket, and handed it across. 'How about that for a turnaround? I thought she was shacked up in the north!'

Rusopov drew out the small sheet of blue paper and read the laboriously written message with mounting excitement. Here, concealed in this spiteful missive, was the big hook.

'I am so sorry. A bad shock.' He leaned forward earnestly. 'You will need a lawyer, my friend.'

'There's one in Frampton who advises the movement.' Norris had been worrying about this on the train. 'I could go to him.'

'Listen.' Rusopov rose with a gesture of decisiveness. 'You are assisting us. The least we can do in such a crisis is to help you.' He went to the desk and pulled open the drawer in which he had placed money earlier. 'Lawyers are expensive allies. By good chance I went to the bank today. I meant it when I said you could rely on us in emergencies.' He thrust out the wad of ten-pound notes.

'Are you sure?' There was no strength in the query. The cash would be useful, very much so.

'Completely,' said Rusopov warmly. 'Take them. I only wish it were more.' He handed over the money. 'Tell Mary you had an old savings-bank account.' He went back to the desk and wrote on a blank slip of paper 'Received £150' and the date. 'Forgive a small formality. This is my own money and I shall have to reclaim it. Without a signature they might not believe me.' He laid the slip and a pen on the table in front of Norris and, rather than watch over him, occupied half a minute copying the address on the letter. To his relief, when he turned round again the receipt was signed. He picked it up casually and sat down again. 'Let me know what happens.' He shook his head with the air of a perplexed student.

'Women are so unpredictable.'

'I'll let you know when the job's done,' said Norris, aware that he was now under some kind of obligation. 'Would you like me to phone?'

'Preferably not. We have given deep thought to this.' Rusopov did not want to overplay his newly strengthened hand. Yet the moment had come to obey the Centre's instructions. 'You have spent two holidays in our country, correct?'

'And had a very nice time, too.'

'Good. However, it has occurred to us that as a result you may be of interest to the counterintelligence.'

'The fuzz, you mean?'

'More or less.' This wasn't the time to deliver a lecture on the varying roles of the police, the Special Branch and the Security Service in Britain, well briefed though he was on them himself. 'A campaign of vilification is being mounted against us in the British press. We suspect it is inspired by the counterintelligence. It will be prudent for you and me to have a more secret method of communicating.'

'I see what you mean.' Norris pondered this uncomfortably. 'They can't prove anything, though, can they?'

'Absolutely not,' Rusopov reassured him. 'Anyway, many trade unionists are guests at the Embassy. To meet me is no crime. None the less, it will be safer if you mail me a simple message to this address.' He handed across another slip of paper. 'It is a small newsagents where I have arranged to collect letters. Say either "Everything OK down here" or, if you have problems, write "Aunt Edith is ill. Do you know of a specialist?"'

'I get it. Sort of hidden meaning.'

'Exactly. You should memorize the phrases.'

'And then you write back to me?'

'We will send you the time and date of the doctor's appointment. On the next Saturday after that date you will go to the central post office in Bristol and ask for a letter addressed *poste restante* to William Rogers. Inside will be a small sum for expenses and instructions, or if you have indicated an emergency, a time to meet me. Now listen carefully, this is most important. As a Soviet diplomat I am only allowed to travel thirty miles from London without official permission. Therefore you must come to me. The time will always be the day after you collect the letter, the Sunday. The place will be the towpath by the Thames at Strand on the Green in Chiswick. You will walk from the end nearest Kew Bridge station and you will find me. Is that clear?'

'Sounds a bit complicated.' If he hadn't just pocketed £150 Norris would have expressed himself a lot more strongly.

'Better to be safe than sorry, my friend. Now, please repeat back our arrangements.' He listened carefully, corrected Norris once and then said, 'I have one final gift for you. It will be posted.'

'What's that, then?'

'A driving licence in the name of William Rogers. You may have to identify yourself to collect letters.'

'Jesus Christ, you've thought of everything, haven't you?' Norris was genuinely amazed. 'It's like something out of a bloody film.'

'No,' said Rusopov confidently. 'It is better than something out of films. In films they make mistakes. We do not.' He glanced at his watch. 'Now, I imagine you should catch the next train. If Mary thinks you are in Bristol she will not expect you to be too late.'

When Norris left the house he was again shadowed from the street intersection onwards. What the thick-set man with the umbrella failed to spot, for all his expertise, happened in the railway station itself. A long-haired, saturnine-faced young man dressed in jeans and an anorak ceased studying the departures indicator board and boarded the Frampton train shortly after the shop steward. The young man was glad to sit down. He was out of breath because he had run like hell to get ahead by a different route.

5

'The thing is, Mr Burnett, I'm the last to want trouble for a fellow worker, but we are all on the same productivity scheme, aren't we, and what one doesn't do, the others lose out on.'

Burnett nodded non-committally. Whatever it was Norris had asked to see him about, it had unpleasant undertones.

'So what are you trying to tell me, Ken? Lodging an official complaint, are you?'

'Fair is fair, Mr Burnett. If the pyrometry men on the night shift don't finish their job then the day shift can't function, can it? I wouldn't want to make any official complaint about a member of another union.' Norris shifted on his feet. 'All the same, certain of the night shift are sleeping when they're on the clock and my blokes are bloody choked off about it. Twice lat week we had to stop work and call the pyrometry to check controls which should have been serviced the night before.' He was on safe ground here. He had made sure production stopped. 'As I say, Mr Burnett, I'm not a stirrer, but the lads feel it's time action was taken in appropriate quarters.'

'I see.' Burnett looked up from his desk. It was his gospel that management had to be seen to be fair. He applied it rigorously, too rigorously some people thought. The snag with this was that the accusation related to men not under his authority. The pyrometry men who maintained the many electric controls and gauges monitoring processes throughout the factory belonged to a special department called Production Services. All he could do was pass the word to the Manager there. For that he needed facts.

'Couldn't you be more specific, Ken?'

'I'm not naming names.' Norris paused, trying to give the impression of struggling with his conscience, then yielding. 'Well, if I say it's a young electrician who sells papers outside the gate at dinner time . . .'

Hell's teeth, thought Burnett, of all the two-faced hypocrites. But he knew exactly whom Norris was talking about and there had been persistent rumours about the night shift.

'OK, Ken,' he said resignedly. 'Point taken. Anything else?'

'That's all thanks, Mr Burnett.' As Norris turned to leave the office he added, 'I wouldn't want him to get his cards or anything. The lads just reckon enough's enough.'

When he had gone Burnett picked up the internal phone and spoke briefly to the Production Services Manager. Then, with a feeling of relief, he turned his attention to the Planning Process sheets listing subassembly parts due to pass through the treatment shops next week, noting with satisfaction that sets of the 207 details were ahead of schedule. The Director of Manufacturing was keeping a close eye on the new airliner's progress.

Both executives would have been surprised to know that Ken Norris was equally conversant with Production Centre Three's expected workload: surprised, yet not disagreeably. By every medium possible, through local press releases, through the company newsletter, through notice boards and by word of mouth, they were trying to instil a sense of purpose, commitment and urgency into their employees' attitude to the project.

The information which had triggered Ken Norris's complaint was very precise indeed. It was that forty parts detailed as Lots F/12660 to F/12699 were due into the first stage of heat treatment on Tuesday. They were the forty individual pieces which would be assembled into five rear-fuselage pressure bulkheads for 207 aircraft.

He had checked out their subsequent moves very carefully. The first stage dipped the 'blanks', as the roughly sized sheets were known, into a salt bath for up to three hours at a temperature of 500° C. Thus softened, they would be rushed across to the adjoining press shop within sixty minutes and moulded to shape under a pressure of 4000 tons. Only if the blanks were immediately deep-frozen could the pressing wait up to forty-eight hours. The schedule evidently allowed for a delay because the batch was not due back for the second stage until Thursday. Late that afternoon all forty would go into the heat treatment ovens for 'age-hardening', a sixteen-hour overnight baking which would precipitate the aluminium-copper molecules out of solution again and make the alloy tough and stress-resistant in its new shape.

Ken Norris knew he could not wait a day longer. If Brunner was caught asleep it was nine to one he would be more than just disciplined: he would be suspended for three days. If so, his first night back at work would be next Thursday. Even if he was only disciplined, and the Night Superintendent concerned was notoriously weak-kneed and might play down the offence, Brunner would still need time to prepare. So he laid his charges with Burnett in the morning and at midday, when the whistle went for dinner, he walked out to the car-park gate, near the hourly paid employees' canteen.

Sure enough, there was Brunner, a sheaf of newspapers under his arm, ready to catch people as they went to eat. Norris strolled up, waiting until there was no one else near and handed over a coin.

'By the way,' he said, 'take some advice from a friend. Get that sleeping bag of yours out of the works.'

'Who the hell are you?'

'One of the stewards. Don't kid yourself, mate. The bosses are in a sacking mood. You're asking for it with that bag.' He reached out for the paper, disregarding the hostility in

Brunner's red-rimmed eyes, and moved off again. The trap was laid. All the boy had to do now was walk into it. And from the look on his face he'd do exactly that.

Fairfax picked up the red scrambler phone and recognized Chief Inspector Sturgess's voice.

'The registered owner of the car is Kenneth Arthur Norris, address 44a Harold Wilson House, Minehead Road, Frampton. Do you want us to bring in Somerset and Avon?'

Would the Security Service want the local police Special Branch involved at this stage? Two seconds' consideration suggested they would not. 'Thanks for the offer, Colin, not yet though.' Fairfax put down the instrument, reached into the desk drawer and filled in a trace request for the clerk to take downstairs.

Two hours later the clerk brought a precis of information not dissimilar to the registration card maintained by the KGB, though much less up to date and including some startlingly trivial items. The Security Service's computer was programmed to dredge up any conceivably relevant facts from its memory. A mere parking offence could reveal an important date and time. After studying the results, Fairfax took them along to the Assistant Director.

'It was the first trip to Russia in 1969 coupled with the Communist Party membership which seem to have alerted us. Three trips to the Soviet Union altogether.'

The Assistant Director studied his junior's face and reflected, not for the first time, that if Fairfax made herself up differently, she could be a most attractive woman, but perhaps not so unobtrusively successful at tracking spies. As it was, she did nothing artificial to accentuate her steady grey eyes, kept her fair hair trimmed well short of falling on her shoulders and barely touched a generous mouth with lipstick.

'The significant point,' he brought himself back to it, stabbing at the paper with his finger, 'is that Norris quit the Communist Party in 1972. The very year the Labour Party's

General Secretary came back from Moscow and announced "a firm foundation for understanding and friendship"; only months before the Party lifted the ban on its members belonging to Communist organizations – the most important political event in Britain since the war, in my opinion.' His thick eyebrows knitted in a scowl, reminding her irresistibly of a certain Cabinet Minister. 'There's only one possible inference, Kit. Our friends in Moscow had plans for him. Long-term ones. They wanted him to look nice and clean within a few years. By now, perhaps.'

'It's hardly a crime. Becoming an entryist, I mean. If the Labour Party wants to welcome incognito Communists . . .' She let the remark tail off. She believed in spies but not in witch-hunts. 'And why on earth do we cherish the fact that he defaulted on the hire-purchase payments for a tape recorder?'

The Assistant Director grunted, faintly riled at her refusal to accept departmental procedures as gospel, though he admired her capacity for independent thinking. 'Could conceivably be a different Norris,' he admitted. 'The computer's not God, I agree.'

'I'm relieved to hear it!' Kit had been in the service nine years now, since she was twenty-six, but she retained a questioning mind. The daughter of a schoolmaster, she had gained a good degree at university, then gone to work for a Bond Street art dealer. There she learnt to accept nothing about an Old Master painting at its face value: to look for wrong attributions, gaps in the provenance, even forged authentications. It was the help she gave Scotland Yard's Fraud Squad in tracing a stolen picture that led to a discreet approach from DI5. She still remembered the lunch at Brown's Hotel with amusement. Would she be interested in a less conventional job, the man had asked her. So Luttrell's had lost an art historian and the Security Service gained a trainee who was now acting head of a section, yet had not allowed her talents to be buried among the files and memos which proved so inseparable from counterespionage.

'I know what you're going to say.' Kit quoted, 'An intelligence picture is like a newspaper photograph, made from hundreds of tiny dots, each meaningless by itself and the computer helps arrange them.'

'Touché.' He smiled. It was indeed his favourite simile, one he used when lecturing the new entrants.

'Well, I admit I'm instinctively certain this man Norris is up to no good, but I'd like to be certain the facts are relevant ones. I want to check that Kenneth Arthur Norris is the man who drove the Ford away from Frampton station that night.'

'That's reasonable.' The Assistant Director pushed the paper back to her across his desk. 'You'd better send Ingram down there again. With a camera. See about a phone tap, too. I imagine we'd get clearance for one.'

The Production Services Manager faced Brunner across the table. On his left sat the Night Superintendent, on the right the pyrometry men's Electrical Trades Union steward. Brunner was unshaven, the fair stubble bristling on his pallid skin, and he had thrust his hands deep into the pockets of his white coat, as though he didn't trust himself to leave them free. He was shaking as if cold. It was 9 a.m. on Friday.

'I can't accept excuses, Jack.' The Manager's tone was kind. He was getting on in years himself and he knew what it was to be tired. 'You chose to do permanent night shift. Everyone knows you don't rest properly during the day. A month ago I had to deliver you a verbal warning for slipshod work. You don't dispute you were found asleep at four ten this morning behind the stores cage in Centre Three. You know that sleeping while you're on shift is a serious offence. Have you anything more to say?'

'I'd done what I had to,' protested Brunner sullenly. 'I had the bag with me for the weekend. I'm going hiking.'

'It won't wash, Jack.' The Manager pulled a small sheaf of forms out of a drawer, took a couple, inserted a sheet of carbon paper between them, and began filling in details with a ballpoint pen. When he had finished he signed the form and dated it. Then he stood up and thrust the top copy out towards Brunner.

'I've no alternative to giving you three days' suspension, starting Monday. You'll report again for Thursday's night shift.'

Brunner did not move, except to shake his head imperceptibly. His hands remained fast in his pockets. The Manager wavered, unable to hand over the form, then laid it in front of the steward.

'We'll appeal this, Mr Jackson,' said the steward. 'A written warning would be sufficient.'

'I'm sorry, Tom. He was lying on a sleeping bag which he can only have had on company property for one purpose.'

'On, Mr Jackson, not in. He was tempted to lie down for a minute. I don't dispute he was wrong, but it shouldn't be suspension.'

'Well, we all know the procedures.' Jackson spoke without emotion. The steward had to be seen to defend his member, just as the management had to be seen to enforce discipline. 'In my view this is the minimum action I can take.' He glanced back more coldly at the electrician. 'That's all, Brunner. You can go.'

When they were outside the steward steered Brunner to a quiet corner. 'Listen, Jack, I'll stand up for you, never fear that. But you're in the wrong. If there's a next time they'll be handing you your cards.' He moved to lay a friendly hand on Brunner's shoulder. 'If you can't sleep days, ask for a change of shift.'

Even as he spoke Brunner ducked away, then rounded on him. 'I need the days! They were out to get me. Don't tell me they weren't.' He was beginning to shout. 'It was all set up!'

'Go and get some kip, lad.' The steward's patience was fading.

'You're in it with them! They set me up!' There were tears in Brunner's eyes now, both of exhaustion and rage. 'Stuff the bosses. Stuff the whole bloody system.'

'Don't be such a bloody fool.' This time the steward took

him forcefully by the arm and propelled him out of the building, picking up his small toolbag for him. 'Here, don't leave this. Now go home and get some kip like a good lad, will you?' He watched as Brunner walked unsteadily away towards the factory gate. Some mothers do have them, he muttered to himself, some mothers certainly do have them.

'You're very late. What happened?' Lee was perched on the typist's chair, the bed unmade behind her, busy with correspondence. On the wide desk lay a file marked 'Trotsky Anniversary Rally'. She stopped writing as Jack entered.

'They caught me kipping. I've been suspended.' He slumped down on the bed. 'A bloke at work warned me yesterday.'

'You mean you were framed?' For all that she organized the Frampton cell of the movement, Lee had only a hazy idea of how a factory operated. Her own working experience was almost entirely in the theatre and television.

'They set me up,' he said wearily. 'Stands to reason, doesn't it? They know I sell the paper every dinnertime. They want me out.' With a spasm of energy he pulled himself up. 'Can't be anything else, Lee. Half the blokes on night shift finish their jobs quick then sleep. Christ, there's one even has a spirit stove and cooks himself eggs and bacon every morning. The foremen don't object. Never have done. This is a witch-hunt. Straight political victimization.' He lay back on the bed. 'Christ, I'm tired.'

'We must fight back!' Despite her illness Lee had astonishing dynamism. 'We can't let ourselves be defeated by corrupt organizational manoeuvres.' She slipped off the chair and knelt beside him. 'Don't give up, Jack. We are going to rally the masses and nothing will stop us. You must show your mates you're not defeated. You must be there with the paper today like any other day. In Vietnam and Iran and Nicaragua people gave their lives for the struggle. This is the least you can do.'

Brunner raised himself on one elbow. 'I suppose you're

right. We must fight back.' He stood up unsteadily. 'I'm going next door.'

'I'll wake you,' she said relentlessly. 'Don't waste time taking your clothes off. We have to reach our target for the fund.'

When Norris went across to the canteen at midday there was no sign of Brunner outside the car park. The buzz was already around the factory about him, swollen by rumour to stories of a camp bed and summary dismissal. Norris had rapidly ascertained both the truth and that there wasn't much sympathy for the electrician on the shop floor. The joint productivity scheme had been one of the management's more shrewd innovations.

I was dead right about that, Norris thought as he hunched over his plate of fish and chips, it's all worked a treat so far. But he still had to exploit the situation he had created. If Brunner did not continue selling his papers outside the gate he would have problems. Peter had been emphatic about not seeking him out. At the same time the electrician had to be caught when at his most resentful, and there must be time for the idea, when planted, to ferment in his mind. Today ought to be the day, or at worst tomorrow.

To his relief as he left the canteen he saw Brunner's slight figure, shifting nervously from one foot to the other, standing some twenty yards from the gate. A couple of others coming out saw him too.

'Bloody red,' one commented. 'Deserves all he gets.'

The remark hit Norris like a hammer, reminding him that the more persecuted Brunner could be made to feel, the better. With twenty minutes in hand before the end of the dinner break he strolled out through the gate, turned right for the car park, then made a show of changing his mind and walked up to Brunner.

'Things aren't so good, I heard,' he remarked sympathetically.

'The bastards set me up. I know they did.'

'I told you the management was after a confrontation.' Norris foraged in his trouser pocket for money, acting out his part. 'What's new today, then?'

'Haven't had time to read it even.' The bitterness was there in Brunner's voice all right, but it wasn't intended for Norris. 'You were bloody well right,' he continued, handing over a copy. 'They were out to get me.'

Casually, as he would when he wasn't in a hurry, Norris scanned the paper, dismissing the colour photos of a football match, searching in the columns for a suitable quote. 'I'll say one thing,' he remarked, without looking up. 'Whoever writes this has got the message. Young peoples' rights *are* being smashed. Look what's happened to you.' He glanced sideways at Brunner, who was shivering as if it were mid-winter. 'Your steward's appealing, is he? Well, don't expect anything from that. You're being busted for your beliefs, mate.' He paused to let the idea sink in, but Brunner said nothing, though his face flushed.

'You know why, don't you?' Norris was still pretending to read the paper. 'This 207's a military project, that's why. They had the airforce brass down only last week. They're scared in case someone who's not afraid of them decides he doesn't want the next war on his doorstep and wrecks it.'

'What d'you mean?' Brunner's voice was a croak, as hoarse as if he was being strangled.

'It's you or them, mate. Like you said, they're out to get left-wingers. That's what it's all about.' He folded the paper. 'See you around, then.'

'Here. Don't go. I want to talk.'

'I've got to be back. I'll be copping it myself next.' He began to move off.

'Can we meet after work?' The words had more desperation in them, more pleading, than Norris could recall hearing in a grown man's voice ever before.

'If you like.' He sounded as offhand as he could. 'OK. There's a pub down the docks called the Shakespeare. After I've had my tea. Seven thirty.' He stuck the paper in his coat pocket, hurried to his car, pretended to search for something, then came back through the gate with five minutes to spare.

'He's off his head, that bloke,' he commented to the policeman as he showed his pass.

Brunner still stood there, as desolate as a scarecrow in the wind. The policeman checked his watch, then walked over to him.

'Why don't you just f... off?' he said. 'We can do without your kind.'

Ten minutes early Norris settled himself in a dark corner of the Shakespeare's public bar. It was an old-fashioned place, the ceiling tanned nut brown by smoke, the wooden benches worn, sawdust on the floor. The landlord had his sleeves rolled up, as if ready to eject brawlers. Norris had chosen the Shakespeare, on Peter's advice, because it was in a section of the city he never normally visited. Waiting, taking an occasional swig of beer – he wouldn't draw attention to himself by ordering whisky – he thought about Peter. The Russian was pretty switched on, he admitted. Of course he hadn't dreamed the whole thing up, but he had made some shrewd observations. Like allowing Brunner time for discussion with the Chinese bird, after the idea was sown in his mind. From the sound of her she'd plump for the violent option every time, the bitch. And Brunner would serve up any scheme as his own in order to impress her. 'We call such people the useful idiots,' Peter had said. He was dead right. It didn't occur to Norris that he might fall in the same category himself.

The door swung back and Brunner entered out of breath, his hair dishevelled. Conversation in the bar died briefly, then resumed.

'Sorry I'm late. Couldn't find the place.' Once he trusted someone, his language fell back into the polite phrases barracked into him by his father, an army sergeant. He had broken irrevocably with his family, yet their influence lingered in minor ways.

'What'll you have?'

'No, I'll get it.' He returned with a lemonade shandy. 'I don't drink much,' he explained, sitting down. He seemed more in control of himself and Norris guessed this might be because he had come to some decision. 'Were you on the march last weekend?' he asked abruptly, as if seeking a credential.

'Which one?'

'Frampton against the missiles.'

'No.' Norris shook his head, faintly amused. He had grown cynical about these mushrooming protest fronts. 'We were busy trying to keep a primary school open. I'm not exactly a right-winger myself, but a lot of these anti-groups are just so much hot air. All speeches and no action.' He took a quick sip of beer. If Brunner didn't mention the factory, he wouldn't. But he could spur him on. 'Now that slogan in your paper, "Youth on the March". That's positive.' He took out a folded page of the paper. 'I reckon this bloke's got it right.' He showed Brunner a sentence he had ringed, just visible in the poor light.

'The youth must be trained as revolutionaries and disciplined fighters.'

'Now that's something like it,' he said approvingly.

'I came to Frampton as part of Youth on the March,' said Brunner, a quiver of emotion in his voice. He sat silent for a couple of minutes and Norris sensed he was screwing himself up to ask a direct question. When it came, it was with unconcealable intensity. 'Were you serious about the 207 being military?'

'Never more so.'

'Two-faced bastards. You know what that scab on the gate said? They didn't want my kind there.' He paused, breathing heavily. 'We have to fight capitalism with its own weapons.'

'Well, you'd better get a shift on,' said Norris cheerfully. 'Next thing you know you'll be given your cards.' He was keeping it cool, playing disinterested. Why couldn't the silly sod get to the point? What he needed was a wet-nurse. One thing was for sure, when the revolution came in Britain, it would be no thanks to this bunch.

'Could the 207 be wrecked?' Brunner shifted towards him on the bench.

Norris chuckled softly. 'Brother, there's a hundred ways you could snarl it up. How long have you been in this business, for Christ's sake?' He wanted it to sound like public knowledge, guessing that Brunner was basically ignorant of aviation.

'Only four months. I was in a power station before.' The way he admitted it was a confession of weakness.

'Well, it's like any other factory. The bosses think the safety checks are infallible, but are they ever?' He was into the spiel he had prepared, making it all sound a doddle. 'Take the heat treatment.' He swigged some more beer. 'You know those tandem ageing ovens?'

'We service the controls.'

'Of course, you do. I'd forgotten. Well, suppose those were switched off one night? So long as the recording machine went on registering, no one would be any the wiser.'

'What would that do?'

'Take next Thursday night, OK.' Norris knew exactly where he was heading now, talking like a teacher to a child. 'Keep it always theoretical,' Peter had said. 'Be the experienced man who is astonished others do not know these things.' The line was working a treat. He wanted to emphasize the day. 'Thursday night,' he reiterated, 'there's a batch of pressure bulkhead detail going through. If those weren't properly heat treated they'd get metal fatigue way ahead of time.'

'And?' Brunner was really excited.

'So they'd fail in flight, wouldn't they? Bye-bye one 207.' He grinned at Brunner as though it were all a lovely joke. 'The bosses think the system's infallible.' He laughed. 'It's bloody not, mate. Any of your lot could fix that recording to go on running.'

'It's fed off an output from the oven.' The electrician

mused for a few seconds. 'You're right. It could be wired to an alternative source . . . '

'See what I mean. The place is wide open.' He got up, wanting to give Brunner a break to think. 'Have another whatever it was.'

'Shandy,' said Brunner mechanically. He obviously was thinking.

'Of course,' said Norris when he came back with their re-filled glasses, 'someone would have to get at the heat treatment inspector's Barcol impressor. Change the calibration for him. That would be no problem, though.' He laughed again. 'Old Charlie Brook never minds blokes borrowing the odd screwdriver. Not exactly security conscious, our Charlie, you could get at *his* toolbox easy.' He lifted his tankard, careful not to spill any beer, and took a deep swallow. 'Then there's the milling machines. All the computer programmer has to do is put an error on the tape, out comes a defective spar.'

The fault would be discovered for sure, but Brunner wouldn't know that. Then Norris realized he had lost his audience anyway, and stopped talking.

'What's this impressor?' demanded Brunner suddenly.

'Thing with a gauge on top and three short legs underneath. One isn't a leg, it's a steel needle. Press it into the metal and a hardness reading comes on the gauge. Has to be calibrated regularly.'

'Like a stylus on a record-player?'

'Bit like that.'

Brunner fell silent. When he spoke again Norris reckoned he must be satisfied, because he veered back on to his original theme.

'What you were saying about Youth on the March. You believe in that?'

'Well.' Norris had to distance himself a little. 'Personally I'm not a Marxist. But we're all workers in the same struggle and if young blokes don't change the system, who will? Not the bosses, brother, no way.'

'I must go!' Abruptly as ever, Brunner jerked himself to his feet, leaving his shandy half finished. 'We've a meeting tonight. Thanks for the drink.' He made for the door as if pursued and was gone.

Norris wiped the back of his hand across his brow. To his surprise he was sweating. He drank down his beer. There was nothing more he could do, except wait. Christ, he thought, of all the mixed-up characters. Reckon he had a date with the Chinese bitch. He looked as though the hounds of hell were after him, not to mention her. He got up, nodded goodbye to the bartender and left. As he walked back through the dark streets it occurred to him that it was time to start looking after number one. The election for Convenor would come before the first 207 flew. He ought to remind Peter of their bargain.

At night the factory was an illuminated ghost, patrolled by works police with the same circumspection as if it were a series of deserted warehouses. Noises which passed unnoticed in the day acquired sinister significance. Only the cats seemed at ease, stealthily pursuing their own obscure objectives in dark corners.

A mere seventeen men made up the night shift for Production Centre Three. Even so Brunner was tense and apprehensive when he clocked in, fear of his workmates' recrimination screwed tighter by the knowledge of what he had to do. For three days he had rehearsed the moves, action by action, Lee urging him on. 'You have to do it, Jack. For the sake of the movement, for all our sakes. This is our chance to smash the capitalist warmongers.' But Lee's had not been the loudest voice. Inside him burned a stinging resentment at the Manager who had humiliated him.

In consequence he was totally unnerved by the foreman's responses after he clocked in.

'Sooner we're back to normal, the better,' the foreman remarked. 'Let bygones be bygones, that's what I say.' The pyrometry men were all weekly paid staff, a cut above hourly paid workers, and it grieved him that young Jack had fallen into the ways of his inferiors.

Brunner stuttered a reply and made off, confused and then even more angry at being patronized, his thoughts still dominated by the plan.

The tandem ageing oven, as the heat treatment oven was properly called, stood like a huge steel container on the shop floor. Brunner knew it was on from the relative warmth long before he reached it. The first necessity was to check what the contents were. Since there was no night shift here, there was no one to query why he took the route cards from their rack. He flicked through them. The first bore the part number F/12660. Below was the description: 'Bulkhead'. He scanned the instructions. 'Precipitate to MP38 sixteen hours at 190° C.' The start time noted was 3.30 p.m. He thrust the cards back and looked around cautiously. Further down the building a man was opening up the inspector's cage. There was nobody close. He moved across to the control console.

Somehow he had never doubted the information Norris gave him. Seeing the green button which activated the oven depressed, and the temperature control set at 190°, it occurred to him that he had been too trusting. All the effort of the past days might easily have been wasted. He tried to put the thought aside, and concentrated on the task. Norris had talked as though one could switch the oven off completely. Luckily Brunner had appreciated that if he did he might be unable to re-start the Kent recorder linked to it. Pretty stupid of Norris not to appreciate the danger, he considered. But it was like that when people boasted, talking off the top of their heads. They missed the really crucial points, and it was in interfering with the Kent recorder that the crunch would come.

Fastened up on the wall near the console, the recorder was basically a large box with a glass panel front. Through this could be seen a broad band of paper, winding all but imperceptibly on to a large spool. The paper was gridded and a delicate arm protruded over it slowly tracing a record of the heat treatment. The horizontal grid lines were an inch apart on the paper and represented hours, the vertical ones registered degrees Centigrade. For the past two-and-a-bit hours the trace had wobbled gently along the 190° C line.

Brunner ferreted in his small toolbag for the key. It was a legitimate possession. He could not service the Kent recorder without opening the casing. He swung open the front, nervous that his memory of the inside might be wrong. It was not. There was space enough for the small dry cell battery he had brought.

He glanced around. He was still unobserved. Indeed, except for handling the battery, he was doing nothing out of the ordinary. The temperature recording was actuated through a thermocouple from the oven. If the heat declined, so would the difference in potential and the mini-voltage involved would sink, moving the arm. If his calculations were right, the battery would replace this voltage when he disconnected the thermocouple wire. He could not switch the oven off completely, otherwise the rotation of the spool would cease. That was what Norris had failed to appreciate. He pushed the battery firmly down behind the cables, then crossed quickly to the console, twirled the temperature control down from 190° C to 19° C, returned and stood facing the recorder, tools in hand. Now for it.

Time stood still. The spool seemed motionless. He thought he heard footsteps, but they came no nearer. Biting his lip apprehensively, he reached inside, undid the thermocouple leads and linked the battery to the terminals. The arm twitched, leaving a tiny V on the trace. He closed the panel, locked it, pocketed the key. The battery was hidden, but would it work? Concentrating all his willpower, he walked away and began routine checks on other machinery. To hang about could arouse suspicion.

Fifteen minutes later he went back. The path of the trace now registered 192° C, but was steady after the jerk. Two degrees was within an acceptable tolerance. There would be no fuss about that. Jesus Christ, he thought, I've done it.

As the realization of success sank in he was caught with such a violent fit of trembling that he could scarcely stand. Clutching his toolbag, he staggered away from the area to sit on a step, panting, his head in his hands.

'You all right, son?'

Startled, he found himself gazing up at a dark blue serge uniform. He levered himself upright, stifling the impulse to run when the policeman reached out to help him, searching for an excuse.

'I'm OK,' he muttered. 'Felt a bit faint.' He felt like telling the bastard pig to f . . . off, but that would be asking for it. 'I'll be OK,' he repeated. 'Must have eaten something.'

'Or nothing, more likely.' The policeman recognized the scraggy, drawn features of one of those young fools who spent their pay on drink and smokes and girls and didn't see a square meal a week. 'Get along for a cuppa and a wad. I'll stand bail for you.'

Brunner obeyed and stumbled away, suddenly frightened of being sent off sick. That would be the finish. He had to last out the night. He should have had some proper rest while he was suspended, instead of selling the paper all day, going through the ritual of self-criticism at political education meetings with Lee every evening, and then puzzling over the functioning of thermocouples half the night. It had not occurred to him that the movement used the weapons of exhaustion and fear to keep its rank and file docile.

Fear of the most immediate, haunting kind kept Brunner going through his round of maintenance tasks, broken only by a snatched half hour at one in the morning to gobble ham and chips in the canteen. He was too preoccupied with the problem of Charlie Brook's micrometer to eat more. At five, when the end of the shift seemed within measurable distance, and the light of the coming day began to filter in through the overhead windows, he came to a decision. The oven would take time to heat up again. By six he would have nearly halved the effective treatment of the bulkheads. He would restore normality before taking the final risk.

As the others disappeared for the last teabreak, he darted back and turned the console control up to 190° C. Again it took all his self-discipline to retreat until the thermometer by the oven, which provided a backstop check on the recorder, showed the full temperature. He reckoned on fifteen minutes, misjudged it, had to wait longer, and at last, in a lather of apprehension, reconnected the thermocouple wires and pocketed the battery. There was now little more than thirty minutes before the shift ended at seven.

Keeping within sight of the inspection staff's wire-mesh-protected cage, he prolonged his own last task and concealed his own Phillips screwdriver under a pile of waste. The Phillips had a cross-shaped tip. No other screwdriver could do its job. He would pretend to be looking for one to borrow.

At 6.50 the lone night shift inspector was called away. Brunner hurried across. The cage was roughly six yards by four and each inspector had a workbench inside. On the right of the door, itself only a hinged grille, he spotted a toolbox with the name Brook neatly lettered on it. There was no padlock. In seconds he had the impressor out of its own small box. The glass-faced gauge was on top. He felt the sharp steel needle beneath. But how was it calibrated? There was no visible mechanism. Christ, he thought, it has to be dismantled. There was no time for that. In desperation he searched for something that might blunt the point, saw a carborundum stone, lifted the impressor and crashed the head down on it. Even if the needle was undamaged, and he noticed the point had pitted the stone, surely the calibration must be upset. The resistance the instrument would register must be less. He thrust the impressor back in its wooden case, replaced that in the box and began searching through the other tools for a screwdriver. He had just found one when a shout made him spin round.

'What the hell d'you think you're doing?'

The white-coated inspector was five yards away, approaching the cage. A moment later he was through the open doorway.

'You've no business to be in here.'

Cowering back, Brunner held up the screwdriver. 'I lost my Phillips. I was just borrowing one for a sec.' The excuse sounded lame and he was trembling all over.

The inspector strode up to him and peered down into Brook's toolbox. 'Is that all you've taken?' he demanded menacingly. He knew who Brunner was and he didn't like him.

'Honest. I must have dropped mine somewhere.'

'Well, you can bloody find yours and put Charlie's back.' He seized the screwdriver, replaced it and slammed the box shut. 'You're the one who was suspended, aren't you?' He gripped Brunner's arm. 'We're going to have a little word with your foreman, lad. Come on. March.'

Ten minutes later it was clear to Brunner that despite the inspector's indignation he had seen nothing more than the taking of the one tool.

'Look,' he pleaded. 'I'm not stupid. I don't want trouble. I just needed a Phillips.'

The foreman drew in his breath, shook his head vexedly, then fumbled in his overall pocket. 'Here, take mine. Cut off back and finish the job.' When Brunner had gone he turned to the inspector. 'I'll tell the Superintendent, Ted. But I doubt it'll go any further.'

'He's no right to be in our area.'

'And it's no crime to borrow a tool. Be fair, if it was anyone else you would't have minded.'

'Maybe.' The inspector wasn't giving in so easily. 'I'll be making a written complaint,' he said tersely. 'Brunner ought not have been in there.'

When Norris arrived for the day shift, barely half an hour later, he soon heard how 'that bloke in pyrometry' had been involved in another row. The inspector had been vocal about it to everyone he met when he came off.

'What was he up to, then?' asked Norris of his informant.

'Caught having a go at someone else's toolbox. He's got a nerve.'

It was bad news. Norris agonized the whole morning, wondering how far Brunner might have bungled the whole thing. All he could discover without causing comment was that the bulkhead batch had come out of the ageing oven at ten, apparently satisfactorily.

At the dinner break he escaped as fast as he could. Drizzling rain was falling outside. Would Brunner sell papers in the wet? He turned his coat collar up and hurried to the canteen. To his surprise the boy was there. Norris checked his pace and approached, hands in pockets, to ask for a paper.

'Back on last night?' he asked off-handedly.

It was the first time he had seen Brunner smile.

'I did it.' He jerked his thumb up in a gesture of success.

'You what?'

'They'll pay for victimizing *me*.'

'Christ alive, you mean the heat treatment?' Norris managed to look flabbergasted. 'You must be joking? You didn't take me seriously?'

A spattering of rain whipped their faces.

'I never said a thing,' said Brunner grinning. 'You didn't hear, OK? It was off nine hours.' He thrust out a paper. 'Why not take out a subscription. That way you'd get it delivered.' He wasn't interested in Norris any more. He was twenty-three years old and he'd successfully pulled the plug on £300 million of the bosses' money. They'd tried to get him and he'd got them instead. Lee had congratulated him, kissed him even in her excitement. He was totally happy. He turned his back to the wind as Norris went off, shielding the papers from the rain.

That afternoon parts F/12660 to F/12699 went through to Flaw Detection. Norris saw them there and knew they had passed Charlie Brook's inspection. What he couldn't determine for sure was whether that was because the impressor reading was wrong, or because a nine-hour break in treatment wasn't enough to leave the bulkheads weak.

6

Ken Norris was collecting his usual *Sunday Mirror* from the corner newsagent when the *Echo*'s headline caught his attention.

THE KGB'S SPYMASTER IN BRITAIN

The accompanying photograph showed a group of three men at a party. Norris stared at the one on the left, picked up the paper, suddenly became aware that he hadn't paid for it, fumbled for more change and went out into the street. Once alone he studied the picture closely. There was no doubt about it. The thin, rather academic man on the left was Peter. But apparently his name wasn't Peter at all. The caption in small type underneath explained:

Soviet 'diplomats' at an Embassy reception. Centre: the KGB's spymaster, Colonel Maxim Petrovich Grigoriev. On the right the Air Attaché. Left the 'Second Secretary Scientific' Vladimir Sergeyevich Rusopov.

The report which followed was too long to read on a windblown street corner. Norris hurried back to Harold Wilson House, ran up the stairs because he was too impatient to wait for the lift, and let himself into the flat. Marion was evidently still asleep. He spread the *Sunday Echo* out on the living-room table and hunched over it.

The story was a long one. But the passage which chilled

him in spite of the central heating was short.

> The government is understood to be deeply concerned about KGB contacts in the trade-union movement. Only one thing holds the Security Service back from more aggressive investigations – the Tory Party's fear of 'union bashing' accusations from the left at a time when industrial relations are critically sensitive.

Sunday Echo readers were not to know that this paragraph was a condensed re-draft of a clumsier text devised for 'our special correspondent' by the Security Service. The paragraph was the price he had to pay for continued cooperation from DI5 in the face of the Managing Editor's sensation seeking. It was intended to offset the effects of the photograph by making Grigoriev's and Rusopov's trade-union acquaintances feel they enjoyed a kind of immunity. The snag – there was bound to be a snag when the government did not control the press – was that in making the thought punchier and more acceptable, the reporter had also made it menacing. In Norris's case it completely misfired. The whole thing worried the hell out of him.

Of course he had realized from early on that he was dealing with the KGB. He was not especially surprised that Peter had used a false name, though it implied a disquieting degree of mistrust. What caught him in the gut was the fear that this article would drive Peter out of Britain and that, having achieved the sabotage of the airliner, the KGB might drop their side of the bargain: namely fixing his election to the Convenorship.

It was already October. The shop stewards election nominations would be going in soon, in January the JSSC would choose the new Convenor. Would Peter honour the bargain? Even if the Russian tried, it would be extremely dangerous for them to meet again. He mulled over more of the considerations. Carol's solicitors were demanding 'half their joint marital property'. He was going to need more money and he'd reckoned to ask Peter for help with that. Even though he now knew the Russian's name was Rusopov, he went on thinking of him as Peter.

Half an hour later, with still no sound from Marion to disturb him, he had come to one conclusion. The Russians had reasons for keeping him sweet now he'd done their dirty work. Peter was no fool. The way of sending each other letters ought to be safe. With careful deliberation he roughed out a message saying he hoped things were being arranged as promised and that there were more legal costs. He decided against the risk of signing it. Then he remembered a detective story he'd read where a poison-pen letter writer had used words cut out of a newspaper. He did the same with the *Echo*, making up the sentences and sticking them on a piece of paper with sellotape. Luckily he had a stamp. He went out again, posted the letter and crumpled the remains of the *Echo* into a dustbin. He didn't want that lying around the flat, for Christ's sake.

Whereas his assistant was required to live as any other Second Secretary did, in a north London block of flats owned by the Embassy, Colonel Grigoriev was allowed a residence appropriate to a Counsellor: a comfortable house in the Notting Hill Gate area. By ten o'clock this Sunday morning there was a ragtag group of reporters and photographers waiting impatiently outside. The *Sunday Echo*'s Managing Editor, appreciating that his front-page story was short on facts, had included Grigoriev's address, as published in the Diplomatic List. But by midday it became clear to even the most optimistic pressmen that the Colonel was not at home. One by one they used the callbox at the end of the street to phone their offices and drifted away to console themselves over pints of beer, swearing volubly. Their language would have been completely unprintable if they had known why their quarry was absent.

Colonel Grigoriev had been tipped off the night before by his contact in the *Sunday Echo*'s composing room, and was safely ensconced with Rusopov. They too had the newspaper spread out on the table, while Rusopov's wife kept them supplied with coffee and made occasional pointed remarks about the damp patches on the walls: the flats were badly built and she seldom had the chance to show a senior officer their deficiencies.

'We can offer you lunch,' she remarked, adding tartly, 'if there is not an electricity cut.'

Grigoriev thanked her absent-mindedly, shifting his bulk in the chair as he thought out the tortuous implications of what had happened. His assistant had more serious problems than rising damp and power failures. 'We must assume that all your agents now know your true identity,' he said at length. 'Even though this does not say you are a KGB officer, there is an implication. Some of your undeveloped contacts will be frightened off, others may panic. Has Yuri broken his silence?'

'No. But he will if the factory elections are not favourable for him.' Rusopov frowned. 'We are heavily dependent on the other one to steer the vote.'

'Someone else will have to take them both over.' He grunted reflectively. 'I do not entirely trust our friend Yuri.'

'He carried through the task.' Like most good controlling officers, Rusopov had a degree of prejudice in favour of his own agents.

'We shall only know that for certain when a 207 crashes. Meanwhile he could be a nuisance.'

'I am confident I can handle him.'

'My dear Volodya.' A wry smile creased Grigoriev's broad face. 'I respect your ability. But for the time being you must abandon fieldwork. When outside the building devote yourself to overt diplomatic jobs.'

'And you, Comrade Colonel?'

'Me?' Grigoriev affected surprise at his assistant's concern. 'I imagine the Centre will recall me. A new Resident will be appointed. You might find yourself in charge for a few weeks.' He looked steadily at Rusopov. 'Which is another excellent reason for precautions. We don't want you suffering embarrassments.'

*

'There was no question about the voice.

'None at all.' Kit Fairfax was emphatic. She was satisfied about that. The saturnine-faced Ingram, the microphone of a miniaturized recorder concealed in his lapel, had chatted briefly to Norris in a pub. 'It was Norris who rang Rusopov from the callbox in February. Since then he's been leading a blameless life down in Frampton: if helping a left-wing take-over can be called living blamelessly.'

'I don't like it, Kit.' The Assistant Director of the Security Service clasped his hands together in front of him, cracking his knuckles in a way which had distressed a whole generation of his juniors. 'I don't believe the Russians have dropped him, not with the 207 project starting up there. He's either on ice or he's been fully recruited.' He cracked his knuckles again and swore. 'I could murder the editor of that damn newspaper. Everyone concerned will go scuttling back into the woodwork now.'

'I never understood why we took the risk of that leak.' She looked at him enquiringly. 'Surely it was always liable to blow back on us.'

'The DG only agreed because the Prime Minister insisted. As you say, Kit, it's liable to be counterproductive trying to embarrass the KGB. All the PM's achieved is to give men we're not yet ready to arrest the fright of their lives.'

'So what next?'

'Run some spot checks on friend Norris. See what he's up to a couple of days a month. We might be lucky. And keep the surveillance on Rusopov round the clock.' He swore again. 'That's all we can do. We're virtually back where we started.'

Trade-union power was a favourite topic for British politicians. Whether they attacked the unions, or defended them, the honourable members of the House of Commons were as mesmerized by the subject as a fangless cobra by a snake charmer's flute.

In theory the elected majority party in Parliament ruled the United Kingdom of Great Britain and Northern Ireland under what amounted to the non-executive presidency of the monarch herself. But a very great deal of power lay outside the elegant Cabinet room in the Prime Minister's official residence at 10 Downing Street. The portentous stone bulk of the Foreign and Commonwealth Office overshadowing Number 10 gave one clue to where it rested. Britain's massive army of public employees were supposed to serve their political masters. Nowadays they sometimes did more to frustrate policies than to implement them. This was especially the case if the lower level public-service unions disliked the policy. So, in analysing where power lay, back one came to that other great bastion of entrenched power: the Trades Union Congress.

For all this, and despite the Labour Party's depending upon funds from the unions for its election campaigns, there was amazing ignorance even among Labour MPs about how Britain's most powerful single union was organized.

Norman Huntley, the Member for Frampton North, did know. He was one of twenty Labour MPs sponsored by the Transport and General Workers Union, which meant that he had been approved by the T&G's Executive in London and the T&G gave financial support to his constituency organization. Though he had easy access to senior union officers in the capital, and important day-to-day dealings with the South-West Regional Secretary in Bristol, Huntley tried to keep in regular touch with the District Secretary in Frampton, an energetic, competent and, beneath the surface, imaginative Welshman of forty-three called Vic Parry.

The two men usually met on a Friday evening at the former shop premises near the docks which were now called 'Transport House', as were the majority of District Office buildings in the South-West, the thirteen Regional Offices spanning Britain and the Headquarters itself in London's Smith Square. The T&G had many of the monolithic qualities of a large corporate concern. It was big business with national funds of around thirty-six million pounds and a membership of over two million workers.

The South-West Region alone incorporated 580 Branches with more than forty fulltime officers such as Parry, 200 other staff, and a turnover in union dues of two million pounds a year. Its membership ran from dockers and truck drivers to construction workers, technical staffs and priests: seventy-three clergymen to be exact. Historically the T&G had roots in the Methodist Church. In the words of the Regional Secretary, 'A Union is about caring for people.'

People and personalities rapidly became the focus of Norman Huntley's conversation with Parry this Friday evening as they sat in the Secretary's bay-windowed office above the shop, once the owner's bedroom.

'Anything of special interest?' Huntley asked, when they had settled down with a couple of bottles of beer brought from the pub along the road. 'All quiet on the Western front?'

Parry laughed politely at the pun, then became serious. 'There's some kind of take-over afoot which I am none too happy about, Norman, not happy at all.' Though Vic had left the valleys as a boy, he had never lost the lilting Welsh speech. 'For what reason should Ken Norris be having himself nominated for Convenor at the Branch meeting last week?'

'You mean the militants are moving in on Western too?' Huntley had half expected it.

'Let us say there are certain overactive members.' Parry was more cautious in his terminology. 'And there's a definite campaign against Fred Dixon. Now, Fred's been a good Convenor. One of the old school, maybe, I'll not deny that, but dependable, has his head screwed on.' The Secretary's concern showed in his tone of voice, which became more emotional. 'Someone's trying to fix old Fred. There's not only Norris in it, that I'm certain.'

'There are people gunning for Charlie Brook, too,' observed Huntley reflectively.

'So I heard. There's much the same accusations flying round about both of them. In the bosses' pockets, seen having a pint with one of the managers, betraying the interests of the working class, all the usual dirt. Blatant bloody lies, but some of them'll stick. Dirt always does.'

'Will the other shop stewards support him?'

'Ken Norris, you mean?' Parry considered the point. The Convenor, the top union official in the factory, would be elected by the shop stewards from their own number in January. He would then be on fulltime union business for the two years until the next election. A dedicated Communist Convenor could wreck a factory's output in half that time. 'Some'll be behind him, though, God knows, the man's a newcomer. They're a basically conservative lot at Frampton, with a small "c", mind.' Parry hesitated, then decided to risk a revelation. 'Still, it's my belief they'd mostly not want to be electing a Party member.'

'Communist Party, you mean?' Huntley was startled.

'Former. Left it a few years back.' The Welshman sipped his beer. 'Have to be careful who I tell that to, could be self-defeating, like – make him sound victimized even. So keep it to yourself, will you?'

'No one believes in Reds under the bed anyway,' remarked Huntley bitterly. He did not trouble to ask how Parry came by the information; a good union official did not merely organize, he was a behind-the-scenes mediator, a sounding board for ideas, sometimes a private investigator. More information came his way than people realized. 'The last thing we want is trouble at Western,' Huntley went on emphatically. 'Not when the 207 promises five to ten years' work for the factory and unemployment elsewhere's at the level it is.'

'Very often,' Parry remarked, 'I would say the cure for an overactive person is to give him responsibility. Sobers a man up wonderfully it does, having to justify what he's doing. But Ken Norris is no wildcat. Here, let me show you.' He rose, went next door to his secretary's room and came back a moment later with a sheet of paper. 'I had this from him yesterday. Now, Norman, I ask you, man, how many of your average part-time shop stewards writes a letter like this and has it all typed neatly into the bargain?'

Huntley examined it briefly, noting the professional setting out of the paragraphs and the polite, yet terse language. He handed it back, half amused. 'Seems a somewhat formal way to ask for confirmation of an election procedure.'

'Too bloody right it is. The answers are all in the rule book anyway. If you ask me, brother Ken intends to be Convenor and he's taking no chances. He's a very fly boy, our Ken. One mistake in our conduct and he'll be down on me like a ton of bricks. That's what makes me suspicious. I reckon he thinks he's got it all sewn up. Looking at that,' he waved the letter, 'I wouldn't be surprised if he has a solicitor advising him into the bargain.'

'So yet again we have to rally the moderates,' said Huntley wearily. After a day in Parliament and the long train journey he suddenly felt too tired to cope. 'What's their game, Vic? What are they after?'

'Taking over the Branch at Western Aircraft.' Parry looked at the MP steadily. 'Taking over as much as they can – including your constituency, Norman. If you don't fight for it, take my word, you'll lose it.'

'Not while Charlie Brook's the Chairman.' Huntley attempted a confidence he did not really feel.

'I wouldn't rely on it. Charlie's in the firing line too.' Parry leaned forward seriously. 'I'm told he could be voted out next time round. I'll tell you straight, Norman, there's a lot going on behind his back – and behind yours.'

'What exactly d'you mean?'

'Try joining the Labour Party in your constituency! You could find it surprisingly difficult if you're not a left-winger. Application forms get lost, payments don't get recorded. When you are a member meetings are changed without warning.'

'Is it as bad as that?' Huntley took off his glasses, rubbed his eyes and sighed. 'Norris is on the GMC too. I might have guessed.'

'He's not alone.' Parry paused, his instinct for drama momentarily taking control of him. 'Listen to me, Norman.

The place to fight back first of all is in the factory. The workers at Western always have been the key to Frampton North and I don't believe the rank and file are interested in political confrontations. In fact I know they're not. They're not extremists. They want a decent job, decent conditions, decent pay. The union gets them all three. Now I'm a fulltime paid official. I leave it to the stewards to make speeches.' He grinned. 'Not that I don't put in a quiet word here or there occasionally. But never over personalities in an election. That would be asking for it. Now you're different.' In his excitement Parry jabbed his forefinger into the MP's waistcoat. 'You can lay it on the line in public, if you've a mind to. And the right occasion's coming up. I heard today they'll be rolling out the first preproduction 207 three weeks ahead of schedule. Old Wormley wanted it by Christmas. He's getting it on the 3rd of December.' He gesticulated with his finger again. 'Ahead of the shop stewards' elections.' Parry realized he was close to shouting and quietened down. 'Let's box clever, Norman. You be there to welcome the plane. The whole workforce will be watching. Congratulate them. And leave a thought about the militants to take home along with their pay packets.' He was suddenly very serious. 'Don't think of it as a factory, Norman, think of it as a battlefield.'

The 207's first public appearance was being adroitly stage-managed and also blessed by fitful winter sunshine. The expanse of concrete hard standing outside the huge assembly hangar had been carefully divided up with portable railings. Two lines of this fencing ran out from either side of the massive folding doors, now shut like a theatre curtain beneath the great arch of the hangar roof. The weekly and hourly paid employees were being marshalled into a solid crowd on both sides. Facing the hangar, far enough out to leave room for the 207 to emerge, stood a large red-carpeted dais for the VIPs, with rows of chairs and a cluster of microphones at the centre. Flanking the dais was standing space for the management personnel. Loudspeakers had been fixed to the hangar sides and to special masts so that all would hear the speeches. Television crews were perched on a gantry with their cameras, while other cameramen and reporters had positions close to the dais.

'So, where are the dancing girls? I can't see anything else missing,' remarked Jim Donaldson in a quiet aside to the test pilot, Bill Broughton. The two men were seated at the extreme end of the dais. Like everyone else they were waiting for the arrival of the Chairman and his guests.

At five minutes before midday two of the company Daimlers purred up to the rear of the dais and disgorged the top VIPs: the Secretary of State for Trade, to whom Donaldson's own chief was directly responsible, the Lord Lieutenant of the County, a Director of British Airways, a Vice-President of Atlantic Airlines, Norman Huntley, and a couple of senior civil servants. The Chairman ushered them to their seats, surveyed the expectant crowd, checked his watch, then stepped up to the microphones.

'Right Honourable Minister, my Lord, ladies and gentlemen, it is my proud pleasure to introduce the Western Aircraft Series 207 airliner: the first, we hope, of many.'

There was a burst of handclapping from the management and ragged shouts of applause from the workforce.

The relayed echoes of the Chairman's voice, thrown back by the bulk of the hangar, were drowned by warning hooters as the fifty-foot-high doors began grinding open, folding away to reveal first the squat shape of an orange-painted airfield towing tractor, then behind it the black nose cone of the 207 itself. Suddenly the dark interior was illuminated by arc lights, rivalling the weak sun outside, and the whole shape of the 207 stood unveiled.

The tractor driver gunned his engine and with majestic slowness the plane was drawn out of its birthplace, aluminium glinting, the gaping mouths of two jet engines slung low beneath the wings, the rearing tailfin all but scraping the hangar roof.

This time the applause was spontaneous, as men and

women who had laboured to construct tiny parts of the 207 appreciated what their efforts had added up to.

'She looks a winner,' Donaldson said to Broughton. 'Better than that, she looks right.'

'I think so.' The Chief Test Pilot knew what his friend meant. Aeroplanes which looked right usually flew well. It was an alchemy defying logical analysis in a business where performance was analysed to extreme limits. The inspiration for the famous Spitfire had come to its designer, Mitchell, from watching seagulls in flight more than from slide-rules.

'Should be no problems,' Broughton reiterated, surveying the 207's clean lines as a trainer might look over a horse. 'We'll be starting the taxiing trials this afternoon. First flight next week, God willing.'

'I'd like to come . . .' Donaldson was silenced by the loud-speakers. The formalities had begun.

In the front row on the dais Norman Huntley listened to the Secretary of State's platitudes, wondering how it was that some Tories made everything industrial sound like a boy-scout attempt to recreate the Empire. 'World markets to be opened up . . . peaks of achievement to be scaled . . . aviation prospects never brighter for Britain.' As the sonorous clichés boomed from the loudspeakers men on the edges of the crowd began to drift away. The canteens would soon be open. At last the Minister finished, the management clapped dutifully and the Chairman turned to the MP.

'Now we welcome the member for this constituency who has so warmly encouraged the 207 project from its inception. Mr Norman Huntley.'

He rose, moved to the cluster of microphones as the cameramen clicked away, thanked the Chairman in an aside and launched into a peroration which he had not merely rehearsed but timed. He felt the same tenseness as at his first meetings all those years ago, when he set out to shock in order to establish himself. Today he was no longer the thin, anxious research worker turned politician. His frame had filled out, his hair thinned, his self-confidence become a protective mantle. But it wouldn't protect him against the left and this morning he knew he was firing the first salvos in the battle to hold on to Frampton North. Once again he was out to shock.

'Friends and brothers!' As the words echoed back he let their impact sink in. None of this Lords, ladies and gentlemen stuff. A number of workers who were sidling off stopped to listen.

'The management here may not like what I have to say. That won't stop me.' A careful pause. 'This plane is ahead of schedule thanks to you, the workers on the shop floor. You built it.' The crowd was silent. He had their attention all right. 'Brothers, as a fellow trade unionist, I ask you to think about that. The 207 is more than just a fine aircraft, more than an order book and pictures in the papers. It's your plane. And it's your future work.'

He could hear the VIPs fidgeting behind him, feel their eyes on his back. He disregarded them, concentrating on making every phrase punch home.

'Brothers, you know I'm no supporter of this Government's policies.' He glanced at the Minister, saw him flush slightly. 'But don't fall for one story being put around about this plane. It's not a military project in disguise. Look at it! Can you see bomb doors, missile racks, gun-sights? No. You cannot. Why not? Because this is no war plane. It's a commercial airliner that's going to give you all five to ten years' work.'

A murmur came from around him, but many of the workforce seemed perplexed.

'Some people would have you think the 207 project should be stopped, by fair means or foul.' There was an audible gasp from the crowd. 'Believe me, brothers, this isn't like jet fighters for Chile or South Africa. There's no sense in activists attacking it. All they're attacking is your livelihood, your pay packets.' He was close to the crunch now. 'Brothers, I'm talking to you as a fellow trade unionist. This month you have important shop-floor elections. Think about who you vote for. Where are they going to lead you? None of us can afford to make this airliner a political football. We have to build it and sell it because we need the jobs. We all know the saying "What's good for Western is good for Frampton." It was never more true than today. If there's one thought I want to leave you with, brothers, it's this. What you're looking at now isn't only a magnificent piece of engineering. It's all your futures.'

As he sat down, sweating in spite of the cold, there was a shout of acclamation from someone in the crowd which triggered an outburst of applause. The VIPs and management clapped nervously. Huntley heard a man behind him mutter, 'Suppose he means well'. Then it was over, he was being ushered down to a limousine, en route for the celebratory lunch, still not certain whether he had touched the right chord or not. He didn't like being separated from an audience by barriers.

Donaldson went along with Broughton to eat at the test pilots' mess and arrange a date to come down again.

Norris, angry and a little frightened, gave vent to his feelings as he walked to the canteen. 'Call himself a socialist, the bastard's as much in the bosses' pockets as old Charlie. A right pair, they are!'

'I don't know, Ken,' said one of his companions. 'There's sense in what he said.'

'You going soft in the head?' asked Norris scornfully. But he recognized the dangers. Someone had woken Huntley up to what was happening. The speech had been a declaration of war.

After his meal he spotted Brunner near the gate and wandered across. 'Haven't seen you for a while,' he said casually. 'How's yer luck?'

'They sacked me.' Brunner looked more haggard than ever, his fair hair long and tousled. 'I went north for a bit.'

'What are you up to, then?'

'Got a job nights at Kinghams. Here.' He thrust out the paper. 'They did a special issue for today.'

Norris took it and almost lost his self-control. Above a picture of the 207 reared the scarlet headline 'FIGHT THE FRAMPTON WARMONGERS'.

He skimmed through the article. It ended by urging the workers in the factory to strike against the bloodstained militarist bosses. So this had been the inspiration for Huntley's speech.

'I helped with that,' said Brunner proudly. 'Gave the inside facts.'

'Did you?' He wanted to kick the silly bastard's face in. 'Well, it won't make you top of the pops today, mate. I'd scarper if I were you.'

He walked off angrily, wishing he could get Brunner out of the way. It was good that he'd had his cards. It would be better still if he got the hell out of Frampton for good and all.

The election of shop stewards in mid-December went smoothly enough for Norris personally. However, there was a procedural change to which he objected as vociferously as he dared. The management announced its willingness to have the elections held in working hours at the factory and the Joint Shop Stewards Committee agreed by a small majority. The idea was an awkward one to oppose, since it was already the practice in many factories. Its snag from the militants' standpoint was that it made voting easier. Whereas many shop-floor workers would fail to attend an evening meeting at Transport House in Frampton, moderates especially being inclined to leave decisions to others, they were all available during working hours. Although Ken Norris himself won a convincing majority by a show of hands, a militant in the tool room suffered the ignominy of a count in which he was defeated, while the word was soon all round the plant that Fred Dixon's win at the Press Shop was overwhelming. The Member of Parliament's speech had evidently struck home.

Although the 207's flying programme resumed in early January, the static tests did not. A dispute arose over bonus payments for the men operating the vast rectangular steel tank inside which a complete 207 airframe was subjected to pressures similar to those of flight. The fuselage had air pumped in and out of it to simulate the changes in atmosphere pressure at altitude, the wings, projecting out through the sides of the tank, were flexed by jacks to reproduce flying stresses. Normally an airframe was tested to destruction in this way and could be put through strains equivalent to many years' flying within weeks. If any part of the structure was going to collapse, it would fail in the tank long before it failed in the air.

The moment Norris heard about the dispute it flashed through his mind that this was too much of a coincidence. He tried chatting casually to the shop steward of the technicians involved, but the men's grouse sounded legitimate. None the less Norris decided the KGB must be behind it and became worried at their failure to tell him. How much did he really matter to Peter? Did they trust him? On the other hand it was comforting that the Russians were as powerful as they claimed.

When he came home from work on 6 January he found an unstamped envelope lying on the hall floor. Inside was a money order for £50 and a greetings card inscribed 'Happy New Year. Love from Aunt Edith.'

There was an eerie quality about the letter, delivered by someone who must know about him, but of whom he knew nothing. Thinking about it, he realized that Peter had never said communications would reach him through the post – except at the *poste restante* address. He had simply assumed they would. Like the dispute over the static tests, it was menacing as well as reassuring. He began looking at his activist acquaintances suspiciously, wondering which of them might also be involved. He still thought of Peter as a friend rather than a paymaster, but there were moments when he felt isolated and insecure.

The events of 8 January were the more unnerving because of these demonstrations of the KGB's strength.

The twenty-six shop stewards at Western's met at

9.30 a.m. in a room provided by the management. The Committee's Chairman presided over the choice of a Convenor. Although he was aware of the intense lobbying which had gone on for weeks beforehand, he opened the proceedings with a breezy cheerfulness which he prayed would mask not only his apprehensions but also the rigidity with which he was observing the rules.

'Well, brothers,' he announced as soon as they were all seated. 'We all know what we're met here to do. No need to remind you that nominations were received in due time for today's Branch meeting as follows. Brother Dixon has been nominated and seconded, brother Norris has been nominated and seconded.' He paused, knowing Ken Norris wasn't going to like this. 'Brother Kingston was nominated and seconded but has withdrawn.' Only the Chairman was aware that Frank Kingston, a moderate rival to Dixon, had been persuaded by Norman Huntley not to split the moderate vote. None of them knew that Rusopov had earlier adopted precisely the same manoeuvre, instructing another militant not to stand. The contest was reduced to a straight fight.

Before he had finished speaking the Chairman felt the tension rise. The word 'withdrawn' precipitated interruptions, Norris demanding 'what the bloody hell's going on', Dixon catching the eye of two or three who ought now to support him, someone else rising angrily to his feet and half shouting, 'Why weren't we told?'

The Chairman held up both hands in a pacifying gesture. 'Order, brothers, order. I would have told you earlier if I'd known myself. Brother Kingston is entitled to withdraw if he so wishes. There is no time requirement for standing down. He is within his rights.'

'Bloody bastard,' muttered Norris under his breath.

The Chairman could not let this go. To call a man a bastard to his face was one of the worst insults possible. Kingston, physically a less robust man than Norris, was already colouring and about to get up. The last thing anyone wanted was a fist fight.

'I must ask you to withdraw that remark, brother Norris,' he demanded firmly, and was rewarded by a murmur of approval from the rest.

'OK, I take it back!' Norris submitted grudgingly. He could see defeat coming.

'Thank you, brother Norris,' he said quickly. 'We can now follow the normal procedure of a show of hands. Those in favour of brother Dixon?' He scanned his small audience as eleven raised their hands. Kingston was abstaining out of embarrassment, then he realized this was an empty gesture, since Norris could not vote for himself and must lose. So he slowly lifted his right arm. The only abstainer now was Norris.

'Twelve for brother Dixon,' the Chairman intoned. 'Hands up for brother Norris.' He looked round as though fearful of making a mistake. 'Brother Norris receives eleven votes. I hereby declare brother Dixon elected.'

The tumult which broke out precluded the Chairman asking if there was any other business. He declared the meeting closed to a hubbub of discussion as the moderates congratulated Dixon and the activists fulminated against the result.

Norris, conscious that his outburst had been a serious error, approached Kingston. 'Sorry,' he said. 'No offence meant. Just the heat of the moment.' He thrust his hand out. 'Shake on it, OK?'

Reluctantly Kingston acquiesced.

That night Norris posted a letter to London, first class. It stated that Aunt Edith was ill and urgently needed to see a specialist.

'Is this aircraft doing all the performance flying?'

'Correct.' Broughton was about to take Donaldson for his second flight. 'Zero Two's on systems tests and Zero Three is basically just an airframe being tested to destruction in the pressure tank – or would be but for a bloody idiotic strike over bonuses.' He glanced up at the gleaming fuselage of the 207 by which they were standing. 'So Zero One's getting all the glory.' He turned back to his wife. 'Well, darling, we must be off.' He kissed her goodbye and led the way up a metal ladder to the forward door of the plane. Donaldson looked back briefly as he stepped inside, steadying himself with one hand on the slightly curving doorway.

'See you for tea, I hope.' He waved to Margaret.

She gazed up from the tarmac, unable to keep the apprehension from her face, and tried to smile back.

The six other members of the crew, white-overalled like Broughton and Donaldson, followed on up. Inside, apart from a dozen rows of passenger seats the whole length of the cabin space was devoted to grey enamel consoles with rows of dials and switches, recording machines and electronic instruments. Cables snaked along the floor. It was a flying laboratory.

'Hardly need to remind you how closely we're monitoring everything,' Broughton remarked. 'Only reason we have the passenger fit is for tomorrow's demonstration. This afternoon,' he went on, 'we'll be having a look at her limiting Mach number. Should be around point nine five.'

Donaldson made no comment. Mach ·95 was 95 per cent of the speed of sound, close to the moment when a subsonic plane could become uncontrollable. The 'sound barrier', they used to call it; and a barrier it was still to anything not designed to fly through it. In normal operations the 207 would never be pushed anywhere near there, but it was essential to study what would happen if it was.

Broughton pulled aside the curtain which closed off the flight deck from the cabin. 'The right-hand seat's all yours.'

Donaldson edged himself into the co-pilot's position. The 207 was as cramped up front as most airliners. He wondered if moisture condensing inside the fuselage skin would drop into his lap as it tended to in the Britannia. Such speculations did not last long. Broughton was wasting no time. Heaving himself into the captain's seat on the left, he began reading through a long printed list of checks attached to a clipboard, calling them out either to the Flight Engineer behind him or to Donaldson, who found himself fumbling slightly. It was only his second flight in the 207.

Broughton started the engines one after the other, checking the temperatures and fuel flow, the first grumbling whine developing into a low roar.

'Call for taxi clearance, please.' The requests were as authoritative as if Donaldson was a normal crew member.

'Clear for runway 23, QNH 1002, QFE 1004, wind three zero zero twelve knots, gusting eighteen.' The controller's voice came back clear, his weather details reflecting a typical February day of ragged grey cloud and occasional rain.

'Zero One,' Donaldson acknowledged and repeated back the figures.

'She's all yours, then,' said Broughton crisply. 'We'll climb out on a heading of three one zero until we're over the sea, then two five zero to take us roughly parallel with the north Devon coast. At thirty thousand I'll take her over again and we'll start finding out about her limits.'

'Understood.' Donaldson released the brakes, eased the throttles forward and as the engine noise rose the huge plane began to move.

Fifteen minutes later he was lining the 207 up at the end of the familiar wide runway, its tarmac seeming to stretch to the horizon. He was given take-off clearance, held the brakes as he built up the engines' thrust, then let go and Zero One began to lumber along, rapidly gathering speed, until Broughton called 'V One' then 'Rotate' and 'V Two' and he eased the control column cleanly back, lifting the huge bulk effortlessly into the air.

On the ground Margaret Broughton watched her husband's plane thunder down the runway, spray cascading up from the wheels. She saw the nose tilt, the plane rise and begin its climb. It always seemed impossible to her, these hundreds of tons of metal clawing their way into the sky. A minute later Zero One was swallowed by the low clouds, vanishing like a lost mirage, only the receding noise telling her it was still there. She gave up straining her eyes for another glimpse of it and walked to her car. The wives are always left behind, she thought, and then told herself not to be stupid. The very last place she would want to be was up there. She hated flying and feared the dangers of her husband's profession.

'OK, Jim. I have her.' Broughton took over control. They were level at 30,000 feet in clear air, the clouds a cotton-wool blanket far below, hiding the waters of the Bristol channel. 'Let's see if the boffins got their figures right.' Slowly he put on more power. 'We'll go gradually up to Mach point nine five.'

Donaldson watched the round dial of the machmeter. In normal cruise the needle showed ·83, or 83 per cent of the speed of sound. Now it crept round to ·86 and Broughton was having to trim the nose down slightly to reduce drag and get the speed higher. There was no other indication of their acceleration, save a little wind roar. The noise of the huge engines streamed out behind, unheard by the pilots. Donaldson remembered the rough passage he had years ago when he first took a subsonic Vampire fighter past this speed in a shallow dive. Then he knew what to expect because other pilots had found out before. Today all Broughton had were the designers' calculations, the computerized output of factors which could never be totally predictable.

'The limiting Mach number recommended to airline operators will be this,' commented Broughton calmly. 'Feels all right.' The needle was at ·87. 'We'll be fitting a chicken clucker.' The warning device installed for airline service sounded like an agitated chicken, but he didn't want his concentration disturbed during test flying.

Donaldson laid a hand on the control column. It was trembling very slightly.

'Stress on the tailplane is rising, sir.' The voice of one of the technicians in the cabin crackled over the intercom.

Donaldson could imagine the men back there trying to keep calm as they monitored gauges showing what forces the airflow was exerting on important parts of the aircraft. What happened near the speed of sound was frighteningly simple. There was a shock wave ahead of the aircraft similar to the bow wave created in water by a motorboat. But the plane caught up with this shock wave and it drastically changed the flow of air over the wings and tail, sometimes altering the effects of the control surfaces, always putting tremendous stress on the construction. A supersonic plane like Concorde, made of special metals and with a nose like a needle, was designed to thrust through the shock wave. Ordinary transport aircraft were not. Therefore Broughton had to discover at exactly what speed the 207 would become dangerously hard to control. This was the true limiting Mach number, though the one recommended for less experienced pilots would be a percentage lower for additional safety.

At ·93 Broughton himself was tense. The aircraft was shaking perceptibly. 'Keep watching,' he said. 'I'm taking her further.' He edged the throttles forward a fraction. The needle of the machmeter wavered on ·94, flicked beyond.

Broughton was sweating. Donaldson felt a sticky clamminess on his palms and wiped them on the legs of his flying suit. No one spoke.

The needle reached ·95. Without warning the whole aircraft bucked and began juddering violently as though running on a rutted road. The control column jumped out of Broughton's hands and before either of them could correct it the nose plunged down. The 207 was out of level flight and diving, straining and shaking. Over the intercom came the technician's voice, distorted by fear.

'Bring her back, for Christ's sake bring her back.'

7

The moment he realized they had lost control Broughton abandoned normal flying and pulled the throttles right back. But the 207 continued juddering insanely, the control column immovably forward, the vertical speed indicator on the stop at 6000 feet per minute descent as the airliner dived on down.

Donaldson felt the shaking right through his body. Yet every action possessed an extraordinary drawn-out clarity, as though watched on a slow-motion replay. He saw Broughton flipping the toggle switches on the side of the control column, actuating the 'flying tail': on the 207 it wasn't only the elevators which moved, the whole horizontal stabilizer could be used to balance the plane's flight. He saw the realization in Broughton's face that this was no longer effective, found himself wondering of the stabilizer had somehow jammed, or if all four separate systems of chain links to the hydraulics had failed together. The hydraulics operated at a pressure of 3000 pounds to the square inch. Their power was such that the column needed artificial restraints to give the pilot 'feel' and prevent him overreacting. Yet so violent were the forces on the tail now that they were overriding the hydraulics. Donaldson thought this through in split seconds, though they felt like minutes. He was about to reach out for the throttles himself when Broughton arched them back in their quadrant, his big hand clasping both levers at once.

Perhaps twenty seconds later the angle of the airliner's dive began to lessen. Donaldson felt responsiveness return to the control column. With the thrust from the two huge engines dying away, the nose came up further, the needle of the machmeter reversing its frightening progress, dropping down to ·94, then ·93. The nose eased up to the horizon. Broughton held it there and the speed fell more rapidly. At ·82 he cautiously restored the power. They were in level cruise again.

'So now we know the limiting Mach number,' Broughton remarked quietly, only the sweat on his face betraying the strain.

'It reached point nine seven.' Donaldson was keeping a grip on himself. It was always worse being an observer. The slow-motion feeling had gone now and he was conscious of the acute danger they had been in. 'A less experienced pilot might have failed to recover.'

'It was an exceptionally sudden nose-down pitch,' Broughton admitted.

'It's a dangerous characteristic.'

'Possibly.' Broughton would commit himself no further. Not until he and the chief designer had analysed all the readings from the stress and airflow gauges back in the calm of an office would he come to conclusions. He gave a deep grunt. He wanted to make notes while the incident was fresh in his mind. 'Take her over, will you?' he said. 'Call Brawdy for a radar heading and get clearance to pass through Amber two five.'

Half an hour later they landed.

'Will you go ahead with the demonstration flight?' Donaldson asked as they walked to the Flight Test Centre.

'Postpone it, I should think. The whole aircraft will have to be gone over.'

Later, as they drove back to the Broughtons' cottage for a late tea, the test pilot asked Donaldson not to say anything to Margaret. 'She'd only worry and there's no reason. The worst of the test programme's finished. Not in terms of time, of course. But we'll soon be concentrating on operating procedures, engine handling, fuel economy and all the other tedium.' He chuckled. 'Making the beast live up to the Sales Manager's claims.'

'What about the technician who panicked? Won't he be telling tales out of school?'

'I hope not.' Broughton was suddenly grim again. 'Can't sack him, of course, but I gave him a piece of my mind. Men who are paid danger money should expect to earn it occasionally.'

'Do you have to go to London tomorrow? It is my birthday.' Marion's resentment had been accumulating all week. By Saturday evening she was ready to disregard Ken Norris's taciturn moodiness and argue. 'Couldn't you go later on?'

'I told you, Carol said if I don't meet her this weekend she'll tell her bastard solicitors to go ahead.'

'Take you to court, you mean?' Marion felt particularly bitter at his deserting her to see his estranged wife. At the same time her upbringing had drummed into her how calamitous divorce could be financially. She didn't want Ken surrendering a third of his pay each week to a woman who could perfectly well support herself.

'Too right!' The way he spoke made it sound the first thing Marion had understood in weeks. 'I have to talk her out of it, don't I?' He looked up from the armchair where he was reading the Frampton *Evening News*. 'Anyway it's not your birthday. Your birthday's Monday.'

'Well, it starts at midnight and we can go out somewhere on Sunday.'

'Like Boxing Day, I suppose!' She'd insisted on a Christmas visit to her parents. Inevitably the occasion had developed into exchanges of excruciating forced politeness, with her mother asking, 'What's work like at the factory, Mr Norris?' and 'Whereabouts do your family live?'

'Not everyone thinks celebrating one's birthday is a stupid

bourgeois convention, you know.' Marion was stung by his sarcasm. 'Most working-class families make a tremendous thing of birthdays.'

'And what do you know about the working class?' He threw the newspaper aside angrily and stood up, all the tangled agonies of childhood raging in his mind. 'Nine tenths of f... all, that's what you know about how things are! OK, I put up with Christmas for your sake. But I'm not going through that f... ing nonsense again.'

His explosion into obscenity shocked her. She sat silent.

'You want to celebrate your birthday!' he shouted. 'Go off and drink champagne with your f... ing mother. But don't tell me that's how the working class lives!'

'How dare you speak of my mother like that!' Trembling, Marion found her voice. 'You don't give way on anything, you don't understand anything. It's just you, you, you.' She was facing him, her cheeks pale.

'I tell you, Mary. I was lucky to get a cold pork pie most Christmases.' He was rapidly calming down, regretting insulting her. 'Why do you think I joined the Labour Party?' He was careful to add the word 'Labour'. She knew nothing of his Communist links.

She looked at him, remembering those jargon phrases of his about 'redistribution of wealth, social justice, the class struggle'. She had always said you couldn't have a heart and not be a socialist when you were young. But Ken was no idealist now. She realized that his lean good looks seemed to have hardened even since she had known him. He didn't care about other people. Only himself.

'You may have joined the Party for good reasons,' she said slowly, unaware of the chord the phrase struck in him. 'But all you really want is power. That's why you were so upset at not being elected Convenor, isn't it?'

'Don't talk bloody nonsense, Mary.'

She sat down on an upright chair and blew her nose. She had made a decision. 'You go to London,' she said. 'Sort things out with Carol. I'll go to my parents' for the day.'

'Shall I make some tea?' He was suddenly worried. He'd never known her like this before.

'That would be nice.' There was no need to be difficult now she had made up her mind. But there was one thing she wouldn't do.

Later on she said, 'I've a terrible headache, Ken. Would you mind if I go to bed now?' She made a show of taking some aspirins and feigned sleep when he joined her.

Colonel Grigoriev had gone to Moscow for 'home leave' early in January and, as predicted, had not returned.

A KGB Major was given temporary charge of the Residency. However, the Major could not be transferred from his cover post in the Trade Mission without alerting the British to his function. In consequence Rusopov gained a small measure of autonomy. Three weeks later a routine memorandum came from the Centre announcing that the Colonel would assume responsibility for Department Three on 1 April.

The promotion was logical, London being the most important Residency under the Department's aegis, and also demonstrated one of the strengths of KGB policy. This was to keep the same officers either controlling or supervising agents for many years at a time. By contrast their Western counterparts normally handed over agents when they were posted away from a station. Grigoriev would now maintain his watch on the operations he had initiated, with consequent advantages in continuity and feel for the way they were developing.

Yuri's letter was followed a month later by another message from Frampton which made the Russian wish Grigoriev was not on leave. Because it demanded consultation with a superior he went across to the Trade Mission straight away.

The Major could scarcely have been less like the Colonel. He was a rolypoly, fat-faced man with heavy jowls and pig eyes, an embryo Khrushchev, whose podgy fingers handled the two brief texts Rusopov brought as if they were banknotes and he could deduce their quality by feeling them. He had a reputation for smelling out treachery and for methods devious even by KGB standards. Rusopov felt none of the same confident rapport with him which had illuminated the relationship with Grigoriev. In consequence he decided to face the worst implication of the two messages first. Better to raise it himself than have the Major reason it out.

'It is disturbing that Yuri did not inform us of the near-incident with the aircraft.' Rusopov chose his words carefully. 'If Edward could inform us, why not Yuri? I am forced to suspect that the sabotage may have failed.' He paused. 'Edward is not conscious of the plan.'

'To what would you attribute failure?' The Major did not add 'on your part' but he meant it.

'With respect, Comrade Major, Yuri was well briefed. The weak link was always the Trotskyite we named Tourist. He may have exaggerated what he actually did out of bravado.'

'Could the technical planning be at fault?' Again the Major was trying to pin the blame on Rusopov.

'No. Of that I am certain. However, without details of the flight test programme it is impossible to forecast precisely when the plane's bulkhead could crack.'

'Is it possible the measuring gauges. . . ?' The Major hesitated fractionally. He was not a scientist yet did not want to sound ignorant. 'The equipment on board revealed the fault in time to avert disaster?'

'That is conceivable.'

'Then why is Yuri, an agent in the net, not reporting what has happened?' The Major spoke softly, his speech sibilant, the flesh creasing heavily around his eyes. 'Where is his sense of obligation to us, where is his loyalty? These are questions you must ask yourself, Comrade Captain.These are questions the Centre will ask.' His face was as expressionless as his words were menacing, every sentence distancing him further from problems he might have inherited.

'Comrade Colonel Grigoriev feared Yuri might panic.' Rusopov thanked his stars that the Colonel was taking over the Department and was the Major's immediate superior. 'In my view his estimate was correct.' He pointed to Yuri's letter. 'Words cut from a newspaper! Childish. I imagine Yuri was upset over not being elected Convenor at his factory. The Comrade Colonel anticipated this might follow from the British counterintelligence plot against us.'

'Who is either of us to dispute the Comrade Colonel's analysis?' The Major laid his podgy hands flat on the table, as if considering every aspect of the affair, while he reflected how much better it would be to lay any blame at his senior's door rather than his junior's. 'I agree,' he went on portentously. 'On balance, I agree. Furthermore, since Yuri must be presumed to know your identity, any indiscretion on his part could be dangerous. We must speak soothingly to him, what those Americans call using soft soap.' His faint smile was lopsided, as though the thick lips had some muscular deficiency denying them a pleasant expression. 'We must avoid adopting a negative attitude, Comrade Captain. We must not assume the agent is going bad. Rather we make a gesture: a reassurance. A little money perhaps.'

'He has already asked for more money.'

'A little, I said. Where would a man in his position obtain large sums? Never give an agent the means to betray himself. Nor can you yourself meet him, Vladimir Sergeyevich.'

So you're on to patronymics now, are you, thought Rusopov. Worried because I have the Colonel's confidence? Well, it'll do no harm to reinforce that impression. 'The Comrade Colonel laid down a procedure for the next contact,' he said. 'He felt it essential there should be no hitch at the next rendezvous. The only person who can recognize Yuri without fail is our coopted collaborator Kirichenko.'

'The Aeroflot office manager? Hardly an ideal choice.' The Major pursed his lips. In KGB parlance, a 'collaborator' was a Soviet official who was not a KGB officer, a cadre worker, but had been coopted for espionage tasks. Usually collaborators' normal jobs were quasi-diplomatic, like information officers. Employees of the Soviet airline were useful for their freedom to travel. Thus Kirichenko could visit Frampton in an emergency. And he understood aircraft. The disadvantage was his relative lack of training.

'We have used him for countersurveillance of Yuri', explained Rusopov.

'Well, if the Comrade Colonel nominated him . . .' The Major let the sentence die away, its implication clear. 'Make him understand the importance of Yuri keeping calm and fulfilling his obligations to us, as the Soviet Union always will to him. Mention plans for Yuri's future.' The Major's tone hardened. 'And find out why he did not report the incident. That is what I really want to know.'

March brought a false spring of blue skies and temperate wind. From his seat in the train Ken Norris watched the countryside unroll past the intercity train with little appreciation. As instructed he had destroyed Peter's letter sent to the *poste restante* in Bristol. It wasn't difficult to remember. 'Appointment confirmed as arranged. Do not worry. What has happened is according to new plans.' He wished he was meeting Peter after, not before, he knew the extent of Carol's demands. For the first time, the excuse he had given Marion for visiting London was half true. He was meeting his estranged wife in the afternoon and was intensely worried that she might ask for half his savings, as a solicitor had warned him was possible. The Sunday delays in the underground did not improve his mood, nor did the discovery that Kew Bridge Station, which Peter had mentioned, was not on the underground system. He ended up going to Kew Gardens and walking back across the Thames. Strand on the Green was difficult to find, hidden away along the river. It was a wide paved pathway, lined with elegant old red brick houses and stuccoed cottages, relics of a Queen Anne village once far from the city. A few small boats were moored to the embankment and the weak sun made it a picture-postcard scene.

The beauty was lost on Norris. He walked along, becoming more and more tense as he failed to spot Peter. There were courting couples wandering hand in hand; as he passed a public house he thought a burly man leaning against a wall eyed him suspiciously and he increased his pace, angrily wondering why the hell Peter had chosen to meet here.

Oleg Andrevich Kirichenko, positioned near the City Barge Inn, was ostensibly enjoying the sunshine, his overcoat unbuttoned, watching both for Yuri and for the safety signal from a colleague. On the Major's orders elaborate precautions had been adopted. Six other KGB cadre workers were involved, two of them women. Strand on the Green was staked out, with men covering both its ends and the three narrow alleyways leading back to Thames Street behind the gardens of the houses. The river itself winds through London in a series of loops and one of Strand on the Green's advantages was its crescent shape. From his perch Kirichenko had no problem observing the Kew Bridge end of the pathway. He would see Yuri coming towards him and he would equally see the signal from the woman cadre worker who would have tailed the shop steward from the moment he passed the barrier at Paddington Station. The meeting would be under continual observation as would the rest of Yuri's day in the capital. He himself had spent three hours driving from Kensington to Chiswick in the Chrysler motorcar, a direct distance of barely four and a half miles.

The motorcar, as the administrative officer back at the Centre in Moscow pedantically referred to it, belonged to the KGB Residency, though it bore no CD plates and was registered in the name of a Briton. As an Aeroflot representative, Kirichenko already had an official car. The airline was the Soviet flag carrier. Naturally its managers were provided with Russian cars. Kirichenko's was a Lada, a version of a Fiat assembled at the vast Togliattigrad factory. However, he could hardly go for a rendezvous with an agent in the Lada. Therefore the Major decreed that he should use the unobtrusive blue Chrysler for the day and faithfully reported this minor administrative matter to the Centre. Had the Major known the consequences which would follow, he would have decided not to mention it. Had he merely been endowed with greater imagination, he might have guessed that allowing Kirichenko the use of a second official car would provoke comment from someone. As it was, with Rusopov a potential enemy, he did not intend to be caught out through failing to obtain official sanction for every detail of the way Yuri's case was handled.

Kirichenko himself had suffered from other worries, chiefly that he might be under British surveillance. But by the time he had completed his circuitous route, which began with taking a bus to where he picked up the motorcar and concluded by parking it at Chiswick station and going one stop on the train to Kew Bridge, he was satisfied that he was clean. Nor did he think a tail could go unobserved by the team as he walked the last few hundred yards.

Now, at last, he saw Yuri approaching and deliberately let him go past, knowing he would turn round at the end of the Strand and come back. Half a minute later the safety signal was given. A stout, middle-aged woman, her hair protected by a bright red headscarf, waddled along the pathway. She stopped a few yards off, foraged in a shopping bag for a newspaper, laboriously spread it on the stone edge of the embankment and lowered her considerable bulk to sit and watch the river. Kirichenko relaxed. All was well. He could introduce himself. When Yuri returned he moved forward, a cigarette pack in his hand, and asked for a light.

When the stocky man confronted him, Norris almost turned and ran. Already nervous at Peter's non-appearance, he imagined he was being arrested. Then, even as he flinched back, he realized this could not be a policeman. The heavy accent and the man's bullet head, hair close-cropped beneath the black homburg hat, told him this was a foreigner. He felt in his pocket for a box of matches, and fumbled to extract one. As he struck it, a gust of wind blew out the flame.

'How is Aunt Edith?' The man was saying. 'Peter is unfortunately ill. My name is Steven.'

Norris looked at him apprehensively. 'Ill?' he asked. 'What d'you mean?'

'Please, have you a light?' Kirichenko waved his cigarette. 'If you can be so kind.'

Sensing the man's agitation, Norris decided this could not be a trap and tried another match. He held it in his cupped hand. Kirichenko leaned towards him, lit the cigarette successfully. 'Let us go from here,' he murmured.

Norris followed, his heart still thumping. They went back towards Kew Bridge. A dumpy woman sitting on an outspread newspaper glanced up at them as they passed and Norris thought his companion might have known her because he nodded his head fractionally in her direction.

'We will go to the Gardens,' said Kirichenko quietly. 'There we cannot be overheard.' He remained silent as they crossed the bridge and approached the ornamental entrance gates on Kew Green. Once inside, he guided Yuri along the avenue known as the Broad Walk. 'You are in trouble?' he suggested at last. 'You have problem? Tell me, please.' The word 'problem' featured heavily in his Aeroflot work.

'Don't you know?' The stroll had enabled Norris to regain his confidence. 'I didn't bloody get elected. That's the trouble.'

'But you received our message?' Kirichenko lacked Rusopov's academic education and his English tended to consist of phrases useful at the Aeroflot office, dealing with schedules and ticket sales. 'There are new plans for you.'

'Well, you might have bloody told me!' Norris stopped and Kirichenko had to urge him to keep moving. 'Listen,' he went on, undeterred. 'I've done my bit, OK? What about your side of the bargain? Peter promised I'd be Convenor.'

'Not all at once, my friend.' Kirichenko made calming gestures as he walked. He might have been escorting a delayed VIP passenger to a waiting room. 'We have not forgotten you. What I have to explain is this. It has been decided to be Convenor is not so important. You should become Branch Secretary. This is a more sure route to power in your union.' He put all the conviction he could into the assertion. 'It is correct, no?'

'Maybe.' Norris was uncertain. 'But you might have warned me.'

'And then you are half hearted in that election.' The Russian glanced sideways at the shop steward, beneficent in his explanation of the KGB's wiliness. 'We are not so stupid, eh?'

'You mean you led me up the garden, deliberately?'

'Excuse me?' Kirichenko knew perfectly well what was meant, but the moment was coming for him to be indignant himself.

'For Christ's sake, you might have bloody told me!' Norris had long perfected his displays of righteous indignation, and he had been working up to this one for days. To his surprise, the Russian came back at him in a way no factory manager would have dared.

'You might also have reported to us. Why do you not tell *us* of the airliner's problems?' Kirichenko's voice toughened. He looked around to make sure no one was in earshot. 'You did not report to us the near-disaster.'

'What are you talking about? What disaster?'

'Two weeks ago. A crash was avoided by seconds. It is possible our whole plan has failed. Why do you not inform us?'

For once Norris was lost for words. He gazed at the bare trees half hiding the little lake, then stopped and turned to face the Russian. In the distance the high glass roof of the Palm House glittered in the sun, catching his eye.

'Listen.' He was guessing. 'I did hear a buzz about a technician panicking.' He shrugged his shoulders. 'Didn't seem important. Why should it?'

'Everything is important. Why do you not inform us?'

'I had other things to think about, didn't I?' An edge of acid defiance came into Norris's voice. 'Like losing an election, for instance. Who told you about it anyway?'

'We have our sources.'

A runner in a blue track suit appeared, jogging down the path towards them.

'Let us go on,' said Kirichenko, hurriedly striking out across the grass towards the lake. He stayed silent until the man passed, checking over the Major's instructions in his mind. At this stage it was more important to keep Yuri sweet than to obtain explanations. 'Very well,' he said at length. 'I accept this. But please. We wish to know precisely what accident might have happened. We must know if the problem was in the bulkhead.'

'OK.' Norris agreed reluctantly. He didn't want to risk poking his nose in places where he didn't belong. 'I will if I can. But don't forget, Comrade, the management's bloody secretive about some things. Right?'

'I am confident you will succeed.' Kirichenko became benign again. 'We have important plans for you, my friend. Important for the future.'

'Talking of which, I have a problem too.' Norris took the cue instantly, he'd wondered how to get onto the subject. 'Money. My ex-wife wants money. Peter always said he could help.'

'He told me.' Kirichenko had come prepared, though the bluntness of the demand shook him. 'Shall we sit?' He indicated a bench a few yards away. He had been explicitly ordered to make any handover invisible to an onlooker. 'Yes,' he said, when they had moved across and sat down. 'Peter is of course anxious to help. He was sorry not to come. We hope his illness will not last long.' As he was speaking he slid the plain brown envelope out of his overcoat pocket. 'This is from him.' He slipped it into Yuri's hand. 'No! Do not look, conceal it.'

'Thanks.' Norris stuffed the envelope into his leather jacket as unobtrusively as he could. 'Don't know how much there is, do you?' He liked to see money on the table, spread out so you could count it. He hadn't forgotten being conned once by a trickster who had wrapped a couple of genuine notes round a wad of paper.

'Peter did not tell me. My instructions are to give you. Also,' his glance was averted from Yuri as he scanned the park, 'we are to make proper arrangement for passing things. You read the *Sunday Mirror* newspaper, that is correct?'

'Too right.' He wondered how Steven knew.

'Next time you bring with you. Myself too. Then is easy. You take my paper, I take yours. Inside is message, money, whatever we want.' He turned towards Yuri, taking a crumpled copy of the *Sunday Mirror* from inside his overcoat. 'Be careful to fold like this one. Exactly, you understand. It is important. Both copies must look the same. Now I leave it on seat and you pick up.' He leaned close to Yuri. 'Remember, please report to us anything new from your factory.' He straightened himself and stood up. 'Now we should go, I think. It will be better we leave separately.' As Norris rose, he reverted to his Aeroflot manner, shaking hands formally. 'It has been a pleasure. I look forward to see you again.' He walked briskly away to the Victoria Gate.

Norris, on unfamiliar ground, retraced the way they had come and went round two sides of a triangle to reach the underground station. On the way he tore open the envelope. It contained ten old five-pound notes. He swore, angry and disappointed at the small amount. The KGB man who had been in the City Barge car park earlier had no difficulty tailing him the whole way to Islington.

Approaching the house of his ex-wife's parents, Norris felt an unexpected, almost unwelcome, sense of returning to a familiar and safe background. Although he was abusive about her to Marion, on principle virtually, he wouldn't be surprised if Carol's threatened legal action might not be her way of asking for a reconciliation. She'd hated abandoning hopes and projects. Her family had lived many years in this small, neatly kept Victorian terrace house. The neighbourhood had 'gone up', as people said, with your professional couples moving in. But the Greenfields weren't worried by that. They joked about the rising value of their property, which they had no thought of leaving, and went on with the business of living. Norris had always been torn between admiring and resenting the stability of their existence.

Nervously he rang the bell by the brown-painted front door, hearing the tones chime inside. After a pause Carol appeared, wearing a print dress and a chunky hand-knitted cardigan, her dark hair as carefully brushed as ever. She hasn't changed, he thought, she always was a good-looker.

'You're a bit late,' she said. 'Mum and Dad'll be back before we know where we are. They wanted to be out of the way when you came.' She noticed his hesitation. 'Well, come on in then. I'm not going to bite you.' She ushered him in, neatly avoiding the kiss he tried to give her, then went to make some tea.

He sat waiting in the front room, amazed at how unchanged everything was: the china ducks still flying along the wall, the picture of sea and cliffs by moonlight hanging over the tiled mantelpiece, the moquette upholstered three-piece suite as pristine as ever. Everything was the same except Carol. She was clearly going to do the talking.

'Now,' she said, returning with the cups. 'I thought maybe we could settle things ourselves without wasting a lot of money on solicitors.'

'I don't want to be unreasonable, love.'

'I'm glad to hear it.' She knew from hard experience that when Ken said that he was normally about to be not just unreasonable but totally impossible. 'I've got a good job with this firm in the City. I can support myself. It would be different if we'd had the baby.'

'Everything would be different!' His bitterness was unconcealed.

She flushed. 'You never forgave me for the miscarriage, did you?' He'd caught her on the rawest nerve. She bit her lip, determined to keep calm.

'Sorry, love. I didn't mean that.'

'Well, even if I haven't got a child, I can't go on living here for ever.' She was getting to the point now. 'I have to find a place of my own.' She was trying to keep her voice steady.

'We were married seven years, Ken. We furnished the flat together. If you can afford to have another woman there, you can afford to give me the half of our property I'm entitled to.' She stopped, biting her lip again, trembling in spite of her resolution.

'Listen, love, all I've got is my savings.' He wanted to tell her about Peter and his disappointment. She would understand that. But he checked the impulse. 'Here,' he said, pulling out the envelope. 'It isn't much, but it's a start.' He got up and gave it to her. 'Sort of on account, if you like.'

She counted the notes, and looked at him incredulously. 'Fifty pounds! Are you trying to be funny, Ken?' It was half her own weekly earnings as a secretary. 'What about the colour telly, what about the fridge and the furniture? All the things we bought on the never-never and took with us to Frampton. I paid as much of the instalments as you did. What about our joint savings account? There was over six hundred pounds in that when I left.'

'There isn't now, love.' He regretted saying it immediately, just as he'd regretted the remark he made to Mary.

'You mean you've spent it on her, I suppose.' She stood up, furious. 'Our money! It's not even yours to spend, rightly.' She threw the money at him. 'You can take your wretched fifty quid and think again, Ken Norris.' She could hardly believe he could be so mean. 'And you'd better come up with something sensible, or I'll be seeing you in court.' As he scrabbled to pick up the banknotes, she opened the lounge door, 'Now, get out of here before Mum and Dad come back!' As he left the house she lost the last of her self-control. 'They told me it was a waste of time talking to you and they were right! You haven't changed, not one tiny little bit. You're still the most self-centred, egotistical man I ever met.'

When he had gone, she collapsed in tears on the sofa. She'd been prepared to make things up, to say now we can be friends; she couldn't believe anyone could be so impossible.

Norris trudged slowly back to the Angel underground station and was shadowed until he passed through the barrier to the Frampton train at Paddington. Even three beers in the buffet car failed to cheer him up. He had been reminded today of how much Carol had meant to him. She was a decent, straight, uncomplicated girl, who didn't swear, kept the house clean and had stuck by him whenever things went wrong. At least until the row that had made her leave. Too late, he told himself he should have made it up, begged her to come back. Instead, like a bloody idiot, he'd got himself hooked up with a mixed-up bourgeois bitch who had to be driven to wash his shirts and whom his mates laughed at behind his back. He reached Frampton shortly after eight in the evening, irretrievably depressed.

He knew something was wrong about the flat the moment he entered the door. He shouted and there was no answer, went into the living room, then the bedroom. Mary's make-up bottles and jars had gone from the dressing table. Her slippers were not kicked off on the floor. The bed was properly made for once. Then he saw the letter, lying on that white counterpane she'd insisted on having. He picked it up and tore it open.

'I've gone back to my parents. Please don't write or ring. It's over and I don't want to see you again. Ever. Mary.'

8

It was Question Time in the House of Commons. This Monday less than a third of the honourable Members were present for the useful ritual which took place in the afternoons between 2.30 and 3.30 p.m. It was one of the few parts of parliamentary proceedings which were broadcast: not that it appeared anything but mystifying to most listeners. For a start they had to imagine the scene. Although physically rebuilt after bombing in the Second World War, the layout of the Chamber was as formalized as it had been for many generations. Rows of green leather upholstered benches rose on either side in gentle tiers.The front benches were the preserve of the Government Ministers on one side, of Her Majesty's Opposition on the other. Between them ranged a long polished table, bearing the Speaker's mace, a weighty golden symbol of his authority. The Speaker himself presided from an ornate, throne-like chair above the table. Whereas the Members lounged or even sprawled on their benches, he sat upright, a sombre figure in black court dress, his shoes silver buckled and on his head a white-powdered, full-bottomed wig.

Norman Huntley, placed two rows back from the Opposition leaders, kept his eye on the Speaker, who must soon call out his name. He had a question down on the order paper and intended to ask a further one, or supplementary, as well; one which he hoped would be reported both nationally and locally. Parliamentary questions were often loaded. Characteristically, Huntley's looked innocent enough in print – a straightforward reminder that he was concerned for his constituents' interests.

'To ask the Secretary of State for Trade and Industry about progress in the construction of the Western Aircraft 207 airliner and when it will come into service.'

The Secretary of State had quietly told him that the answer would be satisfactory. When their interests coincided Government and Opposition collaborated more than they let the public realize. Huntley reckoned the Minister would also play along with his more provocative supplementary question.

The fourth question was dealt with. The Speaker glanced at his copy of the order paper, and called out, 'Mr Norman Huntley.'

Huntley stood up. 'Question number five,' he said firmly and sat down again.

The Secretary of State now heaved himself up from the Government front bench, a single sheet of paper in his hand. This was the answer prepared by his staff and given great priority within the department. Huntley's printed question, stuck to a piece of backing paper and marked 'SOS to reply' had circulated with a red 'immediate' label pinned to its top. Civil servants lived in dread of parliamentary questions.

'It is impossible to give a firm date for the entry of the 207 airliner into service.' The Minister paused, briefly adjusting his thick-rimmed spectacles. 'However, the testing of the two pre-production aircraft is proceeding satisfactorily, positions have been reserved for ten production models by Atlantic Airlines and negotiations are at an advanced stage with several other international carriers.'

There was very little stir as the Secretary of State resumed his seat. Anyone who read the aviation press knew as much as he had revealed, including, of course, Norman Huntley, who now quickly stood up to ask the question which mattered. It had to be phrased as a question, but in practice it was a statement.

'Is the Secretary of State aware that the overwhelming majority of people in Frampton fully endorse the 207 project and welcome the support which the Government is giving to it?' He cleared his throat, anxious to make the crucial sentences fully audible. 'Will he pay no heed to the opposition which has been expressed to the project, opposition which has little if any support in my constituency? Will he remember that seven thousand jobs in the Frampton area depend on this airliner and give an assurance that the plane will come into operation with the minimum possible delay?'

Again the Secretary of State rose. This time he could have no prepared reply, but he was ready to reveal more.

'Yes, sir. I can give that assurance. Furthermore, I can reveal that a demonstration flight will shortly be made to show off this magnificent machine to airline and press representatives from all over the world.'

A murmur of interest rose from both sides. Up in the press gallery the reporters scribbled shorthand notes. But the sequence was not finished. A well-known left-winger immediately got to his feet, the impromptu phrasing of his supplementary less polished than Huntley's.

'Is it not a fact,' he threw out, giving his antagonism the merest shred of cover as a question, 'that this plane, which is ostensibly a civil aircraft, is destined to be part and parcel of the NATO war machine, is designed for troop-carrying purposes and is being funded secretly out of the defence budget?'

Angry at such propaganda, the Secretary of State shot to his feet again amid a chorus of jeers from government supporters.

'No, sir!' he snapped. 'Such assertions are totally untrue.'

A counter-chorus of hisses and cries came from other left-wingers. But it died down before the Speaker felt he should intervene and the House passed on to question six.

Afterwards, in the Members' lobby, several fellow moderates offered Huntley congratulations. However, the man he really wanted to see was Gordon Tait, one of those privileged reporters known as 'lobby correspondents' who could mix uninvited with MPs in this part of the Palace of Westminster. They varied greatly in power and prestige. Some, whose editors allowed them free rein for sarcasm and innuendo, could do much to destroy a rising MP's career. Tait was not that kind. The articles he wrote for the West Country newspaper group which included the *Frampton Evening Post* were straightforward, enabling voters to appreciate what their elected representatives were doing for them at Westminster. Or were not.

To Huntley's relief, Tait approached him, asking for a moment's chat. Although there were no licensing hours in the Royal Palace of Westminster, it seemed uncomfortably early to go to Annie's bar for a drink, so the MP suggested tea and a few minutes later they were ensconsced in a corner of the tearoom.

'One thing I don't follow, Norman,' said Tait eventually, munching on a buttered scone. 'Why should the militants attack the 207? Doesn't make sense to me.' He reached out to spoon more jam on to his plate. The House of Commons catering always lost money. He had no compunction about adding to the deficit. 'Yet you evidently feel strongly on the subject.'

Huntley sipped his tea. Could he risk telling what he believed was the truth, trusting Tait not to quote him verbatim? He decided he could.

'Off the record,' he observed cautiously, 'I have reason to think there is a militant plan to gain control of the workforce in the factory.' It sounded faintly absurd and he tried to strengthen the assertion. 'There is certainly a take-over bid within the Joint Shop Stewards Committee.'

'As well as in your constituency?' Tait asked laconically.

Huntley flushed at so matter-of-fact a reference to the plotting against him. 'Neither is home grown,' he insisted. 'You know that, Gordon. The militants are being moved in from London and the Midlands.'

'Maybe,' Tait conceded, reflecting for a moment. 'You know, Norman, we tend to think of Frampton in isolation, as though it was still the independent West Country city it used to be. But it isn't. The aircraft industry's too international, too widely based. How much of the 207 will be manufactured at Western's? Not the engines, not the undercarriage, not the electronics, not the instruments, not the radios, not the wiring, not even the seats. Yes, the airframe's made there and it's assembled in the big hangar. But workers all over Britain will have contributed to it. You made enemies outside Frampton when you opposed state ownership of Western Aircraft. Isn't there a more positive angle to this somewhere?'

'Only the demonstration flight.' Huntley leaned across the table, speaking quietly but earnestly. 'Surely we can agree on one thing. Frampton has a lot to offer. We want the world to see the 207. We want to be proud of it. Success is the best answer to the wreckers.'

Tait nodded. 'Can I quote you?'

'You can indeed.' Huntley relaxed. 'In fact I hope you will.' But he knew the story was weak. There'd be a small headline in the *Evening Post*; only a small one. And precious little mention of the militants. Yet he knew in his bones there was some kind of plot afoot, just as Vic Parry sensed it. This continual sniping at the 207 project didn't happen by accident. Someone must be orchestrating it. He felt as if he were treading the margins of a bog with the earth quivering beneath his feet, knowing there was firm ground somewhere but not how to find it.

'Can we confirm Thursday for the flight?' Wormley looked up from his wide mahogany desk at the chief test pilot, simultaneously reaching out and pressing the stud on a silver-mounted stopwatch. The Chief Executive limited the time of all interviews with his staff.

'I'm happy with Zero One, sir.' Broughton stood self-assured. 'All she needs is a final polishing.'

'And you can seat thirty?'

'Thirty-five. Unless we remove some of the test equipment.'

Wormley considered this. 'No. I don't want people thinking we're slowing up the programme for public relations purposes.'

They were doing precisely that, of course. Zero One would have been flying tomorrow and Thursday, if she were not being kept in perfect order for the demonstration. 'How long a trip will you give them?'

'An hour or so, sir. Down towards Land's End to demonstrate the cruise. Fly a holding pattern perhaps. Then back again. We can make it longer if you want them served drinks.'

Again Wormley pondered briefly. He knew there was no galley fitted yet. 'Can you serve coffee?'

'I think we could manage that, sir.'

'Right. Coffee, champagne or orange juice.' He glanced at the second hand of the watch, sweeping round in tiny jerks. 'Take-off eleven thirty. I won't be coming, but the Sales Director will. If there are any problems, any problems at all, come straight to me.'

'I will, sir.' Broughton prepared to retreat.

'There's a lot at stake on this flight. We now have options taken on fourteen production positions. I'm looking for those to be confirmed. You'll have the Vice-President of Atlantic Airlines on board, not to mention British Airways, that Air Commodore from Defence Procurement and the press. I want you to make damn certain they appreciate what you're showing them.'

'I'll rehearse my best party piece.' Broughton grinned. He was not overawed by Wormley's pretensions, least of all by the stopwatch.

'I'm relying on you, Bill. And there's one other thing.' A shade of unease passed over the Chief Executive's face. 'A man from the *Evening Post* is nosing around. Evidently thinks he's got wind of something, but the PR chaps can't get out of him what it is. He may have heard about that limiting Mach number difficulty you had. I don't want any of the Flight Test Department staff talking to him, unless it's a formal interview with someone from the Press Office there. We need publicity, but not for troubles.'

'I'll tell them to keep their mouths shut, sir.' Broughton required no prompting. He didn't like reporters at the best of times.

As he left the room Wormley noted with satisfaction that the interview had lasted only three minutes and twenty seconds. In a moment of vanity he had calculated the value of his time including his car and chauffeur. It ran out at £45 an hour. None the less he spent the next fifteen minutes debating whether to invite representatives of the shop floor on the flight. Then he remembered Huntley's speech and decided he should. It would be a token presence, but one the workforce ought to appreciate.

The flat seemed lifeless without Mary, as though the clutter and untidiness Norris had railed against possessed a vitality of its own when she was there. He missed her calling, 'Is that you, Ken?' when he came in, missed shouting back, 'Who the hell do you think it is, the milkman?' The queen of the daft question, Mary was. Not like Carol. The thought left him as breathless as a punch in the belly. Carol was going to want half of everything here, his savings, the telly, the bloody cups and saucers probably. Carol wasn't stupid. She'd handed back that fifty quid fast enough.

He felt crushingly alone, and not only because he was womanless. The Russians might have reason to mistrust him. He had probed as far as he dared in the factory and learned that there had indeed been some kind of high-altitude drama in the 207. People said the pilot only just saved the plane. The management had clamped down on all details. Taking a further risk, he had searched for Brunner, ready to question him. But Brunner had vanished. Left Frampton, he was told, gone north. So he remained depressingly uncertain of whether the bastard Trot had cheated him, invented the sabotage as part of some self-fulfilling dream, or had simply fouled it up, not turned the oven off long enough. Peter could be right that the whole plan had failed, in which case there would be no further help for his own ambitions, and no more cash.

One evening, unable to assuage his need to talk to someone, to confide even obliquely, Norris made a rash decision. He tried to telephone Mary, all his worries coalescing into a single, driving urge to get her back. He feared it was a mistake as the number began to ring. Having to use a callbox made him embarrassed and nervous. The booth stank. A drunk had evidently been sick in it. When the mechanism pinged, demanding money, he pushed in two coins for fear of being cut off. Over the line came her mother's voice, patronizing and nasal. Marion did not wish to speak to him. Would he kindly leave her alone. Click. He slammed the receiver down, his pride savaged, and stumbled home, cursing the bourgeois bitch.

Back in the flat he forced himself to start frying the hamburgers he had bought for supper, then noticed some cartons of spices Mary had bought, lined up like a memory on the kitchen shelf. He used to tease her about them. Now he lunged out, crushing them in his fists and stuffing them into the waste bin. If she'd skipped, then her bloody middle-class pretensions could go with her. The physical action gave him a kind of relief.

The next day brought different preoccupations, though scarcely more welcome. The Joint Shop Stewards Committee was invited by management to send two representatives on the demonstration flight. A meeting was hastily arranged by Fred Dixon, the Convenor.

'Well, brothers,' he announced in his slow, ponderous voice. 'This is a bit of a last-minute offer of management. Still, I feel we should accept. Is there anyone in particular wants to go?' He looked at Norris. 'How about you, Ken?'

Norris shook his head instinctively, thoughts racing

through his head. Did Fred guess the plane might crash? No! How could he? Was he leg-pulling, then? Or what was he getting at? Whatever it was, Norris knew he had to kill the idea. No way would he be on the flight.

'You're the natural choice, Fred,' he said, struggling to keep his voice steady.

'And as runner-up, if you'll take no offence at the expression, I thought maybe you'd come too.' In fact there had been no guile in Dixon's suggestion. He was simply attempting to be fair. However, he sensed apprehension in Norris's reply and, since he basically disliked the man, he reacted to it. 'Not frightened of flying, are you Ken?'

Norris stood up, his lean features angrily set. 'Frightened?' he demanded aggressively. He knew he had to make a scene. 'Me frightened? You must be joking! You've got me wrong there, Fred. No, I don't like this so-called offer by management.' He stuck his thumbs through the braces of his blue overalls and swung his gaze round the others. 'What exactly are management asking us for?' He paused, thinking on his feet, thinking fast. There could be political capital to be made out of refusing to go. 'Approval, that's what they're after. The hell they want the shop floor to feel part of the whole bloody project! They want us up there cavorting with the VIPs, swilling back the champagne, for just one reason. To make it look like we're in their pockets. For my money, brothers, we should only go along with them for a price.'

'I don't agree with that, Ken,' said Dixon. 'I reckon this is a gesture we ought to take at face value. Any road, what price did you have in mind?'

'What are you getting at, Ken?' asked someone else.

'No military orders accepted without the shop floor's consent. We ought to have a say in who buys the planes we build.'

A couple of the other more militant members agreed. An argument started.

'We can demand that any time,' pointed out a moderate. 'Not that it makes any sense. We need all the work we can get.' He nodded at the Convenor. 'I agree with Fred. I reckon most of the lads will be turning out to watch.'

'Not bloody surprising when management's paying them to,' said Norris cuttingly. 'I say we shouldn't be represented.'

He was outvoted, but achieved his object. The Convenor and another moderate from the AEWU were nominated to represent the committee. As he walked back to Production Centre Three, Norris reflected wryly that if the aircraft did fall out of the sky it would avenge his election defeat very nicely. Bye-bye Fred Dixon. Yet the man he really wanted out of the way was Charlie Brook. Even though the councillor was not on the Joint Shop Stewards Committee, he was more respected than anyone else in the factory.

That evening Norris spent more than two hours with Bruce Gardner, the Secretary of Frampton North Labour Party, discussing ways to ease Brook out of the Chairmanship.

On Wednesday Jim Donaldson was due to lunch with Colonel Daly of Atlantic Airlines. He knew Daly was returning to New York in the evening and would miss the demonstration flight; the airline's Vice-President, William J. Conrad Jr, was already in London. It was inevitable that Daly would be briefing Conrad before he left and highly probable that the lunch invitation was a politely cloaked way of obtaining more information. Donaldson was by inclination and by training extremely circumspect over giving opinions. However, Daly was an old friend and he could hardly spend an hour or more stonewalling. The alternative was to bring himself up to date. He picked up one of the four phones on the table by his desk, and rang Bill Broughton at the Flight Test Centre.

Broughton sounded confident and happy. 'You can tell Harrison Daly there are no problems, repeat no problems. Since you were down here the engineers have been all over Zero One, outside and inside. They haven't found as much as a strained rivet.'

Donaldson doodled on a pad as he listened, the inconsequential lines making a pyramid, then growing into an outline like an aeroplane's tail.

'Your Chief Designer must be pleased,' he said.

'Everyone is. We're hoping the VIPs appreciate what a great plane this is. We'll have her on at Farnborough this year, but Wormley hopes Atlantic will have confirmed their options well before then.'

'Gives you a few months.' The celebrated Farnborough Air Show would be held in the first week of September. It was April now. Donaldson's doodle grew jagged speed lines streaking back from it.

'Put in a word for us if you can, Jim. We need Atlantic's order to set the ball rolling.'

A rapid sequence of clicks interrupted their conversation. A woman's voice asked if the shop was open.

'We have a crossed line,' he said, 'could you possibly ring off?'

'Please.' The woman was shrill and impatient. 'I am on this line. Is that Damien's?'

Trying to speak over the interruption he promised Bill to do what he could and put down the phone, defeated, though the message was clear enough. Harrison Daly had to be reassured. He pushed aside the scribbling pad and tried to concentrate on a report for the Secretary of State. The AIB did not owe responsibility to any junior Minister, as other parts of the Department of Trade did. Its chief dealt direct with the ultimate political boss. Though this was a mark of the Branch's importance, it was also a burden. One couldn't afford to make mistakes. Lunchtime came all too soon.

London's Victoria Street is neither an architect's nor a gourmet's paradise; most of the eating places are as drab as the slab-sided office towers. However, there is one notable exception, a fish restaurant called Overton's close to Victoria Station. When Donaldson walked in the American was waiting for him at a table, studying the extensive menu. Daly rose, shook hands warmly and immediately set about ordering.

Unhappily aware that he had to complete a report in the afternoon, Donaldson restricted himself to grilled sole and some white wine. It was a shame. He could not normally afford the luxury of coming here, in fact a sandwich and a half of bitter was his usual lunch.

'I have something to ask you, Jim.' Daly came to the point immediately. 'Just what is going on down at Western Aircraft?'

'You mean problems with the 207? We had a spot of bother two weeks ago with the limiting Mach number. However, Bill Broughton assures me the plane is fine.'

'I accept his word. But that isn't what I'm concerned about.' Daly's expression was so serious and he was speaking in so conspiratorial an undertone that Donaldson wondered for a second if something disastrous had gone wrong in the past two hours. 'Do you realize the ground test programme is not even half complete?'

'You mean testing an airframe to destruction? I knew there was an industrial dispute.'

'You can say that again! Those technicians have had a guerrilla strike going over pay differentials since New Year. They've been banning overtime and taking days off for four months!'

'Is it as bad as that?' Donaldson was genuinely taken aback. He had been fully absorbed with the flying programme on his visits to Frampton. 'The management have been keeping pretty quiet about it.'

'I guess they hoped the men would see reason. I don't blame them. I just want to know something.'

Donaldson spread his hands. 'Fire ahead.'

'Are the Communists infiltrating that firm?' Seeing the mystification in his friend's face, Daly repeated the question another way. 'Those ground tests are vital. We have to know if there are any weak spots in the airframe. So why are the technicians deliberately slowing the programme. Are there going to be disputes in other areas soon? Do we have to expect the kind of delivery hold-ups there've been in other sectors of your industry: in automobile plants, in shipyards, in. . . . For Christ's sake, Jim, don't sit there looking like such a thing never happened. It's the history of Britain since the war.'

'Western has a good record.'

'I accept that to date production of the 207 is ahead of schedule. And I still want to know why the management can't settle such a crazy damn dispute in such an important area.'

Daly's increasingly emphatic gestures were interrupted by a waiter arriving to serve the wine, then dunk it into an ice bucket. The pause gave Donaldson a chance to think.

'It's not like the United States,' he suggested. 'Partly because of inter-union rivalries, we suffer from strikes which seem inexplicable to Americans.'

'Not if you knew the inside story of Communist-organized shipyard strikes.' Daly's tone grew harsher. 'Nor if you'd been concerned with building bomb-proof shelters for our Air Force over here in East Anglia.' He waved an admonishing finger. 'Don't tell me the hardening of those shelters wasn't screwed up by the Communists. We know it was. And you know why I think something similar could be in progress at Frampton? It's those accusations about the 207 being secretly a military project.'

'No one takes those seriously. Any transport aircraft can carry troops. In wartime British Airways' fleet would.' It was Donaldson's turn to be firm. 'This still sounds to me like simple resentment at another group of workers catching up with the technicians' pay rates.'

'Jim.' Daly was becoming heated. 'These guys started their industrial action, as you call it, three months before their current pay agreement ended. You ask me to believe it's coincidence that New Year was also the time when the ground testing was scheduled to start? I won't buy that. We're worried this could be just the beginning of flash-fire disputes in other departments, ending up with production of 207 airliners falling further and further behind schedule.

Atlantic Airlines is embarking on a five year re-equipment programme. We like the look of this plane. We like it a lot. But we need guaranteed delivery dates.'

'Aren't Western offering those?'

'They are. But what are they worth? We don't want penalty payments. We want airplanes to carry passengers in. This is what John Conrad wants to be briefed on this afternoon.'

'I'm sorry.' Donaldson sighed. 'I can only say that industrial relations seem all right down there and I don't believe in deep-laid Communist plots. Perhaps there are a few militants at Westerns. That doesn't mean someone's masterminding disruption in the manner you suggest. The mass of British workmen are not as gullible as the papers make out.'

'The local Member of Parliament seems worried.' Daly wasn't giving up so easily.

'I read the parliamentary reports. My feeling is he has no evidence. Why don't you go and see him?'

'Sure.' Daly looked vexed and he rubbed his chin irritatedly. 'So you think everything's OK. Well, I hope you're right.'

When the fish was brought the conversation lapsed and later Daly concentrated on technical points. Both men left Overton's feeling that far from having had a meeting of minds, they were like explorers who had blundered past each other in a fog.

'Breakfast's ready, darling.' Margaret Broughton cooked her husband a substantial start to every day. Years ago she had read that a pilot's reactions could be dulled by a deficiency of blood sugar. She had thought then, and still did, she'd rather have him alive and overweight.

'Will you be flying again in the afternoon?' she asked, when he had come into the kitchen and she was dishing up the bacon and eggs.

'Doubt it.' He settled himself down at the kitchen table. 'They want me around at the lunch and that'll go on some time.' A grin spread across his broad face. 'Who knows, I may be able to have a drink for a change.'

'You've certainly dressed up for it.' He had put on his newest tweed suit. 'They'll mistake you for one of the directors.'

He laughed. 'No flying overalls today. We want to remind them this is an airliner.'

Twenty minutes later, waving him goodbye outside the cottage, she felt the rain spattering on her face and wondered if the flight would take place at all. The weather was terrible, the hills were completely hidden by rags of cloud and gusts of wind shook the rose bushes, just coming into leaf.

As Broughton drove to the airfield the rain intensified. The cold front which the forecasters had predicted was evidently coming through, sweeping a mass of moist warm air before it, creating this murk. Behind the front all would be clear. But that could be two hundred miles away. As soon as he reached the Flight Test Centre, he consulted the Met Office and learned that by eleven the front would be lying over Frampton and would not be completely past until around three. He phoned Wormley.

'Do you want to postpone the flight, sir?'

Although there was standard routine for VIP visits, the nightmare of a hitch on this important occasion had unnerved Wormley. At his order two plans had been drawn up, the second providing for the 207 being grounded either by weather or technical faults and substituting a guided tour of the factory for the flight. However, Plan B was a poor alternative.

'Will you be able to take off at eleven thirty?'

'No problem, sir. The snag will be landing again. We might have to divert. The guests won't see much either. The cloud's up to twenty-five thousand.'

The word divert made Wormley shudder. It meant thirty-odd VIPs being separated from their limousines and chauffeurs, denied their train schedules, very probably having their evening arrangements ruined. But they could only get the feel of the 207 by flying in it. How else would they appreciate the handling characteristics and the quietness? He consulted his silver-mounted watch. The time was 9.08 a.m.

'When do we have to make a decision?' he asked.

'Entirely up to you, sir. We'll be ready to go from eleven fifteen on.'

'Very well. If the worst happens, you'll simply have to show them the aircraft. At least it'll give the cameramen something to film.' The press coverage was a major consideration. Both the BBC and Independent Television news teams had been invited, plus a score of radio and newspaper reporters. Barring the intervention of some international crisis, the occasion should receive wide coverage.

As he put the phone down, the intercom unit on his desk buzzed. He flipped the switch and his secretary's voice came through. 'A message from Mr Huntley.'

'Oh.' Since that curious speech at the roll-out ceremony, he regarded the MP with suspicion. Wormley didn't believe in airing problems publicly.

'His secretary says there's a three-line whip for this afternoon's debate and he's had to stay in town.'

'Thank you.' Just as well, he thought, then turned to the brief speech he would make before the presentation. 'Honoured to have such distinguished guests . . . Now leave you in the capable hands of our Sales Director, John Smyth. . . .' He was hardly going to explain that his absence was because he hoped, by the afternoon, to tie up a new financing package for Atlantic Airlines which ought to tip their choice away from Boeing and towards the 207. With British interests rates so high, arranging credit terms through the London market could be a very real barrier to export deals. The consortium he was stitching together involved banks as far apart as Hong Kong and Frankfurt. He had a fair idea of what Boeing were proposing and hoped to match them on cost so that the 207 would now be evaluated on a straight consideration of its performance and design.

By 10.15 he was back in his spacious office, having

delivered his welcome to the VIPs, fitted in a tactful few moments confirming dinner with John Conrad of Atlantic in the evening, and checked with the Press Officer that the media would be well represented. Western Aircraft had devoted many years to cultivating the press, partly because the local papers were a useful channel of communication to the company's own employees. At 11.10 precisely, Wormley rang Broughton. He could see by looking out of the window how bad conditions were. The far end of the long runway was shrouded in mist.

'At the moment we can take off, sir,' Broughton told him. 'But the cloudbase is below the two-hundred-foot minimum for landing. However, the Met is forecasting a gradual improvement between midday and four.'

'So what do you think?'

'Our projected track down towards Land's End will take us into the clear. If we had to divert we could go into St Mawgan.'

'God forbid we leave them down in Cornwall!'

'An alternative might be Bournemouth. Or we could fly ahead of the cloud to Gatwick.' Broughton had done his homework. 'The front won't reach there until around three.'

Wormley considered this possibility. The majority of the VIPs came from or via London. 'Very well. If you must divert, go to Gatwick and bring the West Country people back later.' He hesitated. 'You are confident you can find decent weather for the main part of the flight? I don't want this trip memorable for its discomfort.'

'The Scilly Isles are CAVOK already, sir.'

'Right. The the demonstration's on. Do your best, Bill.' He rang off and buzzed for the Finance Director.

At the Flight Test Centre, Broughton adjusted his planning figures for the flight. In order to achieve the shortest possible take-off, he would fuel the 207 with no more Avtur than was needed. The capacity of the tanks which filled a large part of the wings was 12 metric tons. In normal cruise she consumed 3 tons an hour. He reckoned finally on allowing 3½ for the demonstration flight, 2 for a possible climb and re-routing to Gatwick, plus 2½ for a further forty-five-minute diversion. With this total of 8 tons on board she would still handle better than normal and he would have plenty in hand for emergencies. He ordered the extra fuel to be loaded.

Frampton airfield had no terminal building or covered ramps, so the 207 stood parked close to the Flight Test Centre, where a group of cameramen and reporters sheltered from the slanting rain, shepherded by an anxious company Press Officer. Dead on 11.30 a company bus drew up. One by one, shielded by executives carrying umbrellas aloft, the visitors hurried up the steps into the airliner, while the cameramen stoically filmed them, cursing the poor light.

Inside the cabin, newly carpeted and with a galley installed, Broughton shook hands with each guest, introducing himself. Some of the people he knew: Air Commodore Stringer; the burly Vice-President of Atlantic, accompanied by two technical advisers, young Americans with short haircuts and a brisk uncluttered manner; the middle-aged, portly Editor of the *Frampton Evening Post*. The names of others he remembered from the list, like a trio of British Airways executives. The shop stewards were immediately identifiable too, the Convenor uncomfortable in a blue suit. He gave them a special grin. 'Hope you'll enjoy the ride. You'll be able to take the wife on holiday in one of these soon.' When they had all sat down, he realized that of this exclusively male audience, almost half were either government employees or journalists. He watered down the technicalities of his speech accordingly.

'Gentlemen. Sorry about the weather. That's one thing we can do nothing about.' He paused, hoping he was hitting the right note. 'Happily our trip this morning is going to take us clear of cloud. We shall cruise down the Bristol Channel at thirty-five thousand feet and a speed of Mach point eight three. You should get a good view of Land's End. We shall land back here at about twelve forty-five. I hope you'll notice how little runway this plane needs to get off the ground and the overall quietness. If anyone would care to come up front, I'll be glad to talk about her handling. This section of the cabin is as it will be in the service airline. Behind you, the curtained-off area contains flight test equipment. It's not manned. We shall be doing nothing out of the ordinary today – except that the girls will be serving champagne.' He smiled and was rewarded by appreciative laughter. 'Now, if you would make sure your seat belts are fastened, we'll be on our way.'

A murmur of conversation followed as he disappeared through a door to the flight deck. Stringer, in a window seat, caught only a glimpse of sodden countryside before the plane lifted into the cloud. The man next to him, silver-haired and benign, clutched the armrest. Broughton's voice came over the loudspeakers.

'Please keep your seat belts fastened until the sign goes off. We may encounter a little turbulence.'

'What's your interest in the 207?' asked Stringer of his companion.

'The *Evening Post*, of which I am privileged to be Editor, believes in supporting British aviation.' The sentence did not come out as smoothly as was intended due to the plane lurching momentarily. He lapsed into silence.

Fifteen minutes later, after passing through occasional breaks in the cloud, the 207 emerged into bright sunlight at 22,000 feet. Everyone relaxed. The two stewardesses began serving drinks. Below the outline of the coast became visible, Cornwall and the jaggedly tapering westward extremity of England. Broughton was kept busy with visitors to the flight deck. Over Land's End, he put her into a gentle turn, and headed back towards the towering complex of clouds which lay like a barrier across his path. It was one of the best-defined frontal systems he had seen, straight out of a meteorological textbook. Nor did it appear to have shifted much. He spoke to the co-pilot.

'Let's listen to the London Volmet. Then call Frampton.'

Over the radio came a mechanical-sounding voice reading out weather conditions at airports in Britain. Both Bournemouth and Bristol had seven-eighths cloud at 100 feet, 500 metres visibility. Exeter was a fraction better. Gatwick was much better, but every report terminated with the melancholy word 'rain'.

The co-pilot called Frampton. The weather was as bad as at Exeter. However, the controller advised signs of improvement. With thirty minutes in hand before the landing was due and no fuel problems, Broughton decided to try for the home base. Ten minutes later he began a gradual descent into the gloom of the cloud.

In the cabin the euphoria of champagne and sunlight faded as the 'fasten seat belts' sign flicked on. The Editor found himself involuntarily holding his armrest again, and wiped his forehead with a silken handkerchief. The descent seemed interminable.

'I'd like to see how he handles this one,' muttered the Vice-President to his aides and struggled forward, steadying himself against the bulkhead as he opened the door. 'Mind if I join you?' he asked.

Broughton glanced back over his shoulder, and indicated a spare seat immediately behind his own, positioned for a check pilot. 'Take a headset.' The American unhooked one from a bracket and pulled it on.

'We'll be on to the Frampton ILS in a few minutes,' said Broughton. 'But it's pretty thick down there and I'm not taking any chances.' It was getting more and more grey outside as they descended.

'You mean we're in for a diversion?'

'Possibly.'

They came over the outer marker of the Instrument Landing System, its code bleeping in their ears, lights flashing on the instrument panel. Heavy rain was spattering the windscreen panels, the wipers beating an arc of clarity. But all they could see was the ever-darkening cloud, blanketing the plane like fog. The ILS inner marker signals winked, then died as they passed it. At 300 feet above ground, with the instruments showing them lined up for the runway, a sudden rift in the cloud revealed a field and stone houses close below. Broughton strained to see more. But the murk closed in again.

The needle of the altimeter crept down towards 200 feet.

'Overshooting.' Broughton thrust the throttles forward firmly, and eased her into a gentle climb, letting the speed build. 'Undercarriage up, please,' he asked the co-pilot. 'Flap twenty degrees.'

No one spoke. As they felt the wheels clunk into place Broughton steepened the climb. 'Tell the tower we're diverting to Gatwick, then ask London for clearance to join Green One.' At 2000 feet, with the speed approaching 250 knots, he banked the plane around from its westerly direction and headed north-east to intersect the main airway known as Green One, which brought traffic in from the Atlantic and Ireland to the London Control Zone.

In the huge room where staff sat monitoring radar screens at the West London Air Traffic Centre, one of the duty controllers considered the flow of airliners on the way in and out along Green One and gave concise, unhurried directions.

'Good afternoon, Western Zero One. Understand you are diverting from Frampton to Gatwick. You may join Green One west of Lyneham, at Flight Level 19. Routing via Midhurst and Mayfield. Call joining the Airway.' He made rapid notes on a slip of paper and slotted it into a rack in front of him. From now on the 207's flight was being monitored and before long it would appear as a tiny yellow blob of light on the radar.

The co-pilot acknowledged and Broughton handed over control to him. They were steady now, the speed settled at 280 knots, climbing at 3000 feet per minute. He turned to the American.

'Sorry, sir, but you can see what it's like. I'd better break the bad news.' He picked up the handset telephone through which he spoke to the cabin. 'Gentlemen, as you all realize, we had no option there. Instead we shall be landing at Gatwick in approximately thirty minutes. Any instructions you want to be sent to your companies or chauffeurs can be radioed back. In the meantime, the girls will serve some more champagne.' He put down the handset, unclipped his safety harness and heaved himself out of his seat. 'I'm going back to have a talk to them,' he said. The American followed.

As Broughton expected, and as Wormley had feared, the reaction from the VIPs was not entirely charitable. He and the Sales Director briefly discussed arrangements and made notes, balancing themselves against seat backs as the plane rocked in the turbulence. It had resumed straight and level flight for less than a minute when there was a dull crackling noise from the rear.

In the same instant the gold-patterned curtain hiding the back of the cabin flew up as if in a gale, ripped from its fastenings and whirled away. The violent draught threw Broughton to the floor, seized hats and coats, dragged at seats. Everything loose tumbled backwards. Like a hurricane the wind clutched at Broughton's body. As he grabbed for a handhold he felt his eardrums burst and knew, in the same moment of stabbing pain, that the 207's hull had fractured.

From above the seats yellow oxygen masks tumbled out of ceiling panels, opened automatically by the drop in pressure. But the passengers, rammed into their seats, could not reach out for them. The plane was pitching forward. The gale died, leaving only a roaring noise from the rear. In this fraction of a second of quiet someone screamed. Then Broughton realized he was sliding the other way, forwards. He tried to raise himself from the floor, desperate to get back to the flight deck, and tumbled headlong against the door itself. Another man fell too, pinioning him. With horror he realized that the plane must be in a vertical dive. He was lying across the door and briefcases, coats and packages were cascading down towards him. The roaring had mounted to a shrieking crescendo. The air was full of dust. He was still struggling to free himself when Zero One impacted in a field, cratering the soil like a missile.

A second later it caught fire, a gout of flame shooting towards the low cloud.

Two hundred yards away a farmer's wife heard the explosion, ran outside, saw the swirling column of black smoke and hastened back indoors to phone the police.

9

The brown plastic bleep Jim Donaldson carried in his pocket could be triggered unintentionally: a chain saw had set it off once. But when it began emitting its insistent note in the pub this Thursday lunchtime he didn't question the summons. Kingsgate House was only a hundred yards away. It was hardly worth ringing in. He swallowed the remains of his drink and hurried back, going straight to the Information Room on the fourth floor, where the crash phone was.

'The 207's gone down near Chippenham,' the Information Officer told him. 'Came through from the Wiltshire Police. Sounds like a non-survivable accident. Either caught fire on impact or was on fire.'

'When?'

'The alarm was raised just after one, West Drayton declared an uncertainty phase at 1304. The aircraft's last transmission had been Green One at Flight Level 19 at 1248.'

Donaldson checked his watch, trying to sum up the immediate implications. It was now 1346. Barring a last-minute postponement, the 207's demonstration would have begun at 11.30, so unless the other 207 was flying it must be Bill Broughton who had crashed. Together with a load of VIPs and senior officials. The Minister would very soon be breathing down all their necks.

'I'll go down there myself,' he decided. Chippenham was, what, ninety miles west of London? By the time he was there the blaze would probably have been extinguished and countless rescue workers would be trampling the site. 'Did you warn the police to leave the wreckage alone?'

'They sounded reasonably switched on about that.' The Information Officer, a Principal Inspector, began recounting his other actions. 'I've alerted McPherson. He'll make his own way down. D'you want another operations man? Dave Langton is next on the roster.'

The AIB was a small organization. Its staff included only twenty-three Inspectors, some engineers, some pilots, plus himself and the Chief. A major accident like this would rapidly involve as many as six of them. The routine was for one pilot or 'operations' man and one engineer to go first, followed by whoever specialized in the aircraft type, in this case Donaldson. Normally, as Deputy Chief he would let others do the donkey work and concentrate on directing the overall efforts. But there would be a great deal riding on this investigation.

'Yes,' he agreed. 'Ask Langton to follow. He'll take charge on the site. We must have Dick Hearn down, too.' Hearn was a specialist in unravelling the digital account of the flight stored in the plane's flight recorder. 'Now, where exactly was the crash?'

The Information Officer spread out a 50,000 scale map. 'Here,' he said, picking up a pencil to indicate with. 'Four miles west of Chippenham, near the village of Yatton Keynell.'

Donaldson leant over to make a note of the map reference, then straightened up again. 'We'll need the caravan if it's on farmland. Get it scrambled, will you? I'll take my own car. We'll all need wheels down there.' The Inspectors had a rule-of-thumb method of assessing transport requirements. It was quicker to drive oneself, especially since the first stop was for collecting kit at one's own home. Hiring a car locally wasted time and time was extremely precious in the wake of a crash.

Having learned all he could from the crash room,

Donaldson went to his office and unlocked the green ministry-pattern steel cabinet there. On the floor of the cupboard was a light blue RAF navigator's holdall, a large cloth-covered briefcase held by a chromium lock and two black leather straps. He hefted it out and began checking the contents against a list. The bag was one of those items which, once endowed with a role in one's life, become indispensable. Among other necessities its capacious interior held a Pentax camera, with both wide-angle and normal 50-mm lens; another bleeper; a torch; an airways route chart; a map of Britain; notebooks; neatly folded lightweight oilskin trousers and jerkin, coloured bright yellow; and two dayglo orange armbands, printed with a royal crown in black and the words 'ACCIDENTS INVESTIGATION BRANCH'. He also picked up a pocket-size walkie-talkie radio from the cupboard.

Five minutes later he was down in Victoria Street, hailing a taxi. During the short ride to Kensington he remembered a police Inspector's comment when asked if they had a drama every day in the force. 'No,' the Inspector, whose name was Sturgess, had replied cheerfully, 'only at weekends.' Sturgess was damn right. Things always seemed to go wrong just before one. He packed a change of clothes into the grip, grabbed his gumboots and set off again.

Driving out of London to the M4 motorway, spray clouding the windscreen, he switched on the car radio. The crash was the lead item in the brief news bulletins. 'Tragedy today overtook the white hope of Britain's aircraft industry,' announced one station, 'when the 207 airliner plunged into a Wiltshire field killing all on board.'

Inevitably, he found himself wondering if the cause could be related to the limiting Mach number problem he and Broughton had encountered only a fortnight ago. But everything he knew about the test pilot spoke against such a possibility. Broughton would have flown the demonstration with meticulous care.

Then, when he was not far from Chippenham, a BBC local radio reporter revealed a clue of real importance. A labourer near the village of Box, eight miles south-west of the crash site, had found what he thought were pieces of wreckage. The police were investigating.

Predictably, the reporter speculated about sabotage. Though no one could rule that out, to Donaldson the corollaries were more clear cut, though less conclusive. If wreckage was spread so far, then whatever went wrong had begun at high altitude, must have involved some kind of structural failure or malfunction, and happened very quickly. Bill Broughton had been in contact with West Drayton. If the plane had not been overwhelmed in seconds, he would have sent out a distress call. But within that general situation the possibilities were wide open. Hearing the broadcast quickened Donaldson's impatience to reach the scene and he had to discipline himself to keep within the speed limit.

Smoke was visible as he turned off the motorway, a dwindling black column, drifting with the wind, faintly smudging the clear sky. Incongruously it was now a beautiful spring afternoon. He'd been told to take the Bristol road out of Chippenham and turn right where a sign indicated Castle Combe. A mile after this, he came to Yatton Keynell, a straggling village, its stone houses built of typical honey-coloured Cotswold stone. He swung left to go down by the church and found himself at a police checkpoint.

A constable peered through the car window and inspected his identity card. 'It's a couple of hundred yards along, sir. The Chief Superintendent has a control van there.'

Driving down the narrow lane, the hedges still dripping from the storm, he came to a gateway into what had become a morass of mud. Another constable directed him to park in an adjoining field, where he pulled on his yellow protective clothing and his boots. Then he walked back, camera and notebook in hand. The air was acrid with the fumes of burnt rubber and kerosene. He stumbled through the slippery mud, gained firmer ground and paused to take stock.

The field was some two hundred yards wide, shielded down its right hand edge by a line of tall trees, their bare branches catching the late afternoon sun, a faint blush of green promising future foliage. At the far end stood three red fire engines, near the source of the eddying smoke. Two ambulances were conspicuously white by the trees. Everywhere there were police and firemen, the latter in yellow oilskin trousers and high-ridged black helmets. Yet the way they were milling around, some aimlessly standing still, told its own story. The plane must be burnt out. As the radio had said, there could be no survivors. But where was the wreckage? Nothing of the 207 was visible. What the hell had happened to it?

Restraining his urge to run straight across, he walked briskly to the dark blue police van with the emblem of the Wiltshire Constabulary painted on its side. The door was open. Inside there were maps on the walls, two constables operating radios, a young police Inspector, and a tall man whom he recognized from his silver shoulder insignia as a Chief Superintendent.

The Superintendent was stooping slightly in the confines of the van. He had greying hair, a high-bridged nose and a rather melancholy expression. Donaldson judged him to be near the end of his career, rather than still on the way up. Not that it mattered. The important thing was obtaining co-operation. He introduced himself.

'So you're from the AIB? Good. My name's Cradock.' He shook hands and smiled wanly. 'Not much left for you to investigate, I'm afraid. I'd never have believed this one if I hadn't seen it. About the only thing that's identifiable as part of an aeroplane is the tail. 'I'll take you across.'

'Before we do that,' Donaldson interrupted, 'is it correct about wreckage being found near Box?'

'There may have been. You'll be the best judge of whether it is or not.'

'Can we ask the public to report anything they find, but on no account to move it?' Donaldson stepped across to the map. 'We think the plane was at nineteen thousand feet. If it did start to break up in mid-air the wreckage trail could stretch ten or twelve miles.' He traced with his finger. 'We know the pilot had diverted from Frampton, so its path could have passed east of Bath.'

'Thickly wooded down there, you know.' Cradock looked as gloomy as a schoolmaster confronted with an impossible equation. 'Might be years before anything was found.'

'We have to try.'

'Very well!' Cradock turned and gave instructions to one of the constables manning the radio. 'It'll be worth your while speaking to the press about it too. There are enough of them here, God knows.' He immediately seemed to regret this implied slur and added, 'The local boys are all right. Very cooperative usually. Shall we go then?' He beckoned to the Inspector to accompany them.

As they started to walk across the churned-up grass a young man in a raincoat ran up.

'Are you the accident investigator?' he asked breathlessly. '*Frampton Evening Post.* Can you tell me what happened?'

Donaldson was about to say 'No comment' when he was silenced by a clattering roar overhead. They all looked up. A brightly painted helicopter was circling low, a film cameraman leaning out of the open door.

Cradock angrily raised his arms and made gestures with his upturned palms, ordering it to climb. Whether the pilot saw him or not, the machine shortly went away.

'Our Editor was killed in the crash,' the reporter went on. 'Have you any idea what caused it?'

Donaldson shook his head. 'I've only just arrived. All I do know is, we'd be very grateful if any eyewitness would come forward. And if anyone finds fragments which might come from the plane – don't touch them. Just ring and tell the police where they are.'

The reporter scribbled diligently on his notebook. 'Any reason for the accident?' he pleaded.

'Sorry, at this stage I can't say anything.'

Three minutes later he realized how crushingly true this remark was. In fifteen years of investigations he had never seen anything quite so mangled and incinerated as the remains of the 207.

At the far end of the field, where the fire engines stood, the ground fell away into a steep-sided though shallow valley, barely more than a hundred yards wide. They approached this, picking their way among snaking fire hoses, slipping in the mud, fumes stinging their eyes and nostrils. Finally reaching the edge, Donaldson found himself looking down through eddies of smoke and steam at a huge crater fully thirty feet wide, its lip and surroundings overlaid with a layer of dirt-streaked spume from the firefighters' foam.

To both left and right shapes projected from the scattered earth which he realized were the twisted outer sections of the wings. Of the fuselage there was no sign, except a confusion of charred metal projecting from the water which almost filled the hole. How deep it might be he couldn't guess.

'May mean something to you,' muttered Cradock, 'but the only bit that makes sense to me is over there.'

Beyond the crater, lying at a cockeyed angle on the slope, was the high tail fin of the plane, still emblazoned with the words, 'Western 207'.

Donaldson grunted agreement. 'Can you have the area around the wreck cordoned off?' he asked. 'White tape would be enough. No one at all to be allowed past without my permission.'

'See to that, will you, Tom?' Cradock dispatched the young Inspector.

'Thanks.' Donaldson was about to start taking photographs with the Pentax when they were interrupted by the Fire Officer in charge, distinctive in a white helmet, his face smeared with sweat and grime.

'We can pump out the water,' he said, more to the Chief Superintendent than to Donaldson. 'But there's no way to get the bodies out without a hoist. It's like a bloody scrapyard down there.'

'They'll be at the bottom,' cut in Donaldson, thinking of the 207's layout. 'And there won't be much recognizable to bring out. There was a lot of heavy equipment in the cabin behind them.' He gazed down at the muddy water, slicked with oil. Nothing could be done for Bill Broughton or the others now, except discover why they died. He felt a surge of anger at the waste of life and wondered if the news had been broken to Margaret yet, then forced himself back to decision-making. 'As things are,' he said to the Fire Officer, 'I'd rather wait until I've made a survey of the site, then bring in lifting gear and remove the wreckage carefully by daylight. If we can't save life, we can at least save evidence.'

'You don't want us to fetch out the bodies?' Both shock and protest were in the Fire Officer's voice.

Donaldson shook his head. 'This kind of crash causes massive decentralization. Everything disintegrates. There may not be any bodies. And on top of that kerosene burns at around eight hundred degrees Centigrade. Did it catch fire immediately?'

'According to the farmer's wife, yes,' said Cradock.

'We had appliances here from Chippenham in under twenty minutes.' The Fire Officer suspected he was being criticized.

'Even so, with several tons of kerosene on board, do you think any of the wreck will be unburnt?'

It was the Fire Officer's turn to shake his head. 'Unless lack of air stopped it.'

'Then let's leave salvage until tomorrow and concentrate on finding the flight recorders. It'll be dark soon. Have you seen two orange or red boxes anywhere? They'll be near the tail.'

'Like what?'

Donaldson gestured with his hands. 'About this size. Rectangular. Two feet long, seven or so inches high. One has "Digital Flight Data Recorder" on it, the other "Cockpit Voice Recorder". They're both fire-resistant.'

'Not yet.'

'Can you spare me a couple of men?'

'Nothing else you want us to do?' Again the Fire Officer

sounded incredulous.

'Until I've photographed the whole area, no. Unless you think the fire could break out again.'

'How many tons of kerosene did you say there might be?'

'Three or four at least.'

The Fire Officer turned to Cradock. 'We'll keep one appliance here tonight then, sir.' He beckoned to Donaldson. 'Come across.' He led the way to one of the fire engines, the chatter of radio transmissions coming loud from the cab, and detailed two men to help. Donaldson briefed them and then continued his photography, noting with relief that the area was being cleared of people as constables laid out a boundary of broad white tape around it.

Gradually a picture of what might have happened was forming in his mind. The airliner must have come down almost vertically at four or five hundred knots to crush and bury itself so completely. He worked his way round to the remains of the tail. The fin lay some fifty yards from the crater, sticking up like a grotesque piece of modern sculpture, while metal fragments, some large, some small, strewed the ground between. Almost on the edge of the whole was a large and crumpled heap of comparatively flimsy curved metal. He photographed it, slowly realizing from its position relative to the tail that these broken panels had once been concave and must be the rear end of the pressure hull. He called the firemen.

'Over here. What I'm looking for must be somewhere here.' He knew the flight recorders had been positioned on a rack behind this bulkhead.

The two men ran across, one reaching for the hand-axe at his belt. He didn't need it. Within five minutes they had located the two boxes, jumbled together near the battered bulk of the auxiliary power unit, which had partially embedded itself in the turf.

'Are these them, sir?' called out one fireman.

Donaldson hurried over. 'Hold it,' he said, snapped the boxes and the surrounding debris, then went down on his knees beside them. The flight recorders were badly dented. He looked around and could see no sign of the half-inch cables which would have been plugged into the boxes' ends, then told the firemen to remove them carefully.

'This what they call the black box?' asked one, as he pulled it clear.

'That's right. Assuming the tapes aren't damaged, these'll tell us everything about the aircraft's last flight; speed, engine settings, the lot. We're lucky to have found them so easily. All the crucial clues are in these two recorders. Let's get them across to the control van.'

The firemen hefted the boxes on their shoulders and trampled through the mud after him, skirting the wreckage. To his relief, McPherson was waiting with the police, his expression as dour as ever.

'It took me a wee while to get here,' he said apologetically.

'Never mind. It'll take a lot more than a wee while to extricate the 207's powerplants.' Those four tons of jet turbine would be deep down. 'Has Dick Hearn arrived yet?'

'No. Langton's around, though.'

'Well, let's hope he gets here soon.' Donaldson ran up the short steps into the control van and spoke to the Inspector. 'Would you safeguard the flight recorders until my expert arrives? No one is to touch them. Then if he needs transport, can a police car take him and them to Farnborough?'

Ten minutes later, the two red boxes were locked in the boot of a patrol car and a radio message had been sent to warn the AIB's flight recorder laboratory that they would soon be on their way. If the technicians there worked all night, as they would in an emergency, Donaldson knew he could have preliminary readouts tomorrow. When Langton appeared, he was glad to hand over the organization of the site and continue unimpeded with making his photographic survey. He had started the job and wanted to finish before the light failed. While he was doing it, Hearn reported in and left again.

Shortly before six he reluctantly shut the Pentax in its case.

It would be dark in half an hour. But he had made one salient observation. Although the 207's fin was largely intact, the horizontal parts of the tailplane – the stabilizers, as they were called – had been partially snapped off, while the aluminium skin seemed to have been ripped off both their inboard surfaces and the extreme end of the fuselage. He went back and told Langton, who was in the control van.

'Could that have caused the crash?' asked Cradock.

'Impossible to tell yet. It explains why she came down vertically. There's roughly a ten-ton down load on the stabilizers, balancing the plane's flight. Remove that and the nose pitches hard forward. She'd have literally fallen like a bomb. The question is, did the stabilizers themselves fail or did something else affect the aircraft so violently that the stress tore the tail apart?' Again he remembered the limiting Mach number test. The 207 might have broken up then. Equally, if there was a malfunction of the hydraulics and the elevators jammed, the airliner would have been thrown out of control. 'There could be a number of explanations,' he said. 'The flight recorder readout should tell us which to rule out.'

'Could it have been a bomb?' Cradock's curiosity was aroused. 'There were all those VIPs on board.'

Donaldson shrugged his shoulders. 'If it was, we'd need X-ray examination to find the indications of blast. It could be six months before we had answers to fit the questions. Now,' his manner became more brisk, 'I need a telephone.'

'We've already asked the GPO,' said Langton. 'The caravan should arrive this evening and we'll have two lines early tomorrow.'

'The people in the manor might let you use theirs,' suggested Cradock.

'Is that the large house I passed?'

'Correct.'

Donaldson didn't linger. He sloshed his way out of the field and back along the lane to an old stone mansion he had noticed before. Lights showed through the high mullioned windows. He stood in the darkness of the porch and knocked on a massive wooden door. Dogs barked inside. After a minute or so, the door creaked open and an elderly man appeared. Two small terriers yapped round Donaldson's feet.

'Down, boy, shut up.' He silenced the dogs. 'I'm so sorry. I imagine you want to use the telephone?' He spoke with a considered courtliness which took Donaldson unawares.

'If I may. It won't cost anything. We use a telephone credit card.' He found himself ushered into a stone-flagged hall, with coats and magazines piled on an old oak chest. 'We shall have communications tomorrow,' he explained, pulling off his mud-caked boots with slight embarrassment. 'Was it you who called the police originally?'

'I think that must have been the farmer next door. We were out. The telephone is through here.' The man, who wore an old tweed coat with leather patches on the elbows, led the way into a sitting room. A log fire blazed in an enormous chimney. 'I'll just leave you to it,' said the man. 'Shout if you want anything. My name is Barnett, by the way.'

Donaldson settled himself in a chiar, trying to think of the right words, and dialled the Broughtons' number. It rang eight times before there was an answer and he heard Margaret's voice barely under control.

'Frampton 243. Who is it?'

'Margaret, it's Jim.'

'Oh, Jim.' She sounded infinitely lonely. 'Are you there? I mean, where it happened.'

'Yes.' He still could not find the right phrases. 'They were all killed instantaneously.' If a man had to die violently, that was the best way. One almighty bang and oblivion. 'They'd hardly have known what was happening.' He had to stretch the truth. The reality was insupportable. Even a minute knowing you were doomed must be a lifetime, seeing the ground racing towards you. 'Margaret, is anyone looking after you?'

'Mrs Pope's come in. She made me have a brandy.' The

voice was bemused and flat.

'If there's anything at all I can do, ring me.' He tried to decipher the number on the telephone and gave it to her. 'I'll come down to Frampton as soon as I can get away. We have to find out what went wrong.'

'I understand. I'll be all right. Everyone's being very kind.' She paused and a quiver of emotion came into her words. 'You will find out, won't you?'

'We will. It's the least we can do. Bill was too good a pilot to make mistakes.'

'Thank you for phoning, Jim.' She was near breaking down, and he knew she could not say much more. 'Thank you very much. Goodbye. God bless.'

He sat for a long moment gazing into the fire, into the depths of the tiny inferno the burning wood created. The room was quiet except for a ticking clock. He watched the flames leap around the logs and thought of the monstrous fire out there in the field. He had told Margaret the absolute truth in one respect. Bill was too experienced a pilot to make mistakes. Even though the possibilities he would enquire into must include pilot error, because error was the greatest single cause of aircraft accidents, he knew he would never be satisfied with that explanation alone. For no logical reason, he had a sudden fear that the truth, whatever it was, might not prove palatable to everyone concerned with the 207. There was too much at stake.

That evening Mrs Barnett escorted him the short distance to interview the farmer's wife who had first reported the crash. As he had feared, she could offer no worthwhile evidence. She had been cooking lunch when a tremendous bang made the whole house shake. 'I thought it was a bomb at first.' She ran out, and saw flame and smoke through the trees. No one she knew had seen the plane itself. 'They hardly would have,' she remarked sensibly, 'not with the cloud lying so low and the rain. It was as dark as evening.'

The news so stunned Norman Huntley that he was forced to

find a chair and sit down. After a minute he went back to the teleprinter, now clacking out an item about an oil tanker, and held up the paper inching out of it.

1437 FLASH. PROTOTYPE AIRLINER CRASH. WILTSHIRE POLICE SAY NO KNOWN SURVIVORS AMONG 38 VIP PASSENGERS AND CREW ON 207 AIRLINER DEMONSTRATION FLIGHT. PLANE PLUNGED INTO FIELD NEAR CHIPPENHAM ABOUT 1255 TODAY. ENDS.

He re-read it several times, then sat down again, trying to calm himself and clear his mind. No normal human could fail to say to himself, 'There but for the grace of God go I.' However, Huntley was not a self-centred person and he rapidly dismissed his own escape. What horrified him was that the airliner in which they all had such faith should meet disaster on an occasion for which it had been meticulously prepared. It was unbelievable. As he sat there, oblivious of other MPs walking past, the idea became a conviction. If the devil himself had wished to ruin the chances for the 207 and the workforce who built it he could not have chosen a more effective way. Airliners did not simply fall out of the sky. There must be a public enquiry.

Politicians have the same advantage over ordinary men in most democratic countries. Practically anything they demand is news. Furthermore, having made the demand, their responsibility for what follows is minimal. If he had realized how the pressures of a public enquiry can hinder an aircraft accident investigator, Huntley might have held back. But more probably he would have done precisely what he now did; namely hasten to the Members' Lobby and tell Gordon Tait and other reporters that he was asking the Secretary of State for Trade to institute an enquiry. Next he went to the Minister's office and handed in a rapidly drafted written request. Within an hour and a half editions of the *New Standard* coming on to the London streets bore the headlines 'MP DEMANDS PROBE'.

The debate which had recalled Huntley to Westminster so urgently overran its time. In consequence the Secretary of State secured a moment to discuss the crash with the Prime Minister in her House of Commons office, where they were joined by the Home Secretary. A public enquiry, with its legal ramifications and the examination of witnesses, was not to be embarked on without consultation.

'We're going to be under a great deal of pressure, Prime Minister,' remarked the Secretary of State. 'Several newspapers had representatives on board. The Vice-President of a major American airline has lost his life. Three hundred millions of the taxpayers' money is invested in the project.'

'I presume an investigation has already started?'

'It has indeed. And due to its highly technical nature the AIB would much prefer not to have it turned into a public enquiry. I spoke to them immediately. The Chief also pointed out that witnesses will say much more in private than under oath in a courtroom.'

'We do have to be seen to be taking the matter seriously,' murmured the Home Secretary.

'Is that the only political consideration?' The Prime Minister was not a woman to waste time on trivialities. 'If so, I should discount it. What we must ask ourselves is whether this is, or ought to be, a question of major public concern. Surely that is the criterion.'

'Norman Huntley believes there is something untoward afoot in the Western Aircraft factory,' said the Secretary of State cautiously. 'We've all heard him at Question Time.'

'And what precisely does he mean by "untoward"?'

'He suspects there is a militant plot to undermine the factory's production, but he seems to have precious little evidence.' He turned to the Home Secretary. 'Is it worth asking the Security Service?'

The Home Secretary had always been contemptuous of Britain's spy-catchers and the Blunt affair a few years ago had intensified his mistrust of them. However, the Prime Minister took a different view.

'There's no point keeping a watchdog if you don't let it bark,' she remarked tartly. 'Let's hear what they have to say. If they're uneasy too, then this ought to be a matter of very great public concern. You may inform Huntley that we shall make an announcement tomorrow.'

News of the disaster had reached Atlantic Airlines in New York within an hour. Although Wormley himself was in London, his assistant at Frampton appreciated how vital it was that the bad news should reach the airline direct rather than at second hand via the Associated Press teleprinters.

Consequently when Colonel Daly reached the airline's Manhattan offices he had barely stepped out of the elevator before he was summoned to the President, Hugh Johnson.

Minor events seldom worried Johnson. He left them to subordinates. But if something occurred which mattered he could be abrupt to the point of rudeness. He did not waste words now.

'John Conrad's been killed. That goddamn British plane went down.' He held out the telex message across the desk.

Daly scanned it quickly, remaining standing.

'Deeply regret inform you 207 crashed on demonstration flight today. All on board killed. Among passengers was John Conrad. Reasons not yet known. Fullest investigation being mounted. Wormley, Western Aircraft.'

'I don't give a damn about the others,' Johnson continued, 'but John was a good friend. I want to know what went wrong. I also want to know if we should cancel our production positions on that plane and to hell with our deposits.'

Daly handed back the slip of paper, his thoughts momentarily confused. Was it only yesterday he had lunched with Jim Donaldson and then briefed the Vice-President? It seemed much longer. Despite a night's sleep the time change still affected him. He recalled Donaldson's words.

'I was told that airplane had been completely checked out beforehand,' he said. 'They did have trouble on the limiting Mach number flying a while back. The airframe could have been overstressed then.'

'You reckon it was?' The latent anger showed in Johnson's face. 'Jesus Christ, the sons of bitches must have made sure.'

'They had engineers all over it for three weeks. The chief test pilot was happy and he was flying the demonstration.'

Daly considered all he had learned about Western Aircraft over the past six months. 'They're a pretty reliable bunch,' he said, 'They don't take undue risks.'

'So it has to be a design fault?'

Daly hesitated. His boss was jumping to conclusions.

'Not necessarily,' he temporized.

'Harrison, you'd better get right back to England. We can't afford to buy a faulty design. Even if it isn't, we can't buy a plane that's gotten itself a bad name. You find out what exactly did go wrong and meanwhile I'll telex to say the deal's on ice until we know more.' He paused. 'Make arrangements for John's body to be flown back too, and soon. We don't want Fran going across. It'll only upset her worse.'

Consequently Daly found himself back at Kennedy International that afternoon waiting to board Pan Am's Flight 2 for Heathrow. Unusually for him he took a tranquillizer, hoping to sleep on the journey. He knew he was going to have little rest once he arrived.

The rumours spread around the factory in minutes. Someone heard about the 207 crash on a transistor radio, long before the management could put up typewritten notices announcing their 'deep regret at having to inform all members of the company . . .' Most of the work in Production Centre Three involved waiting for the completion of electrical or chemical processes, and there was little noise apart from the background roar of the ventilation system, so the news was shouted or passed by men briefly deserting their equipment.

Norris himself listened amazed, thoughts tumbling through his mind. So Brunner hadn't fooled him after all. The plan had succeeded. And, Christ alive, the Convenor had bought it. There would have to be another election and next time it would be his turn. Couldn't fail, with two moderates out of the way. As for Peter . . . well, the Russians could bloody pay up now.

His fevered speculation was interrupted by the need to shift pressings out of the chrome sulphuric acid tank and into the swill before they were anodized. The bar from which the silvery aluminium pressings hung was moved electrically. A long thick cable hung near the tank with a bulky black control box at its end. As he pressed the button to raise the bar and lift the pressings out of the acid, his mate made a comment which brought him sharply back to earth.

'I can't believe it, Ken,' he said, his expression a mixture of disbelief and horror. 'Has our plane gone down?'

'We'll bloody want to know the reason why,' he replied, responding instantly to the mood, realizing that this was the moment for him to give a lead.

As soon as the pressing had been lowered into the twenty-five-foot-long anodizing tank, and he could escape for a few minutes, he went round the men in his shop to gauge their reactions. There was no doubt about it. The overwhelming emotion was one of shock. The disaster had done more to make the shop-floor feel the 207 was their plane than months of exhortation by management. As he listened, Norris formulated a plan to capitalize on the mood. He felt no emotion himself, but he knew how to arouse it in others.

'We ought to raise a subscription for the families,' he began saying. 'Fred had three children. How's his missus going to manage?'

Agreement was immediate. This was something positive with which everyone could identify. At 4.30 p.m. when the mass of workers streamed out, punching their cards, he stayed on to catch other stewards and enlist their support. Then, shortly before five, he marched briskly along to speak to the Manager. The sound advice Peter had given him long ago had struck him. 'When our project succeeds, my friend,' the Russian had said, 'it will be wise to show yourself a little more moderate. Cooperate for a time.' The emergency fund provided an opportunity both for this and for obtaining information.

Burnett's secretary was in the small outer office. She poked her head round the door, asked if he was free and told Norris to go in.

'Sit down, Ken. What's your trouble?' Burnett tried to mask his tiredness. He'd had a hard week as it was.

'The lads feel something ought to be done for the families of the deceased.' As always he put forward the idea as though it had emerged by consensus.

'The two stewards, you mean? You ought to speak to personnel about that.' Burnett passed his hand across his forehead wearily. 'You know I'm not responsible for welfare. But in the tragic circumstances, I've no doubt the company will do everything it can.'

'We'd be expecting so.' Norris could not quite abandon his habitual antagonism to management. 'We're starting a shop-floor fund as well. Will there be any objection to my going round collecting next week?'

'On the clock, you mean?' Burnett considered this, wondering what suddenly made Norris so anxious to help the family of his former enemy, then gave him the benefit of the doubt. 'So far as I'm concerned,' he said, reaching into his jacket pocket and hefting out his wallet, 'you have permission. And five quid from me for starters.' He pulled out a note.

If Norris didn't smile, at least he managed to sound conciliatory. 'I'll tell the lads you helped,' he said, pocketing the money. 'Does anyone know what caused the crash yet?'

'It's early days for that.' Burnett thought of the traumas ahead for the company. 'All we know is the 207 diverted from here because of weather and was en route to Gatwick. Couldn't have come at a worse time, just as we were hoping for confirmed orders.'

Norris stood up. 'Thanks, Mr Burnett.'

'Any other problems?' He could hardly believe there

were not.

For a second Norris was tempted to think of one. 'Not right now,' he said. 'It's Fred's wife and kids we're worried about.'

After Norris had gone Burnett sat quiet for a minute, speculating on this turn around. True, Norris always had been hot on welfare. The main reason for his success as a steward was the effort he put into defending T&G members' interests, individually as well as collectively. Yet, Burnett suspected, this was not an adequate explanation. Maybe he was trying to show himself in a responsible light in order to succeed Fred as Convenor. That was more likely. There'd have to be an election within six weeks or so. Trouble would only build up later. Burnett had no illusions about Ken Norris's true character; he just wasn't the kind who loved his fellow men.

When Norris reached the flat in Harold Wilson House, he half expected to find an envelope lying inside the door; a discreet message from Aunt Edith. Driving back he imagined it. 'Aunt Edith recovered. Sends her thanks.' Something like that. Sure enough there was a cheap brown envelope on the mat. He tore it open excitedly. A printed notice fell out, a reminder of bye-laws concerning the keeping of pets in council property. He swore and threw it down again, then made himself a cup of tea. They'd been quick enough to criticize when they thought he'd failed. Why the hell were they silent when he'd succeeded? He toyed with going to the callbox and ringing Peter, asking him straight, then decided against. If he was ill he might not be there anyway. Better to go to Bristol on Saturday and check on the *poste restante*. If there was still nothing he'd send a telegram. He didn't like his efforts passing unremembered.

The Royal Aircraft Establishment at Farnborough, some thirty-five miles west of London, housed the AIB's own laboratories. The staff included technicians who could decode the digital information on flight recorder tapes, painstakingly re-creating the only 'eye-witness' accounts there would ever be of what had taken place aboard the 207 airliner. No living person, not even the air traffic controller who had authorized the plane to join the Green One airway, would ever be able to speak with the same authority as the tapes. Theirs were voices from the grave.

The flight recorder, on which much of the original development work had been done at the RAE, spelt out the aircraft's height, speed, heading, engine power and many other parameters of performance, revealing in amazing detail what had happened mechanically. But it is the crew who make the in-flight decisions and the reasons for their actions would emerge from the cockpit voice recorder. The age-old wish 'if only walls could speak' was made reality by the microphones positioned on the 207's flight deck, taping both speech and background noise.

Dick Hearn, who brought the recorders from the crash site, was an established specialist in their interpretation, though even he became tense and nervous during the process of unscrambling their information. Each presented different problems. Furthermore it had been known for complex legal actions to hinge on allegations that a flight recorder had been tampered with. Consequently he would have to certify officially that the machines had not been out of his sight from the time Donaldson handed them over right through to the making of master copies of the tapes.

In spite of his natural desire to solve the mystery of the crash, Hearn could not rush the process. He reached Farnborough shortly before 7.30 p.m. Helped by the waiting computer operators, he carried the two rectangular boxes, still muddy, straight to a laboratory for examination and photographing.

'So it's one of the new Sundstrand Universals, is it?' commented one of the men looking at the deep dent in the flight recorder. 'Someone take a sledgehammer to it?'

'We may have problems there,' Hearn conceded. 'Let's get on with the check.'

They surveyed the physical condition of the boxes, noted their serial numbers, jotted down the amount of tape run as shown by a counter visible through a tiny window in the side, and took photographs from various angles.

But it took them half an hour to open the flight recorder, finally chiselling free the damaged casing to reveal the modular array of equipment inside. The chief computer operator grunted, peering at the thin metal tape running from an enclosed circular reel box through small magnetic recording heads, and protected by stainless steel armour.

'Looks OK,' he muttered. 'Considering the bashing it's had, the shield's protected it pretty well. Do you want to play it back through its own heads or fit it on to our rig?'

'On yours,' said Hearn emphatically. He wasn't taking any risks. He watched the technicians prise out the reel assembly, holding his breath lest the quarter-inch-wide tape should break. The Sundstrand company made their Universal Flight Data Recorder able to withstand forces a thousand times that of gravity and the heat of an intense fire. What they could not guarantee against was careless handling later. The last inches of tape to pass through the head would carry the last moments of the 207's flight. In those inches was concealed the reason why £300 million worth of aircraft development had fallen out of the sky.

'We'll make a master copy first,' Hearn ordered when the reel was safely out, 'then copy it again and run it through the computer.'

'What speed do you want it at? The tape's only a fraction used.'

Hearn reflected. This type of recorder ran for twenty-five hours, and was only removed and played back if there had been some malfunction in the aircraft. He remembered that there had been one; when Donaldson was co-pilot on the Mach number test. After that the tape must have been restarted.

'We'll have all of it,' he said. 'Run it at fifteen times.' To speed things up it could be run at a hundred times the speed of the original recording, but there was no need.

The operator fitted the tape onto the rig which would make a master copy on a big reel, and switched on. The runthrough began with a faint humming sound as the reels spun. In five minutes it was finished. After a brief check the operator announced that nothing had gone wrong.

'Thank Christ for that,' said Hearn, relieved. 'Now let's get a readout through the computer.'

Whilst Hearn sealed the original tape against any possible interference, the operator took the newly made master copy across to the computer console, with its large teletype keyboard and a television-type cathode ray tube display above. He began typing in their requirements; first the Sundstrand code, which would select the correct computer program; next the parameters which they wanted extracted from the thirty-three on the tape.

'I'll have the lot,' Hearn ordered. The Federal Aviation Authority in the United States demanded these thirty-three, which even provided such refined information as both fine and coarse altitude. With an important American airline executive dead, Hearn wasn't going to miss any out.

As the operator tapped out the order in which the details of the 207's performance were required, they flashed up on the screen for checking.

Hearn waited impatiently for the process to be finished, although the ease with which the computer would shortly untangle the four tracks on the tape never failed to fascinate him. Altogether they noted 768 'bits' of information a second, each single digit 'bit' combining with others to make 'words'. These digital words related in turn to each of the thirty-three parameters. Yet the tape which held this lexicon was a mere quarter-inch wide. Now the computer would separate the parameters and print them out on a wide sheet of graph paper. Although they would have to undergo further conversion before they could be shown to an outside authority, anything odd would strike an expert's eye at once.

As the clock crept round to midnight the printed readout

began emerging from the teletype machine. Hearn could hardly restrain himself. At last the subdued noise ceased and the operator severed the long coil of paper, handing it over with a curt 'Stage two complete, sir.'

Hearn took the printout and held it in both hands, puzzling over the digits as a professor might decipher the hieroglyphics on some ancient scroll. The tiny lines all either went up one square on the paper, or along one square, like a child's game. From these jerky lines he slowly read the 207's take-off from Frampton, its cruise south-west, its turn back, its descent and the aborted landing. He saw how the pilot had levelled out at two hundred feet, applied power, raised the undercarriage and flaps, climbed away again, swung through a 150° change in course at 2000 feet, adjusted the power and finally regained straight and level flight at 19,000 feet. He read the speed of 550 knots, the heading of 045°, the power settings, the fuel flow, the jet pipe temperatures, the cabin altitude. He read all the thirty-three parameters and of them all not one was aberrant when the printout ended. All were normal, though there was a mild fluctuation in the cabin altitude. Probably an adjustment made when the plane reached its cruise level. At a real height of 19,000 feet the cabin pressure was equivalent to 5000.

Puzzled, Hearn read through again. There was no indication of trouble. No loss of height, no engine failure, nothing. The printout simply ended.

'Here, John,' he asked the operator. 'Are you sure you got the end of the tape?'

'That's all there was, sir.' He came and looked over Hearn's shoulder. 'Can't be right, can it?' he said perplexed. 'Not if the plane crashed, I mean.'

'I'm sorry,' Hearn's voice was taut. 'We'll have to check right through from the beginning. As you said, it can't be right.'

For two hours more they tried to find fault with their own procedures and could not. The flight recorder tape bore no trace of the accident. The voice recorder tape was equally unrevealing.

When Hearn left the laboratory to snatch a few hours' sleep at the RAE mess it was 4.18 a.m. He reckoned to break the incomprehensible news to Donaldson as soon as the Deputy Chief could reasonably be expected to be up.

10

Donaldson woke with a start. Someone was knocking on the door. He felt for the bedside light. It wasn't there. Then he remembered. The owners of the manor had insisted on his staying the night. The knock was repeated. Unable to find the switch in the dark, he called out 'Come in' and huddled the bedclothes round himself.

The door opened, outlining the spare figure of Mrs Barnett. 'I hope you like morning tea', she said. 'It's seven fifteen.' She deposited the tray and withdrew, while Donaldson mumbled his thanks.

As soon as she was gone, he swung out of bed and drew the heavy velvet curtains. Even in this dim early light he could see through the leaded panes that it was raining again. He had meant to be back at the crash site soon after dawn. He rubbed the sleep out of his eyes, poured tea gratefully from the little porcelain pot, then took the cup next door to the bathroom and shaved. Fifteen minutes later he was downstairs, ready to go and protesting that he didn't need any breakfast.

'Nonsense,' Mrs Barnett declared. 'You can't possibly go out without it.' She was already busy with a frying pan on the Aga.

Reluctantly he accepted and before long was glad he had. The telephone rang and it was for him. Dick Hearn was speaking from Farnborough.

'Jim, we have a problem. A real problem.' There was no

disguising Hearn's exhaustion. 'I've been up most of the night working on the tapes and there is nothing on them; no indication of trouble.'

'Say again? What do you mean?'

'The flight data ceases when the 207 was in straight and level flight at nineteen thousand feet with seventy per cent power.'

'Speed?' Donaldson asked impatiently.

'Mach point eight two. Every parameter is normal. The last bits show a slight rise in cabin altitude. Otherwise there had been no significant change over the previous fifty seconds, since she'd been trimmed at nineteen thousand feet, in fact.'

'And the cockpit voice?'

'The last call was to London Air Traffic. Routine.' Hearn sounded exasperated. 'The only explanation I can think of is complete electrical failure.'

'The standby as well? Come on, Dick. Let's talk probabilities.'

Ever since a Viscount airliner had suffered in the way Hearn was suggesting, it had been mandatory for British commercial aircraft to fit an emergency power source for the recorders.

'You tell me, then.'

For a moment Donaldson considered going to Farnborough himself, but dismissed the idea. Hearn was extremely competent. 'Could you bring the printouts down here? Get the voice on a cassette as usual.' He thought further. 'And have them make a flight recorder readout in engineering units as well. I'll need to discuss it with Western's Chief Designer.'

'That'll take time,' Hearn warned.

'When you're ready.' Donaldson rang off, puzzled and apprehensive, despite the calmness with which he had been speaking. He did not even know if the 207 was on fire before it hit the ground.

Thanking his hostess profusely, he persuaded her that once

he had a telephone in the caravan he would be happy putting up at a hotel. At heart he was a shy man and more of a loner than he cared to admit. Though the Barnetts' hospitality was gratifying – he had known people blame him bitterly for the intrusion of a crash on their lives – he preferred to be independent.

Outside a rivulet of water was running down the lane. However, the field itself was noticeably more organized. The gate had been removed, posts and all, to widen the access while the thick mud had been filled with rubble and bridged with metal mesh, which he recognized as airfield construction material. Sure enough, a high RAF five-ton truck had been manoeuvred to the site. More welcome still, the white AIB caravan was there, parked close to the police vehicles, its orange-painted Land-Rover alongside.

The caravan was a complete mobile office. Fitted with its own generator, it carried shortwave radio for communicating with the inspectors' walkie-talkies, tape players, draughtsman's equipment, charts, even a gas cooker. The investigation team did everything except sleep in it. As Donaldson approached he noticed that telephone cables were already connected. Thank the Lord, he thought, we're in business.

Dave Langton was waiting inside, his tubby figure bent over a large-scale local map. 'Morning, Jim. I got this from the police,' he said. 'I'm starting to plot a trace of wreckage. Mac's out there. D'you want to talk to him?'

'Ask him to come over. I'd like to hold a prayer meeting.' Donaldson grunted. 'It may be that literally. I could do with some divine guidance. We've hit a serious snag.'

While Langton called McPherson, he began to arrange his own kit on one of the built-in desks. Though not unimaginative, he believed that the intuition born of experience only led to breakthroughs as the result of methodical thinking.

When McPherson heard about the recorder tapes his gaunt face became more dour than usual. 'What you're telling us, Jim, is that we're back in the steam age. Am I no' right?'

'Pretty well.' The invention of the flight recorder had marked a momentous advance in accident investigation. 'We're down to what the wreckage can tell us.'

'Man, have you seen that pit since firemen pumped it out?' It's a terrible mess, I'm telling you. Like the inside of a crucible. A lot of the metal's melted.'

'Did you find the engines?'

'Aye. Or rather, I know where they're buried. We'll need a Scammell tractor and a crane. Ideally I'd rig some kind of gantry overhead. That pit's all of twenty feet deep. If we're no' careful we'll have the Scammell slipping down the side of it.'

'The RAF's been pretty quick off the mark,' put in Langton. 'Had the five-tonner here last night. Maybe the Lyneham workshop could rig something for us.'

'Hmm.' Donaldson pondered this. Although their support usually came from the RAF at Abingdon, the major transport base of Lyneham was barely ten miles away. 'Let's try to make some kind of schedule, shall we? Dave, when do you reckon you'll have everything plotted?'

One by one Donaldson checked off the procedures they would follow, right through to finding out if Western Aircraft had or had not arranged for a firm of undertakers to remove the human remains: in public statements they would refer to 'bodies', but they all knew there would be no recognizable corpses. The impact and the heat had both been too intense.

'Let's meet again this evening,' he decided. 'Dick Hearn should have brought the readouts by then. Now, have you seen any Western Aircraft engineers around? I want some general arrangement drawings of the 207's rear bulkhead and tailcone. Whatever cut off the inputs to the recorders was probably in that area.'

'They've a whole squad here,' said Langton. 'Including the Chief Executive, name of Wormley.'

Donaldson left the caravan and walked as rapidly across the field as the squelching mud permitted.

Wormley, sheltering under a black umbrella, an incongruous figure among the rescue workers and police, stood gazing into the crater. He was noticeably more pleased to see Donaldson than on previous occasions at the factory and grasped his hand as though welcoming a saviour.

'I came as soon as I could,' he said apologetically. Appalling business. Poor old Bill.' He was silent for a moment, then reassumed his normal demanding manner. 'How soon will we know what went wrong? We must clear this up. The whole project's in peril. Have you seen the papers?'

'Not yet.' Catching up with the press reports could wait. Donaldson loathed reading about his own activities.

Wormley attempted to spread out a rain-soaked copy of the *Daily Telegraph*, while his assistant tactfully took the umbrella. The story was the front-page lead, with photographs of the VIPs embarking on the 207 at Frampton and of the wreckage. The publicity he sought had rebounded on Wormley with a vengeance.

'Our shares fell fifty pence before yesterday's close,' he complained. 'God knows where they'll be on Monday. We must make a statement.'

Donaldson choked back an angry retort, vividly recalling the Chief Executive's original antagonism to his flying the 207. He and Bill Broughton had been outside the Flight Test Centre when Wormley made some snide remark about never becoming involved with the AIB before. Well, Western had a disaster on its hands now and they were lucky the AIB had gained experience of the plane's characteristics.

'I remember your saying once that you knew very little about our work,' he said coldly. 'Even so you surely understand how impossible it is to make a statement yet. All I can tell you is that your 207 was flying straight and level at nineteen thousand feet when an unexplained phenomenon caused it to descend at a steep angle. Unfortunately the flight recorders stopped before this occurred. And I'd rather that wasn't published.'

'You realize there have been parliamentary calls for a

public enquiry?'

'There very often are.' Donaldson was unmoved. 'MPs seem to have even less understanding than most people. They want to pressure us when what we need is cooperation and time.' He looked straight at Wormley. 'This is going to be a rough ride for Western's, I'm afraid. There seem to have been no eye-witnesses and you can see the state of the aircraft. It could be months before we have enough information to issue one of our special bulletins, let alone submit a report. Meanwhile, I'd like carte blanche to visit your factory and question your staff.'

'Naturally.' Wormley made a faint gesture of submission, then nodded to his assistant. 'Arrange whatever facilities are needed, will you?'

'Thank you. This morning I'd like to obtain design drawings of the tail section.'

Wormley wavered, then said in a more agreeable tone, 'There's nothing I can do here. I'll take you myself. A company car will bring you back.'

As they departed the *Frampton Evening Post* reporter came up, notebook in hand. 'Any statement, gentlemen?'

Wormley stopped. 'The company is giving the fullest cooperation to the accident investigators. It is in the interests of all of us, and indeed of the country, to establish the cause of this terrible tragedy as quickly as we can.'

Donaldson listened, sceptically wondering how long this new spirit would last. But a minute later he was forced to give the Chief Executive full marks for having driven himself across in a Land-Rover, instead of being chauffered in a Daimler. Wormley might appear autocratic and insensitive, but underneath he was no fool.

During the hour-and-a-quarter drive to Frampton, Donaldson learned that Wormley possessed an acute and ruthlessly commercial brain. The Chief Executive had already analysed the minimum hindrance the crash could cause the 207's development programme.

'Even if you isolated the cause tomorrow,' he remarked,

'we should have lost six months. We manufactured the detail for five aircraft. Three were built. While we assemble a fourth, the whole flying programme will have to be carried out by Zero Two. The insurers will pay for the hull of Zero One. No one will compensate us for the additional production costs.'

Donaldson sat silent, thinking of the further six months his investigation might add to this schedule. Then he remembered Harrison Daly's concern at the delays in the static testing and enquired about them.

'It's a thorn in our side,' Wormley admitted, with unexpected candour. 'Those technicians are determined not to yield. They won't even go to arbitration.'

'Completing the static tests would almost certainly speed up my work. At the least they would rule out major structural failures.'

Wormley shot him a quick glance. 'I'm glad you assume there was no failure rather than the reverse.'

'I'm making no assumptions as yet.' Donaldson decided to press the point. 'The static tests would of course stress the wingspars and fuselage until they did fail, but that ought only to occur after the equivalent of more hours than a 207 would ever fly. I need facts and it would be helpful to know the results,' he said.

'Do you appreciate the cost? If we accept the technicians' claim, we'll have every other skilled operative in the plant demanding more. It's not the four per cent extra for twenty men, that's a flea bite. It's extending the same to nine-tenths of the workforce, which we'd be forced to do as each union comes up with its annual negotiation.' Wormley's grip on the Land-Rover's steering wheel whitened his knuckles. This was clearly something over which he had agonized before. 'You're talking about two million a year, give or take a point. I'm sorry, Donaldson, it's not on. Anything else you want, I'll do my best to provide.'

When they reached Frampton, Wormley lived up to the undertaking. The Chief Designer, Frank Golding, was summoned. He was as benevolent looking as ever, though his extravagantly thick eyebrows were knitted with worry.

'I wish we didn't have to meet again in these circumstances,' Donaldson said tactfully, and then outlined his search.

'Curious,' commented Golding, 'I can't immediately think of a reason.' He led the way across to the design staff building, where on several floors open-plan offices were occupied by rows of specially inclined desks, at which draughtsmen produced the many thousands of drawings required for any project. From the smallest machined part to the largest pressing, every single piece of the 207 was produced in exact accordance with a detailed drawing.

Within a short time, they were examining the layout of the tail area. The 207's flight recorders were mounted in a tray attached to the frame of the aircraft, behind the rear pressure bulkhead. Since they had to be checked regularly, there was an access panel close to them.

'You are certain they became unplugged in flight?' asked Golding, pulling on his left eyebrow, an unconscious habit when he was puzzled.

'No.' Donaldson's statements to anyone outside his own team were considered and precise. Misunderstandings sprouted like mushrooms after a disaster. 'No. I can only say that the flow of data ceased.'

Golding grunted and stopped twiddling his eyebrow. 'Let's go and look at the beast itself. Zero Two should be in the hangar.'

They drove down in the designer's car. The second pre-production 207 stood inside one end of the vast assembly hangar, the cowlings of its engine removed while mechanics carried out checks. The sight of the plane made Donaldson shiver involuntarily. How could this gleaming, streamlined bulk become the blackened tangle in the pit near Chippenham? Even knowing how insubstantial an airframe is when pitted against anything more solid than air, even after occupying fifteen years of his life with accidents, the ugliness of the transformation still horrified him. Indeed, trying to lessen the risks, to provide forewarning from experience, had been a key reason for his joining the AIB originally.

Steps were brought, the inspection panel unscrewed, and in a few minutes he was standing with his head and one arm inside the conical cavity which lay behind the 207's cabin. He flashed a torch on the two gaudily painted boxes. They were mounted end on to the fuselage, so that the tiny inspection windows in their sides could be seen easily. To take them out one would have to get further in. He heaved himself up. The cables from them did not hang loose, but curled back to be clipped nearby to a stringer, then looped again and disappeared. He directed the torch more accurately. Sloping up above into shadow was the convex end of the pressure hull. In shape the bulkhead was not unlike an open umbrella seen from the outside, except of course that it was vastly larger, the panels radiating from a circular centrepiece. Even viewed from this uncomfortable position, balanced on his thigh and right elbow, he understood what Golding had meant in attributing it 'a certain structural elegance'. He swung the torch down again on to the cables, noticing that where they passed through the bulkhead there was the bulbous shape of an airtight gland. The linkages to the flying controls must be similarly fitted. He flashed the torch and spotted the thin hydraulic pipes and rods. Then he wriggled back through the opening and lowered himself on the steps.

'Any the wiser?' asked Golding, as he climbed down.

'You did tell me that all the flight data leads come together near the flight deck?'

'That's right. Then the two single cables run back under the cabin floor and through the bulkhead to the recorders.'

Donaldson stood on the concrete, gazing up thoughtfully at the curving hull of the plane. This was one of those rare occasions when the germ of an idea tugged at his brain, incomplete, not even expressible, yet imperative. Every instinct told him he had been looking at the area where something major had gone wrong. What the devil could have disconnected those cables? Even if, as seemed just conceivable, the tailplane controls had jammed, causing unendurable stress on the stabilizers, it ought not to have affected the recorders. He felt sure that the clue lay in what had prevented data reaching them.

'If a technician was removing the boxes,' he demanded, 'and accidentally yanked the cables, what then?'

'They'd simply come free of the clips.' Golding smiled a trifle patronizingly. 'The possibility did occur to us. There'd be enough slack to prevent any damage.'

The images in Donaldson's mind began to coalesce, focusing on the bulbous airtight gland in the bulkhead. 'And when the slack was taken up, could more be pulled through?' he asked.

'Only very gently at the best. Unlike the control links, it's not intended to shift.' Golding was puzzled. 'You're not suggesting the boxes broke free in flight and severed the cables, are you? That is highly improbable'.

'Oh, no, I am aware that the assembly is designed to withstand a substantial impact.' Donaldson spoke not in rebuke, but abstractedly. He had come to a conclusion so unpalatable that he did not even want to suggest it to the designer in case he was wrong. 'I'm going back to the crash site,' he said abruptly. 'That was most useful. The bulkhead is one of the few identifiable pieces left of Zero One. I now know what I ought to find.' He scarcely paused before asking for the company car that Wormley had promised.

As the chauffeur turned out of the factory gates, Donaldson dismissed a vague plan to visit Margaret Broughton on the way back. It would be worse to dash in and out than not to see her at all and he was now in a hurry. His thoughts were dominated by a theoretical explanation of the crash. For once the living would have to wait on the dead.

To his slight surprise Harrison Daly was waiting at the caravan when he reached the site. Commenting that the former Colonel must have made a fast turnaround in New York, he found an AIB armband for him.

'I think you qualify as a fit and proper person to have one;' he said. 'Now come on, I want to examine something. You too, Dave.'

With Langton and Daly following, he strode across the field past the crater, and stopped where the rear bulkhead lay like an outsize metal saucer, crumpled and torn, muddied but untouched by the fire. It took him little time to identify which was its lower side. Immediately he began searching for the holes through which the recorder cables had run. When he found them he could not contain an exclamation. At that precise spot the panel was split in a four-foot-long rent, the jagged edges of the metal peeled back in places, as well as badly buckled by the impact.

'So that's what cut them,' he muttered and turned to the others. 'We're after any pieces of half-inch cable you can find. They must be here. There's nowhere else they can be.'

The task was not difficult. In fact Donaldson kicked himself for not searching more thoroughly when he and the firemen retrieved the recorders. What remained of the cables aft of the bulkhead proved to be lengths of less than two yards each, severed at one end, the plugs partially intact on the other.

He made a preliminary examination of them at once, standing with the others round him. There could be no question about it. The plugs had been torn from their sockets, and then – logically it had to be afterwards, if only by a fraction of a second – the cables had sheared at the point where they passed through the bulkhead.

Daly looked at him enquiringly. 'Langton here told me about the tapes. You figure the bulkhead panel failed?'

'There's no other satisfactory explanation!' Donaldson was as quietly exultant as a chess player who has won a particularly tricky game. 'When I first saw it, I assumed it had split when the plane hit the ground.'

'Anyone would,' put in Langton with unnecessary loyalty.

'In fact it must have gone at altitude, cutting the data cables during level flight.' He remembered a minor comment of

Hearn's. 'Didn't Dick say there was a slight decrease in cabin pressure shown at the end of the tape? By God, that's it! The first loss was recorded, then the hull blew open and everything stopped.'

'I'll buy that,' said Daly. 'You reckon the pressure forced the skin off the stabilizers?'

'Or the control links were also affected and she went into an irreversible dive. Whichever it was,' Donaldson concluded, 'it happened bloody fast. Now, let's get a vehicle organized to take the bulkhead to Farnborough. The sooner the metallurgists confirm or deny this theory the better.'

Back in the caravan Langton made coffee, while Donaldson pored over the design drawings with Daly, trying to fault his explanation. They could not. Nor in his turn could Langton.

'So now we wait until the boffins tell us if that damn great crack is due to stress corrosion or fatigue or what.' The techniques of metallurgical analysis would reveal indisputably not merely whether the metal was defective, but over what period the crack developed, and whether stress or impact caused it. Donaldson sighed. 'I wish those static tests could be hurried up. Assuming this panel isn't a freak, the equivalent one on the test airframe will fail too. Could save us a certain amount of argument. I can't see Wormley liking my theory much.'

'He's damn well going to have to end that so-called industrial action,' said Daly grimly.

'He refused to this morning. Says the cost is too high.'

'Mind if I speak to him?'

'He may be out at lunch.'

'Lunch,' said Langton. 'It's three thirty, Jim.'

Donaldson laughed apologetically. He had lost count of time. 'Go ahead, Harrison.'

Daly picked up the phone and a conversation ensued which reminded Donaldson of the gulf between what civil servants could say to their superiors in rank and what businessmen were prepared to.

After listening to Wormley's explanations, Daly said curtly, 'So you could add two million a year to your wage bill? Correct? Well, it's your decision, sir. If I were in your shoes, I'd ride that to keep the eighty million we pay for those ten planes. Not forgetting we anticipate needing a fleet of twenty within four years.'

'What precisely are you saying?' The chill harshness in Wormley's reply was audible to all of them in the caravan.

'I am saying, sir, that I discussed this question with Mr Johnson yesterday. If your company places any obstacle whatever in the path of the investigation, I have authority to cancel our options immediately. Without further reference to New York. Mr Conrad was a close personal friend of Mr Johnson and I also have instructions to start compensation proceedings against your company in such an event.'

Two minutes later Daly put the receiver down. 'He'll buy them off,' he said succinctly. 'Johnson told me to play it rough if necessary.' Suddenly he laughed. 'Talking about being in his shoes, I sure need to get out of mine. They're soaked.'

'I expect we can find you some boots,' said Donaldson. 'You know, it crossed my mind to put an armlock on Wormley myself. But I was going to get the Minister's backing first. I didn't want to be accused of exceeding my powers so early on.'

'You think we're going to have more problems?'

'Not for the same reason as you.' Donaldson grimaced, 'It's not Communist plots I'm worried about. It's the reactions there'll be to public exposure of a serious design fault. If that's what it is'.

'Which reminds me,' put in Langton. 'The Secretary of State announced a public enquiry in the Commons this morning. And a Member of Parliament called Huntley's on his way here!'

On the Saturday the whole West Country was again shrouded in misty rain, cloud clinging to hills, the damp seeming even to penetrate Norris's leather coat as he made his way to Frampton station. The Bristol trains left every hour, he could be there easily before the general post office closed. Yet he was as apprehensive as if he might be too late.

Tossing in the wide bed last night, all but moaning in his need for physical contact, for the feel of Mary's thighs and firm breasts, he had distracted himself by thinking of the letter. Then thoughts of the letter had begun to trouble him more than memories. There must be some word from Peter. He knew there must. Hell, he'd taken risks, hadn't he? Bloody great risks. More than he ever realized until now. Only appreciation of them stopped him ringing Peter when he got up. Fetching the letter was safer.

He waited at the post office counter in a lather of impatience and when his turn came almost forgot his assumed name as he showed the driving licence.

'Mr William Rogers?' The clerk retreated, burrowed in a rack, and came back. 'Yes, there is one for you. Express.' He eyed Norris suspiciously. 'Ought to have a proper address if you're getting urgent mail.'

'And have the wife open it? You must be joking'.

'Oh, like that, is it?' The clerk winked lewdly. Plain wrappers meant only one thing to him. He handed over the brown envelope. 'Hope it's up to expectations.' He winked again before turning to the next customer.

Anxious for privacy, Norris went to a phone booth outside the building and ripped open the letter. A single sheet of office paper, folded twice, contained three used ten-pound notes. Typewritten on the paper was the message.

'The news is good. Further information essential. Appointment this weekend. Steven.'

He stared at it, pleased, but stunned both by the peremptoriness of the summons and the paucity of the cash. Even a day-return to London was more than fifteen quid.

A rapping on the glass interrupted him. A middle-aged woman with shopping basket was gesticulating outside. Reluctantly he abandoned the booth, stowing the notes in his jeans pocket, and hurried away, his thoughts disjointed.

With nothing fixed until the afternoon, he had time to kill. He bought a copy of the *Western Daily Press*, then hunched his shoulders against the continuing drizzle and was plodding back circuitously towards Temple Meads station when he realized the pubs would be open. There was one he liked near the T&G Regional Office. He went there, treated himself to a whisky, settled by himself at a table in the corner and glanced through the paper.

The crash dominated the news, with a full page of photographs and biographies of those among the dead who were from the West Country. He recognized Donaldson in one of the pictures, remembering him from the Air Commodore's VIP visit. So he was an investigator, was he, nothing to do with the RAF at all.

That did it. His hands actually shook as he stared at the page. Why had an investigator been going round the factory a year ago? The very period when Brunner was doing his bit! For the second time in forty-eight hours he was forced to look at the implications of his involvement with the Russians in a completely fresh light. Fresh and frightening. He took a substantial swig of whisky and tried to concentrate on thinking things out.

Until yesterday, he realized, there had been a strange detachment about his relationship with Peter, as though all the meetings and discussions took place in a parallel life to his own – a life without sharp edges, private, almost a dream. Now you see it, now you don't.

Of course, he had known since the *Sunday Echo* article that Peter belonged to the KGB. It stood to reason. But the Russian was also a real scientist, he was human, he was concerned. His suggestions sounded natural, harmless, almost. Well, if not exactly that, certainly not violent. There was no physical element to them. If you shattered a car's windscreen, or thumped a blackleg in an alley one night, as he'd done before now, then there was noise, pain, blood stinging on your knuckles. You felt it. But passing the heat treatment ovens, as he did most days, aroused no feelings. They stood there, parked side by side, the size of freight containers, the control consoles over to the side with their dials and switches, and he couldn't visualize what changes happened to the metal being baked inside. Or didn't happen. He had only half believed anything would go wrong with the plane, and if it did, well, that was equally beyond his experience. All Peter had ever asked him to do was talk.

But on Thursday, everything altered. He had not been prepared for the genuine shock in his workmates' faces. Nor for himself worrying about Fred's family, feeling responsible even. On Thursday the secret life he had so carefully hidden from Mary began to overwhelm his own. It had been one thing fantasizing about Fred going down with the plane, imagining it like some episode in a TV serial, quite another when it took place. Fred wasn't a positive enemy like Charlie Brook. Fred was just in the way, or had been. OK, he'd reacted. Bloody fast. The families' fund was an inspiration: salved his conscience and showed him as a leader. But he knew that from now on he was caught up in a different game, one with no rules and very sharp edges.

He had finished his whisky. He crossed to the bar and ordered another, a double. He was close to a decision and the Dutch courage helped.

Back in the corner he pulled out the letter. So they instructed him to come to London again, they wanted a report. And it was Steven, not Peter. He didn't trust Steven. The man behaved like a spy in a thriller, he was asking for trouble. Nor did he believe Peter was ill. That was a load of old cobblers. Peter had gone to ground because of the picture in the *Sunday Echo*. Because of the danger. He thought about it for a bit, until the truth hit him. The threat wasn't to Peter. He was a diplomat. Diplomats had immunity. The danger was to Peter's contacts.

Quite suddenly Norris knew he had everything sorted out. He gulped most of the spirit down, feeling the fiery warmth trickle into his gut. The time had come to break the connection. On Sunday he would demand the money to pay off Carol and tell fat-faced Steven it was goodbye. They'd got what they wanted and he himself didn't need them any more. He was 99 per cent certain to be elected Convenor. From now on he could build his own power base unaided. If responsibility for the crash could be pinned on Charlie Brook, that would wind things up nicely. But even if it couldn't, the KGB bit was over. For ever. Finish. In the circumstances they couldn't object. He left the pub in a much more cheerful mood.

In the mid-afternoon, his self-confidence substantially restored, Norris called on the Frampton North Constituency Secretary, Bruce Gardner, and his wife, Joyce. The couple lived in a semidetached council house, known jokingly to their neighbours as 'the library' because of their many books. Both were teachers: she at a primary school, he at a local comprehensive. The books revealed their interests. India, which Bruce had visited as a student; the struggle against colonialism; post-Keynesian economics; above all, Marxist ideology. Copies of militant newspapers and of a recent National Executive Committee pamphlet lay on a table.

'So what have you come to see us about, Ken?' asked Joyce as soon as she had brought a cup of tea. 'The crash? That's a terrible thing. Whatever we may think of Western's management, it's still awful. And the pilot was supposed to be so experienced; think of the widows and the kiddies!

'That's right.' Her compassion was so unforced, it hit him all over again. The disaster really had affected people.

'I'm starting a fund for Fred and Harry's families,' he said, thankful again for his prescience.

'Now that's a damn good idea,' said Bruce. 'Show people we care.'

'I thought you might call an emergency meeting of the GMC to support it,' Norris suggested blandly. 'Might pass one or two other resolutions as well. If certain comrades found it difficult to attend at short notice.'

'Such as Norman Huntley?' Joyce's eye twinkled. 'Forgetting the tragedy for a moment, we've got him on the spot this time. He wanted the demo flight. Now it's him demanding a public enquiry. Did you think we might have a go at him?'

'Something like that.'

'We must stick by the rules. Friday's about the earliest day we could give notice for.'

'Friday would do.' Bruce Gardner was already on his feet and consulting a diary. 'That's a good day too. Huntley'll be making a speech in London that night. Committed himself ten weeks ago.'

'More fool him,' commented Norris laconically.

'Friday it is then.' Joyce made many of the behind-the-scenes decisions in Frampton North Labour Party. She was the de facto coordinator of the militants.

'We'll post the notices Monday morning,' said Bruce, 'after Huntley's gone back to London. You know he's down here? Arrived last night to see the victims' families.'

'Was that in the paper?'

'Owing to an unfortunate misunderstanding on the telephone,' remarked Joyce equably, 'the press weren't informed. Another cup of tea, love?'

'A lot of things are going astray in the office these days,' Bruce commented. 'We lost twenty membership applications last week. He grinned foxily. 'They'll probably turn up in the end. After we've elected a new Chairman.'

'But listen.' Though Norris derived some amusement from these conspiratorial remarks, he was suddenly worried. 'What if bloody Huntley starts a fund himself? He'll have us snookered.'

'No, he won't.' Gardner was confident. 'For one good reason. We'll announce it to the press now, this instant. Tomorrow's paper will have the story; the Sunday which everyone reads. That will snooker *him*, Ken. Good and proper.'

'But then he'll know about the meeting.'

'Come on, love,' interrupted Joyce. 'Are you out of sorts or something? The letters will be delivered Tuesday. That gives three days' notice. He won't cancel his speech. He'll just send a telegram of support. And the meeting won't be well attended either. Not on a Friday. People are too busy spending their pay packets.' She waved a schoolteacher's finger at him. 'You always have to use the machinery, love. We've captured Frampton North's, all except the Chairmanship.'

'When Charlie's out of the way, we'll be there.' Norris grinned.

'Clever boy! I thought you were a fast learner, Ken. You're a bit slow today. Are you sure you wouldn't like an aspirin? Maybe you've a cold coming on.' She smiled. 'Don't fuss. We'll have our bit of fun on Friday. We'll put a nice little wedge between our Chairman and our Member. Absence doesn't always make the heart grow fonder, you know.'

Translation of telephone tap material from the Aeroflot office in Piccadilly was thorough but relatively slow. The Russian speakers on the Security Service staff were permanently overburdened. Although Kirichenko had been called to the Residency to be briefed on the emergency meeting with Yuri on Friday morning, at the same time as the express letter had been posted to Bristol, the obliquely phrased request did not attract anyone's attention until early evening, when the tape was being run through. Then the tone of urgency in the message, coupled with a noticeable apprehensiveness on Kirichenko's part, prompted the expert to try and check the voice of the other person. He decided it was almost certainly Rusopov's, and alerted one of the duty officers who in turn rang Kit Fairfax at her flat.

One good thing about Kit's cover story of being employed at the Ministry of Defence, paper thin though it might have become to her more worldly-wise friends, was that she could always quit a party if 'the Ministry' rang. Annoyingly, on this occasion she had to quit her own. She told her drinks guests to go on helping themselves, arranged to meet them later in a restaurant, and drove straight to Mayfair. Her decision to put immediate surveillance on Kirichenko was half hunch, half deduction. He was suspected to be a KGB collaborator. Rusopov calling him and the way they spoke suggested something that could not wait until Monday.

When Saturday passed without the Russian doing anything out of the oridinary, Kit became convinced Rusopov would put him to use on Sunday. With the Assistant Director's agreement, she added herself and John Ingram to the surveillance team.

More than almost any other modern invention, the automobile has power to stir the envy, malice and bad temper latent in the human soul. The Centre's first reply about Kirichenko and the Chrysler simply confirmed the Major's decision, authorizing him 'to place the motorcar at the disposal of Airman for operational purposes.' The trouble started when this instruction was notified to the administrative officer responsible for cost accounting.

To anyone unfamiliar with the Kremlin bureaucracy and the complex privileges of rank in Soviet society, the occasional allocation of the car to Kirichenko might have seemed to present no problem. However, the administrative officer was not himself entitled to an official car. Whilst he was forced to admit that Kirichenko could hardly go to meet agents in the Lada, he was outraged that a mere coopted collaborator, and a Ukrainian at that, should enjoy the absurd, undreamed of luxury of two official cars. He immediately queried every expense so far connected with Airman's use of the Chrysler. The Major zealously pursued these trivial enquiries, with the consequence that Kirichenko became terrified that he might so much as scratch the paintwork on the sacred Chrysler. The meticulous care with which he therefore drove it was to have unfortunate effects this Sunday.

The Ukrainian's plan was similar to the previous occasion, though he varied it by walking a mile to where the Chrysler had been left. Then he embarked on a two-hour tour of south London. He did not begin to suspect he was being tailed until after he had driven across Chelsea Bridge and was nearing Clapham Common. He had left the main route south and taken a side street short cut. So had a small dark green Marina saloon. Ten minutes later, swinging back into the south circular road at Streatham Hill, he realized the Marina was still behind him, not close, but visible in the rear-view mirror. Even though fine weather had brought out the motorists, and some presumably knew the short cuts, it was a disturbing coincidence.

Steadfastly keeping his nerve, he continued on to the long stretch of main road approaching Croydon where he had planned to lose a pursuer. There were petrol stations at intervals. He slowed almost to a crawl, looking for a suitable one. When he saw a garage with cars at all pumps except one he pulled in to it. Now the Marina driver had a tricky choice. Would he make his pursuit flagrant by pulling in behind the Chrysler, or stop a few yards on, pretending to have a problem? Either way Kirichenko anticipated outwitting him.

The Marina halted beyond the petrol station and the driver climbed out and began peering underneath. Let us play charades then, said Kirichenko to himself. Already another car had drawn in behind him. He went through the routine of hosing in a couple of gallons of petrol, paid for it at the cashier's glass-enclosed counter, then prepared for his escape. Leaving the garage he could turn and go back on his tracks. The road was clear. He was about to accelerate across when a motorcyclist appeared, bearing down from his right, way above the speed limit. Caution prevailed. Why risk an accident when the Marina could never make a U-turn fast enough to follow? He let the motorcyclist snarl past, then made his escape back towards Streatham as fast as he dared drive.

Kit Fairfax in the car behind did not hesitate. As Kirichenko waited for the motorcyclist, she slipped across into the driver's seat. The engine had been left running. She let in the clutch and moved forward. Ingram saw what was happening and leaped in again just as Kirichenko pulled out and set off back towards London.

'That's not a nice thing to do to your boyfriend,' he said mockingly.

'Just get busy telling the others, will you?' She concentrated on trying to catch up with the Russian, who was already out of sight ahead.

Kirichenko was pleased with himself. He had unquestionably evaded the Marina. There was no sign of it. He was making reasonable speed too, overtaking occasional vehicles. But he had never become completely accustomed to driving on the left. At Streatham Common, an expanse of grass on his right, with men walking their dogs and children playing, he was passing a delivery van when he realized that the lane he was in turned right alongside the Common. Approaching the traffic lights he tried to cut back into the left-hand lane. But the van caught him up and stayed relentlessly in his way, coming to within inches of the Chrysler's hitherto unmarked paintwork. Kirichenko flinched and remained in the wrong lane. It took nearly two minutes and a lot of contemptuous horn blowing from other motorists to extricate himself. In the confusion he failed to notice that the car which had entered the garage behind him was in position again.

Thereafter Kit had no problem keeping track of him. Taking turn and turn about with the third car, a red Volkswagen, she trailed the Russian up through Wandsworth, across the Thames, through Fulham and then out to Chiswick. It was a very different kind of chase to the wailing siren pursuit of police cars. She kept the Marina well back, reckoning it was blown.

'He's parking by Chiswick station,' the Volkswagen's driver informed her.

'Go in and buy yourself a ticket. We'll follow him if he walks.' She turned to Ingram, who was doing the map-reading. 'Directions, John?'

'Left and it's two hundred yards.'

'This must be the run-in.' She stopped the car fifty yards

before the bridge over the railway. 'You tail him if he walks. Assuming he doesn't, I'll be along after you, well behind. When you reckon he's at the RV, stand off, wait and we'll have our lovers' meeting.'

'I'm looking forward to that.' Ingram grinned. 'Not often I'm ordered to hold the boss's hand.'

'Just keep your mind on your work.' She smiled in spite of herself. 'Now get moving.' She knew John fancied himself as a hearthrob and an action man. 'Karate-chop Ingram' was a nickname he'd acquired after doing a course in unarmed combat. Girls were alleged to find him irresistible. She could see why, but wasn't going to start falling for a man seven years her junior, even if business did require them to get into a clinch. None the less she'd spent more time than usual on her make-up this morning. The Assistant Director, were he able to see her, would have remarked that she was making something of herself at last. She certainly looked more like twenty-eight than thirty-five.

Ingram jumped out and she drove on over the bridge, seeing to her relief that the Russian was plodding up the incline from the railway. Confronting her was a choice of four roads, and very little time. In a couple of minutes he would be at the T-junction by the bridge. If he came over: fine. But if he went the other way she could be caught out. She parked the car under a tree and watched in the mirror. To her relief the Russian appeared, came down slowly over the hump of the bridge, then turned right. She consulted the street map again. He must be going to the river, she thought, unless they have a safe house down here. Then she saw the name Strand on the Green, remembered its pubs and its narrow alleys and knew, with a shiver of excitement, that her guess must be correct.

Trusting Ingram not to lose their quarry, she ordered the driver of the Marina to circle round the area and park near Kew Bridge station.

'Stand off as far as you can. Our man may take a train back from Kew Bridge to Chiswick. Either way he's likely to come out into Kew Bridge Road eventually.' She paused fractionally. 'And watch for the other side. They may have picketed the meet.'

She had disposed her men as skilfully as she could. Now she was going in herself. She slid the microphone of the Storno into its hiding place and made a quick check of her handbag. The smart, brown leather bag went well with the silk blouse, neat blue skirt and light overcoat she was wearing today. More important, it contained a camera, actuated by pressure on the bag's clip, the lens focusing through a number of tiny apertures in a piece of gilded metal ornamentation. She got out of the car, locked it, slung the bag's long strap over her shoulder so that her left hand could reach the clip comfortably, and set off.

A minute later she saw Ingram's back disappear left at the far end of the road. The Russian could only be heading either for the Strand or for Thames Street which arched round behind, rejoining the river path at its far end. She began thinking herself into the mood of a girl meeting her boyfriend, relaxing her face, masking her impatience.

Post Office Alley ran back from Strand on the Green to Thames Street, close to the car park behind the City Barge Inn. Ingram noted the foreigner seated in a stationary car before Kirichenko disappeared into the alley and did not so much as glance after him, but paced briskly on, joining the Strand through the next passageway. He looked round, but trees obscured his view. He took a chance, and went left. A few yards on he saw Kirichenko settling himself at a table outside a pub. Beyond was Kit, strolling slowly towards them both. He walked straight past the Russian, waving to Kit, then caught her in his arms and embraced her.

'Darling, I can't tell you how long it's seemed!' He'd planned the phrase and was delighted to feel her suppressed laughter. He kissed her cheek and whispered in her ear, 'They've had a guy watching all right. He isn't just here for the beer,' then added loudly, 'How about a drink? We could sit in the sun.' Taking her hand, he led to a table two away from Kirichenko. They were the only people outside.

'Gin and tonic as usual?' he asked.

'Please.' She placed her handbag on the table and began surveying the river scene, shifting the bag so that its end was pointing the concealed lens at the Russian. Beyond him a couple were standing watching the swans. A jet whined low overhead on its flightpath into Heathrow Airport. She watched it for a moment, distracted by the noise, then switched her attention back to Kirichenko. He stiffened. Something had caught his attention. Following his gaze, she caught her breath in total surprise. Threading his way purposefully among the strollers came a figure she knew. Slim. Leather-jacketed. It was Norris! Praying Ingram wouldn't return and interrupt, she rested her left hand casually on the handbag.

To her astonishment Norris didn't hesitate, though his expression was wary. He joined the Russian and she heard his greeting clearly.

'Well, how's Auntie Edith then? Been taken ill, has she? Didn't give me much time.' There was an acid, rankling edge to the way Norris spoke, more resentful than bantering. Even so, Aunt Edith was obviously a password. She pressed the handbag clip twice, three times, trying to avoid jerking it as she looked round for Ingram. A moment later he came down the steps from the bar, a drink in each hand.

'Just what I need, darling.' She thanked him affectionately, gazing into his eyes, then flickering her own towards Kirichenko for a second.

'We were in luck coming here, weren't we?' With a completely natural grin, he deposited the drinks, drew a chair up close to hers and put an arm round her in such a way that he had his back to the Russian, but her view was unimpeded. When he wasn't playing the fool Ingram was very professional.

'Cheers.' He raised his tankard of beer.

Kirichenko and Norris were getting to their feet. Kit had not supposed they would talk here. She took another photograph, and a fifth as they walked off in the direction of Kew Bridge.

When they were out of earshot she sent Ingram behind the pub to transmit a message to the others, calling them off. She had enough: the RV, what sounded like a password and above all photographic evidence. To try for more would be to risk blowing her success so far. The KGB would keep countersurveillance on the pair. Five minutes later, as she half expected, she saw the distant figure of Kirichenko, recognizable mainly from his homburg hat, moving across Kew Bridge. He would be heading for the Gardens. They were the obvious place. What she had to do next was rent a room here, and put a man on Norris down at Frampton. It could not be coincidence that the meeting she had just witnessed had been held so soon after the 207's mysterious crash.

'You did not bring the newspaper?' Kirichenko was indignant. They were now seated on a bench in Kew Gardens and he held his own *Sunday Mirror* neatly folded. 'Have you not a report?'

'No.' Norris was trying to keep calm. 'What more do you want to know? The plane crashed, didn't it? What more's there to say?'

'But . . .' Dismay enveloped the Russian's stolid face. 'There are many things we must know. What investigation is there? Are the workers glad?'

'Glad? Are you crazy? Listen, Steven, blokes we all knew died.' He took a deep breath. 'I did what you wanted. Right? Now what have you brought for me? Cash, I hope.'

'Peter told me he has sent money in the letter.'

'Thirty quid, do you call thirty bloody quid money?' His self-control collapsed and his voice rose. 'I spent more than half that getting here.' A woman leading a poodle across the grass began staring at them.

'Please! Be discreet. We must move further.' Kirichenko rose to his feet, agitatedly trying to recall the points Rusopov had made in the briefing. All the *Sunday Mirror* concealed was a list of questions, not money. 'It is not good for you to be seen with too much money. People will ask where you get it.'

Norris got up too, but wasn't going to move. He was furious and he stood firmly in the Russian's path. 'Don't tell me what isn't bloody good for me. I'll be the judge of that. Peter knows I need money for Carol. I've done right by you, why can't you do right by me?'

'We must walk!' Kirichenko tried to push him aside, but failed. Norris was physically stronger than he looked.

'If it's not money, what have you brought?'

'There are important questions, things we must know.' One of Rusopov's instructions came back to him. Yuri must be given further tasks, it is essential to keep him active in the net. Promise money, if there is no other way. 'There are things only you can tell us,' he insisted. 'I will pass Peter your request. He will respond when it is safe.'

Kirichenko meant 'when it was safe for you to have more cash.' But his meaning was not clear enough.

'It will never be. Not after all that in the papers.' Suddenly apprehension mingled with anger in Norris's reactions. His earlier fears about safety were justified. It would be better to quit now, money or no money. 'Listen, Steven,' he said harshly. 'I'm packing this in. Understand? Finishing. The job you wanted's done. I'm not seeing you again. It's all over.'

'But you cannot do that!' Kirichenko was becoming frightened too, though for different reasons. He dare not lose a valued agent. His own career would be in instant jeopardy.

'Tell Peter from me,' said Norris very distinctly, but more softly, 'he's no cause to complain. I've done what he wanted. He should be pleased.' He looked the Russian straight in the eye. 'And even if it wasn't over, there's no way I'd be meeting you again. I agreed to help Peter, not his sidekick. Right?' He turned on his heel and walked away, leaving the Russian bemusedly holding out the newspaper, a pathetic last token of rejected contact.

*

Norris knew someone had been in the flat the second he entered. Though it was dim in the passage he saw the kitchen door was shut. He had left it open this morning. The door stared blankly at him, giving mute evidence. He froze on the threshold, asking himself if he could have remembered wrong. Then he saw the letter, the circular from the council about pets. It wasn't in the same place on the narrow table. Someone had laid it down again too neatly, lining the envelope up with the edge of the wood.

Christ alive, he thought, thieves don't leave things tidy. Who had been here, the fuzz, the Special Branch? How did they know he'd be out? Was he being watched? He felt very cold inside, cold and alone. Fears raced ahead of logic. So they knew. They must do.

Then he heard the noise. A scratching sound, like a drawer being cautiously eased shut. The intruder was still here; in the sitting room, going through his union papers! Now this was something else, he could get to grips with a man, find out what was going on. Norris was no coward. He tensed his muscles. He'd give the bastard a going-over he wouldn't forget. Very gently he shut the front door behind him, sealing off escape, and then charged into the room, fists flying.

Facing him in confusion was Mary, a duster in one hand, a book in the other.

He stopped short, too amazed to speak at first. 'What the . . .?' he began, then fell silent again.

'I came back, Ken.' She had thought he was going to hit her, and had shrunk into the corner. 'I was just clearing up a bit. Tidying.'

He looked round. It was true, the pile of the carpet showed where the hoover had been and the cushions on the couch were plumped up.

'Anyone would think I was a burglar,' she said more confidently, 'the way you came in.'

'I did. Christ, you gave me a fright. Oh, Mary.' He took her hand, kissed her, folded her in a bearhug as his emotions broke free, swung her round, kissed her more passionately.

'Oh, Mary, are you back?' He couldn't believe it.

'I read about your fund in the paper today and I knew I had to come. I was all wrong about you. I thought you didn't care. But it's my mother who was wrong. You do. I'm so glad, Ken, I'm so very glad.' She clung to him.

He shook his head, half laughing, still bewildered. 'Jesus, I've had a day,' he said. 'If only you knew.' He kissed her again. 'Hey, you know what, love. We're going to celebrate. Go to the Berni, have a steak and all the trimmings. Or that roast duck you like. How about that?'

'I'd love that.' She glanced down at her jeans. 'I'll go and tart myself up, then.' She slipped away.

'Not too much, love. Don't want people thinking I'm with a scarlet woman.' He roared with laughter and delight. It was bloody marvellous. Shot of that creep Steven and Mary back, all in the same day. Fantastic.

Later, after a whisky first and sinking a pint of lager with the steak, he told her in veiled terms how he'd been to London to dun a man for money he was owed and they'd quarrelled, finding it a huge relief to talk to someone who sympathized. Though he mentioned no details, he told her considerably more than was prudent.

11

The way Wormley ended the technicians' guerrilla strike was only revealed to Donaldson later. But the effcct was rapid. They resumed normal working from the Tuesday morning, five days after the crash.

The part of the testing Donaldson was most concerned with was basically as simple as inflating a bicycle tyre. The inside of the fuselage was completely unfurnished; no seats; no instruments; nothing except the basic structure. It was as stark as an empty cigar tube. Then it was almost filled with polystyrene foam. Next it had air pumped in and out to produce the same changes of pressure as would occur if it was being flown from ground level to cruising height and then brought down again. Since air pressure declines with altitude, but passengers have to be preserved at something closer to the conditions on the ground, the cabin of an airliner flying at 35,000 feet will be kept at a pressure equivalent to around 7000. The difference creates some 8 lbs per square inch of pressure between the inside and outside of the hull. The static tests would go on and on reproducing climbs and descents until these repeated strains on the construction made something break. If the design was sound, this would not happen until twenty-five years of simulated operation, when the plane would have retired from service anyway.

However, Donaldson was concerned with five months, not twenty-five years. Because the foam enormously reduced the amount of air needed to fill the fuselage, two flights of two and a half hours each could be simulated in a single hour on the rig. Some testing had already been done, despite the industrial action. When he heard the news he calculated that if the airframe was going to fail, it might do so before the end of the week. He rang Wormley to tell him so, and asked curiously how he had ended the strike.

'Read tomorrow's papers,' said the Chief Executive curtly. 'That friend of yours, Daly, forced me to make an offer which I may yet regret.'

In fact he had taken a considerable risk. Bypassing the established conciliation procedures, he had written personal letters to all instrument technicians and had them delivered to each man's home by hand on the Saturday. He also sent copies to members of the Joint Shop Stewards Committee. What the letters said was strictly factual, namely that if the tests were not resumed the company would lose £80 million worth of orders. This wasn't like selling to the state airline, where the government could intervene. No authority in Britain could compel an independent American airline to buy British. If the technicians' desire was to wreck the employment prospects of 7000 others, they could accept the odium themselves. If not, then the management would offer an immediate interim 3 per cent rise plus arbitration which it pledged itself to accept.

The gamble succeeded. The tragedy of the crash had unnerved everyone to some extent. By the time Wormley personally called for a show of hands on the Monday afternoon, the technicians were in a mood to vote for normal working. None the less, Wormley knew it was not a manoeuvre he could repeat. He would put even the moderate stewards' backs up if he tried.

Tuesday was significant for Donaldson in other ways as well. The metallurgists at Farnborough telephoned to announce that, after careful examination of the bulkhead, they had selected which parts to cut from it for analysis. Their qualitative impression, from inspection without the help of a microscope, was that the cause of the fracture was stress corrosion. If he would ring the head of the division on Thursday, they might be able to confirm this.

By the end of the week, he realized, his basic theory might well be proven by two totally independent sets of tests. It was a morbidly satisfying thought.

Meanwhile on the crash site itself the extraction of the wreckage from the crater had begun. An RAF low loader, a sixty-foot-long flatbed truck, nicknamed a 'Queen Mary', stood by to take the pieces to Farnborough. There they would be laid out on a hangar floor, in as near their correct order as their mangled state allowed. Even assuming the bulkhead had cracked, the investigation would still have to determine what happened after that.

Donaldson left the caravan again and walked across. The scene was bizarre. A newcomer could have been excused for thinking the foundations for a building were being excavated. The slopes of the hole were so perilous that it had been necessary to dig out a level gallery round it, on which stood a mobile crane, while a team of RAF technicians in mud-splashed khaki overalls laboured to prise free the crushed and tangled aluminium. Like ants scavenging a carcass, they were slowly detaching and removing segments of wreckage under McPherson's direction, some hammering, some wielding hacksaws and oxyacetylene cutters. The risk of fire was considered so small now, the kerosene having had six days to soak into the earth, that the fire brigade had long departed. So had the ambulances. The sole survivors of the emergency services were the police and a green Women's Royal Voluntary Service canteen van, diligently serving tea and sandwiches.

McPherson looked up and greeted him. 'We're progressing, Jim. I reckon we've most of the rear fuselage out now. We've located the inboard sections of the wing spars and I know where the powerplants must be. Of course the further we go down, the more heavily impacted it is.' He wiped his sleeve across his forehead. 'We'll be reaching the forward cabin soon. And the bodies. I was thinking maybe we should alert the man from Hanson's.'

Donaldson agreed. Hanson's were a firm of undertakers renowned world wide for their expertise in dealing with aircrash victims. Their representative, named Denman, had been in Chippenham several days. He had already brought his own equipment to the site, most notably a stock of opaque, greyish body bags, which zipped up the centre. The RAF had provided a marquee tent for him, which was pitched at the side of the field and furnished with trestle tables. Here, in principle, he would attempt to sort the human remains before autopsies were performed, for which two Air Force pathologists, veterans of many aviation disasters, were ready to come when needed.

However, it was only the next morning that the first human remains were retrieved. Daly, who had been pursuing enquiries of his own, returned from Frampton. He and Donaldson watched in grim silence as a few shrunken black lumps were brought out and laid initially on a tarpaulin. It was hard to believe that they had ever been flesh and bone.

Daly strode across to the undertaker. 'Can you make identifications?' he asked huskily.

'Not of these.' He looked down at the shrivelled shapes. 'They're almost totally carbonized.'

'The man I'm concerned with was on the flight deck shortly before the crash,' Daly persisted. 'We know that. He wore an Omega watch.'

'The casing might be found.' Denman paused. If this man was a relative of the deceased there were details it was preferable not to know. 'Forgive my asking, was he one of your family?'

'He was Vice-President of our company. Atlantic Airlines.'

'Then you must know what an impact at terminal velocity does, sir. These bodies we're bringing out must have been in the rear seats. They lost heads or limbs before the fire.'

'I see that.' Daly reckoned he had a pretty strong stomach, but he was in fact averting his eyes from the tarpaulin.

'There won't be anything left of the flight crew to bury.' Denman looked straight at the American. 'Just splattered blood and tissue. I've already warned the Air Force technicians that if they as much as scratch themselves they'll be in danger of getting septicaemia.'

'So what do we do?' asked Daly, suddenly aware that for all his years in the Air Force, he had never been present at a crash like this. He'd heard of jet fighters going in vertically but never seen the results, and the ultimate details weren't something pilots talked about.

'We might identify a few victims from dental charts.' Denman tried to make his realism sound caring rather than callous. 'Frankly, sir, there's little point. It's not as though this was an airline flight with last-minute additions and cancellations to the passenger list. We know precisely who was on board. The best solution will be to apportion the remains between the appropriate number of coffins.'

'I guess so.' Daly shook his head reluctantly. John Conrad's widow would go berserk if she knew.

'We should do all we could to keep the fact secret.'

'You'll need to,' said Daly harshly. 'I've just been in Frampton. People down there are deeply upset, it's as if they'd all lost relations. So what do I tell our Vice-President's widow?'

'As I expect you may know, sir, International Air Transport Authority regulations demand zinc-lined coffins for corpses being repatriated. We deal with it all. Your Vice-President's family will not be troubled with either formalities or bills. If the remains can be embalmed, we give them that protection. The only thing we cannot do is return bodies for interment without the local coroner's consent. I believe he is opening the inquest today.'

'He'll have to adjourn it until our enquiry is complete'. Donaldson's voice cut into the conversation. 'Should permit burials fairly soon, though.'

'Thanks. That's some relief.' Daly turned to Donaldson. 'Jim, can you spare a minute?'

'Let's go back to the caravan.' Daly's tone told him this was private.

When they got there, the American was abrupt. 'Have you any ideas on why that bulkhead failed?' he demanded.

'I'm here to ascertain facts, Harrison, not to speculate. If the bulkhead did go, the metallurgists will discover why.'

'And if it was a fault in manufacture?'

'Then my enquiries will be transferred to the factory.'

'Tell me something, Jim. Does Western Aircraft have a history of using substandard materials?'

'Not to my knowledge.' Donaldson rubbed the side of his nose with his forefinger, a habit when he was perplexed. He didn't like what the American was implying. Daly was being remarkably aggressive. 'No,' he said calmly. 'It's unthinkable that they would.'

'Which is what everyone there says. So something doesn't add up, right?'

'I told you. I'm not rushing to conclusions.'

'Do you mind my talking to the factory staff?'

'You can't wear an AIB armband there.' Donaldson was becoming irritated. 'And I don't want witnesses spoiled.' He rubbed his nose again. If he was strictly honest with himself, Daly might find out something useful. 'On the other hand,' he conceded, 'you could do better than I do. This public enquiry is a damn nuisance. The moment people realize they're going to be giving evidence on oath in public, they clam up. Do you have Wormley's blessing?'

'I will have.'

Donaldson didn't doubt it. Daly had already demonstrated his ability in that direction. 'Keep me informed, would you?' he asked. 'Now, if you'll excuse me . . . ' Langton was due back with some fragments of aluminium found six miles away. If they were from the 207's tail, they might throw some light on why it went out of control.

As he left the caravan he was buttonholed by the *Frampton Evening Post* reporter. For the rest of Britain the crash had been a twenty-four-hour wonder and the national TV teams had long departed. However, the local man stuck doggedly to his assignment and now, as a prelude to what he wanted to ask, told Donaldson of Western Aircraft's plans for a memorial service for the victims this coming Saturday.

Grateful for the knowledge, because he would want to be there alongside Margaret Broughton, Donaldson relaxed enough to spend ten minutes explaining the guidelines for an investigation to the young reporter.

'So, where are you taking the wreckage to now, sir?' he asked.

'To Farnborough. Basically the idea is to lay out all we have recovered there in the right order, or as near as we can get to it,' Donaldson explained. 'There's a hangar devoted to it. In crude terms we can then see what's missing. And of course there are laboratories at Farnborough. In fact, metallurgical analysis has already begun.'

'You mean there was faulty metal in the construction?'

'Let's just say we're examining parts of the structure.' Donaldson regretted his benevolence. He tried to back down further. 'Since there was no aerial collision, the cause of the accident has to be within the plane itself. I really can't say any more at this stage. Sorry.'

The reporter thanked him and retreated, excitedly certain he had obtained the clue to a story, but far from clear what it was.

The telegram received from the Centre on Wednesday was of unusual length. Rusopov watched over its decoding impatiently. The originator was Department Three, which meant Colonel Grigoriev, now firmly in the saddle as director. The subject was Yuri.

After referring to the Residency's own telegram sent on Monday, Grigoriev stated bluntly: 'The information you have communicated concerning the behaviour of Yuri shows him in a most unfavourable light. This may be due to lack of positive guidance or even ineptitude by Airman. . . .' The Comrade Colonel did not mince words, Rusopov reflected, even when using the conventional phraseology. There followed a keen appraisal of Yuri's past assistance and future worth. The Colonel regarded his self-centred attitude as potentially dangerous. However, after bearing in mind the situation, it was considered essential to retain Yuri in the net.

The telegram ended: 'You are therefore instructed to re-establish contact and obtain regular reports on the effects of the sabotage in the aircraft factory, progress of any investigations, etc. In order to facilitate agreement by Yuri you are authorized to make a payment of five hundred pounds for the benefit of Yuri's ex-wife and undertake to provide a further sum after six months, dependent on the satisfactory fulfilment of tasks.'

Rusopov re-read the text carefully before taking it to the Major, who had now been moved from the Trade Mission to a nominal commercial post within the Embassy building. The Major had been correct in mistrusting Kirichenko's suitability. Since it would not be politic to blame Colonel Grigoriev, and the Aeroflot manager was already the subject of a report which would make this his last job abroad, either for the airline or any other organization, fresh recriminations could land on only one head. His own.

The Major leafed the telegram through his podgy fingers, pursing his lips as he read, and occasionally grunting.

'It is obvious to me,' he remarked softly, 'that the Comrade Colonel's assessment is correct. Yuri is as unpredictable as a Pole. He requires careful and positive handling. I am forced to suspect that both Kirichenko and your briefing were inadequate.'

'With respect, Comrade Major, the briefing was exhaustive.'

'Yet Kirichenko allowed the agent to break contact?' The Major's small eyes fixed on Rusopov. 'Think about that, Comrade Captain. I shall require your observations. And what remedy you propose.'

'I suggest reassuming control of Yuri myself in spite of the risk. We should definitely not involve another cadre worker.'

'Hmm.' The Major could hardly disagree. 'And by what means will you do so?'

'A suitable greetings card will persuade him. A short message from Aunt Edith saying she is sorry for his ex-wife and is sending her five hundred pounds. He will respond.'

'Through greed and anger. Yes.' The Major revolved the idea in his mind and liked it. 'Yes, he will want so much money for himself.'

'Possibly, Comrade Major,' said Rusopov. 'Or it may renew his trust. He is a lonely man, our Yuri. He told Kirichenko his woman had left him. I think he will come back to us. We have let him run a little. Now we shall gently pull again and he will feel the hook. Here,' Rusopov spread his palms on his chest. 'Because he needs friends.'

Had Rusopov known what was taking place at Western Aircraft on this same day, his assessment of Norris's likely reactions might have been different. The twenty-six shop stewards were gathered to elect a new Convenor in the Personnel Department's conference room.

'Brothers, we all know the tragic reasons why we are assembled here,' the Chairman began, 'and before proceeding to business I propose we sit silent for two minutes in memory of Harry and Fred.'

There was a murmur of assent. Ken Norris sat with his head bowed like the rest, but his thoughts were on the voting ahead. If the management hadn't offered the instrument technicians an additional 3 per cent, this meeting might have been delayed. As it was, everyone knew shop-floor resentment was inevitable. Why should a few be privileged? Even though wage claims would not usually be formulated until the autumn, this was no time for the shop stewards to be lacking a leader. Surreptitiously monitoring the second hand of his watch, he wondered if there would be any surprise nominations. If there weren't then the next five minutes ought to see his ambition achieved.

The silence was broken by the Chairman noisily shifting

his papers.

'Now, Brothers,' he said, looking round. 'No need to mess about. We could be facing tricky times. What I'm looking for, and I hope we all are, is someone who can get the most out of management. Nominations, if you please.'

'Brother Kingston.' It was the woodworking machinists' steward who spoke.

'I'll second.' Another moderate raised his hand.

Norris waited, his face set, determined to betray no emotion. It was Kingston who had unified the moderate vote by standing down last time. Would the field now be left clear for Kingston himself?

It was. The next to speak put forward 'Brother Norris' and was instantly seconded.

'Any other nominations, brothers?' The Chairman paused, scanning the room, seeing only head shakes. 'No one else? Let's have your papers then.'

Norris was on edge in spite of himself. The slips of paper were collected, the Chairman went through them methodically, then faced the group. 'Brother Norris receives fifteen votes, Brother Kingston nine. Brother Norris is hereby elected Convenor.'

Such was the blunt, almost expressionless manner of the Chairman that for a long moment Norris could not believe it had happened. Then the realization hit him. He had won. When the meeting broke up his supporters encircled him, clapping him on the shoulder.

'You were right to start that fund,' said one. 'Show we can give as well as take.'

'Mind you, Fred's family'll get fatal accident benefit.' Norris deliberately denigrated his own role. 'But assuming Regional Office approves, the fund'll make quite a difference.'

'Approve?' echoed another steward. 'This isn't just a T&G affair, Ken, this is our whole committee. Shows Fred's widow she won't have to be dependent on any handout from the bosses. It's the least anyone could do.'

By the time they dispersed Norris knew that the fund had been an inspiration, a bloody fantastic idea. The entire factory supported it, because everyone knew how tough it could be bringing up kids without a breadwinner, state benefits notwithstanding. The fund had hugely improved his reputation in the factory. Furthermore, creating it assuaged the unexpected feelings of guilt he had over the crash. For the management he didn't give a damn, the families were something else. Talking about Fred's widow reminded him painfully of his own mother's struggles.

In the evening he jubilantly squired Marion to dinner again, taking more trouble than usual getting ready beforehand. He had a new image to keep up after all, and she was appropriately impressed. That pleased him. He'd read somewhere about women finding power sexy, and now he felt it in her approving glances and the way she kissed him.

'It's an ill wind that blows nobody any good,' she remarked tritely as they settled at the table in the historic pub, restored to be half restaurant and half drinking place, copper ornaments gleaming on dark oak beams and the food served on wooden platters.

'You can say that again, love.' He looked over the big menu card. By Christ, he'd come a long way since pork pie for Christmas. Convenor at Western Aircraft! He explained to her what it meant. 'Management pay me just as if I was still on the solutionizing, but I'm on union business full time. My own office,' he grinned. 'Not that I'll be such a bloody fool as to use it much. Out on the shop floor is where I'll be. Don't want the lads thinking I've become one of the bosses. I'll be speaking for seven thousand men, Mary. I've got to keep them with me.' The challenge exhilarated him.

She readily shared his excitement, but at heart she was more interested in the welfare of the widows.

'Poor old Fred,' he said, his expression clouding. 'OK, he didn't represent the masses like we do, but I wouldn't have wished him any harm. We'll see his old woman right. She should get a thousand quid fatal accident benefit from the union, and if everyone at the works gives fifteen pence we'd double that.'

'By the way,' she asked, 'whatever happened to that man I went to see, the one living with the Chinese girl? Wasn't his name Brunner?'

Norris stiffened and had to stop himself from telling her to shut up. He was making an effective job of forgetting the Trotskyite, consigning those contacts of a year and more ago to the distant past, as though discarding them would make their significance fade. 'Haven't seen him,' he said non-committally. 'They gave him his cards in the end. He was a nutter, that boy. Someone told me he went up north.'

'The girl's in a play in Bristol. I saw it in the paper today.'

'So what?' He shrugged it off, wishing the silly bitch could understand when he wanted to drop a subject, then that thought in its turn caught him unawares. Mary hadn't changed. Still bloody marvellous in bed, pleasant and warm to have around, but there were days when he wished she wasn't. Well, tonight was going to be good, whatever. He reached out and held her hand. 'You're the girl I'm interested in, OK? Let's not hang around when we've finished.'

That night he made love to her with an intensity which surprised even himself, as though all the triumphs the world had to offer were enshrined in her body. He woke in the morning still deeply satisfied. It was only while making breakfast that he saw the copy of the *Evening Post* she had bought. On the front page a headline reared up at him.

WAS DISASTER PLANE FAULTY?

Metallurgical tests on crashed 207

Thursday morning saw the grisly excavations in the crater reach what was left of the 207's nose and flight deck. There was not much. Hitting the ground at over 500 miles an hour had reduced the structure to sticks and slivers of bent metal. Although the interior bulkhead and the galley appeared to have shielded this part from the full intensity of the fire, almost the only objects which had not disintegrated were a few flying instruments, their casings buckled, their glass gone. Miraculously one group, flattened as if by a steam-roller, preserved their pointers and showed that the two engines' power had been minimal at impact.

'So they had enough time to throttle back, then,' commented McPherson, cradling the surrealist shape of the gauge in his hand. 'Which means the engine controls were operating and it's no' likely to be a fault there.'

Donaldson agreed. The engine gauges, he remembered vividly, had been set at the centre of the main instrument panel, between the two pilots. Although nothing was immediately traceable of either the pilots' seats, or the crew themselves, it was a reasonable guess that the gap between had prevented the total destruction of the gauges. He wished he could find out if the flying controls had also been working.

While he and McPherson were patiently sorting more fragments, his bleep sounded. When he reached the caravan a Senior Scientific Officer of the Materials Department at Farnborough was on the line. They had a preliminary result on the metallurgical analysis, would he like to come over? Ten minutes later he was on the road, thankful that scientific civil servants were willing to bypass official procedure with a personal phone call. But then the RAE's staff were a special breed.

Farnborough, world famous as the venue of the air show held every second year in early September, was the main base of the Royal Aircraft Establishment and looked as though it had grown haphazardly, according to need. Hangars, workshops and offices sprawled around one side of the airfield along internal roads named after aviation pioneers. Justifiably named, because this place was almost as old as the art of flying. The black-painted corrugated-iron sheds built to house the army balloon factory in 1905 still stood near a curious metal tree, a commemorative replica of the stunted growth to which S. F. Cody used to tether the crude biplane in which he made the first officially recognized powered flight in the British Isles in October 1908.

Employed here were 5000 men and women, from craftsmen to some of the most respected scientists in Britain, men who could walk into better-paid jobs outside at any time, but did not because the work was so engrossing and important. Yet Farnborough remained obstinately reticent in appearance, concealing its technical treasures in a jumble of buildings which looked more like a site ripe for redevelopment than the largest aircraft experimental establishment in Western Europe.

Very often Donaldson's visits took him to the south of the airfield, to the graveyard hangar numbered T49, where at this moment the Structures staff were laying out the remains of the 207. But today he was escorted to the unpretentious offices and workshops of the Materials Department on the north side. After briefly paying his respects to the Head of the Metallurgy Division, a distinguished Fellow of the Royal Society, he was taken to the man who had phoned him, given a ritual cup of coffee and expected to stifle his impatience while the explanations began.

The Senior Scientific Officer reminded Donaldson of a conjuror. He had a neatly pointed beard, a twinkle in his eye, and clearly enjoyed his technical sleuthing. Last night, he admitted, he had become so absorbed in the bulkhead's defects that he had only realized it was nearly midnight when one of the security guards reminded him of the time.

'So is it metal fatigue?' Donaldson asked, though he could scarcely believe it was. Metal only cracked through 'fatigue' after countless applications of a load, far more applications than the aircraft had experienced in this case.

'Two-thirds of the cracks we examine are caused by fatigue. And superficially this is similar. Have a look at the section we cut.' The scientist slipped off the side of his desk, where he had perched while talking, and picked up a roughly rectangular piece of the wrecked panel, jaggedly riven along one side. 'Under the binocular microscope, it was easy to see where small cracks suddenly flared into one massive fracture.

The texture of the crack changes from shiny where it has been gradual to rough where it goes fast.' He tapped the thin aluminium with one finger. 'Most of this fracture was extremely fast. It took only a fraction of a second to crack four feet.'

'So there was explosive decompression inside the aircraft?'

'Almost like a bomb going off. It would have released a violent force of escaping air into the tailcone.'

'It certainly stripped off a lot of the skin,' said Donaldson. 'And severed the flight recorder leads.'

'As I explained on the telephone, we spent some time on the visual examination. Yesterday we established the period between the origin of the crack and the onset of rapid failure and were able to select some material for analysis.' He laid down the segment of alloy as carefully as if it were a work of art. 'You'll be able to see the fracture surface of the metal under the scanning electron microscope, if you come along.'

The scientist led the way down a corridor, past a bench on which Donaldson noticed shattered parts of an undercarriage leg, and into a suite of cream-painted rooms. The whole atmosphere was different to the offices. Everything was clinically neat and clean. In the centre of a small room off the others stood a large, gleaming white instrument, consisting of a squat base surmounted by a column about a foot wide, and as high above the floor as a man. It would have made a convincing robot in a science fiction film. This was the scanning electron microscope. A cathode ray tube screen was mounted beside it.

'We have been using magnifications of about one thousand on this specimen,' said the scientist. 'And this is what we're looking at.' He displayed a sliver of metal from the bulkhead, attached to the end of a slim rod. 'Taken from the onset of rapid failure.' Very gently he inserted the rod into a recess in the microscope's base, explaining as he did so. 'It has to pass through the airlock chamber. A vacuum is maintained inside.' He completed the insertion of the rod, which deposited the sample safely inside, withdrew it, then switched on the power. With a low gurgling sound the vacuum was restored. Grey images began to move across the screen.

'Won't be long,' he commented. 'Uses up to forty thousand volts. A beam of electrons excites the metal, which in turn gives off others and creates the picture.'

The image became distinct, slowly settling down. Donaldson found himself gazing at what looked like a rough stone wall, but a wall which had cracked from top to bottom, the dark fissure pursuing its course between the stones.

'Reminds me of the builder I had in last year,' he remarked wryly.

'Some people compare the grains to sugar cubes. Anyway there's the intergranular crack, which proves this was a case of stress corrosion, not fatigue. It made us suspect the heat treatment condition of the alloy.' He faced Donaldson, the satisfaction of having solved a mystery evident in his slightly puckish expression. 'Last night I completed the tests of tensile strength on a larger specimen from the panel – thank God there's plenty of it – and bang. The answer. The material in that panel is not strong enough. As simple as that. It was below specification and in a condition susceptible to stress corrosion. BSL 73 aluminium alloy should have a tensile strength of four hundred meganewtons per square metre. This has under three hundred.' He switched off the power and the picture faded.

'But for heaven's sake!' Donaldson expostulated. 'How could it have got through the factory inspections?'

'That's for them to answer.' He motioned Donaldson back to the corridor. 'We'll have more information for you in a week or two, of course. An electron microprobe analysis of the metal's chemical composition is being carried out now and we'll also be compiling tables of its mechanical properties.' They reached the office, where the segment of torn and buckled metal lay on his desk. 'My guess is that something went very wrong in the factory. As I told you, I was here till nearly midnight puzzling over it and there aren't a lot of explanations available.'

'Would you mind if I ring the Chief Designer? I don't see how this could be a design fault, but they'll have to double check.'

'Go ahead.'

Donaldson moved to a desk and made the call, having to quote the scientist's authority to the switchboard. When he did get through, he did more listening than talking. 'So a whole batch could be defective?' he asked at last. 'Yes, I'd like the panel sent straight here. To the RAE.' He put the phone down and looked at the scientist. 'The static tests at Frampton went exponential a couple of hours ago. It's the bulkhead again, but a different panel. Failed at a simulated twenty-five thousand feet.'

There was no chance of keeping the failure of the static test bulkhead secret. Wormley knew his relationship with the instrument technicians was edgy enough without demanding their silence. He therefore did the opposite, attempting to make capital out of necessity, and ordered the issue of a press release underlining the company's concern to identify the cause of the 207's crash as soon as possible.

When the Chief Designer came to him in the afternoon with the news from the RAE, which was a major step towards that aim, he wasted no time at all. He kept the Designer waiting while he barked out orders to his personal assistant.

'I want everything systematically investigated from the very beginning, from the day the metal was accepted by Goods Inward. Get the route card from accounts and check every entry on it, right through from the stores requisition to final inspection of the panels. Contact the supplier of the alloy. Test the sample that went through with the bulkhead parts. I want a report on every stage of production.'

Wormley's demands were not as draconian as they would have sounded to an outsider. One of the reasons a single 207 airliner was going to cost its purchaser £8 million was the meticulous control Western Aircraft maintained over its engineering processes.

His orders given, Wormley restored his attention to the Chief Designer.

'I presume you're satisfied there was no error in your department?' he asked in a tone which implied that if so, this was the last chance to confess it.

'We're going through all the design calculations again,' Golding assured him. 'Fortunately we had a very careful look at the forces exerted on the tail after that incident on the limiting Mach number trial.' He frowned. 'It would have been tempting to attribute the failure to that in some way, if it weren't for the new evidence. As it is, it's not easy to envisage an error. Plenty of other aircraft have employed BSL 73 specification for the pressure hull. The Trident was one.'

'None the less,' Wormley remarked harshly, 'public reaction so far has been to query the design. You'd better give consideration to ways of strengthening the bulkhead.'

'You mean make us the scapegoat?' Golding was outraged. 'When the alloy is known to be defective?'

'Don't jump to conclusions, Frank. Calm down. Now listen.' Wormley leant forward on his desk. 'This company's future depends on the 207. We're going to have two courses of action open to us. Assuming we find out why the metal was defective, we can tell our customers it will never happen again. Or we can re-design the bulkhead to further improve the safety factor, which is a more positive response. And an immediate one. We can't afford to spend months trying to justify ourselves. We have to get the flying programme going again. We have to get orders. It'll be six months before that damned public enquiry is held. We can't wait that long. If the reason for this lack of tensile strength is not identified very soon, we're announcing a re-design. So please prepare for it.

A photocopy of the route card reached Bob Burnett late Friday morning. The original was some seven inches wide and divided into columns ruled across with horizontal lines, one for each operation in the manufacture of the part. In handling it had been slightly blotched by fingermarks and these showed dark on the photocopy, but did not obscure the entries. The batch of part numbers began with F/12660. Description 'Bulkhead'. He scanned the entries. The batch had been through the solutionizing, sent to the press shop, received back, viewed. Item number 90 was 'Art Age Harden'. Number 100, following immediately below, stated 'Hardness check VP 46E'. It was signed off by Charlie Brook with the date. He sent for the inspector.

When Brook entered the small office it was obvious that he was worried.

'Have a seat, Charlie.' Burnett had long been on cordial terms with the inspector. But he wasn't going to skirt around the subject. 'Have you heard what's happened?'

'The bulkhead going, you mean? Yes, I have, Mr Burnett.'

'It's a bit more than that, I'm afraid. The tensile strength of the metal was way below specification. It ought to have failed the hardness test.'

'I wondered about that. Did I pass it?' The apprehension in Brook's voice completely undermined his normal confident manner.

Burnett pushed the photostat across the desk. 'That's your stamp and signature, isn't it?'

Brook nodded silently.

'You don't remember the batch?'

'To be truthful, Mr Burnett, no.' He peered at the date: 2 April last year. He had good reason to remember last spring, but not on account of the factory. The council elections had been in May. He hadn't only been canvassing every evening, he'd been fighting off the militants at the same time. It was in April that he discovered what Joyce and Bruce Gardner were up to. And that bastard Norris.

'You don't even recollect if the batch looked right?' Heat treatment slightly changed the silvery colour of the alloy.

Brook consulted the photostat, trying to jog his memory.

'Had the full sixteen hours, according to this. Must have been all right or I would have noticed.' He stared at the entries as, with horror, he did remember. It was around then that his impressor inexplicably went out of calibration.

'When was your impressor calibrated?' It was as though Burnett could read the inspector's thoughts. The instrument had to be checked every six months by the Quality Control Team.

'It was in calibration, Mr Burnett. I wouldn't let a thing like that slip.' He hesitated, frightened of the truth. 'But it was late spring when I found it was reading wrong.'

'What do you mean?'

'Didn't show the right value, sir. I could look it up in the records. I sent it straight down to Quality Control and they confirmed it was out.'

'Go and look it up, Charlie. Now.'

While Brook was out of the room Burnett tried to decide if he'd been holding back on what he knew, or if he'd genuinely forgotten. Either way, if the impressor was proven to be in date, then technically he had committed no offence. There were very few 'ifs' and 'buts' in the company rules.

Brook came back with his own record sheet. 'Fifth April it was, Mr Burnett. But the calibration didn't need re-doing until June.'

'And it was under-reading?' The presumption was obvious, if it had shown the metal as harder than it was.

'Yes, sir.' He couldn't keep a quaver out of his voice. 'They didn't tell me how much. Doesn't ever vary a lot, Mr Burnett,' he added weakly.

So this was what Brook had been holding back! Burnett had to dig his nails into his palms to contain his anger. If Brook had only told him! They could have brought the panels back from the paint shop, scraped a square inch clean, and re-tested.

'I didn't realize, Mr Burnett.' Brook sounded broken.

'Yeah.' Burnett forced himself to be fair. Quality Control had a share in this too. With hindsight one could see how both could have thought the other responsible. But they'd both been criminally bloody stupid.

'Why the hell didn't you say?' he asked.

But Brook sat silent. To admit he'd been tired, worried and preoccupied with local political wrangling was the opposite of an excuse.

'All right, Mr Brook,' said Burnett tautly. 'That'll be all for the moment.' He couldn't bring himself to use the Christian name again.

When the inspector had gone he rang Wormley's PA. The Chief Executive could decide what action to take next. It looked to him like a classic example of falling between two stools.

The constituency GMC meeting was set to be a walkover for the militants. Not only did they outnumber the others attending. Charlie Brook's normally healthy complexion was pale. Norris knew why, too. Rumours were all round Production Centre Three about his being interviewed by Burnett and returning to the inspector's cage looking as though he'd been given notice. Everyone knew a bulkhead panel had been proven substandard. The conclusion that Brook had been the one who passed it was inescapable and Norris had a plan for exploiting it.

When it came to the resolution supporting the disaster fund, Brook could not conceal his emotion.

'Friends,' he began, 'I don't believe there's anyone among us who can oppose this scheme. We owe it to the dead in this terrible tragedy to help their families. There's no more I can say than that. Let's all in favour show.'

Everyone present raised their hands.

There's bloody more you could have said, Norris muttered to himself, you could have admitted it was my idea. I'll make you pay for that, Charlie boy.

He didn't have to wait long.

'Comrade Chairman.' Joyce Gardner was on her feet. 'I feel there is more we can do. We can admit the support given by certain members to this fatal flight was wrong.' She looked round the room with studied ingenuousness. 'I don't want to criticize our Member when he isn't here, but I do think we should ask Norman to explain his actions at the next meeting. Was it right to risk lives in an unproven plane?'

She paused and was rewarded with grunts and murmurs of approval. 'It's one thing for the military to take chances.' The inflection she gave the word 'military' neatly expressed her hatred of them. 'If Western's wanted to promote a military project, that's who they should have asked along. Comrade Chairman, I put it to you that this flight was premature, ill-advised and – don't let's kid ourselves – downright dangerous.'

Brook flushed scarlet as she sat down to generous applause from all except a few.

'Joyce,' he said tensely. 'Many Frampton people wanted to see the 207 shown off. I did for one. If you're attacking me personally, say so.'

'I'm *not* talking about you, Charlie.' She wanted to propel the proceedings into disorder and personal exchanges were a good preliminary. 'It's certain *others* I'm referring to.' She smiled and let loose a delicately timed barb. 'We all know how you feel about the Aircraft Company.'

A titter of laughter greeted this back-handed remark. Brook's expression hardened.

'Comrades.' Norris rose immediately, deliberately not addressing the chair, but commanding attention. 'Comrades. Let's leave our Chairman out of this, shall we? You may not all know what I do about what's happening at the works. But I'll tell you one thing, the suspicions being cast on Charlie Brook are grossly unfair. He deserves everyone's sympathy and I reckon we should drop the subject until enquiries vindicate him. Let's just support the fund and leave it at that.' He sat down again as abruptly as he had risen.

The amazed whispering which followed was broken by Brook standing up, stung into furious self-defence.

'What the hell are you saying? Are you accusing me?' He

raised his fist, shaking it as Norris. 'You bloody dare repeat that outside this room and I'll have you.'

'Sit down, Charlie,' someone shouted.

'I bloody will not sit down until he apologizes. I'm under no suspicion. I want nobody's sympathy. D' you hear me!'

'Order, please!' Bruce Gardner pulled at Brook's sleeve, hissing 'For Christ's sake, Charlie, sit down.'

'OK. I take it all back.' Norris didn't trouble to stand this time and kept his voice offhand. 'If you don't want sympathy, don't have it.' He glanced round those near him and added quietly, 'But I tell you one thing, Comrades. Aeroplanes don't just fall out of the sky. Someone's negligence caused the crash and when the bereaved know who it is, they're going to want some explanations.'

Only those close to Norris heard the last sentences. That was his intention. When others asked what he had said, the remarks would become distorted and magnified.

'Can we have order?' Brook crashed his fist on the table.

'Hear, hear.' A militant jeered. 'Who lost it?'

Normal discipline was never fully recovered. The militants forced through a resolution, drafted by Joyce, demanding Norman Huntley's attendance before the next GMC. Since the wording was not in itself critical of the MP, Brook was unable to block it. When he finally declared the meeting closed, he strode out by himself into the night, his composure destroyed, his mind torn between anger and self-doubt.

12

'You could find yourself with anyone from pimps to prelates.' The phrase had remained in Kit Fairfax's memory from the early days of her training. Furthermore the prediction had proved accurate. She had once been required to call on a bishop; she had dealt over a period with the Soho pimp who lived off a civil service mandarin's mistress. Yet, curiously, she had never interviewed a Member of Parliament. Ringing the bell of Norman Huntley's modest Westminster flat, she wondered where he would have ranked in the training officer's hierarchy.

Huntley, when he opened the door, was surprised to find himself facing a woman and an attractive one at that. Somehow when the Home Secretary's Parliamentary Private Secretary had asked if he would mind talking to someone from the Security Service he had supposed it would be a man. He shook hands a little awkwardly and ushered Kit through to the sitting room, where last Sunday's papers were spread on the carpet.

'Please forgive the mess.' He started to tidy up, then thought better of it and offered her a drink. 'It's a great advantage being in the Division Bell area,' he remarked, pouring a gin and tonic. 'This isn't much of a place, but at least it saves me having to hang around the House all the time.'

Kit watched, summing him up. She already knew he was

fifty-one, a university graduate, admirer of the late Hugh Gaitskell, happily married, no scandals. She decided he looked dependable. But were his Commons questions and his remarks to the Home Secretary based on factual knowledge, or intuition, or fear because the militants were infiltrating his constituency? That was what she had come to discover.

'I hope you didn't mind Geoffrey suggesting this,' she began tactfully. Geoffrey was the PPS. This was the way DI5 always operated with dignitaries, an initial approach through a third party. It could save a lot of embarrassment. 'We were interested in the background to some of your Commons statements.'

'You're not alone!' Huntley indicated the newspapers. 'The reporters were after me all Saturday.' He picked up the *Sunday Echo*'s front page, where his own photograph was prominent. 'Look at this: "Was crash plane sabotaged, MP asks."'

'Well,' Kit asked quietly, 'was it?'

'I never even said that. They twisted my words. I said it was extremely mysterious.'

'Quite, Mr Huntley. I understand.' MPs invariably blamed the press if they didn't like the way they were quoted. 'But have you any reason to think it was sabotaged?'

'Not that I could prove.' Huntley came down to earth. 'However, let's just go over what's happening.' He began ticking off points on outstretched fingers. 'One, the campaign against the project by the extreme left, not only down in Frampton, in London as well. Two, those technicians using unofficial action to delay the only test which would have revealed the fault *before* there was a disaster. Three, using the wrong strength of metal in the first place. Western has one of the best design teams in Europe. They don't make elementary mistakes. Four,' he grunted and bit his lip.

'Yes?'

'Well, nobody likes naming names, as we say. But the new Convenor they've elected is a militant and even the local union officials don't like what's going on at shop-floor level.'

He shook his head. 'Doesn't necessarily mean anything worse than that they want Western Aircraft nationalized. Just as they want me replaced by a left-winger under the re-selection procedure.'

'And who is this militant?' She wasn't going to reveal that she already knew.

'Name of Norris, Ken Norris.' He clicked his tongue vexedly. 'Maybe I shouldn't have mentioned him. You see, he's not a Frampton man, came from north London via Derby. He's moved around too much. It's no accident he's got where he has.'

'Surely, Mr Huntley, it is precisely because there *was* an accident. A very terrible one.'

Shocked, Huntley stared at her. 'Oh, no,' he muttered. 'That would be out of all proportion. People don't . . .' He left the rest unsaid.

'In many countries they do,' she said coolly. 'They plant bombs on airliners in order to claim insurance, they assassinate rivals, they divert food from the starving. Some people hold life very cheap. Even here. It's just that we prefer to close our eyes to it.' She gestured at the papers on the floor. 'We read about killings every day, yet think it's nothing to do with us. As it happens, in this case, I agree with you. The proportions *would* be wrong. What we're pursuing is much deeper, much longer term. Your first three points, in other words. Can you elucidate them?'

Unfortunately, though Huntley had smelt a conspiracy, the sum total of his suspicions fell far short of proof. She guessed this was one reason why he had demanded a public enquiry. She left after half an hour, giving him a Ministry of Defence telephone extension through which she could be contacted.

Next day Kit reported to the Assistant Director.

'Huntley's completely genuine,' she commented, 'and not as afraid for his political life as I expected. In fact he was very objective. He gives the militants credit for believing they really do represent the masses, even though every opinion poll shows that they don't. But he knows nothing worthwhile about Norris.'

'I hope you gave no indication of our interest in the man?'

She smiled. 'I hope I wouldn't be so foolish.'

'So, we shall have to go on being patient.' The Assistant Director sighed. 'You have Norris under surveillance?'

'Two men in Frampton, and I've persuaded the owners of a house at Strand on the Green to let me use their spare room for painting in at weekends. It has a bay window overlooking the river and the pub.' She smiled. 'Luckily I *can* draw. I've presumed the RV can't be for working days.'

'A reasonable assumption. What we need most of all, though, is the method of communication. There must be a dead-letter box, or else a coded signal, a local newspaper advertisement, a greetings card, something announcing the date of the next meet. We have no evidence that Norris has either received or handed over anything.'

'If we get it, would you want him arrested?'

'My dear girl.' The Assistant Director waved a recriminatory finger at her. 'You're becoming altogether too enthusiastic. We suppose he is engaged in some form of conspiracy, but we haven't a shred of evidence that would stand up in a court of law. It's hardly a criminal offence to have a few friendly drinks with Russian officials. We need solid proof. Even when we have some, I doubt if we'd want to take him in until we have a very clear idea of what he can tell us.'

'Surely the accident investigation will provide that?'

'Possibly. Possibly not. If it gives a good pointer we might want to frighten him a little, try to precipitate an emergency contact with his masters. But arrest him? Not for a long time. Unless, of course, some new disaster appears to be in the making. Then we might have to act.'

For Donaldson the days following the 207's crash had swept past with irresistible momentum, culminating in the proof of the basic cause. Now, as his investigation entered its second full week, the tempo slowed. The AIB team had to work both backwards and forwards from the bulkhead's failure. Forwards, because the sequence of events after the cabin's decompression had to be reconstructed. Backwards, since the public enquiry would have to be told why the bulkhead panels lacked the tensile strength which the BSL 73 sheet ought to have had. He arranged a meeting with Wormley to explain this further.

The first thing he noticed in the Chief Executive's office was a model of the 207 painted in Atlantic Airlines' green and gold livery. The model, mounted on a plinth, stood prominently on the desk, as if to remind all comers that Western Aircraft was undeterred in its sales aims.

Wormley himself was friendly yet brisk, quite different to the sombre-faced, black-suited mourner at last Saturday's church service.

'I was glad you could come,' he said, motioning Donaldson to one of a group of easy charis where he staged informal discussions. 'We needed to get the emotional part behind us and we were enormously aided by your conclusions. There is nothing worse than a disaster remaining unexplained.'

'I'm afraid that what we have found out so far is a long way from conclusive.' He felt compelled to hedge. 'There are still a great many things we don't know. The detailed cause of the crash for one.'

'I'm not sure that I follow you.'

'May I borrow your model a moment?' Without waiting, Donaldson rose and brought it across to the low table. 'It's possible that the tail surfaces were so damaged from the inside by the compression that they lost the ability to keep the plane in balanced flight.' He touched the white-painted stabilizers on the model's tail with his finger. 'If the whole ten tons download on these was lost at once, or the skin simply ripped off, then brmm.' He picked up the model and upended it. 'A vertical dive.'

'Are you implying further structural failure occurred?' Wormley clearly resented the idea.

'Possibly. On the other hand, if the bulkhead collapsing

affected the control linkages to the tail, jamming the elevators down, then tremendous forces would have been exerted on the stabilizers, forces far beyond any design limitation. The tail structure would inevitably break with the same end result. But I can't prove that without piecing together more of the wreckage.' He put the model down again gently. 'It might take several months.'

'Either way it is attributable ultimately to the bulkhead?'

'Oh yes, which is why I would like to start investigating here just as soon as I'm satisfied that your suppliers were not at fault.'

'I assure you we have set the most rigorous enquiry in train.' Despite his earlier assurances of help, Wormley was on the offensive now. 'We already know that the hardness tests were done with an instrument which was out of calibration. Of course we keep samples of every component we make. Everything else passed by that inspector is now under scrutiny.'

Donaldson could see where this was leading. What the Chief Executive needed was a scapegoat and it sounded as though he had found one. But that was not the AIB's approach. 'My brief is to determine circumstances and causes,' he remarked politely, 'rather than to "ascribe blame to any person", as the statutory instruments say. It will be essential for me to interview witnesses and examine evidence here myself.' He kept his voice level and dispassionate. 'Though I'm sure your internal enquiry will save me a lot of time.'

'Whatever you wish.' Wormley frowned again momentarily, then decided to make the best of it. 'The more brainpower we marshal, the sooner we can clear the company's name. When do you want to start?'

'Straight away if it's convenient. The supplier's paperwork should give us the batch number. Once I have that, I can send a man to see them.' He rose to his feet. 'My colleague McPherson will be doing a lot of the donkey work. He's the engineering specialist.'

'He'll have all the facilities he needs.' Wormley shook hands. 'Don't misunderstand me, Donaldson. We're glad to have you here.'

As he left Donaldson reflected that the AIB's policy of speaking softly was not necessarily going to be enough with Wormley. The big stick might be needed too. Whatever Wormley said, he disliked intruders in the factory.

However, the staff at Goods Inward and in the stores proved helpful enough. The paperwork was readily available.

'We still have some of that consignment binned away, sir,' said the senior storeman. 'Would you like to have a look?' He led Donaldson and McPherson to where the sheet aluminium was kept in huge racks. 'There we are,' he confirmed, consulting the batch numbers. 'Twelve by five. I heard they took in enough for a fourth airframe, but haven't built it yet.'

The big rectangular sheet which the storeman pulled out was slightly dusty. McPherson drew his finger over the surface, across which the code L 72 was stamped in green removable paint, then felt the thickness of the edge with his thumb.

'This should be it, Jim,' he said. 'Heat treatment changes the specification from L 72 to L 73. We'd best have a specimen sent to Farnborough.'

For a moment Donaldson felt a peculiar surge of excitement, as if he had successfully traced the source of an unmapped river. The whole story had begun with an uncut sheet like this, from which the fatally flawed panel had been trimmed and pressed to shape and processed. Here was the raw material of disaster, shiny and innocent under its light coating of storeroom dust.

'We're in luck again, Jim!' McPherson was delighted too.

He came back to reality. 'Don't be too sure, Mac,' he cautioned. 'We have to find a hell of a lot more than their inspection system missed.'

But McPherson was in one of his rare good moods and wasn't to be put down. 'Never mind that, man. Find it we shall. We've more resources for a start, have we not? You'll no' deny that, I hope!'

In the evening, Donaldson drove to the Broughtons' house. He had rung beforehand and Margaret had insisted he should stay to supper. It felt strange, arriving at the cottage, knowing that Bill would not be there, when his coats still hung in the low-ceilinged hall and photographs of the planes he had flown were on the walls. One day, he supposed, she would either change things or move away. Sell up, most likely, the past can be painful to live with.

She was putting a brave face on it, though. Holding her emotion in, talking about her children while they had a drink in the oak-beamed sitting room. But he doubted if the restraint could last and thought it wiser to release the unspoken queries himself.

'We've had a lucky break, Margaret. I expect you've read the papers. Given a certain amount of journalistic licence, they're not too far off the mark. It seems to have been stress corrosion.'

There it is, she thought, the oblique reference, the concealing technicality. Like a conspiracy. Nothing about Bill dead in a Wiltshire field. She was glad she hadn't gone there. The press photos were enough.

'But why, Jim? Why?' She suddenly wanted to shout, to beat her fists on the table. 'How do they make mistakes? How? If things had gone wrong the day you were up with Bill, I could understand. If it was test flying I could understand. But this! It's stupid and wasteful and – and criminal.'

He reached her as she burst into tears and sat with his arm round her shoulders, letting her sob. Eventually she dried her eyes, apologized, sat up and poured herself a stiff whisky.

'It's having to just sit here,' she confessed. 'If only I could do something. I feel so helpless. I've been to see the two shop stewards' wives.' She still didn't say 'widows', the connotations were too bleak. 'But they have their own friends. There's a fund for them.' She fell silent. 'Thank God Bill was well insured.'

Gradually she calmed herself and then served supper.

Over coffee afterwards, she tackled something which Donaldson realized must have been on her mind all along.

'There are a lot of rumours about an inspector not checking properly, Jim. Are they true?'

'I'm afraid so. But it doesn't seem to have been his fault. The instrument he used was what they call out of calibration. In any case, as I've been telling the management, he can't be held responsible for the defect itself.'

'Then he ought not to be persecuted, ought he?'

'Certainly not.'

'Well, I think he is being. The shops stewards' wives were unbelievably bitter.' She fell silent again, biting her knuckles. 'Two wrongs don't make a right, Jim. I don't want vengeance on anyone. That won't bring Bill back. Can't you stop it?'

'I can try.' As he spoke he knew this was one area in which he was powerless. If the factory, from Wormley down to the shop floor, wanted a scapegoat, then God help the one they found.

Donaldson's appreciation was correct. As the second week after the crash progressed, the whispering campaign against Charlie Brook gained momentum. Nothing dramatic was emerging from the investigation to satisfy the desire of Frampton people, even people normally of goodwill, to identify a culprit in the mystery. The only fact to which gossip could cling was that Brook had inspected and passed the defective panels. Worse, this was neither refuted by the management nor reported in the *Evening Post*. Wormley declined to make any statement save that intensive enquiries were in progress. The newspaper risked libelling Brook if they mentioned his name in connection with the disaster. So his defence went by default.

At first, he was merely aware of being eyed and pointed at inside the factory. Next the innuendoes spread outside. An unnatural silence fell when he entered a council committee room. Conversations with old friends in the pub became strained, as though they hardly knew what to say next.

Then his wife Angie told him, crying, that their ten-year-old daughter had been taunted and insulted at school. A gang of girls had isolated her in the playground during morning break, dancing round her, chanting 'Whose Daddy crashed the plane? Whose Daddy murdered them!'

'I don't believe it,' he muttered, holding her tight, looking blankly at the wall over her shoulder, tears in his own eyes. 'The filthy bastards.'

Angie concealed from him the insults she herself was now suffering in the shops.

On Saturday, a poison-pen letter arrived, posted three days before. A foul little concoction, made up of words cut from newspapers, it also accused him of murder. He decided to stay in over the weekend. But Sunday brought the first phone call, a woman's voice, shrill and blasphemous. He tried to argue. At least this could be replied to. But she screamed abuse and rang off. Too late he thought of asking the operator to trace the call. For the rest of the day he left the receiver off the hook.

The poison-pen letter did not emanate from Ken Norris. He had less direct ways of settling the score for last Friday's challenge. Countless versions of his remarks at the meeting spread through Labour circles in Frampton, and thence percolated into the whole community. Any campaign of vilification, given so highly charged a background as a disaster, is self-fuelling. Admittedly, Joyce Gardner gave it a little prod with a not completely chance remark to her class at the school, but it was a girl who envied the Brooks' daughter's new pullover who made up the chant. Children can be remarkably cruel.

In any case, by mid-week Ken Norris had other things on his mind than the stage management of the attack on Charlie Brook.

When he came home on Wednesday he found Marion there ahead of him. She had got off work early.

'There's a letter for you,' she said. 'Looks like one of those greetings. It's not your birthday, is it?' She was curious and watched as he tore the large envelope open.

The card inside was of a kind he knew well. A crudely humourous illustration, on the front a horned devil, dancing in flames with the legend 'Have the hell of a . . .' He flipped the card open. '. . . Party.' He didn't laugh. Written neatly below was the message: 'Sending five hundred to Carol, Love, Aunt Edith.'

'I didn't know you had an aunt.' Marion read it over his shoulder. 'That's big of her, I must say! Why doesn't she give *you* five hundred? God knows, you could use it!'

He wavered, holding the card bemusedly. Mary was right. The bastards! OK, he'd told them he wanted money for Carol. Well, he did. But five hundred quid when they'd just allowed him thirty! What were they playing at?

'Where does she live?' Marion's inquisitiveness intruded on his again.

'London,' he said sharply. 'Look, love, why don't you get supper like a good girl? I want to think.'

Solitude helped little. The magnitude of £500 swirled in his brain. Bloody hell, he'd earned the money. If Carol had half, that was enough. What kind of an idiot did they think he was? Tossing it in his head, he realized that there might be another letter in Bristol. How were they sending £500, for Christ's sake? They didn't know Carol's address. There must be another letter. He would have to go to the *poste restante* again on Saturday.

Later that evening, when he had gone out to a meeting and she was clearing up, Marion was bundling rubbish into a black plastic sack for the dustmen. She noticed Ken had apparently been cutting up a newspaper. Lines and paragraphs had been snipped out. She glanced briefly at the page, then threw it away too. He must be keeping references to the factory. He'd become much more publicity conscious since he became Convenor, and he had a whole folder of clippings about the crash.

On Saturday Norris made Marion one of his customary

'union business' excuses and drove to Bristol. He took the Ford because he had a sudden curiosity to go on afterwards and see for himself where the 207 had come down. Photographs were not enough.

The weekend was the time the newly established surveillance on him was tightest. He was an easy quarry. The rain-coated travelling-salesman type who followed behind him in a car with his 'wife' had problems parking in the city centre, but Norris was taking no precautions and walked straight to the post office. When he had collected his letter and left the counter, the man hurried up to the clerk, acting on a hunch.

'Sorry to bother you, but I know that bloke and I just can't remember his name.'

The clerk eyed him suspiciously, then shrugged his shoulders. 'William Rogers. Doesn't want his missus to see the literature he gets. You one of them, too?' The contempt seemed mixed with envy, as though the clerk wished he could afford pornography himself.

'Not me!' He pretended to reflect. 'Stupid to forget! William Rogers! And I meet him often enough. Thanks.'

To his annoyance, the delay had lost him Norris. But his companion was presumably trailing the man. He returned to the car.

An hour later, after earning a parking ticket, he saw Norris come back. They then trailed the Ford out to the M4 motorway, past Chippenham and towards Castle Combe. The village was a favourite spot for weekend trippers and their first assumption was that he had a rendezvous there. But when he stopped in Yatton Keynell, they realized he might have a different purpose. Yatton Keynell was too small a place to hang about in unobtrusively, especially with a police checkpoint by the church. They let the shop steward go his way.

Norris was stopped at the barrier. The shiny orange T&G shop steward's credential card which he always carried bore the Branch stamp inside, but no photograph. Eventually a constable went to the AIB caravan and asked Langton if he could be let in.

'Don't see why not. There's little enough left anyway.'

So he was permitted to wander across the field as far as the white tape surrounding the crater, which a few RAF technicians were scouring for fragments. Although a Scammell crane was still standing by, and an RAF truck, they were unlikely to find anything heavier than a man could lift. In fact, what Langton was most concerned about were any remnants of the control linkages and hydraulic systems. There might still be tiny pieces around which, when fitted into the jigsaw of reconstruction at Farnborough, would reveal whether the elevators had been jammed or not.

Unaware of this, and shy of questioning officials, Norris gazed uncomprehending at the pit. He had expected recognizable wreckage. Why was there none?

'You from the factory?' Langton's deep voice interrupted his thoughts.

'That's right.' He turned to the inspector, nervous at his oilskins and armband.

'We had extraordinary luck, you know. Most of the plane disintegrated when it hit, but the tail broke off and that's where the clue was. Funnily enough, a rather similar accident happened in Belgium years ago.'

Alarm cramped Norris's stomach. What was he getting at?

'Surprised, eh?' Langton smiled. 'Well, it wasn't precisely the same. A Vanguard went down near Arsele after the rear bulkhead fractured. Water and chemicals had accumulated because some drainage holes were blocked and they corroded the metal. Over a long period. Quite different really. Except that in both cases the bulkhead survived.' He turned away. 'We'll be finished here soon.'

Norris retreated to his car, feeling as numb as if it were mid-winter. Peter was a scientist. Why hadn't he known what might happen? He fingered the letter in his jacket pocket. It asked him to take a responsible and constructive attitude, said that Peter would look forward to seeing him again and that he would be given the money for Carol. Bloody hell! He'd have some home truths to tell Peter next weekend. And then it would be over. Finished. With the money paid.

The third week of the investigation brought two painstaking steps forward. From Farnborough came analysis of the metal's chemical composition: aluminium a fraction below 95 per cent, copper 4·5 per cent, magnesium 0·5 per cent, and minuscule amounts of silicon, iron and manganese. In other words, it was up to normal L 72 specification. So was the sample from the store. No blame could attach to the supplier. The fault must have lain within the manufacturing processes at Western Aircraft.

In fact, McPherson was already labouring through the procedures which had converted the original twelve by five four sheet into a tapering bulkhead section, drilled with holes for rivets and the passage of wires, painted, checked and assembled.

Accompanied by a managerial assistant, he was shown how the production control office had sent a requisition to the stores, how the storekeepers had chosen an appropriate sheet and rough trimmed it with a guillotine. This particular grade of alloy did not require solutionizing before pressing into shape, so it had gone direct to the Press shop, been subjected to the 4000 tons of pressure necessary, then been trimmed again against a template by workmen using hand drills and routers. The part number – L12660 – had been etched into its surface in figures the size of typewriter capitals and it had been sent through for treatment.

This sequence of events had taken a matter of days to perform originally. It took McPherson just as long to follow through. He interviewed every man who had handled the batch, checked every paperwork entry, and could find no irregularity up to the time the batch had been taken through on a trolley to Production Centre Three. The time had come to call Donaldson in from the wider organization of the enquiry.

'It seems to me, Jim,' he commented when they met, 'that the crunch comes in this man Burnett's department. It has to. There's no further process could alter the strength of the material after the heat treatment. Cleaning and painting and drilling can't affect it.'

Accordingly next day the two inspectors began the rounds of Burnett's small empire, shepherded by the Manager himself. They started in his office.

'I have one hundred and twenty-three weekly paid here,' he explained. 'Eight foremen, two superintendents, myself, my secretary. So far as I'm concerned you can talk to any of them, any time.'

'Thank you.' Donaldson appreciated Burnett's directness. 'Do the shop stewards know what we're doing?'

'I've told them.' The way he said it made clear that if they raised objections he'd want to know the reason why. 'I don't think you'll have any trouble. On the whole they're sensible men. I'll introduce you as we go round.' He paused and made a wry face. 'Maybe you should meet the new Convenor first. I wouldn't say so outside these walls, but he's the only really militant one.'

'And what was his job?' asked McPherson.

'Solutionizing. He's the steward there – it's only two men – and in the anodizing and the heat treatment. They're all T and G, the AEWU's more on assembly and construction now. Been some rare old battles over membership. The engineer's green card isn't the passport it was. Not by a long chalk.' He chuckled, and shook his head. 'I'm a union member myself. They don't kid me.'

'You say this militant was in the heat treatment?' McPherson glanced dourly at Donaldson. He had a suspicious mind.

'Name of Ken Norris,' said Burnett. 'No fool either. Knows what the lads want. Shall we go and find him?'

Production Centre Three consisted of a series of interconnected buildings, covering a considerable square footage.

They walked through one spacious shed where long grey anodizing tanks stood in two rows, down steps, and into an area split between the solutionizing and the heat treatment ovens. Notices on the walls reminded operators of soaking times and temperatures. This was where they found Norris.

'Ah, Ken,' said Burnett. 'Couple of gentlemen I'd like you to meet. From the Accident Investigation Branch.'

Norris stuck out his hand. 'Pleased to meet you. Here long?'

'That depends.' Donaldson felt the shop steward's aggressively firm grasp, took in a lean, handsome face and calculating eyes and knew at once that this was a potentially hostile witness. 'We hope to find out why the bulkhead was understrength. It may not be easy.'

'We all know the panels shouldn't have been passed.'

Donaldson stiffened. The remark was loaded. All his intuition told him to reject it. Norris was blatantly pointing a finger at the heat treatment inspector. 'Even if that is correct,' he said evenly, 'it doesn't explain how they came to be defective in the first place.'

'Well, I can tell you one thing.' Norris stuck his thumbs through the sides of his blue overalls. 'The lads here can't be at fault. I've talked to them all.' He looked meaningfully at the Manager. 'They're emphatic and they're no bunch of fly-by-nights, are they, Mr Burnett? They take their work serious. Some blokes have been here twenty years.'

'I don't for a moment doubt it.' Donaldson could say this with sincerity because he believed it was true. 'The workers in this industry are second to none.'

For a moment Norris seemed thrown off balance. But he recovered quickly. 'Then we'll have no problems, will we? Anything I can do to help, just ask.'

'Thank you very much.' Like hell, Donaldson thought. It sounded as if he was going to make the witnesses' statements for them.

'He had to lay it on a bit thick,' Burnett said, as soon as they moved away. 'After all there were at least a dozen men listening. Don't take it too seriously.'

'I shall take no notice whatever,' said Donaldson crisply. 'Now, can you show us the sequence of processing?'

Strand on the Green was flooded. Water lapped over the pathway, depositing refuse from the river, cutting off access to the houses. Norris was forced to retrace his steps. Uncertain of the best course, he took an alley through to Thames Street and made his way into the pub via the car park behind, elbowed his way through the crowded public bar and so out to the river entrance. Men were standing on the steps, joking, watching the swirling current.

'For Christ's sake,' he exclaimed. 'How long does this go on?'

'High water,' someone told him affably. 'Give it half an hour.'

A motor boat roared past, the bow wave splashing the steps, making the more adventurous retreat.

'Rather wet, I am afraid. Aunt Edith would not like it.'

He spun round. Rusopov was behind him, thin as ever, smiling relaxedly. 'I apologize that I am late. You like a drink?'

As they went inside a net curtain stirred at the second floor window of a house a few yards away. Kit Fairfax had caught them with a telephoto lens. But she was as flummoxed as Norris by the tide. She decided she must take a risk and go down into the pub. She wanted to observe the RV, to know if they were on good terms or bad, if possible to see what was exchanged.

Rusopov fetched a whisky for Norris and a vodka for himself, even though he knew it would be a poor imitation of the genuine spirit. They had the luck to find seats at a table. No one paid them any attention, the pub was so full.

'So,' he said. 'You receive my letter? Good. How are you? It has been a long time. I am sorry you did not like Steven. He is perhaps not what the French call sympathetic.'

'He can jump in the bloody lake, as far as I'm concerned.

There are things I want to ask you, Peter. Things only you can answer.'

'About Carol, do not worry.'

'It's not only her.' Langton's words rang in his brain. 'Didn't you know the tail . . . Let's get out of here.' He gulped his whisky and stood up.

From the bar Kit saw the incipient quarrel while parrying a man who wanted to pick her up. She watched them go with annoyance. Ingram and two others were around, but with orders to fade away if there was any sign of counter-surveillance, which she was sure there would be. Rusopov wouldn't resume active running of an agent without taking precautions.

Outside Rusopov escorted Norris to a car, not the Chrysler. He was varying his tactics and set off on a leisurely drive across Kew Bridge and along Mortlake Road towards Barnes.

'My friend,' he said quietly, when Yuri's frightened tirade about the bulkhead revealing its secrets was over. 'Please bear in mind two things.' He put them in the Centre's order of importance. 'First you have performed a valuable service to the freedom-loving peoples. Second, to forecast precisely how an act of sabotage will work is seldom possible. On the whole, this worked excellently. Even if the heat treatment is identified as the cause, which I assure you would be very hard to prove, what have you done? Nothing. All that is necessary is for you to keep your nerve.' He glanced sideways at Yuri's tense face, wondering if the man was capable of enough self-restraint. Yuri wasn't the kind who would philosophically count the number of steps to the scaffold. 'You were not in the building and you tell us the Trotskyite has left Frampton,' he continued reassuringly. 'You have an alibi.'

'Come to think of it, I was with Mary. All night.'

'Exactly.' Rusopov was soothing. 'All you have to do is be a little clever. Find out what the investigator is doing. Let us know.'

'I could always block him,' he said speculatively. Industrial action would be a way of heading Donaldson off.

Rusopov deliberated briefly. 'What is the attitude of the bosses?'

'To the enquiry? They don't like it. They've a ready-made scapegoat in Charlie Brook and the sooner they're left to do a spot of re-designing, the better.'

'Could there be reasons for a strike?'

'No problem!' Norris laughed. He was on home ground here. 'Differentials. Everyone's chuntering about the technicians' rise. I could get them out tomorrow.'

'But that could also be counterproductive. We have achieved one great success. I see no possibility of the enquiry reaching the truth. A strike might arouse unnecessary suspicion.' Rusopov fell silent. He would have to consult the Centre. Although his own instincts were against, they might have plans for further industrial disruption. Also they had not indicated their long-term intentions for Yuri in the telegram. 'I will send you instructions,' he said, 'within a week. Until then, do nothing.' Suddenly he was aware that Yuri was tense again.

'I told Steven. I'm not taking any more orders.'

'That is unwise, my friend.' Rusopov did not look round because he was concentrating on the driving. 'You wanted something from me, did you not? On the shelf in front of you is an envelope. Open it.'

In spite of himself, Norris obeyed. It could only be money. He counted the notes. 'For Christ's sake, this is only two hundred and fifty! You said five hundred!'

'The other half will be given in due course.' The steel in the Russian's voice was now undisguised. 'If you display a responsible attitude.' He had turned off the main road and was near Barnes cricket ground. He eased the car to a stop, then faced Yuri, noting the shock on the shop steward's face with some satisfaction. The time had come to pull on the hook and pull to hurt. 'We must understand each other fully. You will not break contact with us unless we decide so.' He gave Yuri a pained look, as if trust was being betrayed.

'When we all labour for the same cause, it should not be necessary to say this.'

'Well, I've done what you wanted, haven't I?' Norris attempted defiance.

'And signed receipts for the payment, which are on our files. Think about that. I will send you instructions by the usual method. In emergency telephone this number.' He handed over a slip of paper. 'Memorize it.' He made Yuri repeat it several times, then took the slip back. 'You will leave me here. Walk to the right and you will see Barnes station. Take the train to Clapham Common, then Waterloo. From there the underground to Paddington. Is this clear?'

'If you say so.' Norris patted the bulge of the notes in his pocket, just to make sure, then left the car and walked away, furious and impotent.

Rusopov drove on. The KGB agent waiting at Barnes station would report on whether his orders were adhered to.

For the second time Donaldson was questioning the heat treatment operator who had handled the bulkhead panels, with Burnett again in attendance. Neither oven was in use. The pair stood side by side, empty and cavernous, each large enough to garage a small car. Beyond them, mounted on a factory wall, were the two Kent recorders which monitored the age-hardening. Inside them reels of graph paper were visible behind small glass-fronted chromium frames.

'When you switch the oven on, the recorders start automatically, is that correct?' Donaldson asked.

'Yes.' The monosyllabic answer was faintly sullen.

'And you normally leave the oven on overnight, removing the batch when you return in the morning.'

'Like I told you before!' The operator didn't like this interrogation, gentle though it was. 'I put things in, I take things out.'

'I'm sorry to sound stupid, but I want to get it absolutely clear in my mind.' Donaldson's interviewing technique was based on establishing what were normal patterns of behaviour. Once that was achieved, the abnormal stood out. Flying accidents often derived from pilots not following set procedures – turning left instead of right in cloud and ending up hitting a mountain, for example. He was becoming increasingly convinced that someone in this factory must have deviated from a set procedure. But he was meeting a solid front of denial.

'Can the Kent recorders be altered while the ovens are on?' he enquired next.

'They're locked and the key is held by an inspector,' Burnett cut in quickly. Not quickly enough.

'I want Ken here before I say any more,' said the operator. Ken had warned him they might try to trip him up. 'I want a witness, Mr Burnett. These kind of questions aren't right.' He scowled at Donaldson. 'If you're trying to accuse me of something, mister, you can bloody do so in front of the steward.'

'He's pretty touchy,' commented Donaldson as they walked away.

'Not only him. I'll have to be straight with you, sir. The lads don't like your investigation, they feel they're being branded. At first they were as keen as anyone to find what went wrong. Now they're resentful. And I can't say Norris is helping any, though to be honest I do see their point. It's they alone in the whole works who are under suspicion.'

Donaldson took a deep breath. If he was going to have a confrontation, he'd prefer it with Burnett than most men.

'There's no balking the fact that what went wrong did so in here. The analysis at the RAE showed it. But it's not the individuals I'm scrutinizing, it's the processes they carry out.'

'I doubt if they'll see it that way.'

'Then you'll have to tell them, Mr Burnett. Show them my terms of reference. I'm concerned with technical explanations, not attaching blame to people. Is Norris about the place?'

'I happen to know he's not.'

'Then let's see Brook again.'

Burnett jerked a thumb towards the cage. 'He's there now.'

It struck Donaldson at once that the white-coated inspector looked ill. He moved as though pained by arthritis and his shoulders drooped.

'I'm sorry to trouble you yet again, Mr Brook,' he said apologetically, feeling genuinely sorry for the man. 'Might I just have one more look at your impressor?'

Brook reached slowly for the small wooden box lying on his workbench, opened it and lifted out the tool. Shaped to be held in the hand, the underneath had a double-pronged rest at one end and a short circular tube at the other, from inside which projected the point of a steel needle. On the top surface was a round dial, connected to the needle. A small sticker on the side recorded the last calibration date.

'Did this go out of calibration over a period?' Donaldson demanded.

'I've asked myself that question a thousand times, sir. One day I noticed it was reading a lot below the value it ought to have shown. That's when I sent it down for checking.'

'It went suddenly, in fact.'

'I suppose it must have.' He sounded desolate and ashamed.

Donaldson slipped his hand into his pocket, produced a magnifying glass and began to examine the needle in its quarter inch tubular mount. 'You never dropped this by any chance, did you?' he asked.

'No, sir. I'm very careful with it.'

'There are some signs of damage to the housing. It seems very slightly out of shape.' He handed both the tool and the magnifying glass to Burnett. 'What do you think? It must be a pretty sensitive instrument to do the job.'

Burnett focused on it. 'I agree there are signs. But it isn't the housing matters, it's the needle. That looks right enough.'

'True.' Donaldson made a quick note, thanked Brook again and said goodbye.

The next morning, leaving for work, Brook discovered with

horror that his car tyres had been slashed. All four. A folded note was tucked under the windscreen wiper. He opened it to find the single word 'MURDERER'.

Distraught, he stood in the road, shaking, not knowing what to do. The cost of new tyres was prohibitive. If he went and told Angie now, she'd be upset all day and he would have to leave her straight away to get to work. The bus stop was half a mile away, he'd be hopelessly late. It was drizzling. He turned up the collar of his coat and began trudging down the street, the horrors he was experiencing churning in his mind.

The weeks since the first letters had been terrible. At first he hadn't wanted to tell anyone. Then, when the phone calls became frequent, often in the middle of the night, he informed the police. His number was routed through the telephone exchange, the letters intercepted. But no one could stop the innuendoes and the jibes at Angie in the shops.

At the factory he had always felt slightly isolated. Despite his prestige elsewhere, the shop-floor workers in the heat treatment were never going to love their inspector, by definition. But after the investigation moved into Centre Three, he became aware of a sustained campaign. Charlie Brook was to blame. Why didn't management sack the sod and have done with it? He'd overheard people say it.

At the bus stop he had to wait a quarter of an hour and then the first bus was only going as far as the city centre. He'd have to change. The driver seemed to crawl on purpose and when it reached the centre he was already half an hour late. He decided in despair that he couldn't face his workmates anyway. Not after yesterday's comments. For two hours he wandered dismally in the rain, scarcely conscious of where he was going. At eleven thirteen by the cathedral clock, he found himself looking down from a bridge at the wet and glistening railway lines below. A whistle sounded and he heard the rumble of an approaching train. In that instant everything fused together and gave him strength to climb the parapet. He fell two yards in front of the thundering diesel engine.

13

'I'd like a word with Mr Burnett.' The uncompromising way Norris spoke to the young secretary, a pretty girl to whom he was normally polite, boded trouble. Burnett heard and called out for him to come through in a couple of minutes. Then he methodically cleared his desk.

'Sit down then, Ken. What's the problem?'

The Convenor remained defiantly standing, feet apart as if facing an adversary in the wrestling ring.

'Well, let's have it!' Burnett was anticipating a confrontation over the AIB Inspectors.

'My lads in heat treatment want the same as those instrument technicians.' Norris spoke with suppressed anger. He had been working the men up to this mood. 'They're bloody choked. What's good for one's good for all.'

'I take it you're speaking as shop steward, not Convenor?' Burnett wanted the facts straight.

'Right. Management's created a privileged situation for those few workers. We want the same increase. An immediate three per cent or else.'

'I heard.' Burnett's expression was equally hard. 'And let me remind you any industrial action will be in flagrant breach of the agreed disputes procedure. Now I'll call the personnel department. You ought to know they handle all pay negotiations.' He picked up the phone and dialled.

'You can tell them from me we want an answer in twenty-four hours and stuff the bloody procedures. They dropped them for the technicians fast enough.'

Burnett spoke briefly, then put the phone down again. 'The Personnel Director will see you in half an hour.'

'I'll be there.'

Norris was halfway gone, when Burnett shouted after him. 'Come back.' Reluctantly he swung round in the doorway, surprised to see the Manager on his feet too.

'You know what you're doing, don't you?' Burnett was a hefty, well built man and he felt this was the moment, probably the only one, to use sheer physical presence to avert a dispute. 'If you bring your lads out, the rest will follow.'

'Top marks, Mr Burnett.' The jeering tone would have invited a punch-up anywhere else. But Burnett kept his hands resolutely to his sides.

'If they come out,' he said with all the restrained intensity at his command, 'the production schedules will go to hell and so will the American order for this plane. You're talking about seven thousand people's jobs.'

'Management may be. What I'm talking about is unfair discrimination and restoring differentials.' Norris's eyes narrowed. 'Don't try to sell us any sob story about production. There's one easy way you'll get that. Money on the table. And no farting about with arbitration either.' He turned again and departed. The other stewards in Centre Three knew what he had in mind, but he needed to coordinate tactics with them. If he started an unofficial strike tomorrow, which was a Friday, then he'd have the weekend to line up the rest of the Joint Shop Stewards Committee. He reckoned the whole works would be shut down by next Wednesday.

'That bastard Wormley's played straight into our hands, brothers,' he told them in his office. Except for victimization, pay differentials were about the most emotive subject. 'We're not going to settle easy. We've got to go all the way with this, make it official, the lot. There's no way we can let the bosses break down the pay structure we've fought for all these years.'

'Might get those bloody investigators off our backs, as well,' remarked the more militant of the two stewards from the Bonding Department.

'That's as maybe,' said Norris guardedly. 'Not that I wouldn't welcome it. Management too, from what one of the blokes overheard Burnett saying yesterday. But that's incidental. It's the rate for the job we're fighting for.'

His stand was unanimously agreed. The other unions represented in Production Centre Three would bring their members out in sympathy. Afterwards, as he made his way to the Personnel Department, he was in no doubt he could turn this into a long-drawn-out, bitter dispute. One which would so cripple Western's that, even though no mention would ever be made of the heat treatment men's true grievance, the bosses would know instinctively that the ending of the enquiry was an unspoken precondition for a return to work. As for the two inspectors themselves, they would very soon find out the facts of life if they tried to carry on. The harrassment which had driven Brook to suicide was small beer compared to the roughing up they'd get.

'We're in an extremely grave dilemma, Mr Donaldson.' The Chief Executive polished his glasses embarrassedly. It was not often that he felt himself completely trapped. As for his famous stopwatch, that intimidating trinket was firmly to one side. This talk could take all morning, if necessary.

'Unless we give in to the heat treatment workers' demands, we face a major stoppage. Possibly total closure. Equally, if we fall significantly behind our revised production schedule, we face the loss of our most important customer. We have literally hundreds of millions of pounds at stake.'

'I hope I'm not being obtuse.' Donaldson was accustomed to Wormley being direct, not oblique. 'I don't see how I come into the equation. It's hardly my affair, but I thought you had pretty well accepted that it was better to pay out two million than lose eighty.'

'We had.' Wormley flushed. 'Unfortunately your investigation affects both sides of the calculation.'

'How?' He was not sure he liked this. 'The public enquiry will put us all in the witness box. There is no way of pre-judging the court's conclusions.'

'Of course not. However, if you were to accept that there had been a failure in our procedures here –' Wormley was not quite skating round what he wanted, but not rushing out on thin ice either, 'a human error for which one man unhappily felt so responsible that he took his own life. A failure which will never recur. If you felt that explanation sufficient, then Atlantic Airlines would almost certainly accept our re-design proposals.'

'And?'

'We would be justified in buying off the industrial action.' Wormley took a risk. 'It would also be dishonest of me to pretend that your enquiry, by its very nature, has not introduced an atmosphere of mistrust in Production Centre Three, which may be a contributory factor in the trouble we are having.' He removed his glasses again nervously. 'May be. I have no proof.'

Donaldson drew in his breath. He had known pressures many times before, some blatant, some discreet like this, though it was rarely that a manufacturer offered to take the blame for an accident. Not that there seemed any possibility of Western escaping censure in this case. However, that was beside the point.

'You are asking me to say that the fault in the metal was inexplicable?'

'Our own engineers are baffled and believe me, I've had the whip on their backs. Look here, Donaldson, it was a freak situation which cannot recur. Compared to seven thousand jobs and six hundred million pounds, it's a very small matter.'

'I'm sure the organism which causes cancer is very small too. That doesn't stop scientists looking for it. This "freak" has so far cost thirty-eight lives. I'm sorry, Mr Wormley, I can't meet your request.'

'The Secretary of State for Trade may take a different view.' The Chief Executive changed his approach. He did not intend to lose this argument.

'I gave you my terms of reference a month ago,' said Donaldson coldly. 'I don't think you can have read paragraph eight. It gives an Inspector power to require any person to answer any question, to retain any document, to examine any equipment and to enter any building "requisite for the investigation". Furthermore, where a public enquiry has been instituted the Attorney-General is a party to the proceedings. Furthermore, the court. . . Shall I go on?'

Wormley shook his head. 'Our view of where the national interest lies clearly differs,' he remarked sourly. 'As far as I am concerned you can continue. But if we do end up with a strike, which God forbid, don't expect your terms of reference to get you through the picket line.'

When Donaldson had gone Wormley realized that the interview had been commendably short. The fact gave him no comfort.

Half an hour before the dinner break, the entire workforce of Production Centre Three downed tools as Norris went round telling them. 'Everybody out, lads. The bosses won't budge. This is an attack on our living standards. Come on, then. There's only one language they understand. Everybody out.'

When Wormley himself returned from speaking at a Rotary lunch in Frampton's County Hotel, his car had to be escorted in by works police. There was a picket line on the main gates and he was hissed and booed at by a group of about twenty strikers.

Irrespective of Donaldson's warnings, his first action was to telephone a Minister of State in the Department of Trade.

The week had already been a hectic one for Vic Parry, the T&G's Frampton District Secretary. He was trying to mediate in a forestry workers dispute, locally employed long-distance truck drivers had a legitimate grievance over subsistence payments, even with the help of the Branch officers under him he was busy.

On top of this routine came the appalling news of Charlie Brook's suicide. Parry was involved both through ties of personal friendship and because Brook had belonged to the staff union section of the T&G. This morning a police officer had called, enquiring into the origins of the vendetta against Brook. Only since he died had his wife Angie revealed how viciously he had been persecuted.

Finally the afternoon brought Ken Norris in person, announcing the start of unofficial action at Western's. The predominant position the firm occupied in Frampton's economy meant everything else was thrust temporarily into the background. Parry's small staff were inundated with requests for advice, while he himself had gone straight out to the factory to talk to the Personnel Department and clarify his understanding of the management attitude. He wanted to know if enough common ground existed for a settlement before the strike escalated. He was as aware as anyone of Western Aircraft's need for stability in labour relations at this time of crisis.

It was late afternoon before he was able to telephone the Regional Office in Bristol with an interim report and Huntley's customary evening visit found him still hard at work.

'We'll have to keep this short, Norman,' he said bluntly. 'Otherwise I'll be here all weekend. Norris has been busy today. To be honest, I've a feeling he's justified. In principle, if not in the speed with which he's acting.'

'I only heard it on the car radio. What are the management saying?'

'That the increase the technicians had reflects a more skilled job and is anyway subject to arbitration. They've produced some pretty hurried statistics to show how the technicians' position had been eroded – a load of bunkum in my opinion – and offered arbitration if our boss will go through agreed procedures. Norris turned them down flat.

He wants money on the table.'

'Will he get the whole factory out?'

'No question about it. There can hardly be a skilled worker in the factory doesn't feel his pay's out of line. Unless the management back down fast it'll go official.'

Huntley rubbed his chin. As always, he was tired after the long drive, and he was still deeply shaken by Brook's death. Was it his business to warn Parry of the Security Service's concern? It occurred to him that he didn't really know what they were concerned about, though he guessed it was Norris.

'Listen, Vic,' he said, lowering his voice. 'This is something we've skirted around before. Our overactive friend, I mean.' He wasn't going to mention the name again, in case they were overheard. 'We thought things might start happening, didn't we?'

'I'll not deny it, Norman.'

'A lot is going on, isn't it? The 207 disaster. Charlie blamed and committing suicide. Now a strike. Can't all be coincidence. Is the strike anything to do with the accident investigation?'

'Could it be?'

'You tell me, Vic.'

Parry thought carefully. 'Everything was fine at first, you see. The shop floor were keen to cooperate. More recently the heat treatment men began to feel victimized to some extent. Being put in the dock, you might say. Why do you ask?'

'Because the authorities have been asking me.'

'Oh, it's like that, is it?' said Parry sharply. 'You'd better keep that under your hat, Norman, or there'll be hell to pay. You know what some of your GMC think of the Special Branch! I'll try to find out. If there is it'll put a very different complexion on this dispute. Very different indeed. Completely unacceptable, that would be. A strike to stop a public enquiry!' The dramatic instincts of his chapel-going Welsh ancestry momentarily broke through and he raised his upturned palms to heaven. 'Good grief, man. That's a kind of thing I don't even like to think about.'

The house was like a hundred thousand others in Britain. Built of brick in the late 1930s, a tiled roof with a chimney at the invisible join with the companion residence, a bay window on the ground floor and a panel of coloured glass in the door.

Margaret Broughton hesitated at the green-painted gate with its chromiumed street number, observing the lace curtains on the windows and the neat flower bed in the front garden, guessing at what sort of woman Angie Brook was. She had sounded strained on the telephone, but who wouldn't when the exchange was still checking every caller? Margaret pushed open the gate and walked purposefully up the narrow cement path.

Angie Brook had prepared carefully for this visit. A tea service was laid out on the table in the front room, she was in her Sunday best grey frock, subdued and plain. She was carefully made-up, and she was in an absolute state of jitters. From her days as a secretary at Western's she remembered that the Chief Test Pilot was a kind of god. She was terrified of meeting his widow, even though Mrs Broughton had said repeatedly that she was coming to sympathize, not recriminate.

When the door bell chimed she darted out of the kitchen as though a fire alarm had gone off and quickly patted her hair in front of the copper-framed mirror in the hall before opening the door.

'I came because I felt so terribly sorry,' Margaret Broughton explained softly when the tea was made and Angie Brook had ceased scuttling round, apologizing for not having any cake, and had slowly come to realize that this tweed-skirted stranger was every bit as nervous as she was herself. 'The more I heard about your husband, the more I felt sure he was being hounded. And you mustn't ever think he was responsible for the crash. Jim – that's the investigator – told me the fault must lie with someone who worked on the metal long before your husband saw it. We simply don't understand why they made him the scapegoat.'

'I wouldn't have ever believed people could be so cruel.' Angie Brook was dabbing her eyes, 'I wouldn't really. He kept a lot of it from me, too. Like the letters.' She bit her lip, determined to keep the tears back. 'He always got a lot of post, being the chairman in the party and on the council. I never knew what people were sending until the police told me. Awful things. I found one he'd hidden away. It must have been one of the first.'

'May I see?'

Still clutching her inadequate handkerchief, Angie Brook fumbled in a cupboard.

'It was still in the envelope.' She handed it across.

Margaret Broughton noticed the Frampton postmark, then drew out the letter itself. Stuck to a sheet of cheap paper were words cut from newsprint in uneven lines, some in capitals, some in lower case.

38 DEAD! not bad for STARTERS! don't worry your FAmily comes NEXT. . . . BloodY MURDEReR

'How foul. What kind of twisted mind . . .' Margaret Broughton stopped short. Angie Brook could contain her tears no longer and was sobbing. She moved across to the sofa and began to talk, quietly and convincingly, about how to get over the tragedy. She knew, because she was learning herself.

An hour later, Angie was calm and the two women were friends. They had begun to talk about their futures, their houses, their children. Before she left, Margaret arranged for Angie Brook and her daughter to come to the cottage. She also made her promise to give the poison-pen letter to the police.

Ken Norris spent the Sunday organizing a total walkout from the factory: cajoling, arguing; in a single instance, browbeating in the name of workers' solidarity. His task, though long drawn out because he was visiting stewards at home in many parts of Frampton, was easy. As Vic Parry had appreciated, there was hardly a group of workers from any union who did not see the award to the technicians as opening the door to legitimate claims from themselves.

When Norris finally reached home in the early evening he was exultant. The exercise of power stimulated him as nothing else he had ever known.

'They're with us, love. They're all with us. We'll have a joint shop stewards meeting tomorrow and the whole works out by Tuesday. The bastard Wormley can pay or else. I'll not have my lads slandered.'

'Say that again, Ken?' Marion was in the kitchen and thought she must have mis-heard. 'Who slandered who?'

'That Investigator. Trying to pin the blame on the heat treatment. It's a flagrant attack on the lads. They're not bloody having that said about them.'

'I thought it was about pay, though.'

'So it is. They're right bloody fed up.' He came through and saw her bewilderment. 'Forget it, love. Give us a kiss.' She probably never would understand what made the world go round. He looked at the stove. 'What's for supper, then?'

'Goulash,' she laughed. 'Beef stew to you. And don't you dare complain. By the way,' she added, stirring the saucepan. 'I saw Jack Brunner today.'

'Brunner?' He was instantly alert. 'You can't have. He's away up north.'

'Well, he must have come down again. He was there in the Cornmarket as large as life, selling his wretched papers. I'm surprised he bothers. Nobody seems to buy them.' She tilted the pan. 'How hungry are you?'

It had taken the Centre a week to reply. On Monday Rusopov was informed by the Embassy cipher clerks that several cables had arrived. They knew, because the last group of five digits in each indicated the Residency as recipient. Those five digits were as much as they could decode. Accordingly Rusopov went upstairs to the room within the cipher section reserved for the KGB where a clerk with the one-time pad would unzip the messages. Each page of this cipher pad was used once only and then destroyed. After decades of use, the system was still unbeatably secure. Word by word he wrote out the text. The first cable began with the index letters 'O' for Intelligence and 'K' for Scientific and Technical. Since the Centre suffered few constraints in manpower, the telegram was little briefer than a letter. Rusopov guessed that it had been drafted by Colonel Grigoriev's assistant.

In the last mail you informed us about the taking of measures with regard to the activities of Yuri. We consider further disruption of the aircraft factory to be undesirable and liable to expose Yuri to unnecessary suspicion. You are therefore to instruct him to defer such action. We ask you to bear in mind that Yuri may be under the surveillance of the counterintelligence. We are also seriously concerned as to his motivation and loyalty. You are to send an immediate appreciation of his character and potential for the fulfilment of future tasks.

After consultation with the Major, Rusopov had a singularly terse reply encoded.

Concerning Yuri. Subject has now initiated strike against our orders. Consider him dangerously unreliable.

Although the Secretary of State for Trade had been endowed by his parents with the soft-sounding, rather theatrical name of Robin Fairlie, he was tough-minded and abrasive. He needed to be. The Department of Trade was a vast ministerial empire employing civil servants throughout the country and consuming an equally vast budget. Fairlie was heavily engaged in trying to prune this expenditure and taking a worried interest in the £300 million the Industry Secretary had allocated to Western Aircraft. When the junior Minister reported Wormley's phone call, he decided to interview the accident investigator himself. After all, the AIB was answerable directly to him and he was thoroughly disturbed about events at the factory.

*

Accordingly, when Donaldson and the Chief Inspector presented themselves at the head office near Westminster Abbey they were ushered straight through to the Secretary of State's inner sanctum. Fairlie did not beat about the bush. They had barely shaken hands when he asked if there was any justification for Western Aircraft's protests.

'Go ahead, Jim,' said the Chief Inspector. 'You're the man on the spot.'

'I fully understand that they would like to put the bad publicity behind them and resume production,' Donaldson said carefully. 'But such considerations are totally irrelevant to the public enquiry.'

'This unfortunate fellow letting the defective part through is not an explanation of the crash?'

'Emphatically not, Minister.'

'There must have been a failure in the manufacturing process,' explained the Chief Inspector.

'We've begun to meet some hostility from likely witnesses,' Donaldson added.

'So I heard.' Fairlie leaned forward on his desk. 'Well, gentlemen, I never doubted that you have been acting correctly. I shall tell Western Aircraft there is no precedent for interfering with a public enquiry and that anyone at their factory who tries it will find themselves in considerable trouble.'

'Thank you, sir.' The Chief Inspector prepared to leave.

'One moment. I'm not finished. Have you any reason to believe this strike is such an attempt? You have not?' Fairlie's strong face showed a flicker of surprise. 'I think you ought to know that the Security Service is making enquiries of which the management is not aware. It is highly confidential. Obviously their presence is no reflection on your own abilities.' He stood up. 'Thank you for coming. You have my fullest backing.'

As they walked back along Victoria Street to Kingsgate House, Donaldson remarked gloomily, 'So I shall have the spooks breathing down my neck as well.'

'Could there be sabotage involved?' the Chief Inspector asked. 'Fairlie must know more than he told us.'

'I very much doubt it.' Donaldson was not a believer in plots. 'I suspect the answer is simple negligence which whoever was responsible wants covered up. Anyway, I'll be in there again tomorrow, strike or no strike.'

Tuesday was a perfect summer day, a few puffy clouds sailing in a blue sky, picture postcard weather. Some of the strikers picketing the factory were in their shirt sleeves, others sat along the low decorative wall which flanked the main gates, sunning themselves. A few policemen were grouped around a minibus a short distance away. The first morning of total stoppage had a leisurely and good-natured air about it. None the less when lorries drove up with deliveries, the drivers without exception backed their loads away again.

Donaldson arrived from London shortly before eleven, stopping his car obediently when a burly man in a checked shirt and jeans raised his hand.

'What are you after, mate? Can't you see there's a strike on?'

'I'm on a visit to the management.'

Another picket came up, whom Donaldson recognized as one of the heat treatment operators. 'It's the investigator,' he said in a nasty tone. 'He's the man.'

'You'd do better to keep away,' said the check-shirted picket. 'We're asking you not to enter, see.'

A policeman, hovering a yard away, came forward. Donaldson showed his AIB card.

'OK, lads.' The policeman turned to the strikers. 'He's on official business. Let him through, please.' He spread his arms wide and waved them back. 'You've had your say. Let him through.'

Inside the factory two works police hastily unbolted the gates and swung them open. Donaldson drove in, catcalls pursuing him. He was more puzzled than alarmed. West Country voices were distinctive and the check-shirted striker's accent was not local.

To his relief he found McPherson already closeted with Burnett.

'Any problems getting in?' Burnett asked.

'Not really. Slightly unpleasant chat with a man in a check shirt.'

'Sounds like the same charming character I encountered,' Mac commented. 'Bob here says he's not employed in the works.'

'I'd say a quarter of the blokes out there aren't,' said Burnett. 'A few may be students from the university. The heavies aren't locals at all. They're not here by accident either. First time we've ever had this kind of thing.'

'Well, Mac and I have other concerns.' Donaldson dismissed the subject. 'I've been thinking, could we go through the procedures of the heat treatment ourselves? I'm sure the answers we're seeking lie in the routine.'

Burnett suddenly broke out laughing. 'I like that,' he said, chuckling. 'I like that a lot. You know something, if you or I or McPherson here so much as laid a finger on one of those machines the whole workforce would walk out. Quick as a kiss your hand.'

'And since they've done just that, what's to stop us?' McPherson asked.

'That's the joke.' He chuckled again. 'They've just themselves made it possible. They'll still raise Cain when they hear about it, mind.'

'They can take their complaints to the Attorney General,' said Donaldson tersely. 'Let's get on with it.'

Production Centre Three was a ghost, a film set with no actors. The ventilators still gave their dull roar, the lights were on, the long iron tank for the solutionizing was still kept hot. 'I'm not letting him cool down,' Burnett commented. 'Let those salts go solid and you need a pneumatic drill to get them out.' But the machinery was idle, nothing moving except the solitary figures of the foremen, carrying out essential maintenance.

'Tell you something,' remarked Burnett cheerfully as he placed a test piece of L 72 alloy inside one of the treatment ovens. 'What I miss most about this job is not handling things myself any more.' He straightened up. 'One thing we've forgotten, though. This should have been degreased before age-hardening. Want to do that?'

'Is it essential?'

'Should be done. If I'm showing you procedures I'd rather show you procedures right.'

'Fair enough.' Appreciating what a stickler for accuracy Burnett was made Donaldson wonder yet again had anything gone wrong in his department.

The Manager dipped the test piece in the trichloroethylene tank, inspected it, then placed it back on a rack in the centre of the huge oven, where it looked absurdly small.

'Now,' he said. 'Press that button.' Donaldson did so and the vertical door slid slowly down into place.

Burnett moved the couple of yards to the console. 'Set the temperature you want. One hundred and ninety for L72.' He pointed. 'Switch on. Note the time. Your recorder trace will begin immediately.'

'You work the controls now, Mac,' Donaldson said. As McPherson obeyed, he watched the roll of graph paper behind the eye-level window on the recorder. A delicate metal arm projected over the paper, which all but imperceptibly began to move. Then, as the oven warmed, the stylus at the end of the arm started to print a series of small dots, slowly curving out to the right because the temperature scale ran left to right.

'Do you want to wait?' Burnett queried. 'It'll take maybe half an hour to heat.'

'I'll stay.' Donaldson continued his observation. 'Is there any means of turning the oven off without stopping the recorder?'

'None whatsoever.' Burnett tapped the chromium frame with its circular built-in lock. 'Nor can the operators open this. The inspector has the key.'

'Are the inspectors working?'

'Are they hell.' Burnett's expression became grim. 'You talked just now about the Attorney General. Even he can't bring Charlie Brook back. What can be done to one can be done to others. They're frightened men, Mr Donaldson, and I don't blame them. If I didn't know how to look after myself, I might be too. I tell you, things are happening here that never did before.'

'And who else has a key?' Donaldson refused to be deflected from his train of thought.

'Only the pyrometry men. They service the recorders.'

'Oh!' Stupid of me, he thought, obviously somebody has to. 'When do they do that?'

'Have to be tested every nine months. The date's there.' Burnett consulted a tiny paper sticker on the frame. 'This one's due for validation before 21 August.'

'I see.' But the information took him no further. He went on watching the thin arm, the procession of dots curving up, certain that they must hold the clue he wanted.

'Are the old graphs kept?' he asked.

'Most definitely. The management inspector will have them. He's here all right.'

'Then I know what I'd like.' If he couldn't get there by intuition, he'd damned well get there by plodding. 'Can you obtain all the recorder traces from the oven which treated the bulkhead? For a month before, and right up to last week. Tomorrow we'll compare them, together with the one we're making now.'

'I'll do that, certainly.' Burnett hesitated. 'We haven't started this one at a good time, though. If you stick to sixteen hours that means turning off at three thirty tomorrow morning. Only the works police are around then.' He shook his head. 'Now if there were a night shift, we could have asked the pyrometry to do it.'

Donaldson quivered. 'Are they on the night shift?'

'There're always a couple on, in case anything electrical breaks down.'

'There's nothing routine they do with the ovens?' He was kicking himself for his own idiocy. Here was a dimension he had totally missed. Everyone he had interviewed hitherto had spoken of putting the part in during the afternoon and taking it out in the morning. What lay between had sounded completely automatic. However, Burnett's answer was discouraging.

'Not really. The pyrometry would only step in if something stopped on an urgent job. Normally the Night Superintendent would report a breakdown and it would be dealt with next day.'

So that led nowhere either. He'd have to interview the pyrometry staff, though. It occurred to him that he'd like to see the factory at night anyway.

'Would you be prepared to bring me in at three tomorrow?' he asked. 'I know it sounds crazy, but I want to run through a complete cycle of this process myself.'

'I suppose so.' Burnett didn't relish the prospect. Then he remembered Wormley's order this morning. Anything the inspectors wanted they were to have. 'I'll pick you up at your hotel,' he said. 'That'll be the easiest.'

'And do you want me, too?' McPherson had been quietly listening all this time.

'Not unless you feel like it, Mac. You'll have plenty to do comparing those graphs tomorrow.'

'Then I'll thank the Lord for small mercies.' He smiled dourly.

When he left in the afternoon Donaldson, to his surprise, was asked by one of the pickets for a lift into the town. He agreed with slight reluctance, remembering the catcalls of the morning.

'Nice motor you've got,' the man commented as Donaldson drove away. He was a thin, sardonic-faced youth of perhaps twenty-three. 'Had it long?' He sounded like an East End Londoner and there was an unpleasant twist in the way he spoke which prompted Donaldson to keep his reply brief.

'A year.'

'Be sorry to lose it, would you?'

'What exactly do you mean?' He could feel the skin on the back of his hands prickling.

'Take it back to London, I would. In your shoes, that is. Tell you that free, for nothing. Stay there myself too.'

Donaldson glanced in the driving mirror, saw there was nothing close behind, braked and pulled into the kerb.

'Are you threatening me?' he demanded curtly.

The man looked at him coolly. 'You might say that, mister. Yes. Or you might just call it friendly advice.'

'Get out!'

The man stretched himself languidly. 'Now I'd call that rude. Downright impolite. Still, seeing as you're an older man, I'll forget it.' He opened the car door with studied slowness and descended, then, still holding it open, surveyed the interior. 'Pity to spoil a nice new motor like this, I must say.' He shut the door with unexpected care and strolled away.

Furious, Donaldson went straight to the central police station. The Trade Secretary's suspicions might be justified. Intimidation was out of character in the aerospace industry generally and although Frampton wasn't quite the paradise its more virtuous citizens pretended, it was equally no Merseyside or East End. There must be a reason for the heavies being brought in.

During the evening he had a visitor at the hotel. Colonel Daly announced himself and came up to the room where Donaldson was preparing to catch a few hours' sleep. He accepted a whisky.

'How are things?' he asked.

'So, so. Things, as you call them, are a little rougher than I expected.' He related his afternoon's experience.

'And you still don't believe in plots?' Daly sampled the drink appreciatively. 'Nice scotch. Well, that's not what I came to talk about. You may recall I was making a few enquiries myself. A foreman who retired recently has told me a curious story. Apparently at the time this bulkhead was being manufactured there was an extremist working on the night shift who tangled with the management and finally got himself fired.'

'What was his job?' Donaldson felt he didn't need to be told. 'Pyrometry?'

'How the hell did you know?'

'I didn't until today.' Donaldson relented from his own self-discipline and poured himself a whisky. 'Then I discovered the night-shift pyrometry men hold keys to the recorders which monitor the heat treatment.'

'Precisely what the foreman said.'

'Anything more?'

'Not of substance,' Daly conceded. 'Except he was always causing trouble. He had a real thing going against the bosses.'

'Doesn't prove anything, does it?' Donaldson sipped his whisky. However, we'll be that little bit more meticulous when we go through the recorder graphs tomorrow. What was the fellow's name, by the way?'

'Brunner. Jack Brunner.'

'Thanks for the tip.' He decided to change the subject. 'Come to any decisions at your end yet? Since you mention it, the bosses are pretty worried about you too.'

'We still like the airplane, Jim.' Daly himself became defensive. 'It's just that Johnson doesn't like excuses, which is really all Wormley has on offer. I thought re-design would do the trick. It hasn't. Johnson really does want to know why there was a crash.'

'Don't we all?'

'You rule out some kind of sabotage?'

'I'll believe it when it's proven.' Donaldson didn't want a discussion on Daly's favourite topic of reds under the bed. He was too anxious to get into his own. He asked to be excused.

None the less, lying awake after the American had gone, he found himself forced to wonder.

His alarm clock woke him at two thirty. He dressed and went downstairs to the deserted lobby, where the hall porter was asleep on a chair behind the desk. Burnett arrived punctually, dressed casually in sweater and slacks. But Donaldson had decided he could perfectly well drive himself back afterwards. He was concerned about the imposition. He told the Manager he would follow in his own car.

'They're banning all vehicles now,' the Manager said. 'We'll go to the car park.'

They arrived comfortably before three and found the few pickets on the secondary entrance half asleep. A makeshift brazier, lit to keep them warm, glowed steadily. One man woke, did not dispute their entering, but was evidently surprised, though hardly more so than the factory police who had to let them into the locked buildings.

The rows of silent machines, the neon brightness unsoftened by daylight, the echo of their own footsteps, all gave Centre Three an eerie quality. Donaldson checked that the recorder was operating. The line of dots ran unwaveringly up the graph paper along the 190° line. Then he switched off the oven.

'There you are, sir,' Burnett said with slight acidity. 'I hope it was worth a night's sleep.' His wife had told him she thought the whole thing utterly ridiculous and he was inclined to agree with her.

'Very different from daytime, isn't it?' Donaldson commented. He could imagine a temperamental person being affected by long-term night shift employment.

The policeman accompanying them coughed discreetly. He could see no point hanging about in the unheated factory when there was a warm guardpost waiting.

At twenty-five past three, they left the gate and strode rapidly towards the darkness of the car park. Ten yards from their cars, Donaldson realized they were not alone.

'What the hell are you doing?' shouted Burnett, running forward.

A thick-set figure, barely more than a black outline, rose up from behind one car, dodged round it and launched himself at Burnett, swearing. In the same second, two others set on Donaldson. He held one off, was hit savagely on the side of the head, but as he stumbled he managed to grasp the whistle the police had given him that afternoon. As he blew it, a savage kick landed in his stomach. He rolled over to protect himself, rasping his palms on the tarmac, hearing shouts from the guardpost, thinking how useless he was in a rough and tumble.

Two yards away, Burnett was wrestling with the bigger man. He threw him successfully and plunged down on him, yanking one arm behind his back so violently that the man cried out. For an answer he got Burnett's knee harder in the small of his back.

Boots pounded across the tarmac. Donaldson, excruciatingly winded, was struggling to his feet, warding off blows with his arm. Suddenly they ceased as his assailants bolted.

'Are you all right, sir?' A policeman was bending over him, hands lifted him up. He stood unsteadily, put his fingers to his head, felt it wet with blood. He couldn't speak and immediately had to bend over to ease the pain.

They took him back to the guardpost, where the burly man was handcuffed. In the light, Donaldson recognized him as the picket with the checked shirt, though now he had on a dark blue donkey jacket as well. He sat, tight-lipped and sullen.

'At least we got one of the bastards.' Burnett was bleeding too, but there was a look of deep satisfaction on his face. He turned on the picket. 'So what's your game, my lovely? Slashing our tyres, I s'pose.'

'Scab!' The man spat out the word. It was all he would say.

A few minutes later two patrol cars arrived, sirens wailing. The remaining pickets watched them, white-faced. Burnett advanced menacingly on one he knew. He was toweringly angry.

'So what kind of bully boys d'you think you are?' he shouted in the man's face. 'We fought fair when we were at school, didn't we? What kind of a filthy little rat have you become since we all grew up? Answer me that, will you? Or are you too frightened of the bloody militants!'

The man recoiled, looking at his fellows for support, finding none. Then he shook his head as though dazed.

'I'm sorry, Bob,' he managed to mutter. 'We didn't mean it to be like this.'

'And I'm glad to hear that. You should be bloody ashamed of yourselves.'

As he walked away the man followed and said something inaudible to the rest, then returned to sit by the brazier.

Burnett crossed to one of the patrol car drivers. 'Can you give us a lift home, d'you think?'

'We'll take that one to the station first.' He indicated the prisoner.

'That's fine by me, friend. That's completely OK by me.'

In the event the cars split up, one driving Donaldson to Frampton Hospital's casualty department. He was only badly bruised, but they kept him in for what remained of the night.

'The dog always returns to its own vomit.' The Assistant Director indulged his infuriating habit of cracking his finger knuckles. He was in good humour. 'I'm surprised Norris didn't go to the scene of the crash before.'

'Compared to what's coming in now, that's rather old news.' Kit Fairfax was pleased too. The year and a half of surveillance was yielding a harvest at last, and a rapid one. 'We intercepted a letter, presumably from Rusopov.' She handed across a photocopy.

We are alarmed at your actions. These contravene instructions and action should cease. Peter.

'The odd thing is,' she added, 'he hasn't collected it yet.'

'The strike may have kept him busy,' the Assistant Director suggested wryly. 'I also have news for you, Kit. The AIB inspector has been beaten up. The time has come for you to move to Frampton. It might even be worth giving Norris a fright if he's at loggerheads with his masters. See which way he runs.'

'If you've no objection, I'd rather try the girlfriend first. She may know more than she realizes and if we do scare him he might shut her up. I'd like to catch her off balance.'

'Well, it's your case. Do as you think best.' He cracked his knuckles again, reflecting that if juniors weren't given their head they could never emerge as seniors. But it spoilt his mood to be reminded of retirement. There might be rather few spies to catch in a Hampshire village.

The call from the police was no surprise to Vic Parry. He had been told about the night's events by telephone at breakfast time. What did take him aback was when a local Chief Inspector arrived at the office and introduced the man with him, who was in an ordinary suit, as Chief Inspector Colin Sturgess of Scotland Yard's Special Branch.

'Nice of you to see us,' said Sturgess affably. He was on his best behaviour. The Frampton Special Branch consisted of only two officers. None the less their decision, made after Donaldson's complaint, to bring in Scotland Yard had not been lightly taken. The growing ramifications of the strike forced them to it. Scotland Yard owned both greater expertise and the computerized Special Branch records for the whole country. Already this morning these had revealed that Donaldson's attacker was known to the police in Birmingham.

'You're treating this as something more than local, I take it,' said Parry, pausing to call to his secretary for coffee.

'There are a number of dimensions to it,' Sturgess acknowledged.

'Let's start with what I know about, then.' Parry didn't like rushing his fences. 'You've arrested a picket?'

'He's been charged with assault,' said the Frampton officer tersely. 'We're holding him in custody. There will be more serious charges later.'

'What the hell was he doing?' Parry exclaimed.

'Attempting to sever the brake cables on the accident investigator's car.'

'Interfering with vehicles is an old trick of his,' Sturgess added. 'Done it before. He's pretty much of a professional thug.'

'And he's one of our members?' Parry didn't like this.

Conversation stopped while the girl brought the coffee in.

'Out of work at present. Here's his union card.' The Frampton officer handed it across.

Parry examined the contribution record. It was only a couple of weeks in arrears on the reduced amount due during unemployment. He noted the man's name, Clark, and gave the card back.

'He'd be calling himself a flying picket, I imagine,' he commented.

'The other charges,' said Sturgess, 'will arise from trying to obstruct the proceedings of a public enquiry. It's a serious offence.' He sipped his coffee. 'I'm told it's unusual for the thugs to move in on an aircraft industry dispute.'

'True.' Parry could not deny it. 'But the dilemma we're in is that this is unofficial. I can only bring union discipline to bear if we make it official.'

'And will you?'

'Be better all round, it would. This differential lark is a legitimate grievance. If we get it official, I may be able to influence the lads to accept arbitration, which at the moment they're refusing flat to consider.'

'In other words, they want a strike rather than a settlement?' Sturgess suggested.

'Hold hard.' Parry wasn't letting that assertion pass. 'Management hasn't given them much option. No one in their right mind wants a strike. If they don't like this one, any five per cent of the branch's membership can summon a meeting.' He picked up the small greenish blue T&GWU rule book lying on his desk. 'Rule twelve, clause seven.' He showed it to Sturgess. 'I will admit, quite a few members are disturbed by the violence. I've had a lot of calls this morning.'

'Lucky one of them tipped the Manager off not to use the cars,' commented the Frampton officer. 'Someone could have been killed.'

'Bloody daft thing to do.'

'Not daft, Mr Parry,' Sturgess cut in. 'Deliberate.'

'Well, I'll go out there this afternoon and try and make them see sense.'

'I take it the overall organizer is Norris?' Sturgess asked.

'He's the Convenor.' Parry felt a sense of alarm. 'What do you know about him?'

'Not enough,' said Sturgess succinctly, following it up with a statement which was technically correct, if misleading. 'He has no police record. We should very much like a specimen of his fingerprints.'

Parry drew in his breath. 'He's an important elected official of this union,' he said. 'I don't think I can do that without very good reason.'

The Frampton Chief Inspector reached for his black briefcase and took out a transparent plastic folder. Inside it, opened flat, was the poison-pen letter Angie Brook had recently found. Without a word he handed it across.

'Did Charlie get this?' Parry was appalled.

'He did. It was the first. We believe Norris began the campaign against Brook. We want to know if this came from him.'

'In that case, I can help. Anonymous letters are one thing I can't abide and I get plenty of them, I can tell you.' Parry went out of the room and returned a moment later with a normal letter. 'This was from Ken. At least it may clear him of suspicion. For goodness sake, he's ruthless in some ways, but not evil.'

'I'll be in touch,' said Sturgess, inserting the letter carefully in a large envelope. 'If you've no objection, I'll bring this back myself.'

The scene outside Western Aircraft had changed by the afternoon. The atmosphere was tense instead of relaxed. The police presence had swelled to thirty, they had a control van and, far from standing back, constables were now actively guaranteeing a passage for visitors through the picket line, albeit allowing the strikers to put their case peaceably. Cars were being admitted again.

Parry's impression was that his members were unhappy, yet determined to stick to their guns.

'Listen here, Vic,' said one, epitomizing a general consensus. 'We don't reckon 'tis fair. What they technicians do have, we should have, and that's all about it.'

Others crowded round, assenting. But there was something else he wanted to be sure of.

'What was up with this investigator then?' Parry asked. 'Where's the sense in beating him up? All you're doing is give us all a bad name.'

'That were a bloody mistake, Vic, to be honest. Reckon he were only doing his job, after all.' The man looked round him cautiously. 'Too many outsiders here if you ask me. Solidarity's one thing, bloody hooliganism's another.'

Parry was left in no doubt that these opinions were the true voice of his members. He went in search of Norris, finding him in a transport café nearby, where he was consulting with a small group over cups of tea. It was immediately obvious that this was a militants' conference.

'Hello, Vic.' Norris welcomed him none the less. 'Come and join us. Comrades, this is Vic Parry, District Secretary. Fetch him a cuppa, someone.' He grinned. 'Couldn't have come at a better time. We were just talking about getting this dispute official.'

'I've sent a report to the Regional Office. Could take a few days,' Parry temporized.

'Today's Wednesday,' Norris persisted. 'Can you do it by Monday? We've got to show the bosses this is dead serious. We've got to bloody show them we mean business.'

Norris was swearing less than usual. Parry suspected he was playing the statesman.

'You don't think we can negotiate a settlement?' he said. 'I've a feeling management could be talked round.'

It was as though he had propounded a heresy.

'We're not bloody falling for that one, mate,' said a man he had never seen before. 'No one's letting the bosses walk all over us.'

'What's your job?' he asked quietly.

There was a momentary silence.

'Long-distance driver.'

'Listen, brothers.' Parry spoke with all the emphasis he could muster. 'This dispute's about heat treatment operators' differentials, right. Or isn't it?'

'We're not bloody having that f... ing investigator back,' muttered another, but was immediately silenced by Norris.

'We want money on the table,' he said harshly. 'No promises. No arbitration. Money on the table.'

'Which it's my job to help you get,' said Parry unequivocally. 'Even so, Ken, my advice is, you've a legitimate claim, but you may have to bend a little. There's no bucking the fact that the technicians did accept arbitration.'

The militants' faces told him enough. They didn't want to hear this. 'I'll see you, Ken,' he said. 'Come to the office soon, will you? Thanks for the tea.'

He left the café, profoundly disquieted. So the militants were riding on the back of the rank and file's grievance. Furthermore, he had a suspicion the strike *could* be about Donaldson. Norris had been altogether too quick shutting up his colleague. And if that was the underlying cause, there was no way he could recommend making the dispute official. By instigating a strike under false pretences Norris would be guilty of conduct contrary to the interests of the union. Rule eleven, clause nineteen. The financial penalty was negligible. 'A sum not exceeding £10.' The real punishment would be administered by a special committee: withdrawal of his shop steward's credential, possibly loss of membership altogether. If he was guilty. But why should Norris want to do such a thing? Parry could conceive of no adequate reason.

McPherson had rolls of graph paper draped everywhere in a spare office. Once the morning's drama was over, and he had seen Donaldson discharged from the hospital with orders to rest for forty-eight hours, he had come to the factory. The police had escorted him through the picket line and he had set about his task with unrelenting energy.

Sorting the graphs had been wearisome too. Heat treatments varied. However, by the end of the afternoon he had a representative sample of L 72 traces and they all followed a pattern. The dots climbed slowly to the peak temperature and, although their line was seldom completely straight, it wavered only fractionally over the whole period. Last night's test confirmed this consistent performance. But, as Donaldson had guessed, the graph from the fatal evening bore two distinct aberrations. The line was kinked twice, once after six hours of treatment and again nine hours later. Anxious to confirm the unusualness of this trace, McPherson had been through a further sample of graphs. None had similar aberrations. He took the crucial roll of paper along to Burnett.

'Something happened,' he said. 'Can you tell me actual timings?'

The manager had the route card for part F 12660 locked away. He brought it out. 'Age hardening began at 3.30 p.m.'

McPherson ran his finger over the paper. 'The first kink must have been formed around 9.30 p.m.,' he said, 'the next at 6.30 a.m.'

'Half an hour before the night shift ends,' said Burnett grimly. 'And the first was soon after it began. That's too much of a coincidence. We'd better find out who was on.'

'Would you mind if I telephone the news to Jim?' said McPherson happily. 'It's the best medicine he's likely to be receiving today.'

Jack Brunner had joined the pickets. His desire to join in was too strong to resist, just as the urge to return to Frampton had been when he read about the crash. Caution warned him to keep away, a kind of pride drew him on. As he had a job by day, he could only do picket duty at night. He was welcomed. There was always a shortage of volunteers in the evening.

Norris's insistence on a twenty-four-hour-a-day blockade was proving hard to fulfil adequately. No one felt like saying so, but the strike was already losing support. The attack on Donaldson had made headline news even in the national media.

Lounging round the brazier, warming their hands as it grew dark, the pickets gossiped, argued politics, discussed the strike. Some squatted, one or two had acquired chairs from the rubbish tip where they found wood for the fire.

'Those f...ing investigators are still nosing around,' remarked a militant. Only the activists turned up at night.

'One is, you mean. The other met with a little accident, didn't he?' There was a guffaw of laughter.

'I heard Joe Clark'll get sent down for five years minimum,' said another. 'They've thrown the bloody book at him.'

'What are the investigators up to?' Brunner asked cautiously.

'Taking the heat treatment recorders apart, they say.' Plenty of information filtered out of the factory. 'That Scots bloke's been going through all the graphs today.'

Brunner shivered and fell silent, memories of the night last year fermenting in his mind. Could they pin anything on him? He'd been on the shift, they'd know that. Trying to calm himself, he leaned against a wall and recounted everything he could remember. The graph had shown a quiver or two. No one had noticed it at the time, though, or they'd have been asking questions then. Fixing Charlie Brook's impressor. They hadn't caught him with it in his hand. But he had been reprimanded for being in the cage. He found himself shaking violently. They'd written a memo, the Superintendent had shown him it when he was disciplined. The memo must be still there, the only evidence that he'd been up to anything: forgotten, but on the files, a bomb waiting to be set off.

'You OK, Jack?' One of the others had noticed he was upset.

'I'll just get myself a cuppa across the road.' He rose stiffly to his feet and left them.

Sitting in the café, his feet warmed, the hot tea reviving him, he decided what he had to do. Steal the memo. He knew where it was. The Superintendent's office only had one filing cabinet. What's more, he'd have to do it now, right away. Tomorrow might be too late.

Instead of returning to the gate he walked along the factory fence to a spot he'd noticed earlier where a pub backed onto the factory grounds. The fence on top of the wall there was already broken and, as he had hoped, the whole area was in deep shadow. He looked around, saw no one, and scrambled up.

Security in large factories is difficult to maintain, especially when buildings are old. Brunner made his way cautiously, keeping out of the pools of light from lamp standards, dodging round corners if he heard noise. Halfway to the pyrometry section in the quality control offices he had to hide behind a container when a pair of works police strolled by, flashing their torches into corners. He kept telling himself he could take it easy, he had time.

Sure enough, the window which always used to be loose still was. He prised it open and wriggled across the sill. Inside the rooms were unlocked. He quickly reached the Superintendent's small office, with its linoleum floor and battered desk. The filing cabinet stood against the far wall. It wasn't locked either. He began patiently going through the files, having to take each one out and hold it to the little available light in order to distinguish the title. The twelfth was the one. Disciplinary proceedings. He laid it on the desk, but the memos themselves were impossible to read.

Risking everything, he struck a match, shielding it with his body, flipping through the contents with one hand. The match flickered out. He lit another. There it was. Headed 'Brunner' and relating the details. 'During the night shift this worker was found . . . etc.' He folded it and shoved it into his donkey jacket pocket, replaced the file and was edging the drawer shut when a torch shone straight on him through the window.

'You! What the hell are you doing?' He could hear the shout, but not see the person. 'Run round the door, Ted. Quick.'

He stood frozen in the beam of light, then recovered his wits and dashed out of the room, only to collide with a policeman in the passage.

'Got you, my lad.'

He felt his arms wrenched back and pinioned, struggled, kicked, but knew he was caught.

Light flooded the corridor.

'Well, I never,' said a voice he knew. 'If it isn't bloody Brunner.'

14

Donaldson woke on Thursday morning in his hotel bedroom, dreaming there was an emergency. Was it the fifth or the sixth week of his enquiry? He knew he had lost time. He pushed back the bedclothes and was transfixed by pain in his arm. Then he remembered. It was the sixth week, he *had* lost a full day and McPherson had located the aberration in the heat treatment recording. Even at the cost of being beaten up, going through the routines had been worthwhile. But he was stiff! His back ached and he must somehow have twisted his arm, torn a muscle perhaps. He began slowly manoeuvring himself out of bed, hoping a hot bath would improve matters, when the phone rang.

'There's a lady to see you, sir.' It was the hall porter.

He looked at his watch. It was 9.45. The doctor must have given him too strong a sedative.

'Can I speak to her?' he asked.

'One moment, sir.' He heard the porter say, 'Over there, madam,' and then a low-pitched, educated voice came on the line.

'I do apologize for just turning up. But it is urgent. I'm from the Ministry of Defence.'

'I'm not even dressed.' He felt ashamed.

'That won't bother me.'

For a split second Donaldson wondered if this was some incredible nymphomaniac come-on; maybe she had the wrong room number? Then the fanciful idea died. Ministry of Defence was almost certainly a euphemism for a rather different sort of proposition.

'All right,' he agreed. 'Could you be kind enough to have them send up breakfast?'

As he struggled to pull on a shirt and trousers, he speculated on what sort of woman this would be.

Even so, when Kit Fairfax entered and introduced both herself and Chief Inspector Sturgess, he was surprised. He half expected a tweed-suited virago, or else the more elegant Bond Street shopper to whom the voice could have belonged. But then he didn't know that the animal which inspired Kit's working clothes was neither the fox nor the leopard. It was the chameleon. Frampton was proud of its university. She had brought with her the African print cottons, loose-knit sweaters and vaguely ethnic accessories favoured by graduate teaching staff.

'I didn't want to mention police in front of the porter,' she said, producing an identity card.

As a formality he compared the small photograph with her face, then realized in embarrassment that he was staring at her chunky amber necklace and that under a flamboyantly coloured shirt she had an appealing figure. He averted his eyes and handed back the card.

'What can I do for you both?' he asked. 'The Minister warned there were people from your, er, department around.'

'Did he indeed?' She glanced at Sturgess. 'Goes to show one can't trust politicians, doesn't it, Colin?'

'At least Fairlie's backing my enquiry,' Donaldson protested.

'Which is what we came about. The police arrested another striker last night. Inside the factory. You may appreciate the significance of what he had stolen better than we do.'

'Go ahead.' He was willing to bet it was a graph.

'He took an inter-office memorandum sent to what they

call,' she had to consult a tiny notebook from her bag, 'the pyrometry Superintendent. The subject was the thief himself. It complained that on the night of 2 April last year he was caught inside the inspector's cage of the heat treatment department "borrowing a Phillips screwdriver". He was subsequently sacked for other incidents of indiscipline. . . .'

'Was his name Brunner?'

Sturgess nodded. 'You evidently heard about him. However, borrowing a screwdriver's hardly a crime. What can make concealing that worth breaking and entering plus larceny, which is what he's up for now?'

Donaldson suddenly visualized Brook's impressor, with its damaged needle housing. He sat on the edge of the bed, his arms folded, rubbing the side of his nose gently with a forefinger, so obviously concentrating that the two remained silent.

The fragments of evidence danced in his mind, refusing to coalesce. When they became a sequence, he so disliked the implication that he went over it again. There was a link missing, namely the way the recorder was made to function when the oven was off. But that might be discovered by interrogation faster than by research.

'I'm ninety-nine per cent sure you've arrested a saboteur,' he said reluctantly, still clasping his arms across his chest.

'We had the same feeling,' said Kit Fairfax. 'He also happens to be a dedicated revolutionary.'

'Which is irrelevant,' Donaldson said sharply. 'I'm concerned with technical explanations, not political motivation. May I explain why the 207 aircraft crashed?' He went to the table, took a sheet of hotel notepaper and began to sketch.

'So,' he said, when he had finished, 'the most logical explanation is that someone contrived to turn the oven off between,' he glanced at the notes from his conversation with Mac yesterday, 'between nine thirty on the evening of 2 April and six thirty the following morning. He made the recorder continue drawing its graph, but the aberrations reveal when he switched the oven off and then on again. During the same night he interfered with the impressor, so that when the inspector did his hardness check, the reading was normal. Or near enough. If your bloke was in a hurry, which sounds likely, he might have simply displaced the needle in some way, so leaving the marks I found.' He looked at Sturgess. 'As a detective, you'll appreciate there is no proof that one person carried out all the actions. Nor can I tell you yet how the circuits were re-aligned.' He hesitated. He didn't like pointing towards a man who might be innocent. 'Pyrometry technicians do carry a key to the recorder's lock. And of course pyrometry is an electrical job.'

'Thank you very much.' Kit smiled self-deprecatingly. 'Even I understood that. Now I've one final question. Could there be any connection between the heat treatment shop steward, Norris, and this sabotage?'

'Technically?' Donaldson shook his head. 'No. He was employed on the solutionizing, which is a later process. Admittedly, as I discovered for myself, ten minutes training gives one the so-called skill to operate the oven so virtually anyone could do it. However, you would have to prove that he did. I'm satisfied that McPherson and I interviewed every operator who was involved on the two days in question.' He stood up. 'Now if you don't mind, I really would like to finish dressing.'

'Would you mind interviewing this man too? If it's necessary?' Kit asked.

'It's not a question of minding. I shall have to, though it may be easier if he's prepared to confess.'

'That's what I like to hear,' said Sturgess exuberantly. 'We'll go straight to it.'

Kit Fairfax shook hands. 'Thank you again.' She smiled meekly. 'I did order your breakfast. I hope it comes soon.'

Frampton's central police station was an imposing stone-faced edifice close to the Cornmarket. It had two interviewing rooms, both rather drab, cream-painted, each furnished sparsely with a table and half a dozen upright chairs.

Before Brunner was brought to the room they had been allocated, Kit Fairfax and Sturgess discussed their tactics. One possibility was for Sturgess to put the fear of God into him, then for Kit, separately, to play the sympathetic counsellor, admiring the technical brilliance of what he had done, but advising him to save his skin. They decided this sophistication was unnecessary. Sturgess would simply go all out to break Brunner, while Kit listened; she needed knowledge of the electrician's character as background material for the far trickier session she foresaw with Norris. Even though she had no inkling of what connection there was between them, she was confident one existed.

When Brunner was escorted in by a constable, who remained by the door both as a guard and as a police witness, Sturgess motioned him roughly to sit down. Kit herself was ready to make notes.

'Let's go over why you're here, right.' The heavy handed approach wasn't his forte, he was a 'college-educated copper', but he could sound tough. 'You're here because you were caught red-handed. Stealing what? A document which shows you'd been indulging in some light-fingered activity with the late Charlie Brook's toolbox.'

'I was borrowing a screwdriver.'

'A likely bloody story. That was the night the defective bulkhead panels went through heat treatment, wasn't it?' Sturgess was beginning to raise his voice. 'And next morning Charlie Brook passed them. With the impressor you'd put out of calibration.'

Brunner did not reply. There was a sulkily defiant expression on his thin face. Kit observed that he was shifting around on his chair and guessed it wasn't only because it was hard.

'Charlie's dead, isn't he? Killed himself because of that tool. Makes thirty-nine, doesn't it? Thirty-eight in the plane plus Brook. That's a lot of dead men to have on your conscience, Brunner. I wouldn't like them on mine.'

Brunner quivered, his jaw clamped shut, his hands gripping the sides of the chair seat.

'We know what you did that night,' Sturgess said, dropping his voice. 'At nine thirty p.m., when no one was around, you switched off the oven. At six thirty, just before you went off the shift, you put it on again.' Sturgess suddenly hammered the table with his fist and shouted in Brunner's face. 'But you weren't so bloody clever after all. It showed on the recorder trace. That's what shopped you.'

'You can't prove anything.' Brunner spoke at last, defiant, running one hand back through his tousled hair, as though the action gave him confidence. He made a curious noise of contempt, half sniff, half snort. 'You're not bloody clever enough.' He wasn't afraid of this flatfoot. If they thought he'd turned the oven off, then it stood to reason they knew nothing, because he'd only turned it down. 'How long do you reckon I'll get for breaking and entering? Six months? Less remission.' He smirked. 'You're not worrying me!'

'I don't believe it!' Sturgess looked at Kit as though wanting an audience, 'Does he think that's all we're charging him with? Why d'you think you were remanded in custody an hour ago?' He leant forward again, not shouting this time, talking confidentially. 'Listen, Jack my boy. You're going on being remanded in custody, week after week, until the *real* charges are documented. Don't think you're going to murder thirty-eight people and get away with it, because you're bloody not! Six months? Who are you kidding? Thirty years is what you're in for.'

Brunner's defiance was fading. He was gripping the chair again.

'Thirty years being locked in a cell every night, slopping out in the morning, calling warders "sir", queuing for prison food. No nice cups of tea like you've had in here. And how *did* you like it last night?' Sturgess shook his head as though Brunner was an idiot. 'Let me tell you, boy. Last night was the bloody Savoy compared to a proper jail.' He paused. 'Life's what you get for murder.'

'I don't believe it. I couldn't be charged with that!'

Sturgess stared him straight in the eyes. 'There's only one

way you're going to earn a reduced sentence. That's by helping us now.'

Brunner took a deep breath, bit his lip, and stayed silent.

'OK.' Sturgess glanced at the constable. 'Take him back down.' As the policeman opened the door and hustled Brunner through, he called out, 'Think about it. You'll be in your mid-fifties when you come out.'

Brunner swung round as far as the constable's grip on his arm allowed. 'Stuff you,' he shouted back. 'Stuff the lot of you.'

'Well,' said Kit, when the door was shut again. 'You almost pulled it off. He's a funny mixture. Intelligent, I think, conceited, yet completely unsure of himself.'

'He's as guilty as hell.'

'I wouldn't dispute that. How do we prove it?'

'We go back to Donaldson.'

'I know you ruled out fingerprints on the impressor thing, but mightn't there be some on the recorder?'

'I'll try anything once.'

'So will I,' she said determinedly. 'I have an idea there's another way to get under that young man's skin. I'm going to have a few photographs sent down from London. See how he reacts.'

Before coming to a decision Colonel Grigoriev went through the entire dossier on Yuri. It had become a long one. He reminded himself of the Black Sea holidays Yuri had taken, of the open quarrel with his wife Carol, reported during the first of the character assessments made by numerous observers. He re-read his own letters and telegrams concerning Yuri's recruitment into the net, his initial reluctance, his desire for money, his ambitions, his bitterness against the bourgeois class and the bosses. He appreciated again how strongly Yuri had resented the poverty suffered by his mother, clearly a dominant factor in the man's whole make-up. So, Grigoriev reflected, how had the Centre made a mistake with this agent whom he had never met, yet felt he knew better than many of his own relations?

'Search for people hurt by fate or nature,' General Pavl Anatolevich Sudoplatov had told him years ago when he was a young officer and Sudoplatov headed the Fourth Directorate of the old NKVD. 'The sense of belonging to an influential, powerful organization will give them a feeling of superiority over the handsome and prosperous people around them.'

Yuri had seemed tailor-made for the requirement. What had gone wrong?

There were occasions when Colonel Grigoriev entertained other officials in the long, modern building of KGB's First Chief Directorate, out on Moscow's circumferential highway. As a departmental head he had an office with a view over the woods, and its excellent furnishings extended to a supply of vodka for guests.

Grigoriev felt in need of a drink now. If he was going to make an unpalatable recommendation to the Chief of the Directorate, he could at least reward his own straight thinking. He opened the cupboard, reached for the bottle and poured himself a small glass. This wasn't the rubbish most Russians had to be content with. It was the real Stolichnaya, the famous old brand which had vanished from ordinary stores in the early 1970s to be reserved for export and senior Party members. He tossed it down and poured another, which he took back to his desk.

The facts concerning Yuri were inescapable, Grigoriev reflected. He had become intransigent. He had started this strike against orders. Even Rusopov now regarded this agent of his own as 'dangerously unreliable'. To cap if all, here was an urgent telegram announcing that the Trotskyite whom Yuri had recruited for the sabotage had been arrested. The danger had become acute. What would Yuri do if he too was picked up by the counterintelligence? The answer had to be faced. He was loyal only to himself and he was mercenary. If his own interests were threatened he would betray the KGB. Grigoriev picked up the telephone and requested an immediate interview with the Director.

The lower bureaucratic echelons of the KGB might work ponderously, but when an emergency arose the Directorate was capable of making extremely rapid decisions.

Colonel Grigoriev found himself part of a minor conference when he reached the office of the Director, the same man whose name had been attached to the so-called Directive by the British. Once his contribution to the meeting had been made, the Director raised its corollary. Kutuzov was a big, broad-shouldered Slav, wearing a general's uniform. 'A year of investigation has failed to root out the traitor who revealed the Plan of Work for the London Residency to the British,' he said. 'But at least our Ambassador's denials that such a so-called Directive exists have prevailed. The subject has ceased to be discussed in the British media. Because the counterintelligence clearly lack proof, the scandal has died. If this agent Yuri squeals, it will be resurrected. And it will be far worse than the situation after the defection of Lyalin.' The comparison was reasonable. Until he sought asylum in 1971 Oleg Adolfovich Lyalin had been tasked to the sabotage of aircraft production.

'Precisely, Comrade General,' put in the Head of Department V, whose fifty officers specialized in various activities, including sabotage. 'Only a few ever understood Lyalin's importance. The British public expect Russian officers to be spies. They treat their exposure like the latest episode in a television serial and laugh and forget. The revelations of a trade unionist will be totally different. Everyone will take note.'

'I agree,' Grigoriev said. He was the officer with the most recent experience of Britain. 'This could wreck twenty years' penetration of the labour movement and frighten off many agents of influence.'

'We cannot afford to lose our resources there,' confirmed the Head of Department V. 'They are too valuable.' Although everyone knew he was thinking in a relatively narrow sense, they grunted assent. For every spy in Britain, the KGB had fifty others ready to assist in occasional minor ways; a booking clerk prepared to issue a backdated ticket to confirm an alibi; a truck driver willing to let his vehicle be 'hijacked'; the left-wing university lecturer who lent his flat in Paddington to Rusopov without asking questions; the salesman with a taste for child pornography in whose name the Chrysler was registered; the list was wide-ranging. If Yuri went bad, this entire network of human resource would be at risk. Only those over whom the KGB had the strongest hold would not be scared off.

'The British government is already anti-Soviet,' the Director commented. 'It will institute a purge of both industry and the bureaucracy. Worse, we shall suffer a major propaganda reverse and every major manufacturer in Western Europe will look to his security.'

'And in the United States,' added the Departmental Head, concerned. 'Our work there will be prejudiced.'

'Then we are agreed. I shall ask higher authority for the elimination of Yuri.' Such a sensitive operation would have to be approved by the Administrative Affairs Department of the Party Secretariat. 'Draw up a plan,' he ordered the Head of Department V. 'Send the necessary personnel to London. Assuming action is sanctioned, it will be essential we get this man before the counterintelligence do.'

The meeting broke up as rapidly as it had been called and the Head of Department V hurried to his own offices in another wing of the building, with Grigoriev accompanying him. Whilst the area departments of the KGB, like Grigoriev's, were identified by numbers, some functional ones bore letters. The 'V' stood for 'wet affairs' in which the KGB had long expertise. The first notable operation carried out by the department's lineal ancestor in the OGPU was the gunning down of Simon Petluva, a Ukrainian, in Paris in 1926. The most pressing assignment for the 'Administration of Special Tasks' in the next decade was only completed on 24 May 1940, when Leon Trotsky, exiled co-founder of the revolution itself, was hacked to death with an ice pick at his villa in Mexico. In 1953 Premier Khrushchev closed the 'Kamera', the laboratory devoted to developing methods of assassination. However, it shortly re-opened as part of Department 13 of the First Chief Directorate and later in the 1950s achieved a notably more sophisticated killing. Captain Khoklov, a defector from the KGB, was poisoned by a dose of radioactive thallium in his food. His death was lingering and painful.

The 1960s brought the curbing of assassinations in favour of sabotage and further re-organization in 1968/69, when the letter 'V' was allocated. However, murder could never be relinquished as a weapon and the department had assisted the Bulgarians in eliminating an émigré in London in 1978. He was injected with a tiny capsule from the ferrule of an apparent passer-by's umbrella in broad daylight.

For most of the afternoon experts in the department discussed the best method of dealing with Yuri. Eventually a telegram was sent to Rusopov demanding certain preliminary administrative arrangements, and the two officers who would handle the case left on the next Aeroflot flight.

In an elusive, indefinable way, Donaldson sensed the respect of the pickets when he returned to the factory on Thursday afternoon.

'Here he comes!' one called out as the police car approached. 'Here's the man!'

'Who's the lady friend?' another shouted.

Others jostled to look, staring at the five occupants, yet yielding to let them through. The works police inside saluted as they held back the gates, knowing Sturgess was from the Special Branch and speculating about the others. The identities of Kit Fairfax and Dick Hearn, who had just reached Frampton, were going to provoke plenty of rumour.

'By the way,' Donaldson asked, 'when are you going to let me have my own car back?'

Sturgess grinned. 'What makes you think you're getting it back, sir? Material evidence like that! We had someone's front door for three months once.' He relented. 'It's OK, sir, in a day or two. But with respect, you're going nowhere without a police escort for the time being. We don't want any more incidents.'

The driver stopped outside Production Centre Three and they trooped in to be greeted by Burnett.

'This is our electronics expert,' Donaldson introduced Hearn. 'Let's go straight to the recorder.'

They walked through and Burnett inserted the key, leaving it in the lock.

'Just a minute,' said Sturgess. 'How often is that opened?'

'Only when a reel of paper's removed.'

'Would our friend Brunner do that?'

'No. That's done by the . . .'

Sturgess cut him short. 'It's a long shot, but let's dust the inside for fingerprints before we go any further.'

Burnett opened the foot-wide chromium door, revealing an inside like a black plastic box, with the thick roll of paper mounted centrally and electric cables running in from underneath to the right-hand side of the mount. There was a lot of spare space.

Kit watched fascinated as the fingerprint expert, a constable who for convenience had doubled as driver coming here, began brushing the interior with powder.

'There's a few here,' he announced. 'Some fresher than others. I did hear of one on a bungalow wall in the West Indies lasted a year. Conditions inside this might have preserved them.' He began lifting off the impressions with translucent tape.

Hearn, meanwhile, was asking Burnett detailed questions about the power supply.

'There's a bit of something lying inside,' the constable called out.

'Don't touch it,' Sturgess snapped. 'Have a look, Mr Hearn, will you?'

The fingerprint expert, slightly aggrieved, backed away and Hearn peered in with the aid of a torch. Resting on the bottom of the casing, almost hidden by the cables but now made conspicuous by the powder, was a tiny piece of wire, a bare quarter-inch length.

'Anyone got tweezers?' Hearn asked.

Kit produced a pair from her bag and he retrieved the fragment, then held it up to the light. 'Copper wire,' he said, half to himself, sweeping the torch beam round, then saw the explanation. The fingerprint powder also showed up a faint circular mark on the bottom of the casing. He summoned the constable again.

'If someone had pressed a small battery into place behind the cables there, would it leave a mark?'

'If there was dirt or grease on it, certainly, sir.'

'Where there any prints just above?'

'Those were the old ones. Forefinger and middle finger. Must have been pressed hard for them to have lasted.'

Hearn turned excitedly to Donaldson. 'I'll have to set up an experiment in the lab to make sure, but I'm ninety per cent certain. What he did was leave the oven on low, so that the recorder spool still turned, while a battery was connected to the temperature recording to replace the lost voltage through the thermocouple. I can see where the battery rested and this piece of wire must have broken off the leads he used. Probably screwed the terminal a fraction too tight. Then when he undid it again the wire fell down and he never noticed it.'

'I'll be . . .' muttered Burnett. 'The crafty devil.'

'Let's keep that wire safe, shall we?' Sturgess took a small envelope from his tunic pocket.

Donaldson looked at Kit. 'So there you are, Miss Fairfax, most physical phenomena are explicable.'

'I wish ideological ones were as easy. Thank you again.' She glanced briskly at Sturgess. 'Well, Colin, we have work to do.'

A couple of hours later, in the central police station, the fingerprint constable demonstrated how he had transferred the images on the tape to a backing sheet and finally produced a photographic print. Now he was comparing them to those taken from Brunner after his arrest.

'One's a little smudged,' he said. 'But I'd go into the witness box that they're his.'

In fact he would not be asked to: evidence was never given by the expert who had lifted the prints. However, his opinion was enough for the moment.

'What about those letters I gave you?' Sturgess asked. 'Any of the same prints on both?'

'Apart from your own, sir. No. I had to take a slight liberty to check those, sir.'

To his credit, Sturgess blushed.

'So that was a false lead,' Kit commented when the expert had gone. 'Still, I think I might take the poison-pen one with me when I go to see comrade Norris's girlfriend tonight. She probably knows more that she realizes and it'll give me a reason for turning up. He and the unfortunate Brook were on the same committee, after all.'

'Slightly unethical, isn't it?' Sturgess had a conscience.

'All's fair in love and war,' she answered with unusual abruptness. 'As far as I'm concerned this is a war.'

In the early evening Donaldson had another visitor at the hotel, a man who according to the porter did not want to give his name. Potential witnesses were sometimes shy. Even so Donaldson was amazed to step out of the lift and find Ken Norris waiting in the lobby.

'Good evening, sir.' Norris advanced in a manner far from his normal self-confidence. He was holding his leather coat and twisting it in his hands. 'I came to apologize on behalf of the lads,' he said. 'The local blokes never meant you any harm.'

'Sit down a moment.' Donaldson moved to one of the unwelcomingly upright armchairs, presumably intended to keep non-residents at bay. There must be a good reason for this approach and it was unlikely to be concern for his health. Donaldson knew from the police that the flying pickets had been summoned by Norris. Several of the 'local blokes' had grassed. He looked at the Convenor. 'Luckily I'm only bruised. Don't you have any control over the pickets?'

'It's all, like, volunteers, sir. Some get a bit over-enthusiastic. I hope it hasn't kept you off work.'

Ah, Donaldson thought, now we're nearing the truth. 'It hasn't delayed the investigation, if that's what you mean,' he said. 'I'm not a one-man band, you know. In fact, during the last twenty-four hours the others have pretty well concluded what we need to do in the factory.'

'Got the answers, have you, sir?'

'Precisely.' Donaldson gritted his teeth. This man was putting on the most sickening performance he'd witnessed in years. He deserved a reward for his efforts. 'Yes,' he said in a steely voice. 'I can tell you two things. The first is that the disaster was no accident. The second,' he kept his eyes on Norris, who was listening attentively, 'is that whoever orchestrated the campaign against Brook will carry that man's life on his conscience to his dying day. Brook was innocent.'

'I always thought he must be,' Norris muttered.

Donaldson stood up. 'It's not my job to deal in personalities or attribute blame. My reports are purely technical. But there are other authorities who do and you can rest assured, Mr Norris, that I am passing them all the evidence I obtained. Good day to you.'

Norris backed away. To Donaldson's satisfaction, he had the expression of someone who has suffered an unpremeditated assault.

Leaving the hotel Norris let fly such a volley of subdued swearing that a policewoman outside stopped him.

'Any more of that and I'll arrest you,' she said firmly.

He stifled a reply and walked off. To be arrested by a woman, after demeaning himself to Donaldson, would have been the ultimate humiliation. Furthermore, at heart he was becoming frightened. Very frightened indeed. Brunner must have talked. The question was: how much?

*

Ingram was keeping the entrance to Harold Wilson House under observation from a car.

'The man's out, she's in,' he told Kit when she joined him.

'Then we needn't hang around. If all goes smoothly I'll ask you to fetch some cigarettes, all right? Don't come back in, just stay around.'

'And if Norris returns? I wouldn't like to leave a defenceless lady all alone.' Ingram could never resist playing the male chauvinist.

'What do defenceless ladies do?' she suggested lightly. 'They scream blue murder! So if someone runs out yelling, you'll know what happened. But it's more likely to be Norris than me, I promise you.'

When they rang the bell there was a delay before Marion came to the door wearing a dressing gown, her head swathed in a towel. She saw Ingram first.

'Not today, thank you,' she said firmly. Salesmen and so-called 'market researchers' infested Frampton.

'It is you we came to see, Miss Robbins.' Kit smiled encouragingly. 'And Mr Norris. Is he in?'

'Oh.' Marion stepped back, confused. 'Ken's gone out and I'm just washing my hair. Could you come back later?'

'We're only here today.' Kit gave her a pleading look.

'Then you'd better come in, I suppose.' She led them through into the sitting room. 'I won't be a moment.'

Five minutes later she came back in a sweater and jeans and with the towel made into a neat turban.

Kit held out her hand. 'How do you do? This is John and I'm Kit. We're friends of Charlie Brook's from London.'

'That's a terrible business.' Marion's sympathy was immediate. 'Quite awful. Not that I really knew him. Ken only met him on committees – not socially much.'

Kit foraged in her bag. 'Oh, damn,' she exclaimed. I've no cigarettes. John, be an angel and go and get some?'

'Here, I'm sure we've some.' Marion started searching.

'No, no. I wouldn't dream of it.' She knew all would be well. At heart this was just a normal middle-class girl. 'There must be a shop nearby.'

'In Howlett Street,' Marion prompted, secretly relieved, since she knew she had none. When Ingram had gone she offered Kit some coffee.

They chattered generalities while she was boiling the kettle, but as soon as they were back in the sitting room, Kit became earnest.

'When Norman Huntley told us,' she explained, 'I couldn't believe Charlie'd killed himself. Until I saw this.' She pulled the poison-pen letter out of her bag, no longer in its protective plastic. 'What kind of a mind does that?'

Marion took the small sheet of paper and read the few words.

'Cut out of an issue of the *Frampton Evening Post*, apparently,' said Kit, her eyes on Marion's face.

'It's horrid.' She felt sick inside. Could Ken have been making up this letter before she found those remnants of newspaper? No, surely not. He hated Charlie Brook, but he wouldn't do this. And he did religiously clip news about the factory. She handed it back.

Kit saw her skin whiten and knew she had struck home in some way.

'Does Ken come to London much?' she asked.

'On union business.' Marion was upset and distracted by the letter. Things like that would prey on a man's mind. 'His aunt isn't well either.'

'Oh, so he has to go on Sundays?' Kit was all sympathy. 'But he has other relations there too?'

'Carol. If you can call an ex-wife a relation. All she's after is money.'

'Some women!'

'Luckily his aunt's been helping.' Marion sighed. Her mind was still on the letter. 'I just don't understand how anyone could do that.'

'Some people do extraordinary things.' Kit wanted to shift the subject. 'Look at this man Brunner, breaking into the factory. Did you read about it in this evening's paper?'

'Jack Brunner?' Marion was clearly intrigued. 'Ken's always said he was crazy. Actually "nutter" is the word he uses. I went round to the house he lives in once. The girl there was interesting, very intelligent. But Ken didn't like her. He doesn't trust the Trots.'

There was a noise from the hall. The door opening. Kit braced herself. This couldn't be Ingram.

'Hallo, love.' Norris's voice came from the hall and a second later he entered the room. 'Who's this?' he asked rudely. He didn't like finding strangers in his flat.

'This is a friend of Charlie Brook's. Kit . . .' Marion stumbled over the introduction.

'Kit Fairfax.' Her tone ceased to be vague and chatty. 'I was hoping you might be able to help me.'

Norris recoiled. He was on the verge of saying Charlie Brook was no friend of his, when he thought better of it. There was something familiar about this woman. Fair-haired, brightly coloured shirt. Christ! He felt himself go rigid with anger. It could only be the bird the pickets had described, the one taking fingerprints with the police this morning.

'Make us some tea, will you, Mary?' The request was as harsh as an order. Marion left the room quickly. 'What are you doing here?' he demanded. He wanted to know, too. Then he'd throw her out.

Kit showed him her card. 'Ministry of Defence. If you want to check my authority, you can phone them.'

'There isn't a phone.'

'I'd like to know about your relationship with Jack Brunner.' Displaying a confidence she didn't feel, she perched herself on the arm of the sofa. Everything about this man suggested potential violence.

'I'm not answering any questions without a lawyer.' He was afraid now, as well as angry. 'You've no right to be in here. This is private property.'

'Council property. There are a lot of things we'd like you to be more exact about. Sundays in London, for example.

Would you and your lawyer care to make an appointment? For tomorrow, perhaps?'

'Get out.' Norris neither knew nor dared say anything else. 'I know my rights. Just get out of here.'

She made a gesture of yielding gracefully and rose to her feet. 'If you insist. We'll be in touch again anyway, quite soon, I expect.' She picked up her bag and looked briefly in the kitchen. 'Thank you so much for the coffee.' Norris stood in the sitting-room doorway, his face contorted, his fists clenched. She walked quickly to the front door, opened it, and glanced back over her shoulder. 'Give my love to Aunt Edith. I'm sure she's longing to hear from you.'

She had escaped with more dignity than she had anticipated. Waiting for the lift, she heard the screaming start.

'Why did you let her in?' As soon as the door was shut, Norris confronted Marion, seizing her by the wrist, glowering into her face. 'What did you tell her?'

'Ken! You're hurting me!'

She tried to wriggle free but he twisted her wrist harder, repeating the question in individually articulated words.

'What did you tell her?'

'Nothing, Ken. She wanted to talk to you about Charlie Brook.'

'Like hell, she did.'

'I promise, she and the man came about Charlie Brook.'

'Man? What man?' He relaxed his grip and Marion wrenched herself away.

'He went for some cigarettes.' She couldn't understand why he was so furious, but she did desperately need to know one thing. 'Ken, they had a letter someone sent to Charlie Brook. A foul, horrid poison-pen letter. Made up of words from the *Evening Post*. You didn't send it, did you?' She was desperate to be reassured. 'Ken, you didn't cut those words out, did you?'

'Christ,' he muttered. 'If I ever meet that bitch again.'

'Ken. Answer me.'

'No, of course I didn't.' He tossed his head impatiently.

How could Mary think he'd be such a fool?

'Do you absolutely promise you never had anything to do with letters like that? I've got to know. You didn't like him, did you?'

'I hated his bloody guts,' Norris spat out the words. 'But I didn't write him any letter. Now will you bloody tell me what else that woman said?'

'Why are you in such a temper?' She massaged her wrist. 'You really hurt me.' Slowly she realized he was as agonized as she herself had been over the letter. 'Well, she said she was from London. She knew you had relations there.'

'Aunt Edith, you mean?' He could hardly bring himself to mention the name, but he knew he must.

'Yes, the one who's been helping with money.' Marion was calming down a little. 'She was only here a few minutes.'

'That was the lot?'

'Except she mentioned Brunner being caught inside the works. Well, you always said he was crazy, didn't you?' The image of the letter came back insistently into her mind. 'Ken,' she demanded, 'you do cut bits out of the paper sometimes. If you hated Charlie Brook . . .'

She never finished the sentence. In an explosion of fury he struck her straight across the mouth with the back of his hand, sending her staggering against the wall.

'I told you, you silly bloody bitch,' he shouted. 'Why can't you keep your f... ing trap shut? You should have stayed with your f... ing mother.' He felt if he stayed another second he'd throttle her. Seizing his leather coat, he went out, slamming the door.

Even as he ran down the stairs, not having any patience for the lift, he realized he would have to phone Peter. If this wasn't an emergency, nothing was. It only needed Brunner to talk and he'd be arrested himself. He went to the pub to get some change, then to the callbox. The number rang six, seven, eight times. Finally the machine began pinging. He thrust in several coins. A strange, guttural voice answered.

'Bill Rogers here,' he said. Peter had told him to use the

other name. 'Is Peter there?'

'He is not here now.' The reply sounded guarded.

'I must talk to him.'

'I tell you he is not here now! Can you please telephone in the morning? At eleven o'clock.' The phone clicked dead.

Norris felt as though he'd been punched. Why wasn't Peter there, if that was the emergency number? He wasn't to know he had been ringing the house telephone of a West German businessman whose mother still lived in the East and who therefore had a strong motive to cooperate. But the West German disliked being used as a cut-out. He did the minimum for Rusopov's interests.

Norris stayed in the phone booth briefly, considering what to do. He wanted quiet to think. It was futile going to the flat. Whether she was merely crying, or actually packing to leave, Mary would still be there, and he wanted no truck with her at this moment. She had landed him right in it, the stupid cow. As for that other bitch, he'd get even with her one day. Of all the filthy tricks! He decided to go to the pub and have a beer and some pie.

Ingram, posted in the car fifty yards from Harold Wilson House, saw Norris leave. Half an hour later the lights in the fourth-floor flat went out and after a short interval a young woman emerged, a suitcase in one hand, the other holding a handkerchief to her eyes. She dumped the case in a red Mini parked by the building and drove away jerkily. Even at such a distance he could tell she was weeping.

The arrangements for the second interrogation of Brunner on Friday morning were more elaborate. The material Kit Fairfax had ordered from London had arrived. Hearn was asked to be available in case technical explanations were required.

Again Kit discussed their approach with Colin Sturgess in the interview room beforehand.

'Norris is showing signs of panic,' she said. 'His first action after I left was to make a phone call and he appeared extremely agitated. His RVs with the KGB case officers have always been on Sundays. If he goes to a meeting this weekend, I'd like to be ready to arrest him.'

'So you'd like me along?' The Security Service had no powers of arrest. 'Are you afraid he'll cut and run?'

'Depends on the advice they give him. We believe they're angry about the strike. It's very hard to say. Honestly, Colin, there are such enromous gaps in our knowledge. Until last night we didn't even know if they were paying him. Or if he knew Brunner. We're still a very long way from being able to prove a connection with the sabotage. The whole thing's hypothesis. As an ardent Trotskyite, Brunner wouldn't willingly take directions from the KGB in a million years. Did he take them from Norris? If so, why? Until we find that out we've no possible justification for an arrest. It's conceivable we never will have. The KGB may be so confident that they'll simply tell him to calm down, do as he's told, and get the dispute settled before he arouses any more suspicions.'

'In other words, you want Brunner broken this morning?' Sturgess grinned. 'You're not the only one who'd like to be home for the weekend. Let's get him in.'

Though he was shaven and clean, Brunner looked as though he hadn't slept and Sturgess seized on this immediately.

'Conscience been keeping you awake, has it?' he remarked. 'Thinking of those thirty years? Sit down, son. This isn't going to take long. Your goose has been well and truly cooked since we saw you last.'

Brunner took the indicated chair. 'I'm not saying anything without a lawyer.' He wished to God he could get hold of Lee, but she was in Bristol. He hadn't even got her address.

'Won't make a blind bit of difference. No lawyer in the world could argue his way round the evidence we've got now. What's his name, then?'

'I said I want one.' Though he was as sullen as before, Kit decided he was distinctly more nervous.

'You might have told us earlier.' Sturgess beckoned to the constable. 'Go and tell the Duty Inspector the accused wants a solicitor.'

He was delighted. They were intending to leave Brunner alone anyway. 'Right,' he went on. 'Well, that may take a little time. Let's fill in some of it studying these.' He picked up one of the two manilla folders on the table. 'Ever seen a fingerprint, Jack my boy? No?' He pushed two photographs across the table. 'Those are yours.'

Brunner could not resist looking. At first he merely craned his neck forward, then he picked them up.

'The ones marked "A",' said Sturgess cheerfully, 'are the routine ones taken when you were charged yesterday. Those marked "B" are from the inside of the heat treatment recorder casing, where you were also foolish enough to leave a short piece of copper wire and the imprint of the battery you used when you turned the oven down. Down, not off.' He smiled as though rueful. 'Not being technical folk, we had a slight misunderstanding yesterday. What do you think of those? Not bad, eh?'

'Those could have got there any time.' Brunner's voice was shaking.

'When you have never yet serviced that machine? Come off it, lad. You've been mucking about in a factory where every damn movement you make is written down. We know which technicians handled that recorder and you weren't among them.' Sturgess shook his head. 'We've got you cold, Brunner. Thanks to a very bright electronics expert who came down specially.' He was close to the psychological crunch and he unobtrusively pressed the bell concealed beneath the table. It would ring in the station office. 'Wherever you got the idea from, it was too clever by half. You'll be up for sabotage of course, but it won't just be that. As I've said before, you've thirty-eight lives on your conscience. Killing those VIPs was murder. No two ways about it: and I think while we're about it, we'll probably stick a charge of treason on you too.'

Even as Sturgess spoke the last words there was a knock on the door. A constable's head appeared.

'Sorry to interrupt, sir. The Super wants you both urgently.'

'Damn!' Sturgess sighed and got to his feet. 'Well, you'll have to cool your heels for a while. Give time for the lawyer to get here.' He gathered up the two photographs and motioned Kit to leave the room ahead of him. The two folders remained on the table.

While Brunner stayed locked in, they had a cup of coffee in the station office, and were told a solicitor had been found and would be along in an hour.

'Excellent,' Sturgess commented. 'With a bit of luck he'll be just too late.'

'Brunner's really on edge,' said Kit. 'But nothing to what he'll be in a few minutes.'

In the interview room Brunner sat staring at the walls. So they'd got him. That bloody copper was right. They'd cooked his goose. Try as he might, he could see no way round. But why the mention of treason? Surely that was a crime against the state. He'd made a plane crash. But that was all.

His gaze drifted on to the two folders. Thought he was a bloody genius that Inspector, and he'd forgotten his papers. His curiosity mounted quickly. No one could surprise him when the door was locked. He slid off the chair and reached out. The first, the folder which had contained the fingerprints, was empty. He flipped the other open. It contained photographs. He shifted them the right way round. The top picture was actually a newspaper cutting. It showed three men at a party. The caption read 'THE KGB's SPY MASTER IN BRITAIN'. Below a longer explanation named the men. One of the names 'Vladimir Sergeyevich Rusopov' was underlined in red ink and an inked arrow indicated which he was in the group.

Brunner was more than intrigued. While he was up north he'd been on a course in Marxism and revolution. One of the things they had done was teach him to identify KGB men. He'd had it drummed into him that the KGB were the assassins of Trotsky and the greatest enemies of the movement. The man named as Colonel Grigoriev he reckoned he would have spotted anywhere. He wasn't so sure about Rusopov, who had more the look of a university lecturer. He pondered this for a minute or so, then, fearful that he might be interrupted, lifted away the cutting to see what was beneath. He took one look and gasped. It was a glossy enlargement of a photograph taken by a river. One was the same KGB man, Rusopov. The other was Ken Norris.

He rubbed his eyes and looked again. There was no question about it. Norris even had on his leather jacket. Then, since there was no caption, it occurred to him to turn the print over. On the back was pencilled 'Agent contact 12 May.'

As the implications sank in, Brunner found himself unable to stand. That was why treason was mentioned. Norris was an agent of the hated KGB and here he was himself, about to be jailed for doing their dirty work. He began trembling, his knees jittering uncontrollably, as if he had St Vitus' dance. If only Lee was here to help him, give him advice!

Kit checked the time by the big clock on the wall. 'He's had twenty-five minutes. If curiosity hasn't overcome him by now, it never will.'

Accompanied by the constable, she returned to the interview room. Brunner was sitting with his elbows on the table, his head in his hands, sobbing.

'Fetch a cup of tea,' she ordered. The constable went out again and she drew a chair up beside Brunner.

'You've been made use of, haven't you, Jack?' she said softly. 'They don't care what happens to ordinary people, you know. They'd have happily seen you hanged, if hanging was still the penalty. Luckily for you it isn't. Now why don't you just tell me about it from the beginning?'

There was a callbox outside the factory fence, not far from the car park gate. It was cleaner than ones in the city centre and had no broken window panes. Not that Norris cared, so long as it functioned. It did. He recognized Peter's accent at once.

'We've got problems here,' he said. 'A certain friend of ours has spilt the beans.'

'Excuse me. I do not understand.' Rusopov, seated at the desk in the comfortable study of the West German's house, cursed Yuri's stupidity. Why couldn't the fool speak intelligibly?

'You know the bloke they've arrested?'

'I do.' The chill in the way Rusopov spoke would have frightened any Soviet citizen rigid.

'He's being interviewed. They came to see me last night.'

'So?'

'I told them to get lost.' The bravado was short lived. 'I want to talk to you, Peter. We've got to do something about our friend. Bloody soon.' The KGB were always knocking people off, why not Brunner? He'd lain awake half the night thinking about it.

'When do you want to come? Tomorrow?' Rusopov had made all the calculations. A Saturday was more suitable than a Sunday, and Department V's instructions were explicit. 'With minimum delay.'

'Soon as possible. Tomorrow's OK.'

'Then we agree tomorrow, Saturday.' Rusopov spoke soothingly now. It was essential his instructions be obeyed. 'The usual place, the usual time. But come by car. That way it is more easy to avoid unwelcome people. You understand?'

'I get you.'

'Good. You must leave not later than nine. Take the motorway route. This is important. Then we can make sure there are no unwelcome people.' It was nonsense, of course. Surveillance was easier on a motorway than any other road, but things were not so simple for the KGB outside the metropolis. They wanted to be able to keep an eye on him themselves without difficulty.

'I'll be there. See you tomorrow then.' Norris rang off.

In the West German's study, Rusopov made a brief record

of the conversation. It would be useful if anything went wrong.

Sturgess went to call on Vic Parry alone. There was no reason for anyone else to go. He gave back the specimen letter.

'Thanks,' he said. 'None of Ken Norris's prints were on the other one.'

'I'm relieved to hear it.'

'Unfortunately something else has arisen.'

'Have a seat.' Parry was tired. The violence accompanying the unofficial strike was giving the union appalling publicity and the Regional Secretary shared his doubts about making it official.

'It concerns Brunner, the thief we arrested inside the factory.'

'Then thank the Lord, that's no concern of ours. He belongs to the ETU, not us.'

'I'm afraid it is. He's made a confession.'

As Sturgess recounted the details of Ken Norris's involvement, Parry's expression became more and more set.

'The little bastard,' he said at last, which since he rarely swore was his ultimate condemnation. 'I suppose you'll be arresting him too.'

'It may not be so easy.' Sturgess had no intention of revealing his plans. 'Depends a lot on the legal definition of conspiracy, which in turn means we would want a confession from Norris himself.'

'I doubt if I can help much with that,' Parry commented grimly. 'Do you reckon the strike is purely a cover-up?'

Sturgess nodded. 'That's why I came. It might be months before Norris appears in court. Every day that strike continues is effectively another day of sabotage.' He rose to go. 'It's none of my business how you run your union. At least you know the score now. Goodbye, Mr Parry. Thanks for your help.'

'Don't you worry,' Parry said as he showed the Chief Inspector out. 'We can handle this one. I've dealt with wildcats before.' He laughed because one can laugh at past battles. 'And got badly scratched for my pains, I can tell you.'

As soon as Sturgess had gone he rang the Regional Secretary and arranged to come straight to Bristol. This was not a matter he cared to discuss on the telephone, though he knew exactly what the outcome of the trip would be. Before the end of the day there would be a letter in the post signed by himself and framed in carefully chosen phrases. He began to sketch it out. 'Dear Brother Norris. It is the intention of the Regional Committee to investigate a complaint made by the police that in the month of April last year, you encouraged the performance of an act of sabotage at your place of work . . . etc.'

The outcome, unless Norris unearthed some incredibly powerful excuse, would be a recommendation to the General Executive Council that he be expelled from the union. But two week's notice had to be given of the Regional Committee meeting. It would all take time. Parry knew that the onus of settling the strike, and meeting the legitimate aspirations for a pay rise which Norris had exploited, would lie fair and square on him. It would be no walkover either. He could see that once the management at Western's knew the facts, they would try to screw the union into the ground. However understandable that desire might be, he wasn't going to let them get away with it. Norris or no Norris, the T&G existed to defend its members' interests.

Since it would be crucial evidence at the public enquiry, Donaldson was given a copy of Brunner's confession that afternoon. He read it with amazement, not because it confirmed the technical appraisal Dick Hearn had made, but at the complexity of the political motivation. Brunner's statement, as he finally wrote it out, was long and profusely larded with jargon about the struggle against capitalism, as though the court might feel this justified his action. He was clearly in an exceptionally confused state of mind. In places he sounded proud of trying to further the cause of revolution;

in others little short of demented at having been so easily tricked by an agent of the KGB, an organization he vilified at length.

Remembering Kit Fairfax's comment about the complexity of ideological motivation, he wondered what the twelve good men and true of a Frampton jury would make of Brunner. Or indeed what a jury at the Old Bailey would. Norris appeared in many respects a straightforward, venal, persuasive villain. But an eloquent QC might swing a jury to thinking Brunner suffered from a diminished sense of responsibility.

However, his own investigation was far from over. He and Langton and McPherson had still to determine whether the elevators of the 207 had jammed after the bulkhead failed, or whether the collapse of the tailcone skin had been enough to bring the aircraft down. They had several more months' painstaking research ahead before the endurance test of giving evidence to the enquiry.

Meanwhile, he was certain of one thing. The widow of the unfortunate Brook should be told that the crash was not, and never could have been, in any way the fault of her husband. The best person to do that was Margaret Broughton. He had managed to retrieve his car from the police and he drove out to her cottage in time for tea.

Usually Ken Norris left for work before the post arrived. On Saturday he heard the spring-loaded letter box snap shut as he was eating a denuded breakfast, consuming the remains of Mary's last shopping expedition. He went into the hall, his mouth full of bread and jam, and saw the T&GWU envelope. It cheered him. Maybe this was news that the strike would be made official.

The first time he read Vic Parry's meticulously formulated sentences, he had a wild feeling that this was about someone else, this was simply a copy for his information. When the truth sank in he shook himself, as if trying to escape a nightmare, and needed to sit down.

The implications were almost beyond comprehension. Ever since he was sixteen his life had centred on the union; it was his foster home, his refuge, his strength. He could not imagine losing his membership. He read the letter yet again, forcing himself to find hope in the dry references to union procedure – the very procedure on which his career was based. Peter would have to help him with this too, with legal advice, with . . . Then he remembered how the Russians had failed to secure him the Convenorship. A thought seeded in his brain, growing like a tumour, sending spasms through his whole body. If the KGB wouldn't help, then the only salvation lay in betraying them. Turning – what was it called? – Queen's evidence.

He looked at his watch. Christ. Nearly nine. He had to go and he hadn't even warned Bruce he wouldn't be at the GMC today. To hell with it. There were enough militants to elect the Chairman they wanted without his own vote. He gathered up his coat, thrust the letter in the drawer with his other union correspondence – habits died hard – and sprinted downstairs.

The Ford started second go. In this warm weather it usually did behave well, though it was showing signs of age. Spots of rust coming through the white paint. Silly colour to choose, really. He'd thought it glamorous when he saw it in the second-hand dealer's two years ago. No way he could afford a new one, though. Money. His mind reverted to Peter, to what he was going to ask, to what they might suggest.

As he drove out of Frampton towards the M5 motorway, following the blue signs, another speculation seized him. Why couldn't they take him to Russia, set him up there? Hell's teeth, they'd done it for that bloke George Blake, even sprung him from the Scrubs. Proved they took care of their friends, someone said once. Well, they could do it for him, couldn't they? He wouldn't mind some fancy Russian bird either. Like the one he met on the Black Sea trip. Be no problem forgetting Mary with a bit like that around. He was so preoccupied that he never noticed the car threading its way through the traffic behind him, a big red Rover 3500.

'If only they were all as easy as this,' Kit Fairfax commented. 'I suppose he has a certain amount on his mind.' She was wearing dark glasses and a scarf over her head in case Norris caught a glimpse of her.

Colin Sturgess laughed from his seat in the back. 'I like your sense of humour, I like it very much. If he's not running scared, then I'm the man in the moon.'

As the white Ford approached the motorway access, he bent down and used the radio to tell the other car to return. There was no need for two surveillance vehicles on the motorway and arrangements had been made with the Metropolitan police to have a patrol car stationed at the London Airport turn off, ready to join them. Additionally two Security Service cars would be on the same radio net.

'Assuming our Russian friends are waiting at Strand on the Green, then we're all set to nick both him and them,' said Sturgess. 'He won't know that if they're diplomats, we can't hold them. Think you can invent a lively account of what they might tell us?'

'I expect so. I have memories of Kew Gardens. A boyfriend used to take me there on Sundays. He must have had more foresight than I imagined. At the time he seemed distinctly dull.'

Ahead of them the Ford continued an unhurried progress, eventually switching to the M4 motorway at the complex series of junctions near Bristol and heading east towards London at a steady seventy miles an hour.

Norris had made some rough calculations about the route. Once he was past Bristol it would take him an hour and three-quarters to reach London. Even allowing that he would have to map-read the last mile or two, he would be early if anything, because there was a turn off the main road in Chiswick itself. So he kept to the speed limit, sticking to the centre lane, letting a succession of vehicles pass without minding, though normally he was an aggressive driver.

Today there was no point and being more relaxed allowed him to think. He was becoming increasingly certain that the answer was to skip. He had a passport, he could go any time. London today, Moscow tomorrow. It would be stupid to betray the KGB. They were powerful, they had money, resources, jobs. And what would he get if he did squeal? A reduced sentence? Maybe not even that. He had no illusions about where Brunner was going to spend the next thirty years.

A truck behind him hooted. He glanced in the driving mirror. Bloody cowboy. It couldn't be more than three yards away. Some long-distance drivers were like that. Believed in steamrollering down the motorway. He wished he could somehow flash his shop steward's credential at the man, say, 'Give over, mate, we're brothers.' He even thought of holding the orange card up. But the driver was persistent, and so close that he couldn't see the truck's windscreen in his mirror, which was filled by the image of the chromium radiator grille and the blue-painted bulk around it. The heavy beat of the diesel engine thundered in his ears. 'Stuff it,' he thought, 'I might as well let the bastard through.' He pulled over into the inside lane.

The side of the truck towered above him as it inched past, a roaring monster, articulated too. Jesus, they had some power, those things. It was bloody close. His eyes were level with the huge mudguards. They crept closer. He eased over a bit. What the hell did the bastard think he was doing – forcing him off the road? The next thing he was on the hard shoulder, the truck dominating the inside lane. The main part of the vehicle was past. The trailer had come alongside. Suddenly it veered across him. He stood on the brakes. Too late. As the Ford's wheels tore up the verge above an embankment, the high arching mudguard of the trailer wheel grated Norris's own side, slicing through the body work in a rending cacophony of sound. The windscreen shattered. He threw himself sideways as the car tipped, entangled with the trailer. His last conscious knowledge was of agonizing pain as the Ford rolled over.

Sturgess was out of the Rover before it stopped, running towards the wreck of the Ford, which lay upside down at the foot of the steep embankment. The car was so crushed that it took him a few moments to see where Norris was. The body lay trapped in a tangle of metal, the head thrown back, as if he had given one last despairing cry.

In the Rover, the driver called for assistance. Norris was dead by the time the ambulancemen arrived, quick as they were. Nor was it any surprise when a patrol car reported the articulated truck abandoned. They learned later that it had been hijacked the previous night outside a transport café on the A46.

15

The blue and white striped awnings of the chalets rose in four long lines from the terraced slope overlooking the main runway at Farnborough airfield. Below them, in a series of static parks, stood aircraft from manufacturers all over the world. The sun shone on queues of cars being marshalled through the airfield's entrance gates by police, a light wind occasionally made a piece of tenting flap. Loudspeakers crackled 'One, two, three, testing'. Down on the static park a team of US Air Force pilots stood by examples of their military airpower, the dark painted strike planes menacing even at rest, geometrically arranged displays of their weaponry laid out in front of them. It was the opening day of the biennial International Air Show in the first week of September, the big week in Britain's aviation calendar.

From the Western Aircraft chalet Jim Donaldson surveyed the airfield. 'Chalet' was a misleading term. The large ones like this had carpeting, glassed-in viewing balconies, a large dining room and a bar, cloakrooms – all the interior luxuries of a permanent building. Here Western would entertain its more important visitors throughout the week of the Show.

The scene always intrigued him. Looking down at the parked aircraft he amused himself spotting types he knew. Prominent among them was the surprisingly sleek bulk of the second preproduction 207, Zero Two, which would be performing in the flying display in the afternoon. Beyond the wide tarmac runway lay the sprawling confusion of the RAE's buildings, predominantly grey in colour, dwarfing the white airfield control tower with its glass-enclosed top floor.

The chalet's reception area was filling up. The men mostly had name tags pinned to their lapels. Much as he disliked these, even Donaldson had submitted to a small adhesive label being stuck onto his coat by one of the hostesses at the chalet entrance. He noticed a rather portly man eyeing it.

'So you're the investigator,' the man said, peering at the label. 'My name's Norman Huntley. Very pleased to meet you. You rendered us all a great service.'

Donaldson flushed slightly. 'I was only doing my job,' he said, and was immediately aware of how absurdly mock-modest that sounded.

'You helped save seven thousand jobs. Have you met Vic Parry, the T and G District Secretary?' He made the introduction. 'We were all glad Western's saw fit to invite him today. But for Vic, the strike could have gone on much longer.'

Donaldson shook hands, thinking that Wormley's attitude to the unions must have undergone a fairly rapid change.

'I can't really claim the credit, though,' said Parry. 'Once the word got around, see, it was the shock of the exposure brought the moderates out of their shells. It was they voted the end of the strike, not me. The pity of it is, not much happened in Norman's constituency party.'

Huntley grunted. 'The days when Party headquarters would send in a national agent to take over running a constituency which had been infiltrated are past,' he said grimly. 'The trouble is, nobody really knows what Norris was up to outside the factory.' He made a deprecatory gesture. 'That would hardly interest you anyway, Mr Donaldson.'

'The subject interests me considerably more than it used to.'

'Norman has been re-selected to stand for Frampton North again, no problem,' cut in Parry. 'But there's not been the clean-out there should have been.'

Their conversation was interrupted by loudspeaker

announcements of a speech by the Chief Executive in the dining room. The guests filtered through and Donaldson seated himself at the back. The journalists took the front seats, as this was primarily for their benefit. Wormley walked up to a small rostrum and an aide made shushing motions at the audience with his hands.

'As you may have guessed,' Wormley began, 'I'm talking today primarily about our 207 airliner. You will all have seen the brochures. It gives me great pleasure to announce that this project has come through what was for this company an unpleasant and anxious experience. We owe a debt of gratitude to someone with us here now,' he nodded towards Donaldson, 'one of whose axioms I am going to adopt. He always says he is not concerned with personalities or apportioning blame. I agree. What is past is past. What I have to tell you this morning is that this magnificent aircraft has had its dynamic systems tested throughout the flight and weight manoeuvring envelope. All systems have been functioned with no major snags and we see no reason that we cannot seal the design to enter into the full certification programme.'

He paused to allow the reporters to scribble their shorthand notes.

'There are plenty of technical experts present who can enlarge on detail. Today's truly important news is that Atlantic Airlines have confirmed the purchase of twenty 207 aircraft, with spares. The entire package,' this time he paused for effect, 'will be worth in excess of two hundred million pounds.'

There was a ripple of applause. Although the announcements of sales contracts were always kept for the first day of the Show, this one had been achieved in the face of such well-publicized adversity that it deserved a clap.

'Johnson actually signed last week.' Donaldson heard an American voice in his ear and looked round. Daly was behind him. 'Say, unless you want to hear the rest of the spiel, let's get ourselves a drink.'

The two men slipped away to the bar.

'I'm very sorry, gentlemen.' The white coated barman had strict instructions. 'Nothing to be served until the briefing is over.'

'Nothing what!' Daly exploded. 'My goddamn company is buying twenty of your planes and I can't get a drink! You want me to go back in there and say the deal's off?'

'You haven't changed much,' Donaldson said, as the barman capitulated.

'I reckon we've earned a scotch. Say, wasn't Margaret Broughton going to be here? I haven't seen her around.'

'I think she's coming in time for lunch and to see the display.'

Donaldson was right. Twenty minutes later she appeared, pale but gratified at the kindness everyone immediately showered on her. The three of them ate the lavish meal together and afterwards sat in the front row of the chalet's terrace to watch the flying display.

When in mid-afternoon the 207 lined up at the end of the runway to take off, the announcer, his voice echoing around the airfield from the loudspeakers, paid an unexpected acknowledgement.

'Here, ladies and gentlemen, the 207 airliner, the very latest example of the state of the art and I am glad to say, a completely British production. It gives me a genuine thrill to say that. And, as you have probably heard, Atlantic Airlines today confirmed their order for twenty of these magnificent machines.' The announcer's robust and cheerful tones had become famous at successive Air Shows. 'Before she goes off, and what a beauty she is, I must pay tribute to the pilot who carried out so much of the development flying and who was so tragically killed earlier this year. Bill Broughton. He's a man the whole industry misses a great deal.'

As the 207's engines roar loudened and the plane began to move, Margaret Broughton was unashamedly crying. Donaldson put an arm round her, his eyes on the airliner as its nosewheel lifted off the ground and it rose effortlessly into the air.

'That was nice,' he said. 'Mentioning Bill.'

She dabbed at her eyes. 'I'm so sorry, Jim. It's all more than I can quite cope with. Thank goodness the worst is over. Things must get better now, mustn't they?'

The 207 turned steeply over the Laffan's Plain end of the airfield, glinting in the sunlight, and flew back almost overhead, the huge crowd craning to watch.

One hundred and twenty miles away, at the Frampton factory, the management posted up notices about the Atlantic Airlines order. One man who read the announcement was the instrument technicians' shop steward. He laughed sardonically and then slipped a folded letter out of his overall pocket and reminded himself of the date and time mentioned. The letter was an invitation to attend an Aircraft Workers Youth Committee meeting in London. He was the man known to the Centre as 'Edward'.